MONKEY'S UNCLE

Monkey's Uncle

JENNY DISKI

Weidenfeld & Nicolson
London

First published in 1994 by Weidenfeld & Nicolson,
an imprint of the Orion Publishing Group, Orion House,
5 Upper Saint Martin's Lane, London WC2H 9EA

A catalogue record for this book is available
from the British Library

ISBN 0 297 84061 4

Typeset by Deltatype Ltd, Ellesmere Port, Cheshire
Printed in Great Britain by
Butler & Tanner Ltd, Frome and London

3094

For Chloe and Anna Diski
with love

He thought he saw an Argument
That proved he was the Pope:
He looked again, and found it was
A Bar of Mottled Soap.
'A fact so dread,' he faintly said,
'Extinguishes all hope!'

Lewis Carroll,
Sylvie and Bruno

I'm a monkey's uncle who's a cousin
to a chimpanzee

Neil Sedaka,
'I Go Ape'

Chapter 1

HARDLY ENOUGH TO MAKE ONE

―――――

. . . this curious child was very fond of
pretending to be two people. 'But it's no use
now,' thought poor Alice, 'to pretend to be two
people! Why there's hardly enough of me to make
one respectable person!'

Perhaps, if Charlotte had known her father better, or if she had not noticed the book on the little table outside the second-hand bookshop on the Charing Cross Road, or if the Berlin Wall had not fallen quite when it did, coming so near to Christmas, or if Miranda had gone to a different party with a different young man on Boxing Day; or if Charlotte had not found herself at the Zoo on the morning of the incident; perhaps, if any of these things had been different, it would not have happened. Charlotte might simply have muddled along in the way that people do, even when they can see no point in the further continuation of their lives.

But, as they always are, things were as they were, and so, in the mid-afternoon, early in the new year of 1990, Charlotte found herself sitting in her living-room, filled to the gills with the diazepam her doctor had just injected into her bloodstream.

Whether Charlotte Fitzroy's descent into madness, at the age of forty-nine, had come upon her suddenly and particularly, say a couple of weeks previously, as an understandable response to a pointless death; or whether the seeds of her madness were strung out like tiny pearls along the length of her life, beginning way back in childhood, was, Dr Lander knew, a matter of doctrine. A Freudian analyst might say one thing; a clinical psychologist another. But whichever way one looked at it, the end result was the same: Charlotte Fitzroy was, by any measure, not very well.

That much had been blindingly clear to Dr Lander, responding to an emergency call, when he reached Charlotte's front gate. It was also obvious to her son when he arrived an hour later, although he, naturally, took it more personally.

'Mother!'

Charlotte, her usually pulled-back grey hair collapsing wildly about her shoulders, looked up from the armchair at her son with an impossible mixture of nonchalance and terror, and drew hard on the last quarter of an inch of her cigarette. The diazepam was surging strongly through her bloodstream now, so that she had to pay attention to the rather delicate task of finding enough space in the crowded ashtray to stub out her cigarette, before performing the even more difficult trick of applying the flame to the tip of the new one she immediately drew from the pack on her lap.

Charlotte's son stared down at his unkempt mother waiting for an answer to the question he thought he had asked. She had not worn her years well. A long time since she had *let herself go*, and whatever it was that goes, had gone, leaving a slightly overweight, slack-muscled, somewhat shapeless and decidedly untidy woman to get on with it.

With the old cigarette extinguished and the new one alight, Charlotte had no other activity to keep her from speaking to her speechless son.

'He called you, then,' she said in a monotone, her exhaled smoke enveloping the words. 'I asked him not to.'

She still tried to achieve a what's-all-the-fuss-about look in her eyes, but fear seeped into them, spoiling the effect. She dropped her gaze and concentrated on the colour of her plaited dressing-gown cord.

'Of course he called me. Who else is there to call?' Julian snapped.

Charlotte glanced up to meet his eyes, hoping to find something ambiguous in them, but seeing nothing other than enraged blueness, returned to the maroon of the cord.

'Have you any idea how busy I am?' Julian continued.

Once again his mother looked up; this time to signal with her eyes that they were not alone, and the doctor was there listening to the way

2

he spoke to her. Charlotte realised that Julian was too angry to be concerned with what other people might be thinking, which surprised her, since there was little else, as a rule, that concerned him more. Things, she understood through the Valium haze, must be very serious.

'Yes, I know you're busy. There was no need for you to come. I'm quite all right now. I'm sorry for being so much trouble.'

'Much help that is,' Julian muttered and turned to the GP who was standing behind him in the doorway. 'What the hell is going on?'

It was clear from his expression that Dr Lander realised he had made a mistake in calling Julian. But the damage being done, he was forced to explain the situation he had found when he was called in by Charlotte's next-door neighbour.

'Mrs Lane called me,' the doctor said in a muted voice. 'She's also a patient of mine. Your mother was . . . she was in the front garden pulling up all the plants.'

Julian stared at Dr Lander, his thin mouth quivering with rage. There was a very real possibility that he might have to trade in his Porsche for something considerably more modest. The waters were rising (if his Porsche had to go: had risen); he had been wondering if he remembered how to swim. He wasn't sure if fear alone would reactivate the skill.

'You called me away from work to tell me that? I was with a client. I had to turn her over to someone else. I can kiss goodbye to *that* commission. So my mother was pulling up the plants. Why didn't Mrs Busybody next door call a gardener? Or are you known in the area for your green fingers? It's not a crime to pull up your own plants in your own garden, is it?'

'Julian . . .' Charlotte tried to quieten the tirade.

'Well, *what*?' he turned on her. 'What's the big deal?'

Charlotte sighed and took a deep breath.

'I didn't have any clothes on, Julian,' she said quietly.

Julian's pale English cheeks flushed a high, bright scarlet.

'What?'

Dr Lander took over.

'Your mother was very distressed. Mrs Lane tried to get her indoors, but she couldn't. I talked her into coming inside and gave her an injection. Valium.'

'In the front garden – with no clothes on?' Julian whispered, as if fearing he might be overheard by his colleagues at work. He turned to stare incredulously at his mother. 'Why?' was all he could manage to say.

Charlotte took a deep puff of her cigarette and her somewhat sleepy eyes took on a slight glint, though her voice remained subdued and dull.

'I think I might have been trying to dig my way out, Julian. I had to get rid of the plants before I could start the digging proper.'

Julian's stare did not falter.

'What are you talking about?' His voice was reduced to a whisper, but it had the quality of a scream about it nevertheless.

'Dig my way out. That's the only way I can describe it. Get digging, I thought. So I did. Perhaps, it wasn't out, perhaps it was in. Or it might have been down. I'm rather confused about it, myself.' Julian had not moved. Charlotte realised that his main concern was not with what her plan had been. She tried to help him. 'I took the clothes off because it was very hot work. Somehow . . . once I'd started with the jacket, and then the cardigan . . . it all came off. I don't remember that well, I'm afraid.'

'Christ!' Julian said dully, shaking his head as if trying to dislodge the image of his naked mother in full view of the street which had entirely filled his mind.

Dr Lander intervened.

'Mr Fitzroy, could we talk outside?' He signalled with his head and raised eyebrows that the two of them should go into the hall.

'Has your mother been under any particular stress, lately?' he asked, closing the door carefully behind them.

'Christ!' Julian said again, as if hearing nothing but the sound of blood rushing to his cheeks.

'Any stress?' Dr Lander asked again, trying to gain the young man's attention.

'What? Oh . . . I don't know . . .' he said vaguely, as if he had other, more important things on his mind. What stress could be worse than his current fear of losing his car, his house, his job, even? Now, his fury at having been dragged away from work redoubled at the new information of the shame and embarrassment his mother had caused him. 'How the hell do I know? I don't live here. I've got a life

4

of my own, you know. It must be the change of life. Don't women of her age often start to go funny? Can't you give her something? Hormones or whatever?'

'We'd have to test for hormonal imbalance,' Dr Lander said stiffly, not pleased. 'Your mother was extremely disturbed when I arrived. Has anything like this happened before?'

Lander was a newcomer to the practice and had had no time to read up Charlotte's past history.

'No. Mind you, she's always been difficult,' Julian said bitterly, his lips compressing in distaste. 'Full of ridiculous ideas. Politics. Feminism,' he spat at Dr Lander's enquiring eyebrows. '*Caring*, she called it. *Idealism*. Well, that's all come to an end, thank Christ. Her beloved socialism's bitten the dust. She was pretty worked up about that. Served her bloody well right.' He noticed Dr Lander looking oddly at him, and brought himself back to the question. 'But she's never done anything . . . well, bonkers, you know?' He stopped speaking for a moment and blinked as if he suddenly remembered something. 'Miranda. That's probably it. But she seemed all right. Well, a bit quiet, but, OK, considering . . .' Another thought dropped like a penny into his mind. 'Jesus, I hope she doesn't lose her job. I can't take on her living expenses as well as my own. You don't know how bad things are out there. She'll be all right, now won't she? Well, soon, anyway? Won't she?'

'I couldn't say,' Dr Lander told him, watching the sweat break out around Julian's collar as he took in the implications of having a mad mother on his hands. 'Where is your father?'

Julian snorted.

'I don't have a father; and she doesn't have a husband. It's not the way we do things in this family.'

'And the Miranda you mentioned. Who is she?'

'My sister. There was an accident on Boxing Day . . . she was killed.'

Dr Lander stared levelly at Julian for a few moments before he spoke.

'Bereavements can take quite a while to get sorted out . . . Weeks, months, even years sometimes . . .' he stopped himself, realising how much pleasure he was deriving from terrifying the young man. 'I'd like to take her into hospital for a week or two for observation, if she agrees.'

5

'What do you mean, if she agrees? She's got to go, she can't stay here on her own if she's behaving like that.'

'There aren't any grounds for compelling her . . .'

'Are you kidding? Running around in public, stark-naked?' The thought burned lurid rings on Julian's cheeks again.

'Well, that might be an embarrassment for you, perhaps, but it isn't dangerous, apart from the risk of getting scratched by thorns. I'll only have her admitted as a voluntary patient.'

'Don't worry about it,' Julian growled, opening the door to the living-room, where his mother sat listlessly, trying to replace some of the hairpins that had fallen into her lap. 'She'll volunteer.'

Since just before the previous Christmas of 1989, when she had found the book called *FitzRoy of The Beagle* in Charing Cross Road, Charlotte had suffered from the growing conviction that she was not herself, or rather, not the self she had thought herself to be, which made her, to her mind, someone quite different. This revelation (or delusion, some might say) about her origins was the only thing which had made sense to her for a very long time. She had not told a soul about it, and no one seemed to notice when she began to capitalise the 'R' in the middle of her surname. It was not that the someone else she thought herself to be was no one else's business – indeed, it was very much Julian's business – but she felt she needed time to think about her discovery and its implications before passing the information on. There was no point in upsetting anyone until it was absolutely necessary.

Charlotte did not consider herself deluded. She felt that she had come upon a discovery which made a great deal of sense of many things which, up until then, had seemed unaccountable. There was a pile of facts, incidents, feelings and inclinations, jumbled together in a corner of her mind as if by a careless sweep of a broom, which turned out not to be there by accident at all, not once they were sorted and put properly in the file with the capital 'R' where they seemed to have belonged all the time.

But, although it was temporarily gratifying being able to find a rightful place for all those apparently separate and curious items, there was little satisfaction to be gained from it in the end. It was much as if she had completed an extraordinarily difficult jigsaw puzzle, only to find the picture she had made was of a monster which then came alive, and leaping up, tore out her throat. Nice to finish the puzzle, but not for long.

In fact, her discovery did not kill her, but it might have had something to do with the unfortunate incident in the garden which looked, at the moment, very much as if it was going to land her in the care of the mad doctors.

As far as Charlotte could remember, it had been a perfectly normal morning. She had eaten her buttered toast, bathed and dressed, caught the right bus, got off at the right stop near Regent's Park, and walked to the laboratory where she worked. It was not until she was actually standing in front of the entrance that she discovered she was not, after all, going to work as usual.

Her hand reached out to pull the glass door open, but her brain flatly refused her arm permission to contract the muscles necessary for completing the task. Charlotte stood and stared at the D-shaped handle, and her own disobedient arm so far from it, perplexed. Perhaps she should wait until someone else came along and then slip through the door behind them when *they* opened it. She held on, for a bit, to the notion that this was still a normal working day and she would be going to work as soon as she could find a way to get through the door, but then, like a garment that was several sizes too big for her, the whole idea fell away, dropping in a lifeless heap to the ground, waiting for Charlotte to step out of it.

She was not going to work, it seemed, and, once this thought had struck her, it was with the greatest of ease that she turned and walked away from the laboratory. She followed the road around the perimeter of the park until she came to the entrance to the Zoo, where she stopped and bought herself a ticket. And although she had never before behaved in such a way, it still didn't strike her that anything was wrong. It seemed a harmless enough thing for a woman so recently bereaved to take the morning off and walk around the Zoo.

'You should take some time off,' Professor Dawes had said to her when she returned to work as normal after the Christmas holidays. But she hadn't wanted to then.

So at the time, a day off work and a visit to the Zoo had seemed to

7

her, as she was sure it would have to anyone, perfectly reasonable, and hardly the first sign of a madwoman on the rampage.

It felt only slightly less normal as she began to walk around. There was barely a soul to be seen. The Zoo had only just opened for the day, and the January weather was not perfect for a wander round the gusty tarmac paths. Clouds were scudding across a dreary sky, blown by a wind which had a real northern bite to it. It was the sort of day when sensible people, planning a visit to the Zoo, changed their plan and found some warmer activity. Only parties of schoolchildren and the occasional shivering tourist were braving the windy walk from cage to cage – and Charlotte, who seemed oblivious to the icy wind as she marched in what looked like an almost purposeful way in her sensible, sheepskin-lined ankle boots.

In spite of working so near to it, it was years since she had been to the Zoo; not since the children were small. It had changed a good deal, though not in its layout. She passed the place where she had queued so that Julian and Miranda could ride the elephant and the camel, and paused to look at the lion enclosure which was new to her. She supposed the lions and tigers were happier stretched out and doing nothing on their little patch of bald grass, rather than pacing ferociously up and down behind the old black railings of the cages in which they used to live. Guiltily, she remembered the old cramped lion houses with affection, perhaps just because they had been there then, and she remembered them. Perhaps, also, there had been something ambiguous about the iron bars which she had appreciated. Now, for all the lion's lolling languor, there was no question which was captive.

Charlotte passed on. Seals and penguins, all charm and something heartbreaking about the purposeful waddle and slide into the water, as if they were going somewhere, instead of round and round and then back out on to concrete. To her right was the parrot house, which she avoided thinking the screeching noise inside the old building was not what she was after. Miranda always wanted to go there first to see the blue parrot which invariably greeted her with a squawked 'Hello!'. It always sounded a little aggressive to Charlotte, but Miranda loved to be specially hailed. She never told her daughter that it said hello to everyone who came and stood in front of its cage. Perhaps if she had, Miranda might have had a different fate.

8

Charlotte reached the monkey enclosures: the tribe of macaques squabbling and chasing each other; the chimps resting in the metal branches of their climbing frame, instead of, when the children were young, taking tea on the central green for the amusement of the human visitors. Shamefully, again, knowing anthropomorphism to be a cardinal sin, she remembered the tea-parties with pleasure, they *had* seemed to enjoy it, and why not, tea and cake was a treat for Charlotte?

She walked on, noting the gorillas, still and solemn, and refusing to let herself think about Guy and his sad, sorry life, and turning the next corner, found herself face to face with an orang-utan.

Charlotte stopped walking.

There were only inches between them, woman and orang-utan, separated by a thick sheet of reinforced glass. The animal sat staring out through the glass, with one hand cupped around its ear, as Charlotte approached. It took no notice of her, keeping its gaze unwavering, off into the middle distance over Charlotte's left shoulder, where – Charlotte turned her head to check – there was nothing to see.

The creature's long straggling red hair, hanging from its shoulders and arms, and seemingly pushed back from its face, gave it the appearance of one of those women who live on the street, bundled into all the clothes they possess, topped by an ancient fur coat, grabbed at a jumble sale, and worn winter and summer, a protective outer layer, not just for the cold, but to keep the world at a distance. Charlotte tried to lose the image, remembering about anthro-pomorphism, but the picture was reinforced by the orang-utan's eyes. It was not just their peculiar humanity – the gorillas and chimps had those eyes, too. It was a curious quality of resignation, of bewildered suffering that struck Charlotte. A mixture of deadness and pain, a look of *resigned suffering*, a package, rather than two separate qualities. Quiet desperation. Hopelessness. A disengage-ment with everything the eyes appeared to look towards.

It was several moments before she realised that there was a baby tucked under the ape's arm; a tiny creature, sleeping, lolled, utterly relaxed. She walked to the side of the cage, where the plaque was.

Suka, and baby Jago, it said.

'It means "delightful",' a woman's voice said behind her. 'We named her, you know, and Jago, too.'

9

Charlotte turned around and saw an elderly couple of the peculiarly matching variety that elderly couples sometimes become. The woman wore a silk square around her head, he had a loden coat, and each carried small folding stools of green canvas.

'We've been coming here every week, for twenty years, to see them.'

The woman seemed to speak for both of them; he simply nodded his assent at her words and smiled.

'Just to see the orangs?' Charlotte asked. 'Where do you live?'

'In Hove, by the sea. The orangs are very special to us. We keep in touch with them. Suka here is the daughter of Bula. She's over there,' the woman pointed off to the left. 'They're a dynasty, you know. Bula's the daughter of Toli and Charlie. They were orphaned and David Attenborough rescued them and brought them back in the fifties. So Jago is the fourth generation. They're wonderful creatures, aren't they?'

'Yes, they are,' Charlotte said. 'How did you come to name them?'

'When Suka was born the keepers asked us if we'd like to choose a name out of the Borneoan dictionary. We were thrilled. Well, you can imagine.'

'Yes,' Charlotte could imagine.

'Do you know what the natives in Borneo think about wild orangs? According to Mr Craven – he's the keeper – they believe orangs can actually talk, but they won't. They pretend they can't because they think if the humans find out they can speak, they'd make them work. He says that after twenty years working with this lot he's inclined to agree with the Borneo natives.'

Charlotte laughed.

'Do you think they know you?'

'Oh, yes,' the man said, suddenly coming to life. 'But it's like one's children. They get used to you, so they take no notice. I think of it as an honour to be ignored like that by another species. We just like to come and see they're all all right.'

'Do you think *she* is?' Charlotte asked. 'She looks so sad.'

'It's only their faces,' the woman said, knowledgeably. 'You mustn't make the mistake of putting your own interpretation on their expression. They aren't us. Of course, it's different from normal being in captivity, but the boys all take very good care of them, and make things as natural for them as they can.'

'Why is she holding her ear all the time?' Charlotte asked.

'She started that when she was an adolescent. They've checked for everything, looked in her ear, done blood tests and whatnot, but there's nothing wrong with her. It's just a bad habit. And now some of the younger orangs have started to copy her. It looks like something's wrong, but it's not really. Nothing physical. They're solitary animals. Not like the chimps. There isn't the space for them to lead normal lives, but Mr Craven says that their faces only *look* sad. It's no way to tell. How can you know what happiness and sadness might be for another species? Sometimes it's hard to tell among human beings.'

Charlotte smiled her agreement.

'Yes,' the woman sighed. 'We do love them. But they're going soon. The Zoo can't afford to keep them. All the orangs are being sent away. It's such a shame. Do you know there have been orangs in the Zoo since the 1830s? Mr Craven told us that Charles Darwin himself used to come here and watch Jenny, the very first one, while he was thinking about his theory of evolution. He said Darwin wrote in his diary after his first visit, how much more human she seemed to him than the natives he met in Tierra del Fuego. They *do* seem human. But they're all going soon. Suka and Jago are off to France in a few months. Mr Craven's been talking a bit of French to get them used to it.'

'Oh, you'll miss them,' Charlotte sympathised.

'Yes, we won't be able to visit them nearly so often, but, perhaps, once or twice a year . . . we might manage . . .'

She looked towards her husband as tears welled in her eyes at the coming loss. He nodded briskly, coughing to conceal his own painful feelings.

'I'm sorry,' Charlotte said, and turned back to look at Suka. She was still staring beyond the three of them, her hand over her ear, exactly as she had been the last time Charlotte looked.

'Well,' the woman said with a brave smile. 'We'd best be off to see how Bula and her little one are getting on. Our train leaves in an hour.'

Charlotte waved goodbye as they walked off. The woman turned back before they disappeared round the corner and called out.

'If you're ever near Hove, do come and see us. We like to talk about the orangs.'

11

Charlotte returned her gaze to Suka, who was now sitting on the floor, gathering up handfuls of straw and dropping them on to her head, while baby Jago, who had woken, tried busily to turn somersaults with only occasional success. She was not quite sure why she was still standing there. Suka the Delightful had taken hold of her imagination, and she wanted to spend time watching her, though for what Charlotte couldn't quite tell. It had something to do with the connection between herself and the ape that she seemed to glimpse when she looked into Suka's eyes.

Charlotte understood enough of evolutionary theory to know that chimps and gorillas were nearer relatives to mankind than orangs, both morphologically and socially. Orangs were solitary and displayed none of the social interactions that the other apes did. Still, her hunch was that it was the orang she must be with if she wanted to make anything at all of her almost fifty years of existence on the planet.

She was there, she understood, because the look she had seen in Suka's eyes – of resigned despair – was tantalisingly close to her own current feelings. For a moment, Suka's eyes met Charlotte's; unintentionally, Charlotte was certain. But there was a brief, accidental look between them. Then Suka turned her head and stared at Jago, who was still racing and acrobating frantically around the cage. Suka followed the movements of her son with what seemed to Charlotte a look of utter weariness at his explosive energy. Why, her eyes seemed to say, what is the point? And then she turned her head back and Charlotte found herself staring into those eyes again. This time, it was not an accident. Suka, Charlotte knew, was *looking* at her, her deeply recessed black eyes making contact with Charlotte's own weariness and sense of futility. 'I am so tired,' they said to one another, across the ray of light that connected them. 'But what is to be done?'

Charlotte smiled a gentle smile that made the forty-nine-year-old creases in her face deepen. If it had been possible, Suka might have smiled back. But a mutual expression of helplessness was more than the two species could manage.

Smiling still, as if there was nothing in the world that required her attention, Charlotte lapsed into thought.

★

Scale, the apparent significance of a thing, was, she knew, only a matter of the distance from which you looked at it. Examine a blood cell through an electron microscope; focus a radio telescope on a galaxy. Either way, what you got was a pattern of information which fitted on to a piece of paper. Only a pattern. Universe or particle. Where was the difference?

And what went for size, surely had to go for time and place. Same difference. It just depended which end of the telescope you used: the universe end, or the particle end. Light years. Centuries. Decades. Minutes. Tick tock. Tick tock. Here and there. Closer and further away. Sooner or later. Now and then.

Now and then, Charlotte had been able to take the godlike view, to stand outside time and space, beginning and end, large and small, and see the absolute lack of absoluteness of the whole damn bag of tricks. But only for an instant, before the heavy curtain of one-thing-or-the-other swung down over her vision and sent her back to the world of the 'scope – micro and tele. It didn't do her much good, her momentary overview, although it had, perhaps, played some part in her decision, years back, to let herself go, at least in the cosmetic sense of the phrase. The overview just came and went from time to time, and when it had gone, there was nothing but a large SO WHAT? hanging in the place it had been.

As a working, practical technician, Charlotte understood how futile was the abstraction of her thoughts about size and time. Practically speaking, she knew that the world of the microscope, and the world of daily-monthly-annual (and so on) life, coexisted without causing any serious difficulty. But as a madwoman, which Charlotte was about to become, she began to feel obliged to try to connect the unconnectable, and thus would cause herself (and others) all kinds of difficulty.

Looked at another way, politically, you might say, the size and time issue could be seen as another version of the old history-versus-the-individual dichotomy. Again, no problem, if you keep like with like: history, you study; life, you live. But Charlotte began to think she could no longer keep the categories straight in her head, whatever label she gave them. History and Life (the world's history, her life; her history, the world's life, and so on and so forth) were not so separate to her, suddenly. They bled into each other, creating a runny continuum of meaning between the entirely unalike categories of historical necessity, random chance, personal history and destiny, which it was now Charlotte's unhappy burden to try to understand.

She tried to make a statement to herself about herself that was simple and made sense. She was Charlotte Fitzroy (though perhaps, since finding the book, with a capital 'R'), forty-nine-year-old mother of two (or one, strictly speaking), genetic technician; daughter of Iris, née Chapman, called Fitzroy (with a lower case 'r') by deed poll, formerly a chambermaid in a seaside town; daughter, also, of Richard Fitzroy (which needed a capital 'R', she was practically certain), absentee father, provider of necklaces, suicide; himself, she now believed, the great-grandson of Robert FitzRoy, one-time captain of the *Beagle*, failed colonial administrator, inventor of the weather forecast, true believer in the word of God; suicide; himself the nephew of the Marquess of Londonderry, latterly Lord Castlereagh, foreign secretary, madman, suicide.

It didn't seem at all simple. The statement contained as she feared – as she knew – all of it, but tangled as hell. Everything was there in the bloodline: random chance, historical necessity, personal history and destiny; living inside her, bouncing together in her blood like bingo balls.

How many sets of chromosomes did she contain? Millions, billions – all the same (except for the sex cells), all containing the complete and true story in a language no one had learned to read much beyond the state of simple letter recognition. As simple as ABC. *I am Charlotte FitzRoy*, every nucleus of every cell sang. So simple. And yet. And yet, although the song they sang was the same song, word for word, letter for letter (not forgetting the capital 'R'), there was no harmony, but only a great and frightful cacophony which lost the meaning altogether.

Charlotte FitzRoy, genetic researcher and former political activist, had, perhaps, become those things in order to untangle the mystery, the very particular mystery, of who and what she was, and who and what she might be. But, of course, the more she had understood about the ABC of it, the less was clear. As she moved from biology lesson, to university, to research laboratory, she got nearer and nearer to the single cell, until, with the magic of technology, she was inside it and actually able to take it apart, even make a picture of it. A picture book for early readers, you might say.

But it didn't help. The closer she got, the further the meaning of herself receded. What she learned most thoroughly, was how much could not be known. When she looked through the microscope at the single cell, she saw all there was to be seen, without being able to make the sense she wanted to make. She had observed the strings of chromosomes, with their letter codes written along their lengths, patterning for this or that characteristic, only some of which showed up on the whole individual. The messages were there, all right, and yet they didn't *speak*. She might, like a wanton boy, break them apart piece by piece, stain them, slice them, clone them, and yet never find the way to put them back together that would amount to the story she was looking for. The why of it, rather than the how. Biology teased her, and then ran, giggling, for cover.

There was another angle: step back from the microscope and use the telescope to look at the finished object the billions of cells had made. Investigate the complete individual, consider the personal story of days, weeks and years which added up to the present and *what she had become*. And when that proved, perhaps, not quite sufficient, turn the barrel to take in a greater distance. Look at what was beyond her own particular individuality and her own history. Trace the larger scale and look at the grand sweep of political forces that made individual confusion an irrelevance. But she had done that and only sorrow had resulted.

What was there left to do, but enlarge the lens still further and see what kind of a creature she was in a species, a planet, if necessary the stars, galaxies and, for all she knew, an infinity of universes? And after that, when the search still yielded nothing that made sense to her? What then?

Charlotte's thoughts in front of the orang-utan's cage that morning jangled backwards and forwards between the large and the small, the past and the present, the theoretical and the everyday. The problem was with the looking, she decided. She realised that the instruments were the difficulty. Whichever lens she put to her eyes gave her nothing more than a view from a distance, and each was hampered by its limitations. It could only see what human beings were able to make it see, which could only be what was known about already.

Lenses were such clumsy things. She could look through them till the cows came home, close up, or from a distance, and never see what she was really searching for.

Then how was a person to find out about their destiny and their doom? Where was it possible to go, and in what direction, now that science, politics and the reasoned life had failed her? And if she did find out? Supposing it were possible. If she found a way to know about destiny and necessity, and chance and choice?

Charlotte stared for a very long time, unseeing, over Suka's right shoulder, while Suka continued to stare, unseeing, over Charlotte's left. Eventually, her eyes focused for a moment and took in the orang-utan.

'*Delightful*,' she whispered, her eyebrows lifting slightly.

And it was then, during her meander through the dialectics of scale in front of the orang-utan cage, that, quite unexpectedly, and without the slightest warning, she seemed to lose her footing amid the treacherous minutiae of her thoghts, and found herself falling headlong through a gaping hole that had suddenly appeared between the one side of one thing, and the other side of the other.

And *then* the unfortunate business in the garden happened.

Charlotte had no recollection of returning home. After that moment of whispering 'Delightful' to herself, she must have stayed at the Zoo for hours because it wasn't until mid-afternoon that she found herself in her front garden. She remembered using all the force her body could summon to wrench well-grown shrubs from the earth and fling them as far from her as she could, uprooting and killing every living thing she could in the garden she had cared for over two decades. She remembered the sweat she worked up, and pulling at her jacket, then her cardigan to relieve herself, and then not stopping, taking off each layer, because she needed to be cooler to accomplish the task in which she was engaged. She remembered the slapping January wind against the exposed areas of her flesh – buttocks, thighs, breasts – which were usually covered against the elements. She remembered, also, catching sight of herself in the hall mirror, as she was manhandled back inside the front door by Dr Lander, and noticing, quite casually, as if she had just stepped out of the bath, the way her large breasts hung, these days, heavy against her torso, and how her pubic hair was now almost completely grey.

And yet, for all the detail of her recollection, and the pain it brought her, Charlotte could not now give any account of her state of mind at the time. She remembered the actions, but they were divorced from any feelings. There was nothing of anger, fear, nor even embarrassment. There were no feelings, and no intentions at all attached to her memories, other than the current, retrospective feeling of shame and perplexity. She had no idea, now, sitting, drugged in her living-room chair, what she had been up to when she made herself naked and denuded her garden.

If it was an experience of madness Charlotte was remembering, and she was sure it was, she was surprised at its secret nature. It was as if a concealed door had suddenly opened on to a new and undreamed-of wing of a familiar house, and then, as suddenly, had closed and disappeared, leaving the occupant with a memory of an arrangement of rooms which could not, in all architectural reason, exist.

She could only think: *that was not me; I couldn't have done that.* Which was not helpful, since she couldn't shake off the knowledge that she had. What she did not know, of course, was that she was right: it had not been her, or rather not that part of her which had been left behind by her wandering mind to provide itself with an alibi.

'Curiouser and curiouser,' Charlotte said under her breath, during the brief moment of silence as the two men stared at her from the doorway. The fraction of Charlotte's mind she had left behind to negotiate for her in the world, slipped into gear as Julian moved towards her across the living-room, glaring with undisguised rage. The world, it seemed, was too preoccupied with its own problems to notice that only part of Charlotte was available. No one, in the world of sanity, had any notion that Charlotte was anything other than present in her entirety. Not even Charlotte herself (or part thereof) seemed aware that anything else was happening anywhere else. Unless, that is, she was remarkably good at concealment.

In the meantime (or, as it might be, meanplace), down and down the rest of Charlotte fell through her dialectical hole, into seemingly bottomless, fathomless space. But, as unexpected falls went, it was not unpleasant, and even seemed an improvement on having both feet squarely on the ground. Charlotte, who had had enough of life on the surface, allowed herself to fall with not the slightest fear of breaking anything, nor any concern about how she was to get out again. The falling was delightful, as if she were a balloon filled with gas, released all of a sudden from its tether, so that she went flying, floating, soaring, away from reality, all finished with weight and the clawing grasp of gravity. Although, she admitted to herself, that wasn't such a very good description of falling, or it wouldn't be if she hadn't decided to let accuracy go hang, along with everything else. And why shouldn't falling be flying, and plummeting be soaring? It was only a matter of where you were when the action was taking place. If this was madness (real madness, that is, rather than mere misbehaviour of the common-or-garden variety), then it was perfectly delightful, and nothing to trouble oneself about at all.

She didn't think she would be missed if the Charlotte she'd left behind to take care of things on the surface kept her real whereabouts to herself. And she was quietly confident that Charlotte-up-there would manage excellently well without the rest of her.

Eventually, Charlotte became aware that she had been quite still for some time. It was dark. No darker than it had been while she fell through her dialectical hole, but no lighter, either. It was the kind of disorienting dark that, had she been a feather in a large, unopened can, she wouldn't have the faintest idea which way was up.

There was no doubt, however, that she was as far away from Charlotte-up-top as it was possible for one person to be from themselves. And she felt nothing but relief to discover that there really was another place to be. It seemed likely to her that madness was a closely guarded secret, in the way that a small, private island might be kept secret, so that the rabble might be kept from overrunning it. But she retained a decent amount of caution. This black otherness was all very well, and very pleasant, actually, but Charlotte guessed that there might be other aspects, other landscapes, as it were, and who could say how nice they were?

Now, though, the darkness was not so utterly black as it had been. There was something of a glimmer, a tiny peep-hole of, if not light, something less than absolutely dark, ahead of her.

She began to move without any sense of having got up, or even of actually walking. Swimming, it might have been, except that there was no water. It was as if she flowed towards the point of half-light, which was really no more than a brightening gloom amidst the inkiness that was everything else. Very like a dream, she told herself, as she arrived in the slightly lighter, but no more definite place. And it was not surprising that madness should be like a dream. Not really.

'Well, here I am,' she thought. 'Here. And now what?'

It was a little disappointing, really. A bit dull.

Charlotte waited.

Nothing happened.

So Charlotte waited some more. She rather hoped *something* would happen, having gone to all this trouble to get here.

After a while she called out, as one would in a shop where all the assistants had gone into the back room for tea.

'Hello?'

But nothing continued to happen in the most alarming way.

Chapter 2

HE HASN'T GOT NO SORROW

*Alice could hear him sighing as if his heart
would break. She pitied him deeply. 'What is his
sorrow?' she asked the Gryphon, and the
Gryphon answered . . . 'It's all his fancy, that:
he hasn't got no sorrow, you know.'*

She had thought, at first, that the greyness in front of her eyes was the
result of eyestrain from reading her book, *the* book she had been
careful to bring with her from home. But when it did not disperse
after rubbing her eyes, she began to wonder if she was dreaming, and
whether the surrounding greyness was the sea, of which she herself
was inextricably a part. But gradually the light lifted towards silver
and became the hesitant illumination of dawn. No longer united with
it, she saw how the light fell in slanting lines of something less than
complete gloom through a small skylight.

Now, there were walls enclosing her, so close a person could have
reached out to touch them. They were made of tongued and grooved
planks of rich, dark mahogany wood, like the floor, and she supposed
the creaking and groaning she heard, as if a creature was in hopeless
pain, were the planks as they stretched and relaxed with the altering
conditions. Beneath that sound was another; a continuous noise
whose colour was the shade of grey-green mildew, whose rhythm was
that of blood pumping through a heart. She recognised it as the sound
of the sea swelling against the hull of the ship she now understood she
was in, and breaking against its sides, both lulling and exciting the
mind with its incessant movement.

As if he had been there all along, she saw the figure of a man sitting
at a desk which took up half the space in the tiny cabin, his forehead

cradled in his hands. His pose might have accounted for him not seeing her, except that now he looked up, straight into her face, and still he continued to behave as if he were quite alone.

She looked long and hard at him in his immaculate uniform, and recognised the fine-chiselled nose, which had been hidden by his interlaced fingers, and the limpid, almost liquid grey eyes, hooded and staring sightlessly ahead of him.

She knew who he was.

She spoke his name, but he seemed not to hear her, just as his unblinking eyes had been unable to see her: impossible in such a small space. He remained in his pose for several minutes, unmoving, as if his stiff, Royal Navy uniform had frozen him inside it. Suddenly, with an excessive, violent movement of his hand, he wrenched the collar apart, making the stud fly, as if he were trying to release himself from its immobilising confines. He stretched his neck, and seemed to focus as if trying now to see out of the skylight.

But there was nothing to be seen, she knew, beyond the slowly brightening sky. Whatever he was looking at could only have been seen in the mind's eye. And whatever he saw there, judging by his expression, appalled him.

It should have been elementary; a matter only of drawing a line, FitzRoy knew. A concavity here, a convexity there. Simple, broad strokes were all that were needed. It was not necessary, for practical purposes, to be too precise: he had just to be detailed enough to be able to pinpoint a position, and know where the next safe harbour was. But what the Admiralty thought sufficient was not good enough for Captain Robert FitzRoy. He knew it to be hopelessly inadequate. Not for the limited purpose of recognition, but for the satisfaction of knowing the task he had been asked to do had been done correctly. It was essential to him that the line he drew on the chart corresponded *exactly* to the reality out there in the world.

Naturally, the first priority was to enhance the safety of those at sea. No one would ever be able to accuse FitzRoy of not taking his responsibilities to others seriously. But beyond that elementary task, it was necessary for his peace of mind that the job he had been ordered to do was done with exactitude.

This was where it had all started to go wrong, although why it went wrong at *this* moment, on *this* voyage was unaccountable. But whatever the reason, on that day's charting, as he took the whaleboat to shore, he was gripped by the phenomenon he must have seen, without noticing, a thousand times previously on approaching land. He saw suddenly the utter impossibility of his task, with a clarity and force which struck at the very centre of his being.

The line of the part of the coast he was attempting to chart was unarguably simple if seen from the distance of the ship anchored out at sea. He could have gone below and drawn his lines untroubled. But then, as he stepped into the whaleboat, and got closer and ever closer to the shore, FitzRoy had noticed how the apparent simplicity altered. The smooth line seen from a distance, a bulging promontory here, an indented cove there, became, the nearer he got to it, increasingly complex and jagged.

FitzRoy longed with all his heart for simplicities, but his mind was committed to precision. And *precisely*, the line he might have reproduced from simple looking turned out not to exist in any continuous way, but became manifold, one outline blurring into another, more and more detailed and intricate, according to his distance from the single contour he had supposed there to be.

The obvious concavity of a cove became a multitude of ins and outs, set within the greater simpler shape, as, coming closer, the outlines of the many rock formations of which it was made up were defined. Then, moving closer still into shallower water, a myriad of individual pebbles on the shoreline grew visible and undulated away all remaining hope of smooth simplicity. Finally, wading on to land, his heart pounding, desperation thudding in his head, FitzRoy sank to his knees on the beach, to the alarm of his men, examining the shingle and even the very grains of sand, each minute one of which also, of course, had an outline of its own – and so many, too many ever to hope to give an account of the pattern they made.

Terror had closed its fingers around FitzRoy's throat as he arose and returned woodenly to his boat. The chaotic horror he had seen remained with him back on board ship, try as he might to bring his mind under control.

He sat at his desk and spread out the rolled sheets of charting paper on which he was depicting the outline of the south-western coast of South America. He could not even dip the pen he held into the glass inkwell. It pointed down, functionless, as he stared aghast at

22

the blank space he was supposed to fill with accurate information, and a simple shape designed to give future sailors certainty of respite from a storm. But his mind's eye saw only his horrid vision of an imprecision which he had not imagined even in his darkest dreams.

And then it came to him that it was not just that he was unable to provide a definite outline of the coast of South America for his masters at the Admiralty, though that was bad enough. But if the coastline was imprecise, then so must be all the rest of the world, and therefore it was not possible to measure *anything*. It was not only navigation at risk. How could plans ever be made about anything and carried out with any certainty of success? Every kind of plan, in such a world as he presently saw, became nonsensical. How could a man conduct his life with any degree of certainty or direction? And how could such a life, devoid of faith and purpose, continue? When plans and bearings fell away, what would be left but an infinity of individual grains of sand, tumbled meaninglessly, one atop the other? And worse, he had come to realise, not even *that* vision was static, but each grain shifted continually with the winds and tides, which, presumably, might themselves be discovered to blow, and rise and fall according to no truly understood season or timetable. There was no end to it.

Captain FitzRoy was not a man to allow his emotions to carry him away without a battle to regain proper control. He had moments of irrationality, but, if his character was flawed (and he knew it to be so, in that respect), it could not be said of him that he willingly indulged his failing. He always fought his temperament with all his strength, and, as a rule, brought himself back to reason quickly enough, so that no more harm was done than a heartfelt apology to bystanders could take care of.

He tried to pull himself together now, pushing the terrible thoughts away from him, but this time, although the clouds in his mind began to disperse, it was not to the usual blue sky of good sense, but to the heaving and surging from the depths below of what he feared most in himself. This time something in his mind had gone too far, or too deep, and opened the way for his wretched fate to overtake him, for even as he was successfully suppressing his fearful thoughts about mapping the coastline, FitzRoy slumped once again, head in hands, as his destiny rose in him like a great wave.

It reached his heart; his throat; soon it would fill his mouth, his nostrils, the sockets of his eyes, until finally his very mind would be submerged, and then it would be done. Like a man overboard in an empty sea, watching his ship journey on away from him, FitzRoy felt the power of the inevitable filling him, and he gave up the struggle against what he could never hope to overcome. He respected that elemental force rising in him, and he no longer had the strength to battle against it.

Other men on board that ship could see immediate practical reasons for the despair that came to FitzRoy hard on the heels of his vision of chaos, and they were reasons which any one of them might find cause enough for dejection.

His anger at having to give up the schooner was echoed by all the crew. Their Lordships at the Admiralty were universally condemned on board the *Beagle* for having refused to pay for what was so obviously necessary to complete the survey *they* wanted done. FitzRoy's rage was righteous. Knowing it to be essential for the proper execution of his task, he had paid out of his own pocket for what was needed; the extra boat itself, and the crew to man it. But the costs were too high even for a man of FitzRoy's private means. His income could not bear the burden of his need to do things *right*. The sale of the *Adventure*, at a loss – of course, at a loss – was taken hard by everyone. No one was surprised that a Captain so easily moved to anger should be enraged at the stupidity of the old men sitting at their desks at the Admiralty. And who could blame him for being more than distressed by his financial losses, if not ruin? The Captain's pride was greater even than his famous temper, so it was to be expected, perhaps, that he would shut himself away in his cabin, isolating himself from the gaze of his subordinates.

Most of the crew knew, too, about the mental burden the Captain carried, as successor to the late Captain Stokes. Some, at least, were aware they had been sailing along the very coastline where (as Stokes had written in his log immediately before putting a bullet through his brain) *the soul of man dies in him*. It was hard for a man sailing those same waters in the very same ship not to feel the bleak spirit of his predecessor, who was said by some to walk, still troubled, to and from the Captain's cabin where he had lingered half-alive for days after he botched that last, what should have been, most simple act.

To step into a dead man's shoes was hard enough, but to be also treading in his footsteps along the exact same path that had brought him to a halt, was, perhaps, too great a burden for anyone to bear. Sailors knew, like no one else, the power of ghosts in a world of jagged coastlines and empty horizons.

But if the crew could see causes for the Captain's mood, if most of them could imagine how the desolation of the coastline might have affected him even without the other problems, they did not know what the Captain himself had brought along with him, in his blood and in his mind, that made him now, locked alone for days in his cabin, bereft of hope. The sailors found *reasons* why FitzRoy should be low in spirit, but they did not grasp the degree of his anguish, for the knowable reasons alone did not account for it.

In any case, what chance had they to fall so low, to feel such private despair, living, as they did, forever in each other's reach, no doors to shut themselves behind, no air to breathe that had not passed through sixty other souls? There was surprisingly little resentment about this. It was the way things were; breeding, and the space that comes with a position in the world, were necessary conditions for the expression of profounder feelings, high or low, that a man might experience. Solitary despair was not for your ordinary, cheek-by-jowl, low-born sailor. They did things differently. A sudden drunken madness which ended, instead of with the usual hangover, with a reckless climb and final dive from the crow's nest, or, for the quieter types, a leap over the side of the ship; that was more their style than silence, a locked room and a silver filigreed pistol.

Yet, for all the known differences in class and power, the men genuinely felt for FitzRoy, not just because their fate depended on a functioning captain, but also because the distinctions of privilege meant less, in the end, than common feeling between men on a small ship at the mercy of the open seas.

Robert FitzRoy, however, had lost touch entirely with the camaraderie of the high seas. The varied reasons for feeling the way he did had vaporised as the power of his certain doom took over. Like the ingredients of a witch's spell (bat's ear, toad's breath), which lost their specificity in the overall brew, the causes of FitzRoy's despair (the Admiralty, financial ruin, the dreadful grey-green gloom), disintegrated into the all-inclusive blackness of his certain fate. Now, he swallowed the potion almost with relief that it was here at last, no longer to be waited for; the loss of everything, the final shame.

He had been expecting it for more than ten years. Now, at twenty-seven, the fear of what had to be, of the poison running in his veins, was over.

FitzRoy remained at his desk, the cabin door locked, no longer pretending to be working, no longer master of his ship. The charts lay in front of him on the desk, ignored, curled in on themselves, in the cabin which was so small his beating heart seemed to press against all four walls. He did not mind that. No sailor was troubled by cramped living conditions. But a man who had lost hope might remark on the similarity between the size of the room he had locked himself into, and the tomb in which his remains would have rested back in England, were his end not, after all, going to come at sea.

There was one comfort: he would not die a failure in the eyes of the world. They would see he had died because he refused to fail. He had never in his life done less than was asked of him, even if he had to take personal risks. They would know that on this occasion, too, he had given his all, and failed only because the means at his disposal were inadequate.

But his pride faltered. He was not a man who grasped the underlying truth of things with great ease, but once it was known, his essential honesty could not allow it to hide behind bold words. The blackness, now, was everything; no principle existed any longer. He had done the unthinkable for a commander of a ship in mid-voyage, where seventy lives depended on him: he had shut his cabin door on the world, resigned his command, and refused to speak to anyone. FitzRoy, whose honour had meant more to him than anything in the world, could no longer care about his discreditable behaviour. If his resignation and retirement into his cabin was a petulant response to not getting his own way, beneath it was a void so dark and deep that in his very heart he had given himself up for lost, and his soul, as Stokes had correctly written, was dying in him breath by breath.

FitzRoy's existence until then had been shored up with the only three things that must matter to a man: dignity, service and a profound religious faith. Now, he had failed all three tenets of propriety. He had embraced despair, which was the deadliest of all the deadly sins. It was rightly thought to be so, because each of his rules for living were utterly and irreparably shattered by it.

FitzRoy had come to a stop, but, in truth, it was his heritage, not his pride in a job well done, which was the real cause.

Not one, but two ghosts had haunted FitzRoy on this voyage. Captain Stokes, of course, had walked parallel with his every step, whispering incessantly of the danger to vulnerable men, to those cursed with a morbid imagination, of the terrible, soul-destroying coast that ran from Chiloé to Valparaíso. On FitzRoy's first journey to those parts, in his pride at taking command at such a young age, he had managed to ignore Stokes's voice, and refused to acknowledge the gloom that all his sailors felt. This time, on the return journey, he did not need the sound of Stokes's mournful warnings, once the ship had sailed round Cape Horn and the west coast came into view, to feel his throat constricting and his heart's blood drain away.

The task was to finish mapping the virtually unknown coast, to find safe harbours for passing ships in those treacherous seas. At first, FitzRoy noted and charted the inlets and promontories they came to with the cool eye of a professional maker of maps. But behind the dutiful gaze of his outer eye, another eye, whose vision seemed to bathe his mind with mood and colour in exchange for light and form, watched unblinking as the granite grey cliffs stained the air with gloom and sucked the very life out of the light.

It was clear that everyone felt the oppression of the area. Voices were subdued, and the songs the men sang came close to dirges. FitzRoy felt his blood thicken and his temples throb even as he told himself that he was merely making scientific observations. He knew he had to pay attention to his every breath if he was to sail past this dreary, desolate place with his mind intact. And all the while Stokes whispered in his ear, 'I warned you. I warned you. The soul dies. The body shrivels. There is no life. I warned you.' How could FitzRoy, whose morbid imagination had come to him with his mother's milk, resist the dying of his soul in such a place?

The other ghost lived much closer to him than his inner ear. It did not only reiterate Stokes's warnings, but surged through FitzRoy's very blood, beating in the pulse at his temple, and sweating through the pores of the palms of his hands. This ghost was another who had died by his own hand, self-killed, but with none of the ambivalence that must have caused Captain Stokes to make such a slow and sorry job of it. The other grimly efficient suicide had changed FitzRoy's life when he was just seventeen. That death had shot fear deep into him, like a bolt of lightning striking the heart of a well-grown tree, when he was still young, sturdy and upright with the certainty of a dutiful and virtuous life to come.

Stokes's crime had been one of place. A man might fight against that, might tell himself to disregard, indeed make himself proof against the danger of the world he passed through. But the other was a crime of mind, of recurrent despair and inevitable self-destruction. How could a man make himself safe from an internal demon passed down to him along the bloodline of his own mother? How could one chart a course safely through *those* dark cliffs and grim, threatening skies? No, one did not dismiss an uncle's doom so easily, merely by deciding to be strong against it.

The memory of that last day of youthful, innocent hope was constantly with FitzRoy. It came to him each time he looked in the glass and saw the face that so closely echoed that of the man whose namesake he was, Robert Stewart, Viscount Castlereagh, Second Marquess of Londonderry. Uncle Robert, whose grey eyes, sloping brow and fine-honed hooked nose were quoted wherever Robert FitzRoy's reflection stared back at him. Uncle Robert had taken his last breath, and ended his torment early on one summer morning that his nephew had thought no more than ordinary, as he'd breathed in, with the warm sweet air, the promise of his forthcoming life and daredevil adventures.

What young Robert had felt most keenly on first hearing of his uncle's suicide, was the loss of family honour. Not just the disgrace of suicide, but the rumours, which had accompanied the news, of an unspeakable scandal which, despite the unspoken words, cast doubt on his uncle's manhood.

Robert was already a midshipman by then, and dreaming dreams of great adventures and of magnificently fulfilling his family tradition of service to his country. On both sides of the family there had been military men, sailors and politicians, and if there was the stain of bastardy at the beginning of the dynasty, it was a *royal* bastardy. Charles II had honourably conferred a dukedom on the love-child who could never inherit the throne. For a young man whose head was filled with the curious mixture of pride and responsibility which the already old-fashioned Tory nobility had made its own, the death of a close relation – and a Home Secretary, in the full public gaze – in such unsavoury circumstances, was a burden too terrible to bear.

And yet, of course, he had borne it, precisely because family tradition demanded it. He rode in the carriage following his uncle's body to Westminster, his face stony against the jeers and cheers from the populace lining the streets as if for a festival of fools. He walked, behind the bier, into the Abbey, upright and handsome in his ceremonial uniform, head held high against the whisperings. His youthful discipline and composure was noted and went some way to make up for the dynastic disgrace.

None the less, when the ceremonial was over, and Robert was returning to his ship, he remembered the stories about his uncle. A strange, perhaps unseemly, companionship with a Russian princess whose reputation was not unassailable. Times when he would shut himself away and refuse to speak. The final, terrible story – a man, a park, letters – that had his noble uncle on his knees, weeping and pawing at the King's breeches, begging him not to take account of any scandal that might chance to reach His Majesty's ears. And His Majesty conferring with Wellington on what was to be done about his mad Foreign Secretary.

Mad, quite beyond redemption, so that, just days later, after his physician, Dr Bankhead, had confiscated knives and razors, and even moved in to keep a better eye on his distraught patient, Uncle Robert, in dressing-gown, and groaning (as Bankhead said: a groan which could never be either emulated or forgotten) had stabbed himself with uncanny anatomical precision in the jugular vein with a secreted penknife, and died within seconds, saying only, as the good doctor rushed in at the commotion, 'Bankhead, let me fall upon your arm. 'Tis all over!'

Although young Robert was not of country stock, he knew enough about bloodlines and breeding to understand that certain characteristics were inherited, handed down from generation to generation. He knew also what his Bible told him about the subject. Were not the sins of the fathers to be visited upon the sons unto the fourth generation. And uncles? What of uncles? Robert had inherited

29

his uncle's nose, his receding chin, his upright stance. He was said to favour that side of the family. What of his uncle's insanity?

FitzRoy remembered strange moods and moments when, even as a small boy, the world had suddenly grown dark, and something terrible clawed at his heart as if he had been transported instantaneously to a bare, barren land from which there was no means of escape. Since his mother's death when he was five, these turns had come over him, and yet they passed momentarily, like speeding clouds causing a sudden chill as they eclipsed the sun, but then moving on to let the warmth return. He had not spoken of these dark moments to anyone, indeed, he had not supposed them to be unusual. He thought those humours merely something that happened to everyone.

Only when his uncle died had he understood. One did not have to be a physician or a philosopher to know that insanity ran in families. From then on, Robert saw more than just the physical resemblance between himself and his uncle when he stared at his reflection in the glass. He saw bad blood and a sorry end for himself. From then on fear lived in his heart and mind, a second circulatory system to complement his tainted blood. Robert had not been especially close to his uncle when he was alive, but at his death, uncle and nephew became object and shadow, held together by their bond of contaminated blood.

And now, in the seas off Valparaíso, a shameful death was riding the waves towards FitzRoy and it was, he knew, as ineluctable, and almost as impersonal, as the weight of those waves which now crashed mercilessly, though without rancour, against the ship in his command.

It was over, he was sure. Almost done.

And she watched the man at the desk, observing his torment, feeling his horror as her own. She called out to him, but although FitzRoy heard the voice of his past beckoning him towards his doom, he did not hear the future, far ahead, yet there for all that, in the same small cabin with him. She was calling out to him with the same blood fear he presently felt. But if he had heard such a call, he would only have supposed it to be the voice of the ghosts that walked the ship and preyed on his heart and mind. And then the voice itself lost power and faded, as her vision returned to the greyness, the eyestrain and the book which waited silently for attention on her lap.

Chapter 3

A MAD TEA-PARTY

'Would you tell me, please, which way I ought
to go from here?'
'That depends a good deal on where you want to
get to,' said the Cat.
'I don't much care where –' said Alice.
'Then it doesn't matter which way you go,' said
the Cat.
' – so long as I get somewhere,' Alice added as
an explanation.
'Oh, you're sure to do that,' said the Cat, 'if you
only walk long enough.'

'*Jenny*, actually,' a voice said.

Charlotte-the-Escapee was just beginning to be alarmed at the prospect of madness turning out to be eternal boredom, and had even started to wonder how things were going back in the world above her, or wherever it was. She hoped Charlotte-up-there was not misbehaving, or receiving any treatment which would make her uncomfortable when she returned to fill the vacancy she had left. It surprised her a little to realise she was planning to return. Not that she had thought she wouldn't, it was just that she hadn't thought about it at all before then. It crossed her mind she had no idea how to set about rejoining herself in the world of the normal.

Her attention, however, was distracted at that moment by the sound of '*Jenny*, actually', which seemed to her to have come after the faintest echo of someone saying 'Delightful'. If it was a conversation she was overhearing, it was a strange one, since '*Jenny*, actually', hardly seemed to be an appropriate response to 'Delightful'. Still, Charlotte reminded herself, appropriate was precisely the opposite of madness, and since she'd opted for the latter (at least in part), what did she expect? Expect the unexpected, she told herself, forgetting that good advice is rarely taken, not even from oneself.

Charlotte's confusion was not helped as she suddenly realised that she was no longer in the dark, nor in the something less than gloom which the pinpoint of light had turned into. She looked about her, and, very like a dream, she found herself to be standing on a grassy bank, a few yards from an ornamental lake.

It was one of those high summer afternoons which seems as if it might go on for ever. The sky was an improbable blue with only the occasional pillowy cloud passing across it. Around the edges of the lake, willow wept into its water, and on its glacial surface, ducks of various denominations dipped and dove in search of food.

'This is very nice,' Charlotte said to herself neutrally, and then noticed, around at the other side of the lake, three elderly gentlemen sitting on the grass with a cloth between them, apparently having a picnic. They were too distant for Charlotte to make them out in much detail, but all three had notable white beards and were rather overdressed for the heat, which could be seen to shimmer in the air above the water. There seemed to be a palpable atmosphere of ennui about them and although they appeared neither comfortable nor relaxed, they sat on as if time was of no consequence to them at all.

Charlotte was just about to set off round the lake towards the three gentlemen, when she heard the voice saying '*Jenny*, actually' once again, although rather more emphatically this time, and coming from behind her. She turned to see an immaculately crisp, white, circular tablecloth covering the grass, laid for tea, and sitting at its edge, pouring a steaming brew from the pot into two delicate, porcelain teacups on matching saucers, was a monkey.

'Ape!' the monkey said. 'Higher primate. *Pongo pygmaeus*. Orang-utan, to be precise. Monkeys: *very* distant cousins. Pleased to meet you.'

By all means, let us be precise, Charlotte thought, though she said nothing, being too preoccupied, for the moment, with staring at the animal. The orang-utan – for that was, indeed, what it was – finished pouring the tea, and looking up at Charlotte, asked, 'Milk and sugar?'

It was no ordinary orang-utan, that was for sure. Quite apart from its ability to talk (which didn't surprise Charlotte as much as it might), it wore a rather pretty floral frock, a pair of white, high-heeled summer sandals, and on its head was a pale straw hat with a large brim garlanded with cherries and apple blossom, which teetered rather on account of the ape's backward-sloping forehead. It was sitting on the grass, quite straight, as stiff-backed as it was possible for an orang-utan to be, its legs out in front and slightly parted on account of their natural bandiness.

'I *said*, "Milk and sugar?" It's very rude to stare, you know,' the orang-utan said tartly.

'I'm sorry,' Charlotte said. 'Milk, but no sugar, thank you.'

'To be strictly accurate, you should have said, "Milk, *please*, but no sugar, *thank you*." And prior to that, of course, you should have acknowledged my greeting with, "Delighted, I'm sure." But it doesn't matter since you're not quite yourself. I know what you mean, and I know you mean well. Not that meaning well ever made much impression on the world. You'd better come and sit down, or the tea will get cold. I *do* hope we will strike up a conversation soon.'

Charlotte sat herself on the grass, opposite the orang-utan, while with great care the higher primate began to slice an apple tart into five mathematically equal pieces.

'Two for you, two for me, and one, in case,' it said.

'In case of what?' Charlotte asked, taking her first slice on the plate handed to her by the orang-utan, and finding her voice at last.

'In case you never do know what,' the creature said. 'Don't you want to talk about something serious, instead of asking silly questions?'

'Well,' Charlotte began hesitantly.

'Being well? Wishing well? Treacle well? Which well did you have in mind as a subject? Please be specific,' the orang-utan demanded briskly.

'No, I meant . . . I didn't mean anything. I hadn't got round to saying what it was I meant to say.'

If the orang-utan had possessed eyebrows, they certainly would have risen high on her forehead. She waited, stirring her tea meaningfully.

'I meant to say: why did *you* say, "*Jenny*, actually"?'

'Because I was trying to explain to you that that is my name, and not Suka, nor Delightful.'

'I don't understand,' Charlotte said, hopelessly confused. 'Why would I think your name was either of those, especially since I didn't know you were here in the first place?'

'Because,' Jenny said, her patience clearly coming to an end, 'that was what you called me when you spoke to me just now.'

Charlotte decided not to argue.

'I see,' she said.

'You do not see. You think I am called Suka, or if you wish "Delightful" because that is the name on the plaque. It's an understandable mistake, but my name is, in fact, Jenny. Our name is always Jenny. Jenny was the first, you see; the first of us to arrive in your cold and clammy climate. Or, at least, the first of us to live long enough to be given a name. Now, with us displaced orangs, we take the name of our ancestors. Normally, we don't bother with names at all, we recognise each other by a variety of other means, which add up to a far more subtle sort of identification. But when Jenny the First got her name, it became a kind of mark of distinction from our brothers and sisters in what you like to call the wild. In fact, the first few of us didn't live for very long – a sorry tale of poor diet and viruses to which we had no resistance – and for some reason (perhaps the impoverished imagination of the species we were being named by) they called them all Jenny. Why waste names, I suppose, on a rapid turnover of individuals? *Jenny* rather stuck with us. We thought of ourselves and our offspring as *Jenny*, although, since waste was to become something of a fetish among your people, after that they started to give each individual a different name. It didn't catch on with us, though. So, the name's Jenny.'

Jenny, having finished her speech, gave a little bow with her head, which caused her hat to fall forward over her eyes so that the cherries dangled dangerously close to her tea.

'But if you're all called Jenny – the living and the ancestors, male and female – how can you tell one from the other?' Charlotte asked.

Charlotte had never imagined that an ape could give one a withering look, but this one managed it surprisingly well once she had shifted her hat back off her eyes.

'Do *you* need to know the name to tell if one of you is male or female?' she said scathingly.

Charlotte was giving this matter some thought when the orang went on.

'We don't tell from the *name*,' she explained, with considerable condescension. 'We tell one from another by their qualities. I explained that. Names are of no use whatever in that respect.'

'I don't know. My name's Charlotte and that makes me different from people who are called other things.'

'Does that mean you're no different from Charlotte Brontë, or Charlotte Corday, or Queen Charlotte, or Apple Charlotte?' Jenny asked, hooting with merriment at her impromptu joke.

'No,' Charlotte said, not amused. 'Because I'm Charlotte FitzRoy.'

'And does that mean that there are no other Charlottes with such a name?'

'Well, there are very few with a capital "R".'

'And is that it? Is that how people know you're you?' Jenny asked contemptuously.

'Not only . . .'

'Quite,' said Jenny.

'I believe I am the only Charlotte FitzRoy who is descended from Richard FitzRoy, who was, or, at any rate, might have been, descended from Robert FitzRoy, nephew of Lord Castlereagh, and descended on his father's side from the first Duke of Grafton, who was the illegitimate son of Charles the Second.'

'Ahh, now we're getting somewhere,' Jenny said. 'And what do all those people, with quite different names, have in common?'

'Blood,' said Charlotte, thoughtfully. 'Also grey eyes and aquiline noses. And a statistical tendency to cut their throats. An outpouring of blood and an inbreeding of chromosomes, you might say.'

'There you are, you see!' Jenny crowed, delighted with her triumph and waving her teacup dangerously. 'Known by their qualities. What runs through and out of their veins. What they look like. What they get up to. It's just the same with us. If everyone in the world was called Charlotte, you'd still be the only one quite like that, wouldn't you?'

'But how can you know about the blood in other people – orangs', I mean, veins?'

36

'Don't you?'

'Yes, *I* do, but I can test it in the lab. I wouldn't know otherwise. And even then, you can't always be sure. And orangs don't do science,' Charlotte said with rather too much confidence.

'My dear, if we had to do science to know what flowed in our veins we'd be in a sorry state. Haven't you got any further than that, yet? I forget sometimes that we are among primitives.'

Charlotte blinked.

'You mean, you just *know*?'

'Well, naturally. We've got our senses, haven't we? That is how we make sense of things. We smell, see, feel, hear, taste, and the other thing.'

'What other thing?'

'The sixth sense, of course. Unfortunately, you don't have an accurate word for it.'

'And you do?'

'Of course.'

'So?'

'There's no point in me telling it to you in orang tongue because we don't use our tongues to tell things. What we grunt, you wouldn't understand.'

'But you're speaking now?'

'One of the peculiarities of this place. It's not usual. Not how we do things in the real world.'

'Which this isn't?'

'Of course it isn't. This is a place entirely of your imaginings. A playground, you might say, of your mind. You're not well, you know. More tea?'

'How do you mean?' Charlotte asked.

'I mean, do you want me to fill up your cup?'

'No, I mean, how do you mean about this place?'

'Well,' Jenny said, filling up Charlotte's cup anyway, 'you should say what you mean. And don't give me any of that stuff about meaning what you say being the same as saying what you mean. It won't wash down here, I'm afraid. This place,' she continued, taking another piece of tart for herself, 'is a place of madness. The only types you meet down here are of the mad variety. Not normal, you know?'

'But I don't want to go among mad people,' Charlotte remarked, suddenly feeling not at all herself.

'Oh, you can't help that,' said the orang (who for a split second looked remarkably like a cat): 'we're all mad here. I'm mad. You're mad.'

'How do you know I'm mad?' said Charlotte.

'You must be,' said the orang (who was still rather catlike for an orang-utan, but beginning to look more like herself), 'or you wouldn't have come here.'

Both of them looked at each other for a moment, and then each shook their head, as if a passing dream had suddenly clouded their thoughts.

'If you must have a name for it,' the ape added, acknowledging the kind of company she had, 'you could call it Chromosome Crescent.'

'Is that where I am? Down among the chromosomes?' Charlotte asked, getting quite excited.

'You might say that. Or you could call it Memory Lane. Or Lineage Alley. Limbo Park. Dementia Place. Idyll Mews. Actually, as I explained to you, you could call it anything you like, it doesn't much matter. It won't help. I'd think about something else for the time being, if I were you. Another slice of tart?'

Charlotte declined, and noticed that Jenny put the other second slice on her own plate rather rapidly.

'This is very nice,' Charlotte said, wondering if tea was all that was ever going to happen in this place.

'Such impatience,' Jenny muttered, displeased with the manners of her visitor even though they had only been thought and not spoken. 'It's usual over tea to have an amiable conversation,' she added, while taking most of a slice of tart into her mouth and then wiping what Charlotte could not quite call her lips very thoroughly. 'Mmmm, this is a veritable queen of tarts. Are you sure you won't have . . . No? Well, I'll just . . .'

A great deal of the penultimate slice of the queen of tarts disappeared very rapidly while Charlotte worried a little if so much sugar could be good for an orang-utan's digestion.

'Nice of you to worry, but I'll be fine,' Jenny mumbled as small crumbs of pastry escaped from her mouth on to the tablecloth. She swallowed hard before continuing. 'Perhaps you would like me to tell you a story?'

Charlotte was not certain that was what she wanted at all. But there was no point in having taken all the trouble of coming here unless she took what there was on offer. So she said that she thought that a story would be lovely.

'Maybe it will, and maybe it won't,' Jenny said, not giving anything away. 'Actually,' she added, relenting a little, 'it does have its lovely moments. Which is more than can be said for your story.'

'What story? I haven't told you one.'

'No, but you will, I daresay. Never you mind, I'll get us going with a story of *my* origins. *My* story is about Jenny,' Jenny began, but was interrupted before she could get into her full flow.

'You?'

'No, the first Jenny,' Jenny snapped.

'Oh, that Jenny.'

'Yes, that one. Now, if you're quite clear, I'll get on with it.'

Jenny looked severely at Charlotte, or as severely as it was possible for an orang-utan wearing a fruited straw hat to look.

'You might think it unusual for an orang-utan to be wearing a dress and hat, and presiding over a tea-party, but, in fact, there are historical reasons for it being perfectly normal.'

'For here,' Charlotte said.

'Yes, of course, for here. That's where we are, isn't it? It all began in 1830, before the time of Jenny the First, in fact.'

'You mean Jenny was not the first, after all?'

'It depends what you mean by first,' Jenny said, rather sourly. 'This was an earlier one, but unfortunately,' and here she gave Charlotte another of those looks, 'she arrived preserved in spirits. Which makes her the first in a manner of speaking, but dead as a doornail, in actual fact. Shall I go on? Thank you. This orang, who was not called Jenny, but since she was female and something of a pioneer, I shall call Jenny *Zero*, was captured and taken on board ship to be delivered to London as the first live specimen of her type ever to reach English shores. She was, being native and open to new phenomena, very interested in her new companions and in the sea, which, of course, she had never seen before. She took to the life of a sailor like a duck to water, if you see what I mean. And the sailors took to her, too. They quite treated her as one of them once they understood the superior nature of her intelligence. The ship stopped for some time at the Isle of France to take on provisions and do repairs and so on, and Jenny Zero went with the sailors on their daily trips to the shore, where they bought goods from the market, and visited taverns and places of like description, such as sailors will. Well, one of these places of like description – '

'There's no need to be coy,' Charlotte interrupted. 'I know about brothels.'

'And well you may,' Jenny said sniffily. 'However, that aspect of the place has nothing to do with my story. One of these places *of like description* was run by an old woman who also sold coffee and hot croissants and so on, and since Jenny Zero knew that several of her human friends were to be found there, she took to going there every morning.'

'On her own?'

'Yes, quite on her own. She was no fool. She was well equipped with a sense of direction. Anyway, since it took a while for the sailors to appear from upstairs, Jenny Zero struck up an acquaintance with the old woman, and by a system of signs evolved between the two of them, Jenny managed to make her requirements known to the old dear. So every morning she would arrive, sit down at her favourite table and wait for the hot coffee (with milk, and especially sugar), croissants and a boiled egg, which was her favourite breakfast, to be brought to her. Naturally, the account was charged to the captain, who settled it before they departed. And that is how us orangs became adapted to, if not positively adept at, the pleasures of the human table. Tea-time, of course, is a particularly English variation which was added to our repertoire somewhat later. In fact, there's a report on Jenny's manners from the captain of the ship himself. Shall I quote it?'

'Please do.'

Jenny spoke in a more formal tone, reciting from memory.

' "His conduct at table, to which he was familiarly admitted, was decorous and polite. He soon comprehended the use of knives and forks, but preferred a spoon, which he handled with as much ease as any child of seven or eight years old." And that is the story of Jenny Zero.'

'That's very interesting,' Charlotte said. 'Quite remarkable. But I thought you said she was a female?'

'She knew she was a female, and we know she was a female, but, unfortunately, the captain and his crew were not so well informed. It quite makes you wonder why they bothered to go to places of like description; it's hard to believe they would have known what to do when they got there.'

'What happened to her?'

'Died, like all of them,' Jenny said resignedly.

'Of indigestion?'

'Not exactly. Nor of a virus. She died of fright.'

'What happened?'

'As I said, she got on famously with all the crew – except one. He upset her whenever he was near. There was a smell about him she found very disturbing. One day, as she was roaming about the ship, she came to a door she hadn't noticed before. Being curious, as are all highly intelligent creatures, Jenny pushed it open, and there in front of her was that man, who was, in fact, the ship's butcher, in an apron covered with blood and unspeakable bits from the insides of an ox he had just been sawing into manageable pieces, the remains of which were lying in several parts on the table in front of him. He was in the process of hacking a leg off when Jenny opened the door, so she saw him, bloodied and gored, standing there with a very nasty-looking, dripping chopper raised above his head. Now, it so happens that us modern, displaced orangs like a bit of protein with our meals, and even the natives get meat in the form of bugs and things that are attached to the leaves and fruit they eat. But Jenny Zero didn't know about any of that and, in any case, eating the odd bug is one thing, but seeing a whole dismembered ox and a man waving a chopper in what looked like her direction, is quite another altogether. She wasn't as sophisticated as we have since become, you see.'

'Being the first?'

'Being before the first. So she took fright. With a piercing scream she fled up the stairs and on to the main deck, where, tragically, she failed to stop at the side and, in despair it seemed, flung herself headlong into the boiling sea. A sailor, seeing her, yelled, "ORANG OVERBOARD!" and the captain stopped the ship. He sent a boat down to look for her, but it was too late. She drowned. They found her body, eventually, and although many of the sailors wanted to give her a hero's (they mistook her gender, remember?) funeral at sea, the

41

captain decided that she had to be taken back to England for the purpose of scientific research, which was becoming quite the thing by then. So they pickled her in a mixture of rum and vinegar with a little salt thrown in. And that is the sad story of the beginning of my dynasty.'

'It's very sad,' Charlotte murmured.

Jenny agreed.

'A tragedy. A terrible misunderstanding.'

'But where is all this getting *me*?' Charlotte wondered to herself, as they observed a moment's silence in memory of Jenny Zero.

'*Getting* you? *Getting* you? Where do you think you are? This isn't any Cook's tour for the bewildered, you know. My, you're an impatient woman. And while I think of it, do you think it's proper to wear your hair all hanging and loose around your shoulders, at your age?'

Charlotte put her hand up to her hair. It had all fallen down.

'I'm afraid my hairpins have dropped out,' she said, apologetically. She realised she was not looking very smart for tea with a well-dressed orang: a jacket and old woollen skirt, a baggy cardigan and sheepskin-lined ankle boots over thick tights. But she had been dressed as a depressed, politically disillusioned and ancestrally haunted middle-aged woman who had let herself go, on her way to work on a cold January day; she hadn't reckoned with tea-parties. She hoped that whatever the Charlotte she had left behind was wearing was more suitable for whatever she was doing.

'Never mind,' Jenny said, a little more generously. 'You can't help it, I suppose.'

'But, about *your* dress,' Charlotte said, remembering. 'You said you would explain, but you've only told me about why you drink tea.'

'Oh, yes. But that's another story for another tea. One thing at a time, that's my motto.'

'Why?'

'It's as good a motto as any, and the best I could think of just on the spur of the moment. Funny that, moments having spurs, but I suppose they ride seconds, like horses, so they need the spurs to race on towards the hour. Do you think that might be it?' Jenny paused to find out what Charlotte thought. She was particularly pleased with this line of polite tea conversation, and resolved to remember it for

42

the next time she had a guest, or even just to tell it to herself when she dined alone.

Charlotte smiled, a little weakly. Jenny thought she didn't have quite the *savoir-faire* to be a *perfect* tea companion.

'Tea's over,' Jenny suddenly declared.

'What do we do now?'

'*We* don't do anything. You get on with your business, and I get on with mine. You'll probably see me later, though.'

'But what is my business?' Charlotte asked, alarmed. She didn't like the way things kept coming to a full stop in this place, with no directions as to where to go next.

'Your business is your business, and my business is mine.'

'Who are those old men over there?' Charlotte asked.

'Oh, you don't want to worry about them. They're not important. That's why they're here.'

'But who are they? If this is a place of my imaginings, they must have something to do with me, mustn't they?'

'Oh, yes. They're here because of you, and you're here because of them. And since that's a nice round circle, I wouldn't let it bother you any further. They're just a nineteenth-century music hall act that ran out of steam and time. Three old has-beens with nothing better to do,' Jenny said airily. 'Which is not my problem. I've got matters to attend to.'

And she pulled a black patent handbag from behind her, slipped it over her hairy red forearm, and with some difficulty scrambled herself upright.

'But who *are* they?' Charlotte insisted.

Jenny said crossly, 'This is your daydream. Charlotte's revenge. You should know.'

'I don't know,' Charlotte wailed. 'What am I to do? Should I go and talk to them?'

'Why not just ignore them? You wouldn't learn much from them. You *already* haven't. So why bother not to again, is what I say. You should have brought a friend if you're so keen on company.'

'I don't think I have any friends,' Charlotte ruminated.

'You're like me,' Jenny approved. 'A solitary type. You don't want to have too many friends. I think three is the right number. Three's enough.'

'I don't even have three,' Charlotte said, feeling a little depressed that she had fewer friends than an orang-utan. 'I think you are my only friend at the moment.' Then she brightened up. 'But I can't say I'm missing the other two.'

'Maybe, if you tried to do something with your hair. That might help,' Jenny suggested by way of consolation. 'Now, I really must go.'

'What *am* I to do?' Charlotte begged Jenny, who was standing with her handbag over her arm tapping her foot impatiently.

Charlotte had always imagined (and she *had* imagined) that madness might be anguish, misery, confusion, fear; but it had never crossed her mind that it might be a grassy bank, an ornamental lake, perplexity and not knowing what to do next.

'You really have to do some thinking for yourself, you know. I can't look after you all the time. I'm a very busy orang-utan.'

Charlotte was about to panic at the idea of being left alone, when she had a thought.

'But if this *is* a place of my imaginings, then I've imagined you, and you can't possibly have anything to do which doesn't concern me. You can't leave if I don't want you to.'

Jenny the orang-utan drew herself up to her full four-foot-sixish height and glared at Charlotte, rather as a white corpuscle might glare at an invading virus.

'Oh, I can't, can't I? Well, you just watch me!' she said in her most queenly voice.

And with that she made a regal exit, or rather, a regal disappearance, for as Charlotte looked at her, she, the cloth and the tea things on it (including the last slice of apple tart for you never do know what) simply vanished into thin air. And there was not so much as a smile left in the place where they had been.

The three elderly gentlemen with beards sat in a languid circle on the grassy bank, around a bright white cloth covered with the detritus of a picnic lunch. They looked neither comfortable in their formal suits, nor relaxed; yet they sat on.

The man on the left was the first to break the silence. His massive head was framed with a shock of unkempt white hair which developed into a equally untamed beard, making the size of his head

44

seem all the more monumental. He spoke in a thick, guttural accent, and although his words suggested perplexity, the tone of his voice was more suited to certainty, so that the doubt boomed out as if he were making a definitive point.

'I did not think this is what it would be like.'

'No, nor I,' agreed the man in the middle, who also spoke with an accent which indicated Teutonic origins. His timbre, however, was softer than the first man's, as if he were better used to speaking into an attentive silence. He was considerably more compact than the man to his left. *His* beard was neatly trimmed and curved carefully around the frame of a thin, rather solemn, if not severe face. The look of calculated neatness was reinforced by the smoothness of his bald head, and wire-framed, circular eyeglasses.

'Well, I never dreamed . . . not since I was a very young man . . .' the man on the right said energetically, with an accent which was unmistakably English and well-bred. His beard was quite the longest of the three, cascading untidily almost halfway down his chest, and his high bald forehead made his overhanging brow ridges seem all the more prominent, giving the small eyes a secluded, almost crafty appearance which was at odds with the boyishness of his tone.

'Of course you dreamed,' the man in the centre snapped, losing his earlier softness. 'Everyone does. It is only that you have repressed the memory. Lie down, I can help you.'

The man with the English accent sighed impatience into his flowing white beard at the literalism of his companion.

'No, no. It is an *expression*. It means that, like you, I did not think this is how it would be.'

'Yes,' the man with the glasses said triumphantly. 'An expression! But an expression of what?'

'Or that it would be at all,' the first man rumbled with a dumbfounded shrug, ignoring the previous speaker. 'And I was so sure there was nothing else. Nothing was more certain . . .'

Apart from their equally unsuitable clothing for a summer picnic, and a certain similarity in their stiffness of bearing, the three men appeared to have little in common, yet they sat on together by the lake, clearly having nothing better to do. They lapsed, once again, into a bemused silence.

45

It was broken this time by the English gentleman who had been dreamily looking over his shoulder.

'I say, do you see that, over there?'

The other two men followed his pointing finger with their eyes.

'I think I do,' said the man in the middle. 'And yet, perhaps it is nothing more than a passing fantasy. A figment . . .'

'Rubbish! It's there, plain as the nose on my face. A phenomenon, not a figment,' the man on the left declared, throwing a challenging look at the previous speaker. His German accent had become more pronounced.

'There *does* seem to be something,' said the Englishman, tentatively, as if not wishing to contradict anyone. 'What do you suppose it is? If I didn't know better, I'd say it was a member of the genus Pongidae. But how would it come to be wearing a dress?'

'*Jenny*, actually, gentlemen, not Genus. Pleased to meet you.'

Jenny the orang-utan appeared through a clump of trees, befrocked, behatted and with her handbag swinging from her arm.

'An interesting case of hysteria,' the man with the soft German accent said, taking out a pipe from his pocket and proceeding, with great deliberation, to fill it with tobacco from a leather pouch.

'A misrepresentation,' the man on the left announced, and turned away to stare in quite another direction. 'The particular circumstances in which we find ourselves inevitably lead to a false consciousness of the state of things. It's no business of ours, this apparition.'

'My dear Karl, surely you can't mean that?' Jenny said, sitting down and joining them.

'The phantoms formed in the human brain are necessarily sublimates of material life-processes – ' Karl said, refusing to look at her.

'Exactly, sublimation!' the man in the middle said, taking a deeply satisfying suck on his pipe.

'You didn't let me finish,' Karl said, a little threateningly. 'I was going on to explain – !'

'The thing is,' the Englishman said, 'there is no survival value in a member of the Pongidae wearing a dress, and therefore, I'm sorry, really sorry, I have to agree with my colleagues, you can't exist.'

Jenny, by now, seemed more interested in picking something very small but fascinating from between the toes of her left foot, having slipped off her shoes with some relief.

'The point is, gentlemen,' she said, without looking up from her task, 'here we all are, whether we exist or not. And I notice you don't have much left of your picnic.'

'I *was* wondering,' Karl said, reluctantly turning around and talking to the orang-utan, 'how we might come upon another bottle of wine.'

'And some more food,' the Englishman added eagerly.

Jenny looked up.

'No dice, Karl. Not possible, I'm afraid, Charles.'

'Isn't there anywhere we could go to get something?' the man in the middle asked.

'Sorry, Sigmund, there isn't anywhere,' Jenny explained.

'Well then, we'd better go,' Sigmund said.

Jenny found a little something to scratch down the front of her dress.

'No, gentlemen, you don't understand. There isn't *anywhere*.'

Something was beginning to dawn on the three men.

'Nowhere at all?' Charles asked, alarmed.

'Exactly.'

'But,' Karl spluttered, 'we can't sit here, in this terrible heat with nothing to do – or eat or drink, for ever. That's intolerable.'

The orang-utan looked up and nodded, making the cherries on her hat jiggle. Something very like a smile crossed her face.

'Yes,' she agreed. 'It's hell, isn't it?'

There was a heavy silence for a moment.

'What about that woman across the lake?' Sigmund asked.

'That's Charlotte FitzRoy.'

The three men looked at the figure of the woman in the distance, standing aimlessly by herself.

'And what is a Charlotte FitzRoy?' Karl wondered.

'Crazy. Off her head. Out to lunch,' Jenny replied.

'Like us,' Karl muttered.

'No,' Charles explained, 'we're out *of* lunch. That's different, I think.'

'It certainly is,' Sigmund agreed. 'Couldn't she help us?'

'It's her show. She's in charge. You could say the lunatics have taken over the asylum. Frankly, I don't fancy your chances; I don't think she thinks you've helped her much. She's very disappointed in the three of you. That's why she's here. But I'd say she's your best bet for lunch. Your only bet, in fact.'

'Did you say "FitzRoy"?' Charles asked.

'Yes, I did.'

'Would that be with a capital "R"?'

'It might be . . .'

'Not a descendant of that idiot Robert FitzRoy?'

'She doesn't know. She believes herself to be doomed. Psychologically. Politically. And genetically. Welcome to the wonderful world of disappointment, boys.'

'Well, of course she's doomed,' grunted Sigmund. 'But no more so than anyone else. The question is whether she will suffer beyond ordinary unhappiness. It depends entirely on her ability to confront her unconscious – '

'Nonsense!' Karl broke in angrily. 'It is not the unconsciousness of men that determines their being, but, on the contrary . . . Or rather,' he corrected himself, puzzled, ' . . . on the converse, or possibly the obverse . . . '

'Women are very difficult,' Sigmund mumbled to himself. 'Complex isn't the word for them. But if lunch depends on her . . . '

'If she's in direct line to Robert FitzRoy, then she's got a real problem. There is nothing fantastical or unconscious in being worried about that heritage. Her chance, according to Mendel . . . '

Charles began doing a calculation which involved the fingers of both hands.

'Gentlemen!' Jenny interrupted. 'Perhaps you'd better go and see her. You're here because she is.'

'Don't see what it's got to do with us. I mean, the three of us are theoreticians; we can't be at the beck and call of every individual who feels disappointed,' Sigmund said moodily, as if his mother had told him to go and play with the little girl next door. Karl and Charles grunted their agreement with their friend and looked to see if there were any clouds in the sky that might signify rain. But the sky was as blue as blue could be, and there was nothing in prospect but the endless, the eternal afternoon.

'But if we *were* to – engage with this lady,' Sigmund began.

'This *person!*' Karl corrected. 'I believe women have made great strides recently. Best not to get on the bad side of them – particularly if they're in charge of lunch.'

' . . . her, over there. You think there might, perhaps, be refreshments?'

'Oh, I should think so,' Jenny said, getting up and straightening her frock. 'You couldn't be expected to *engage* without refreshment.'

The three men looked at each other and came to a silent accord.

'Very well,' Karl said darkly, choosing himself as spokesman for the rest. 'We will do so. But I want to put it on record that I do *not* believe that the situation I find myself in is anything more than a mystification.'

'Yes, exactly,' Sigmund added, nodding his fervent agreement.

'Hear, hear!' said Charles, adding his conviction to the rest.

'Your reservations are noted, gentlemen,' Jenny said, slipping her shoes back on, sliding her bag over her arm and heading off into the trees. 'There's your boat, I believe,' she said, pointing to a small rowboat which had appeared at the water's edge. '*Bon voyage!*'

Chapter 4

REAL TEARS

———

'You won't make yourself a bit realler by crying,'
Tweedledee remarked: 'there's nothing to cry
about.'
'If I wasn't real,' Alice said – half-laughing
through her tears, it all seemed so ridiculous – 'I
shouldn't be able to cry.'
'I hope you don't suppose those are real tears?'
Tweedledum interrupted in a tone of great
contempt.

Charlotte, quietened by the Valium and appalled at herself, had made no objection to putting herself out of harm's (and the curious eyes of the neighbours) way.

Charlotte was not unhappy to be in the hospital, and to have her days arranged for her. There was a time to get up, a time for coffee, lunch and tea, all provided by someone else. All she had to do was get out of bed, dress, and wander into the day-room, where she could sit undisturbed (except for the chirpy exhortations of the art therapist) and read her book, until it was time for some scheduled thing or other. There were other patients, of course, but apart from the occasional chat or dramatic episode they left her pretty well to herself. The young were interested only in the young, and the miserable middle-aged wanted nothing more than to sit alone, brooding, or, at least, seeming to brood.

At the hospital Charlotte was in the care of Dr Davies, whom she saw twice in the first week and then never again. He was a neatly suited man about whom Charlotte had no feelings whatsoever. He made it clear to her that he felt the episode in the front garden was an isolated incident, a case of sudden overload. She was, he told her, in a state of acute depression, a not unusual response to unexpected bereavement, and, in all likelihood, she was also suffering from an erratic or depleted supply of hormones. Charlotte was put on antidepressant tablets, and since she had shown no further signs of bizarre behaviour or untoward thought processes, it was decided that a few weeks' rest in hospital, giving the pills time to do their work, should be enough. Provided she agreed to see a therapist regularly when she went back home, and continued with the medication, she might aim for a return to work within a couple of months.

Julian made resentful, though regular visits to the hospital, resigned to, if not happy about, the fact that he was her only remaining relative. He was reassured by his mother's flattened mood, and the doctor's professional opinion that she would stay that way, nice and quiet, once she was home.

Dr Davies advised Charlotte to try to put the front-garden incident out of her mind, but although she was feeling exhausted and low, so utterly and curiously depleted that she could barely think at all, the events of that awful morning had stayed in her mind like a high brick wall she could never hope to climb.

She only spoke of her perplexity to Matthew Dean, the registrar put in charge of her case. He was a big, bearish man just a few years younger than Charlotte, with long, untidy hair, left over from another decade, who wore shapeless jeans and bright-coloured shirts. She saw him several times a week and quickly came to like his practical humour and relaxed attitude. He seemed almost over-anxious not to fall into the style of a stereotypical therapist, and was not entirely, it was clear, comfortable in the hierarchical hospital setting. Sometimes, when he was on night duty, he and Charlotte smoked cigarettes together in the patients' kitchen, holed up like outlaws because Matthew wasn't supposed to smoke on duty, and Charlotte was supposed to be in bed.

'Are you a Freudian?' she asked him, at their first meeting in the neutrally furnished ward consulting room.

'I think of myself as more of a witness than an analyst or therapist. What do you think you need?'

'Oh, medication and support. Someone to chat to.'

Charlotte was quoting Davies verbatim.

Matthew raised an amused eyebrow.

Charlotte had, in the past, considerable political objections to

51

psychotherapy. It was self-centred, inward-looking. An ugly aspect of Western materialism. She supposed a great deal of her time with Matthew would be spent in silence, and she had no objection to that, but she also knew that she had to find enough words to make him feel she was trying to deal with her situation.

She eyed the open box of tissues on the table beside her chair with deep suspicion, and saw it, not as an inanimate object, but a malevolent little beast which waited, gaping, for her inevitable capitulation into tears. She determined it would not triumph. The Kleenex would stay folded and undampened in their box. Matthew's calm, friendly manner was, she suspected, deceptive. The owner of the beastly tissues also waited for her collapse. She wasn't going to give either box or owner the satisfaction. If there was crying to do, she would do it in private.

'What is the point of this?' she asked Matthew crisply. 'Of going over the past? What's done is done. I'm almost fifty and what has happened won't change.'

'It does no harm,' he said quietly, 'to look at what happened and how it might have been different.'

'Even if it can't be changed?'

'Information is information,' Matthew said easily. 'And anyway we've got to do something if we're going to sit opposite each other two or three times a week.'

Charlotte could have argued, but she didn't. Seeing Matthew would do no harm.

When she worried about the inexplicable garden business to Matthew one evening in the patients' kitchen, he shrugged his shoulders.

'You know why it's inexplicable?' he said, exhaling a long plume of smoke. '*Because* it's inexplicable. Madness is mad. The whole point of it is that it's not reasonable. There isn't an explanation for why you stripped off and pulled up your plants, except that it was a perfectly mad thing to do.'

Charlotte took his point, but even so, sometimes she sat in her chair in the hospital day-room with shame flowing through her as the memory, like an adrenalin rush, threatened to quite overwhelm her. She shook her head slowly against it, and from time to time, as if fending off a re-emergence of the disorder, she raised her hand to her head to check on the stability of her hairpins. Her only activity was to read and reread the FitzRoy book, the one which told her so much about herself and her prospects, and which, without her knowing it, had even begun to inhabit her dreams.

She did not mention either the book, or her conviction about her origins to Matthew. She wanted him to convey her good progress to Dr Davies, and he did. All in all, it was, Davies thought, a very good example of the modern management of mental illness. A textbook case.

During Julian's visits neither of them mentioned what had happened in the front garden, but one evening Julian told her he had called the garden design firm which had created a brick and terracotta patio out of the concrete backyard of the artisan cottage which was now his house. He'd asked them to sort out his mother's devastated garden.

'In any case,' he told Charlotte, although they hadn't discussed why the gardening service was so urgently needed, nor even the reason why she hadn't been home for the past fortnight, 'it's such an eyesore. I don't know how you can bear to live with it. Roses, peonies, *grass*, for God's sake. Appallingly suburban, Mother. They'll do a decent redesign job for you.'

Charlotte didn't care, so long as someone took away the uprooted shrivelling plants she saw in her mind's eye sprawling in her garden like dead comrades. Paying to have the whole garden redesigned would take a chunk of her savings, but she didn't complain. In a way, it made sense to pay an exorbitant fee to someone, and why not a firm of gardeners? It would be a form of just punishment, so that, perhaps, once payment was made, the whole incident would be over and done with, and the shame of it expunged with the laying of London brick and gravel over the wounded remains.

Julian never mentioned what had happened when he spoke to his mother, but did ask at every phone call and visit whether she was taking her pills. She assured him she was.

'Good,' he would say, relieved. 'So you're feeling better.'

Meaning, Charlotte understood, we aren't going to have a repetition of that unpleasant business, are we? The unpleasant business was why Charlotte had agreed, as a voluntary patient, to go on medication; she also did not want a repetition. But, nevertheless, she was *not* taking the pills that were handed to her in a small paper cup, three times a day. She would tuck them under her tongue and then spit them into a handkerchief to hide away in the back of her locker drawer. She herself did not understand why. She was certain that she didn't want that awful morning to recur, but something prevented her from taking the pills that were supposed to ensure it wouldn't. While, around the surface of her mind, she would rather have been drugged into oblivion than have a thing like that happen again, somewhere underground, it seemed to be a risk she was prepared to take.

Charlotte, however, did not think about it, because such a thought was too shocking. She simply found herself hiding the pills she was supposed to swallow, and shrugged away the question her rational, nervous mind tried to ask.

Nothing terrible seemed to happen as a result of not taking the tablets, and she managed to give the doctors and her son the impression that she was a sober citizen once more. She gained time to continue with something urgent, and so secret that she herself didn't understand exactly what it was.

But Charlotte knew it was better this way. She had to keep to herself the knowledge that she was someone other than who she had always thought herself to be, at least for the time being. No one could have the shocking revelation that had recently so altered the meaning of her whole life. That story was for some other sort of investigation, though what that might be, she couldn't begin to say.

She did tell Matthew about the redesigning of her garden.

'What are they going to do with it?' he asked.

'Pave it, according to Julian. He says paving's the only thing, these days.'

'Do you want it paved over?'

Charlotte shrugged.

'It doesn't matter. It'll mean less work.'

'But how will you dig your way out?'

Charlotte stared at him dolefully.

'I can always buy myself a jack hammer if things get desperate.'

'They're not desperate yet, then?'

'I'm not home, yet.'

She liked Matthew's casual view of demented behaviour. He made it seem almost inconsequential. They established a warmth for each other during their conversations, and it had been a long time since Charlotte had enjoyed sitting and talking with someone. Even so, she didn't tell him about not taking the pills, nor about FitzRoy, even when he saw her reading the book in the day-room.

'What's that?' he asked, folding himself into a chair beside her.

'A biography of Robert FitzRoy. He was the captain of the *Beagle*. The ship Darwin was on.'

'Is he a relative of yours?'

'Not very likely,' Charlotte smiled. 'Fitzroys are two a penny.'

'But look,' Matthew said, leaning across and pointing at the title at the top of the page she was reading. 'It's spelt with a capital "R". Don't you spell your name like that? That can't be very usual.'

'I'm afraid it's just a coincidence. I don't have any illustrious ancestors as far as I know.'

'Funny, though,' Matthew said, letting it drop.

'Yes, funny,' Charlotte agreed.

Occasionally, when she was alone in the day-room, Charlotte would allow herself a deep sigh. It was dangerous, because it disturbed the careful equilibrium with which she got through her day. Sometimes, though, she had to release the pressure.

There was no doubt she was depressed; probably what Davies would have called 'clinically depressed'. However, recognise its depth though Charlotte might, what mattered was that no one else did, and funnily enough, no one *did*. Of course, she had been depressed since before the dreadful business in the garden. Perhaps, since long before. But having lived with it sandwiched, as it were, between her epidermis and the first layer of fat beneath, she had managed.

The fact was that no one thought she was unduly depressed. Depressed, yes; they would have diagnosed her as very unwell if she hadn't been. But not unduly so.

But she *was* unduly so. It felt like that top layer of skin had been removed, and suddenly the depression was exposed to the air. Yes, that was it, as if she had been skinned. There was less of herself now, that was how it seemed to her, and that lesser Charlotte was obliged to

55

keep up appearances in spite of having to carry the full load of pain. And yet she knew she must, not for the sake of others, but for herself.

And she had done the job very well, so far. Behaved properly, and been just defeated enough to be both understandable to the doctors and a reassurance to her son. And that, in spite of refusing to take the little yellow pills which were supposed to make her brain produce more (or was it less) tryptophan so that . . . So that she didn't know what. It wasn't bravery, putting up with the pain, but *necessity*, which made putting up with it possible.

Late at night, when the visitors had gone, the other patients secured in medicated sleep, and the doctors were safely at home, she wept. Not the special tears that came in response to private or public tragedy, but just plain, everyday salt tears that had been queuing up quietly behind her tear ducts all the day long, waiting for their moment of release. Patient sort of tears they were, not demanding to be shed before it was convenient, or overcoming her in the lunch queue. They were workaday tears, which fitted themselves in with Charlotte's daily routine.

They came from a place of despair far inside her, a place where hopelessness meant precisely what it signified – that there was not a glimmer, not the faintest, meanest chance of hope. Hope for what? Nothing. Not directed hope. Just none whatever.

She felt, during the times the tears had to wait because there were people to deceive, like a desert: dry, unbounded, parched, so that her skin actually felt as if it might crack from lack of moisture. No feelings of depression had ever been as bad as this, or quite so lacking in the prospect of termination. There was no end to her desert; or so it seemed during the day and on those evenings when Julian came or a colleague popped in to find out, in a normal friendly sort of way, how she was doing.

And yet. And yet, when, safely alone in bed, late at night, she finally let the tears tumble, not bothering to mop them up because it didn't matter and, anyway, she knew more and more would fall, something happened. During the expulsion (there was no sobbing, just the flood down her cheeks and deep, tremulous breathing) a change took place. If it was a watering of her desert, it did not cause it to spring into life, but it made, perhaps, relieving irrigation channels, small rivulets that broke up the vastness of the wasteland inside her.

There *was* something healing, something special that occurred, and she didn't understand it. Eventually, she arrived at a sort of deep peace, as if depression took on its other meaning and provided a profound and comforting trench into which she could curl safely.

Charlotte felt then, in those late hours, almost euphoric; though quietly. She achieved a kind of serenity which was as powerful and mind-altering as a drug. It did not dispel the lack of hope, but changed the anguish that looked to hope for its relief. There was no need for hope, and she didn't find it. What she got was a kind of rest, a place of retreat, in which wounds were healed and sadness transformed itself into a most particular joy, without losing a deeper sadness which seemed to her to be essential. This sadness was global, quite unrelated to herself, and it was not a companion of pain. It was a spirit that flowed through her and made her, in those very early hours of the morning, more human than she had ever felt in her life.

And, naturally, it did not last. Dreams, reveries, revelations, never do.

In the cold light of morning she awoke to take on the task of the day, which was always the same: not to arouse suspicions which would make them wonder about her medication. Why, she still could not tell, because, at least during the day, she did not care for her mind and feelings the way they were. There was nothing logical or reasoned about her secret refusal to allow them to be modified.

But the night-time alterations she underwent were not wasted; they did not disappear without trace. They left enough memory of themselves to whisper to her of other things, other possibilities.

It was much more than she could have hoped for in her desert condition.

One night, after having only seen him a couple of times, Matthew surprised her in the middle of her secret weeping. He was on late call and had just attended an emergency. He walked past the ward and saw Charlotte sitting up in bed. He was so quiet that Charlotte didn't notice him until he was right beside her. Her face was drenched with tears, her breath banked behind her throat with the effort of not crying out loud and waking anyone. Matthew's appearance was too sudden for her to be able to stop herself. He said nothing, but sat down on the bed beside her pillows. He put his arm around her, cradling her silent, shuddering torso against his, and rocked her gently backwards and forwards. He didn't tell her to calm down. He didn't say anything, just sat with her, holding her until the peace came and Charlotte was ready to sleep. He looked down at her face and softly kissed her on the forehead, like a parent settling a child for sleep. Then he left, and didn't mention the episode at their next meeting.

'What was going on with you before your little gardening caper?' was what Matthew asked Charlotte at the next session.

She was surprised to find that she didn't mind him asking, and even more surprised that she wanted to tell him.

'There were two things,' Charlotte said, thinking back. 'One public, the other private. Two losses.'

Matthew invited her to go on with a raising of his eyebrows.

'The Berlin Wall came down and my daughter was killed.'

'You said one was private and one public?'

It was a question. Charlotte smiled. Matthew had impressed her. She had wondered if, hoped, perhaps, the tears she was shedding late into the night recently were for her daughter. But she knew they weren't. They weren't private tears.

'There was a particular terror which haunted me for most of Julian and Miranda's childhood,' she began to explain to Matthew, lighting another cigarette. 'It was that they would die in some kind of nuclear conflagration. It wasn't about kinds of dying. There are other deaths just as awful to imagine that don't require a world war, or nuclear accident. It was about my children being just two among a great many deaths, so that, if I outlived them, even only by moments, their particular loss would disappear among the millions of losses. The terrible thing about death in war or a gigantic accident involving thousands or millions of people is that it's impersonal. It loses its singularity, and I was afraid it would deprive me of the right to mourn for the death of two specific souls.'

Charlotte took a breath before going on, and Matthew waited.

'Now that one of them *has* died, and in quite singular circumstances, I realise how theoretical my old fears were. Or dishonest, rather. As it turned out, I had tears for the death of socialism, but none for the death of my daughter. Of the two fatalities, it was the loss of my ideals which turned out to be the most personal.'

58

It was the first time since the garden incident that Charlotte had allowed herself to remember, in detail, those two near-simultaneous endings. She recollected the first for Matthew, who was so good at listening quietly and with humour, and for herself, choosing to begin on an evening in the autumn of 1989.

She had switched on the television for the nine o'clock news. The time was momentous, of course. For weeks, for months, people had been saying, in the curious, dreamlike sort of way people do when they can't quite believe what they're saying is actually true, that they were all living through an historical moment. Charlotte had thought, rather sourly, that the Vietnamese might feel they had already done so, along with the people of Suez, Korea, Cambodia and most of Africa. But people, particularly those living on the small offshore island which Charlotte inhabited, had got the feeling that history's last stop had been the Second World War, since when very little had occurred that would cause historians to pen more than a paragraph or so. Now, it seemed, history had made a move, and these present times were the ones the grandchildren would be lining up to hear about. So they said in the newspapers, and on television and radio, anyway. And it was true that astonishing things were happening rather closer to home than usual.

People did feel they were living through history. Charlotte had felt more as if, for the past few months, she had been living through a nightmare which belonged, not to her, but to the entire world, which, for reasons that were not difficult to understand, chose to imagine itself instead, at the finale of a fairy story, where everything had turned out all right in the end.

That night Charlotte stared at the screen and saw an uncountable mass of people funnelling through what had once been a fortified checkpoint along the wall which for forty years had separated the socialist East from the rest of Europe. The elated, laughing young faces surged forward like a multi-headed chimera, in a chaotic, good-tempered stream towards the narrow pass of what was once Checkpoint Charlie. Their triumphant salutes and wide open mouths gasping at their achievement when they came through the barrier unhindered, and out to the other side, made them seem not so much conquerers, as newly born infants exploding their way into a new world and taking their first astonished breaths. Above the sea of

59

people at ground level, young men and women, indistinguishable in blue jeans, T-shirts and trainers, stood, legs wide, arms spread high in victory, on top of the wall; or they squatted, wielding hammers and chisels, and chipped away at the cratered concrete. And all the while, bemused guards in uniform, fresh-faced boys themselves, stood awkwardly around, their faces perplexed, firearms limp at their sides, looking embarrassed, even a little shy.

Journalists and commentators babbled their reports breathlessly, the narration coming so fast in their excitement that, above the cheering, singing crowd, it was sometimes only possible to pick out certain words spoken with a special emphasis – *triumph, democracy, freedom, unification* – from the overall tone of wonderment and choking emotion.

Charlotte had watched the celebration late into the night. Her wide, attentive grey eyes remained fixed on the television screen, barely blinking, while a silent deluge of tears streamed from them, for hour after hour, down her cheeks.

Why are they all laughing, she wondered? Why are they talking about *hope* and *freedom*? Why don't they understand? Not since – when? – 1962, the October of the Cuban missile crisis, had Charlotte felt such fear, such dread for the immediate future of the world. For years after that, she had marched and demonstrated against having to live with the terror of a world ending in nuclear conflagration, believing it would happen, that it was inevitable. And now they, the people, the reporters, the politicians were talking about the world breathing a sigh of relief, of the danger being over, while Charlotte watched the carnival barely daring to breathe at all, more filled with fear than she had ever been before.

In the middle of it all, the phone had rung.

'Well, Mother,' a cocky voice had crowed into her ear as Charlotte tried to wipe away her tears with the back of her hand. 'The dream's over. I told you, people want freedom and democracy.'

Charlotte cleared the build-up of tearful mucus from her throat, hoping it sounded like a cough.

'What people want are cars, Julian, and streets paved with gold. This is a dream; any minute now it'll become a nightmare.'

'You can't still believe all that nonsense, Mother. Look at them. Are you watching? Look at their faces. It's freedom, it's the free world they want. You'll just have to admit that capitalism has won, old girl.'

Charlotte looked at the television screen; all she could see was catastrophe.

'No, not capitalism. This is the triumph of *materialism*. They want Mercs in place of the Trabants they've dumped. Is that what you'd call a move towards freedom? And what's going to happen when they find out they're free to be unemployed and homeless? What about when they don't get their cars? What about when there aren't enough jobs for this vast movement of people across the face of Europe?'

Julian laughed.

'Dream on, Mother. The real world has just left you behind.'

'I don't think I care much for your real world if this is what it's going to be about.'

Julian's humorous tone died, to be replaced by old, old fury.

'For Christ's sake, can't you see that you're wrong? Not even now? You're wrong and stupid, and you always have been.'

As he slammed the phone down, Charlotte could hear through the earpiece the faint sound of cheering voices and the clinking of crystal glass.

To Julian, Charlotte was a dangerous dreamer; and not just because he despised her politics. He had suffered from her dreaming as a small, fatherless and needy little boy, living in his own microcosmic dystopia of emotional neglect. He had come to see the betterment of the world and the improvement of the lot of women as direct threats to his own hunger for attention. The more they occupied his mother's thoughts and time, the less he received. Drought and desperation were his own internal state of affairs, but his mother never really noticed her son's deprivation, probably because he was too near at hand. *Utopian* became a term of abuse with him, signifying all those who cared so little for him that he would care for them, and anyone who was not Julian himself, not at all.

Charlotte herself would have denied the word utopian, but she did believe in the innate goodness and perfectibility of humanity on a grand scale. She had been able to imagine the conditions where they might flower, and she understood the forces that were their opposites (for her imagination was dialectical), and the ways in which those dark forces subverted the true quality of the human race. Charlotte had never been religious, although she had an almost mystical belief in the opposing struggle between the agents of hope and despair. But she knew from an early age that the struggle took place in the material world. Good and evil *lived* in the form of political systems and institutions devoted to the freedom or enslavement of humanity. There was nothing and no one in the ether to be appealed to, there was only work and action pushing things in one direction or the other.

And she had done her best for most of her life to push like hell against the wrongs that bedevilled the world. Believing in the idea of justice, Charlotte had made it her business to attend all the major political demonstrations of the sixties and seventies. She went to meetings filled with committed people, and felt good to be sitting in the centre of an angry, concerned crowd who believed as she did. And apart from the fellow feeling, she wanted to be able to tell herself – and her children – that seeing things were wrong, she had tried to do something about it. Perhaps she did not believe, fundamentally, that marching, sitting down on pavements and signing petitions would actually change the real world of power politics, but she couldn't allow herself to do nothing. The battle against injustice and inequality often kept her busy at night and at weekends, but if the children suffered, she was genuinely convinced that in the end it was for them she worked.

By the seventies, she had thrown herself wholeheartedly into the Women's Movement, which was in full swing. She attended consciousness-raising groups, where she met and discussed sexual politics with other women, and the ways in which their actual lives had been disorted by the overriding male ideology. She read every text that emerged over the decade, and she tried to put her new understanding into daily action, both at work and with the children. As the political action of the late sixties and early seventies became increasingly ineffective, feminism provided the fellow feeling and sense of embattled comradeship that was beginning to dissipate. Sometimes, it was hard to reconcile her fundamentally Marxist beliefs with the rather differently perceived fight against the oppression of women in both the First and Third Worlds, but she tried, knowing that essentially the enemy was the same.

But, that evening, at the end of the terrible decade of Thatcher and

Reagan, as she watched the hordes passing through Checkpoint Charlie, she knew she was witnessing the final death rattle of Marxism, and for her it meant the end of hope. She felt the remnants of hope flowing out of her like menstrual blood; unstoppable. And she began while she watched, to mourn. It wasn't Marxist ideology of any particular variety she mourned, since her politics were, in truth, more felt than cerebral, but the end of the possibility of idealism. *Socialism* was not, in itself, to blame for its own demise. People were corruptible and *they* had corrupted the idea. It seemed that living political systems and ideals were unable to coexist. She didn't regret the failure of the political system of the East. It had already, long since, been tampered with by individuals hungry for power and privilege. But it had dragged the principles of justice and equality, the *essence* of socialism, down with it. A terrible spoiling, a catastrophic waste had occurred, and Charlotte wept inconsolably for it.

She wept also for the future. For the disappointment, the anger, and the chaos that was to come to those she watched walk away from the East, and to those who cheered them on so gleefully. She heard the words they shouted – *freedom* and *democracy* – ring hollow in the grim grey future she knew was just around the corner. And she wept. She wept as though her heart was breaking.

'Well, we've made a start,' Matthew said, breaking into her brooding silence.

'At what?' Charlotte asked, grimly.

'At starting,' Matthew grinned at her lopsidedly. 'No wonder you're depressed. Karl Marx has let you down very badly.'

'It's not his fault,' Charlotte said, with a half-hearted loyalty. 'How was he to know what miserable monoliths would be built in his name?'

'What other shape can there be but monolithic if you leave all mention of the individual out of the utopia you're designing? All those minds and hearts can't be ignored.'

'So what about Freud, then? Your man. He concentrated on the individual, and where has that got us? Do you really believe the world's a better place for Freudian analysis?'

'Nope,' Matthew said.

'Well, you're supposed to,' Charlotte said, a bit taken aback.

'Well, I don't,' Matthew said. 'But it's your feelings we're talking about.'

'What I think is,' Charlotte said slowly as if coming to the thought only at the moment of speaking. 'What I think is that Marx and Freud have had us by the throat for most of the twentieth century, and the truth is, *they just weren't good enough*. Oh, I know they tried. They meant well. But they were much, much smaller than we thought them to be, and they left great gaping holes which their followers filled up with shit. And now the shit's hit the fan, and we're left with no real, serious structures to think with.'

Matthew grinned and raised a clenched fist.

'Damn right! Give the woman a soapbox! Mind you, there's Darwin to think with.'

'As full of holes as your socks probably are. Gaps in the fossil record. Carbon dating definitely doubtful. Look what Herbert Spencer managed to do with Darwin. And do you really believe that a rock fish came to look like a rock fish by millions of accidental genetic mutations over millions of years? I say to hell with the lot of them. Off with their heads!'

'You want to punish the three of them for disappointing you and making you tear up your garden?'

'I sentence them to wander helplessly in the historical wilderness. I propose to put them out of my mind.'

'Well, that's them sorted out. Now, about you . . . '

It was inevitable that he would want her to continue the story through those dark winter months.

The next day Charlotte returned to her own story, searching her recent history, forcing her memory to inch its way cautiously along the last weeks of 1989. Those weeks which were bracketed between the liberation of East Germany, and that video, released by the Romanians, and shown on the television on Boxing Day, of the mortal remains of the Ceauşescus. For Charlotte, trying to find the drift that led to her moment of madness, the recollection of that time was like rereading a novel, and hiding the knowledge of the plot from herself, or rather, knowing what is to come, hoping, nevertheless, that somehow a transformation would have taken place in the pages that had waited all those years on the shelf to be taken down and turned again. Perhaps this time Raskolnikov would not kill the old woman, Jude and Sue's children would not die, and Lolita would come to love Humbert. Not exactly a happily ever after, but a turning away from tragedy to what Freud called 'ordinary unhappiness'.

But, as in books, the past does not change. At best it can be ignored and left to sit on a shelf in a neglected corner of the mind. Otherwise, if you choose to dust it off and look at it, it is what it is, and there's no escaping the marks on the page. Charlotte let her recollection run on (while Matthew continued to be an attentive but silent witness), knowing what was ahead, what had to come, but refusing to acknowledge it until it became inescapable.

It was almost two months after the breaching of the Berlin Wall that Charlotte's twenty-year-old daughter became a statistic in the Christmas road-accident figures.

Charlotte's memory arrived at that Boxing Day via the official end of the Cold War at 11.45 p.m. British time on December 3rd, the American invasion of Panama, the death of Samuel Beckett, the heavy-metal music bombardment of Noriega's refuge, and Christmas Day with her two children, Julian and Miranda. On Boxing Day itself, Charlotte was alone, using the Sunday silence that always fell on the country on Boxing Day to lick her wounds from the day before.

It had not been very much out of the ordinary at first. Every Christmas began with and then continued in panic. Panic about what had not been bought and now the shops were shut, panic about the turkey being raw in the middle despite the fact it had been in the oven since eight o'clock, panic about a present which was wrapped but had no name on it, panic about lateness, panic about earliness. All the fuss and dissonance was never really about turkeys and presents – everyone being adult and not really caring – but covered their loathing of the enforced family togetherness of the day. Each of them had something they would rather be doing, Miranda and Julian wanted to be with friends and lovers, Charlotte longed to have the day to herself so that she might ignore it, but still the plans were laid in November, and with gritted teeth and irrelevant panics they congregated in Charlotte's house by midday.

Gifts were exchanged, prettily wrapped by Miranda, and little

65

more than covered with Christmas paper by Julian and Charlotte. Charlotte tried to look delighted by the incredibly expensive cosmetics from Miranda which would never be used, and then pleased with Julian's gift of crystal wine glasses. Later, Julian noticed the book which lay on the coffee table. He looked amused as he read the title out loud; *FitzRoy of The Beagle*.

'I found it in a second-hand bookshop,' Charlotte said, trying to sound casual.

'What do you think, Mother?' he said, flipping through it. 'Is he our ancestor? If he is, as far as I can see, it makes us related to royalty.'

'No, look, his name's spelt with a capital "R". I'm afraid if you want royalty in your family you'll have to marry one of those redundant European princesses.'

Julian was joking, of course, and Charlotte supposed he was laughing at her, for her mysterious silence on the subject of her father. She never spoke to them about her origins. She changed the subject by announcing that it was time for lunch.

Every year it exhausted Charlotte, not so much the work of it – cooking a meal for three people only seemed to be more difficult than the rest of the year – but the tension which wound tighter and tighter through the day between three people who had little in common and who did not like each other very much. Charlotte thought of Christmas as a day of compressed lips, clamped together over the hours to prevent words from slipping out. The displacement panic failed occasionally, however, and sometimes open hostilities broke out, although these themselves were only shadow versions of the major explosion which had never quite happened. But that Christmas things turned decidedly nasty.

All through their meal Julian had been crowing, goading Charlotte about what he called the triumph of capitalism. By the time they got to the Christmas pudding, Charlotte had had enough. She was used to holding her tongue. Once, long ago, she had argued and explained, but it was pointless so she gave up and, as a rule, merely sighed when Julian brought up politics – his admiration for Margaret Thatcher, his loathing of social welfare and all things pinkish. But she had shed too many tears during the past two months and had listened too often to her son's smug satisfaction with the loss of everything that she'd held dear.

'You are a little shit, Julian,' Charlotte said quietly, and began to clear the pudding plates from the table. 'I don't think I ever liked you, not since you started to talk.'

Julian looked up in surprise, silenced not just by her offensive words, but also by something unusually grim in Charlotte's tone of voice.

'And you're not much better,' she added, when Miranda gave a little giggle of nervousness. 'Why don't you do something with your life? Why don't you think about someone other than yourself, just for once? I can't think of anyone more suited than you to live happily in the coming century of shopping which, with any luck, I won't live to see.'

In the ensuing dumbfounded silence Charlotte piled up the used plates and was on her way with them to the kitchen when, as if on an afterthought, she stopped beside Julian's chair. She put the dirty plates down next to his place, picked up his wine glass, his Christmas present to her, and without a word poured its contents over Julian's head.

Christmas Day had ended abruptly that year, with Julian screaming about his spoiled Armani suit and Miranda apparently a little hysterical, making a twittering, high-pitched sound that might have been laughter or tears, as they swept out with a great banging of doors into the late Christmas afternoon. Charlotte got on calmly with the washing-up thinking her momentary loss of composure was rather moderate considering the years she had put up with the two of them with hardly any complaint.

That Boxing Day, like all the others, was for recuperation and the pleasure of knowing there were 364 days before she would have to go through it again, only this time there was just the possibility that she might not have to.

It was true that she didn't like Julian. It was a fact she had come to terms with some time before. It had been her son who had caused her to question one of her most fundamental beliefs: that people were the way they were as a result of their environment. It was still something she believed in a general, public sort of way, but Julian had made her suspect that there was something essential about people that had nothing to do with how they were brought up. Almost from the moment he was born there had been something about him that was *him*, something recognisable which continued throughout his childhood and was there, plain to see, now he was an adult. Not his politics, of course, not his devotion to material well-being and contempt for those who were less fortunate; but something that *allowed* him to be what he was. It was impalpable, and yet Charlotte knew it was there, that *Julian-ness*, and that it was what enabled him to melt in so easily to the spirit of the times. Of course, she knew his politics and social attitudes were a reaction to Charlotte's own, and yet there was more than that. Before he could even say the word 'politics', before he could walk, before the word 'Mother' fell contemptuously from his lips, there was a quality, a streak of something that made Charlotte uneasy. Not a streak of conservatism, not a congenital right-wingedness, obviously, but something harsh, something brash, something that echoed into the future. All small children are selfish and unpleasant sometimes, but Julian was selfishly unpleasant and unpleasantly selfish, and made Charlotte wince. It was only to be expected that he would have his doubts about getting a younger sister, and that he would want to impress her with his seniority. Yet Julian sneered at Miranda's attempts to talk and walk in a way which had never changed, and there was never, so far as Charlotte could see, the other side, the gentleness most older children exhibit towards their younger siblings, or even to animals. You could call it a congenital selfishness or, more negatively, an innate inability to empathise with anyone or anything. Charlotte thought of it more simply: Julian was born cold.

But although Charlotte could accept that people were themselves in some deep way (the idea was not all that disturbing, in the abstract. It suggested, after all, that people might have innately good qualities which could not be entirely distorted by a poor environment), she did not feel the same equanimity when it came to Miranda. She, too, had been her own person.

Miranda was born pretty, lively and manipulative, qualities which blossomed by the time she reached adolescence. Charlotte's sense of hope had made her name her daughter after the child who cried, wide-eyed with wonder: 'O brave new world, that has such people in 't!' Miranda never had. Charlotte suspected that she had never noticed that there *was* anyone else on the planet. She was a child who was too preoccupied with catching reflections of herself to see other people. She missed the ducks in the park for the image of herself that rippled on the surface of the pond. She never discovered the satisfaction of making music or acting a play with a group of people, because when she did so she was too intent on presenting herself to the best advantage. She failed to notice huddled bodies sleeping in shop doorways when she was out in the evening because she was too busy imagining how a dress in the window above might look on her. Miranda existed, like her namesake, in a world of her own, but unlike the child of the magician, she had no desire to share it with anyone else, except those who could advance her in some way. It made her successful, desirable and, by the time she was sixteen, bankable with one of the biggest model agencies in the country. But it did not make her lovable.

Charlotte knew all this, had watched it developing in spite of all she could say and do to make Miranda a little more concerned about the world around her, but unlike Julian, Miranda caused her continued pain. She never lost hope that someday something would make her only daughter stop and reconsider her set of values. It was that hope which made her daughter's obtuseness hurt so much. Probably, it was because she was a girl, and Charlotte's young dream of a gentle, sensitive child walking hand in hand with her, sharing stories and songs and daydreams had been unwilling to die.

Perhaps, if there had been a father for the two of them, it would have been different. But independence had had a higher priority to her than the provision of an involved father for her children. On the contrary, both the growing radicalism of the feminist movement, and her own personal history had made her fierce in her determination, for the children's sake as much as her own, to do without a man. Anyway, she thought, remembering Jamie, he would not have been their father for long. But she immediately let the memory of Jamie go. He was for later, perhaps.

So the children had grown up as they had, for whatever reasons, and sad as it seemed to be to Charlotte, they were their own people now.

That Boxing Day, sitting with her stockinged feet resting on the coffee table, Charlotte shrugged off her disappointment in the children and simply took pleasure in their absence. She remembered it as a small island of peace in the turmoil of the previous couple of months. A moment of silence when her sadness with everything was put aside and she allowed herself to take pleasure in nothing more than a cigarette, a cup of coffee and solitude. To hell with Eastern Europe, to hell with the kids. Charlotte settled down to read her biography of Robert FitzRoy.

The doorbell had rung before she'd finished the first chapter.

For a moment, Charlotte had considered ignoring it, wanting to maintain her peaceful state of mind. Then, almost simultaneously with the second ring, she'd realised that she didn't want to answer it for another reason entirely. By the third ring, she was ready and got up, mouth dry, heart painfully constricted, to receive the unavoidable news on the other side of the door.

Later, Charlotte concluded that, however great her disappointment with her children, there was after all enough blood between her and them to have allowed her to know what was coming when the knock on the door interrupted her Boxing Day idyll. It was another death in another car.

Miranda had died in a tangled confusion of aspirations; a twisted Porsche, the mangled remains of a fashionable fashion photographer, and, over everything, a dusting of white powder.

It made the tabloids the following day. Miranda's photo, moody and wild, hair awry, had been taken by the young man who had died beside her. The papers spoke of wasted youth and beauty and of the suspicion that cocaine was responsible for the tragedy. It wasn't on the front page, but inside the paper, and the photograph was smaller than Miranda would have liked, but at least it was there. And later, the next month, one or two of the glossy magazines which had used Miranda to model for them, had appreciations of her. Nothing very big, but a mention, none the less; a recognition of her passing. Then, of course, the world carried on without her.

Why wouldn't it? Miranda's contribution had been decorative but essentially ephemeral. The world would have carried on without her if she hadn't died at twenty, but lived into her forties and fifties. Charlotte couldn't exclude the possibility that Miranda could have grown up; that the shock of losing her youthful prettiness (it had been nothing more than that) might have kicked her into taking stock and finding a more substantial role for herself in society. There would always be a question mark, a tiny space where Charlotte could imagine the daughter she had always imagined: strong, purposeful, interested, a doer of something worthwhile. So, in the end, she mourned a lost Miranda of the future, not the living being of the past. And it might well have been that she would have mourned that mythical person, even if Miranda had lived.

Julian said, 'Shit!' when he heard the news, turned up to the funeral in a new black suit and looked embarrassed by the whole proceedings. Death and its ceremonies was altogether too mournful for Julian's taste.

The funeral was dreamlike. Charlotte had to keep shaking herself to remember what was happening. Apart from a few of her friends, the mourners were young people whom Miranda had known. They floated around at the cemetery and afterwards in Charlotte's living-room as if they were attending a social event, a cocktail party. It was like watching the fashion pages of a glossy magazine come alive, as behatted, lanky girls with precision haircuts greeted each other with 'darlings' and pecks on the cheek, and beautiful young men posed with hands deep in the pockets of their baggy trousers, their eyes darting about the room to see if they were being seen by the right people. Several people had brought cameras and punctuated the interment with bright explosions of light. Afterwards, Charlotte moved around her living-room pouring wine into rapidly emptying glasses and heard snatches of conversations which seemed mostly to be about planning rosy futures, meetings being set up, locations being discussed, rather than the finished future of the girl they had come to see buried. Charlotte concluded that this was how it should be. What was dead should not be allowed to interfere with the confident optimism of young people who felt they ran the world. It would serve no purpose to stop and think about anything serious. Television programmes could be planned, business deals discussed, love affairs considered, but what was the point of brooding about death, why think about something you could do nothing about? It was, after all, the one thing that could not be pencilled in on the year planner on the wall.

As Charlotte approached each small group with the bottle of wine, their conversation would die, and a desperate glance pass between them. They would have to say *something* to the bereaved mother, but what? They were not equipped with this area of social skill; almost

71

none of them had experience of it. Young people died rarely, and most were not even of an age where they had experienced the death of their parents. Mostly she received a mumbled, 'Sorry . . . ' which seemed to die as the first sibilance passed their lips, because it sounded as if they were apologising for something, which was not what they had intended at all. Charlotte, having no wish to cause them discomfort, smiled her understanding of their embarrassment, and passed on quickly. One or two tried harder.

'It's such a terrible thing, Mrs FitzRoy. An awful waste,' a girl in a huge floppy-brimmed purple hat articulated through vermilion lips.

Oddly, Charlotte felt less generous about this attempt at commiseration than about the incoherence of the others.

'Well, we don't really know, do we?' she answered drily. 'It might not be a waste. Waste doesn't only happen when someone dies, you know.' She gazed into the dark-shadowed, panda eyes of the girl and then took in her modern parody of a Chanel suit, with its gold chains, box jacket and micro short tweed skirt which, parody or not, was clearly the real thing. 'In any case, waste is second cousin to greed, and where would Miranda and her charming friends have been without that? More wine?'

The girl had frozen, and Charlotte passed on, but she noticed later out of the corner of her eye the girl leaning forward towards a small group, wide-eyed and recounting something that was obviously very shocking to them all.

Soon, at around the time for getting to business lunches just late enough, the mourners began to drift away. It wasn't long before Charlotte was alone and clearing away the remains of the gathering.

After the house was cleared up, Charlotte took the phone off the hook and sat in the living-room without turning the lights on as the afternoon slipped by. In the growing dark and silence while the last of the day passed into night, and night into the following dawn, Charlotte sat waiting for the tears to come.

She was still waiting when daylight lit up the living-room and she took herself achingly, but dry-eyed, off to bed.

Charlotte had told her story to Matthew, and there was some relief in putting the words out into the world. The memories had stayed with her, but she had left out the fact that on the day after the funeral she had picked up the FitzRoy book again and, this time, was not interrupted. She had read it from cover to cover over the course of the afternoon.

And that, of course, was when the madness really started, with dreams which she had kept even from herself. Failed political ideals and the death of her daughter were enough for Matthew to make do with. Her blood she would keep to herself. Destiny, after all, was a very private matter.

Chapter 5

IMPOSSIBLE THINGS

'I can't believe that!' said Alice.
'Can't you?' the Queen said in a pitying tone.
'Try again: draw a long breath, and shut your
eyes.'
Alice laughed. 'There's no use trying,' she said:
'one can't believe impossible things.'
'I daresay you haven't had much practice,' said
the Queen. 'When I was your age, I always did
it for half-an-hour a day. Why, sometimes I've
believed as many as six impossible things before
breakfast.'

There was no doubt that time and space were con-
spiring against her. The world of the hospital corridor, along
which she had been walking after another morning reading the
FitzRoy book, evaporated so suddenly that she hadn't time to notice
it had vanished. This, she didn't mind so much; the trek had seemed
endless, the corridor disappearing into infinity and coming no better
into focus however far she walked. But it was disorienting to find
herself in so very different a place without any sense of having
travelled there.

Instead of the glossy cream ceiling, there was sky above her. It was
almost black with a blanket of inky continuous cloud which was only
broken far out at the horizon by the cold silver of a hidden, sinking
sun. At the edge of the shore the silver was echoed, as the frothing
surf caught the dying rays. Underfoot, burnt black rocks doubled the
sense of desolation – of a world charred beyond recognition. Looking
closer only increased the sense of confusion. The rock-hard surface
was neither smooth nor jagged, but swirled in oozy, serpentine

ripples which belied solidity and forced the mind towards the viscosity of molasses. None the less, above the forlorn shrieking of seabirds, a scraping sound of boots walking towards her confirmed that the ground was, in spite of its ambiguous appearance, indeed set solid.

Two men strode across the rocky terrain, side by side, each with their heads down, peering at the lava formations beneath their feet. One she recognised at once as the young naval captain who had been despairing in his cabin. The other, equally young, was not in uniform, and walked with a bouncier step. He was gesticulating excitedly, pointing to the strange patterns of solidified lava and then looking up, bright-eyed with enthusiasm, at his companion. Captain FitzRoy kept his head bowed throughout their conversation, his eyes fixed on terra firma.

'Do you see, Captain, do you see?' the ebullient young man was saying. 'We are treading with our own boots over the proof of Lyell's theory. How could such a landscape be the top of a submerged mountain? What kind of mountain terrain looks so . . . so molten? This is viscous liquid, folding and re-folding over itself and suddenly hardened, raising itself in layers until it emerged from the depths of the sea. What further proof does one need, when your own eyes must tell you the truth of it?'

FitzRoy did not reply immediately, but kept his eyes down and placed one foot in front of the other with steadfast deliberation. He was only in part continuing to examine the rocks, his eyes were lowered also to keep the growing alarm in them hidden from the sight of his companion. Each step he took felt as if he were walking away from everything he held most dear. His essential honesty made his mind keep pace with his feet. After a long moment, he spoke.

'It *is* hard to see how any other explanation would suffice for such a landscape, Mr Darwin,' he said, almost in a whisper.

'Exactly, so you see . . . ' the other man bubbled, but suddenly both his voice and feet came to a halt as if he had been struck dumb and immobilised.

He looked up, astonished, at FitzRoy, who had continued his steady pace and was now a little ahead. Had the Captain realised the enormity of what he just said? Could he leave go of his faith with such ease – speak those heretical words and walk on, without so much as breaking the rhythm of his step? He had just agreed that the landscape they were passing over necessitated his admission that it had been built by accretion, rising infinitely slowly from the depths of the sea, and so gradually that the world had to have been in existence for millennia, its beginning too far in the remote past to be imagined. It was obvious, even to a fervent believer such as the Captain, that they were not walking over a mountain-top drowned by a flood. And if this was an inescapable truth demanded by one's own eyes, how could the Christian version of geology, with its single moment of creation and subsequent cataclysmic dousing also be true?

Either the Lord had created the earth in six days and then, displeased with how things were going, made a great flood, witnessed by Noah and the animals he saved from God's wrath, which resulted in the present landscape, unaltered by later events; or the story was as their eyes and intelligence told them, and Genesis was, at best, a charming fable about moral and social behaviour. It could not be both.

But FitzRoy kept on walking towards the boat that was to take them back to the ship. He did not speak, or even raise his head until they were almost at the *Beagle*, then he looked up and stared directly at Charles, who saw his companion's eyes were clouded, as if pain had become substance and created a film across their normal vivid blue brightness. He looked, Charles thought, as if some familiar ghost had come and spoken to him of his doom, and Charles, alarmed at seeming to witness something terribly private, averted his own eyes and stared out to sea.

'Do you remember, Darwin,' FitzRoy said in a voice so quiet that Charles had to strain to hear him over the sounds of the seabirds and the roar of the sea. 'Do you remember the time, some months ago, when I . . . was tempted to resign my command of the *Beagle*?'

It was said with difficulty, his words forcing themselves through a constriction in his throat. Charles remembered it only too well. He had feared that his adventure might be over.

'Yes,' he said, keeping his eyes on the horizon, alarmed at FitzRoy's sudden need to speak of what had never been mentioned since it occurred.

'I daresay you noticed my black mood?'

He waited for Charles to grunt his embarrassed assent.

'There were certain – practical and personal reasons for my ill humour, but it began with a sudden fear I conceived about the matter of mapping the coastline. About the very reason for the voyage.' He paused as he tried to summon further courage. Then he continued, aware that he had his companion's fullest attention. 'It seemed to me that it was impossible to describe the outline of this coast – or any other – for the closer you came to it, the more detailed and the more different it appeared to be.'

Charles was astonished by this explanation and overcame his cautious silence.

'But, FitzRoy, you had no need to draw an outline in such detail. Surely it only required enough accuracy for ships to navigate by?'

'Quite. But the thought – the vision – came to me unwilled, and would not leave me. The point was this: it seemed to me that the earth – the universe – itself had become unreliable . . . no, not become: must always have been quite different from the certain image I had of it in my own mind. It was as if I, and perhaps everyone else, might be seeing a phantom which had never really existed.'

Charles's appeasing nature rushed to pour balm over the conflict his friend was feeling.

'But, FitzRoy, we are *here*, and it is where we intended to be. That is thanks to your earlier map work, and the works of other sailors for many generations. Your – our – notion of how the world is, works. How can it be wrong if it brings us to the very place we set sail for, and not just once, but time and time again?'

FitzRoy shook his head impatiently.

'Yes, yes. In some way it works. Yet, what I understood was that there is no absolute certainty. And such a degradation of confidence in what one knows in one area, means one can never be entirely confident about anything. Not about *anything*.'

With his final reiteration, Charles felt FitzRoy's eyes burning into him, challenging him to disagree with his logic. He looked directly at the Captain and saw a pain so powerful that Charles thought he felt it in his own breast. His own heart grew cold at FitzRoy's vision, as if he himself saw the horror of scepticism and where it might lead a soul. He felt the foundation of his beliefs, far less rigidly held than his friend's, rock and shake so that he trembled to his very marrow.

Charles ached for the pain FitzRoy was suffering. He wanted to offer comfort to a man who had become enveloped in blackness. Yet he saw quite clearly that he could not. Charles, whose own faith, it was now clear to him, was so diluted, could not offer FitzRoy the reassurance he needed. He could not have summoned the fervour necessary to be convincing. And, in any case, what reassurance could there be, from whatever source, for a loss of conviction such as FitzRoy had experienced? Could Charles say, don't concern yourself, everything is as you thought it was, all's well with the world and God is in His mansion? No, it would not suffice this man who, however much he might try to hide it from himself, had doubted, and once doubting could never feel perfect security again. And in the realm of faith, there was no other kind of security worth the name.

Charles, who so much wanted everything to be pleasant, could offer FitzRoy nothing but the reflection of his own pain as they continued for a moment to stare in silence at one another. Finally Charles broke the stare, unable to bear it. Nothing more was said as they arrived at the side of the ship and climbed back aboard.

The conversation was never referred to again during the voyage. It was as if it had never occurred. It seemed that FitzRoy returned to his ship and to as unclouded a view as he had left it with, if his manner was anything to go by. He did not appear to be a man changed by a sudden crevasse appearing in his most dearly held convictions.

Charles let the matter lie, preferring to assess his Captain as weak in intellectual honesty, than chance the revival of the anguish he had seen in his eyes for that brief moment on the boat.

But guiltily, as well as the pity he felt for FitzRoy, Charles experienced a small surge of delight at discovering himself to be free from such self-lacerating fears. He could not help but feel glad that his conscience could be so untroubled by the very same dubieties as made FitzRoy mad with despair. He guessed, though he didn't understand why, that this thing he had discovered about himself was a gift for which, one day, he might find himself grateful.

Charlotte, of course, did understand why, but Darwin was not her concern. She watched, along with Darwin, FitzRoy's anguished encounter with, and then avoidance of the truth, and felt her heart bursting with pity for the man so lost in his changing times. She followed him to his bunk where he lay desperately trying to achieve a blank, pain-free existence, but no consolation of hers would have helped him, even if he'd had the capacity to hear the chaotic story of the future, which was all she had to tell him.

Chapter 6

JAM TOMORROW

———

'Twopence a week, and jam every other day,' the
Queen said.
Alice couldn't help laughing, as she said, 'I
don't want you to hire me – and I don't care for
jam.'
'It's very good jam,' said the Queen.
'Well, I don't want any to-day, at any rate.'
'You couldn't have it if you did want it,' the
Queen said. 'The rule is, jam to-morrow and
jam yesterday – but never jam to-day.'
'It must come sometimes to "jam to-day," ' Alice
objected.
'No, it can't,' said the Queen. 'It's jam every
other day: to-day isn't any other day, you
know.'

Charlotte-the-Decidedly-Demented gazed mournfully up into the pointless blue sky. She felt she wasn't managing madness very well at all. It was one thing to decamp and get as far away as she could from the miserable mind of Charlotte in the world above, but what was she to do all alone in this place, with nowhere to go and nothing to do? It was begining to look remarkably similar to life on the surface.

Hearing a noise, she turned to look at the lake and saw a small rowing boat containing the three men from the other side coming towards her like the clappers. They were near enough for her to make out their voices.

'Feather! Feather!' the man with the straggly beard was shouting.

'Shut up!' answered the man with the neat beard and round glasses, who was rowing. 'What are you talking about?'

'Look, I'm English *and* I know about seafaring, and "feather" is quite definitely one of those things you say. Unless,' he murmured to himself, putting a memory-prompting finger to his lips, 'unless it was "Belay!". It's been such a long time now . . . '

'The man's an idiot,' the third said, lounging idly at the back. 'Take no notice. Just keep rowing.'

The rower turned and stared dangerously at his adviser.

'Thank you very much, Karl,' he said icily. 'That's very helpful.'

'You mustn't be so sensitive,' Karl said. 'Can't you go any faster, I'm extremely hungry.'

'So catch a crab,' Charles said jovially. 'That's a rowing joke.'

A bad-tempered silence fell over the lake while Charlotte watched the boat arrive.

She hardly needed the introductions.

'How do you do,' she said, shaking each of their hands. 'Marx. Freud. Darwin. I can't believe it!'

'No, we're having problems believing it ourselves,' Sigmund agreed. 'But you're in charge, apparently, according to that monkey. She said we should come to you. It's quite a while now since lunch, and it's very hot – '

'Orang-utan,' Charlotte corrected. 'Jenny sent you, did she?'

'She seemed to think you might want to talk to us . . . ' Karl muttered, shuffling a little. 'But my throat is so dry, I can hardly speak.'

'I wish I could help,' Charlotte said.

'You can. You can. Some wine, a little roast beef . . . ' Charles suggested.

'Sausage would be nice,' Karl added.

'Fried fish wouldn't be a bad idea,' Sigmund said.

'But I don't have anything,' Charlotte explained.

'You don't have to have anything. You just have to think of it,' Sigmund explained, quite in his element now. 'It's a matter of wish fulfilment.'

'It is? Just think and it's there? Are you sure?'

'Well, you could *try*,' Charles said. 'If it's no trouble.'

Charlotte thought, and in the twinkling of an eye, a cloth appeared on the grassy bank in front of them, and on it, a bottle of Moselle, a haunch of rare roast beef, some smoked salmon and a noble-looking German sausage.

Sigmund murmured, 'Never mind, I'll manage with the smoked salmon.'

'Any chance of a drop of claret for the beef?' Charles wondered.

A decent bottle appeared, along with an appropriate glass.

'Well, gentlemen,' Charlotte said, since she seemed to be the hostess. 'Shall we?'

They settled themselves around the cloth and began to eat and drink.

'So how can we help you?' Sigmund asked with his mouth full. 'I understand you are mad.'

'Shh,' said Charles, nervously.

'No, he's right,' Charlotte said. 'I am.'

'Well, are you taking your tablets, young woman?' Sigmund asked.

'No. *She* isn't, up there where they hand them out. She's helping me stay mad.'

'Well, you should take your tablets,' Sigmund said firmly.

'I thought you believed in the talking cure,' Charlotte said, surprised.

'I have been greatly misunderstood. I was a *doctor*. I always said one day they'd identify physical causes for neurosis. I only saw myself as a stopgap. Why, in God's name, would a person want to lay on a couch every day for years on end *talking*, when they could just take a tablet?'

'Well said,' Karl enthused, cutting himself a large slice of sausage. 'Now you're talking sense. Far too much time wasted on personal problems when there's *work* to be done in the real world.'

'Not any more,' Charlotte said. 'That's the problem. Hardly any work at all. They even say history has come to an end, Karl, without the slightest glimmer of world revolution. And somehow, Sigmund, psychoanalysis doesn't seem to have filtered down to enough people to have much of an effect on the extreme unhappiness everyone seems to be feeling. And even those who've had it don't seem a lot better for it. And, Charles, something's wrong with evolution. It doesn't seem to have worked very well, and, quite frankly, might even be said in respect of the human race, to be going backwards.'

'But apart from that, things are all right, are they?' Charles wondered as Sigmund poured the last of the white wine into his glass.

'No, that's what I'm trying to tell you. In spite of each of your Isms having had a really good run for its money, it looks very much as if the coming thing is Barbarism. Frankly, I'm very disillusioned.'

All three men stopped chewing and stared at Charlotte. Once again, it was Karl who broke the silence.

'We seem to have run out of Moselle,' he growled.

Charles seemed to be thinking deeply.

'It's funny about evolution. I think the general idea was all right, but there was always that problem about intermediate fossils being missing. Never did solve that.'

'The missing link?' Charlotte asked.

'Yes. You know it crossed my mind that the missing link between apes and *Homo sapiens* was never found because it was never missing.'

'Pardon?'

'I mean, supposing all along *we* are the missing link? Perhaps we haven't arrived at *Homo sapiens* yet, and we're just the intermediate species. Now, that would explain why there are no fossils, and a few other things too.'

'Reductionist fool!' Karl said.

'Don't speak to me like that,' Sigmund said, looking up in surprise, only to meet an equal look of surprise in Karl's expression.

'I didn't mean *you*,' Karl said. 'I meant *him*.' Karl looked from one to the other of his companions and fell to brooding. 'Still . . . '

'What about this FitzRoy business?' Charles asked his hostess, not liking the general tone of the conversation.

'I found a book about him, by accident. The more I read, the more it seems I am discovering my origins. You knew him well, didn't you?'

'Oh, origins are right up my street,' Charles said. 'But fancy someone bothering to write a book about old FitzRoy, I'd have thought he'd be quite forgotten by now. Nothing but disaster after disaster. The only thing to be said for him was taking me along with him on that trip. And that, quite honestly, was pure serendipity. If his uncle hadn't cut his throat in a manic moment, I'd never have travelled on the *Beagle* and the theory of evolution would have been – '

' – written by Alfred Russel Wallace,' Karl said sourly.

'It *was* bad luck him coming up with the same idea,' Charles agreed.

'Bad luck for him! He was a poor, self-educated young fellow, and you had your fat allowance from Papa, and all those rich, important friends to back you up. An old story!'

'And if Engels hadn't kept paying off your debts so you could sit on your *tochus*, who do you suppose would have written *Das Kapital*?' Sigmund demanded.

'It's not the same thing!' Karl bellowed.

'It's all a matter of chance,' Charles said mildly.

'Necessity!' Karl insisted.

'No, chance. I mean about me going on the voyage of the *Beagle*. FitzRoy had this terror – '

'Neurosis,' Sigmund said knowingly.

' – that he'd inherited Castlereagh's madness, so he wanted someone – a gentleman, that is, not one of the crew – to dine with him, to keep him sane during the long time at sea. And it wouldn't even have been me, because I was just an amateur collector, and actually studying to go into the church. He asked Henslow, but poor Mrs Henslow looked so upset about him going off for four years, he turned it down and suggested me . . . '

'A Tory aristocrat,' Karl spat. 'I don't know why we're bothering with FitzRoy. Just a feudal leftover.' He was still eyeing the empty bottle of wine.

'But a psyche in pain, none the less,' Sigmund said solemnly.

'Pain! Schmain!' Karl exploded. 'A *parasite* on the backs of the working classes. *Is* there going to be any more wine or isn't there?'

Another bottle of Moselle instantly arrived on the cloth, and Karl seemed a little mollified.

'He had grey eyes and a nose just like mine,' Charlotte said dreamily. 'He seemed so desperately to want to do the right thing all the time.'

'And never did,' Charles said sharply. 'He put honour above everything. A proper old-fashioned Tory. It's true his heart was in the right place most of the time . . . he wanted the best for everybody, but, quite frankly, he just didn't know what the best was. When I first met him I was dazzled. Of course, I was very young. He was only in his twenties himself, but he seemed glorious to me. Four years at sea sorted my romantic ideas out. He was a pig-headed idiot!'

'Not your "beau ideal"? That's what you called him at the beginning. It said so in the book.'

'Did I really? It's hard to remember what such enthusiasm felt like,' Charles said rather sadly. 'I was such a *boy* in those days.'

'Too eager to please and be pleased,' murmured Sigmund. 'It suggests trauma in early life.'

'Well,' Charles turned with interest to Sigmund. 'My mother did die when I was nine. Do you think . . . ?'

'Oh, shut up!' Karl snarled, and refilled his glass, draining it in a moment. This clearly made him feel a little better because with a slightly glassy look in his usually fiery eye, he gazed up into the sky and began to hum the first verse of The Internationale to himself.

Charles had also finished and refilled his glass of claret. He reorganised his position so that he could lay down with his head in Sigmund's lap, and began to talk without stopping. Sigmund seemed quite comfortable with this and in a nice, slow rhythm nodded his head up and down while intermittently murmuring 'There, there,' and stroking Charles's shiny bald pate.

Everyone seemed quite settled, except Charlotte, who feeling left out, got up and began to wander down to the lake. If she was in control of this world, it had a funny way of showing it, she thought. She wished Jenny was back again.

'All right. I'm sorry,' Charlotte called into the empty air. She was sure Jenny could hear her, and that only convincing grovelling would wheedle her back again.

'I really am sorry. I know you're busy, and, of course, you've got better things to do than talk to me, but I would appreciate it if you could spend some more time with me. I'm lost without you.'

There was a long, and it seemed to Charlotte, very noisy silence. But, eventually, it was broken.

'Oh, very well,' a voice said huffily in her ear. 'You can walk along with me.'

Jenny had reappeared in all her floral glory, and was now standing beside Charlotte, trying to look as if she had returned only because Charlotte was too hopeless to be left alone. Charlotte was grateful to Jenny for relenting, although she suspected she had nothing else to do in spite of what she'd said. But she didn't want to offend again her only friend in this, and possibly any other world, by saying so.

Charlotte fell in step and they walked, side by side, at a measured pace around the perimeter of the lake.

'I told you those old fools wouldn't be any use. Better leave them to it,' Jenny said.

'They don't seem to be interested in anything but eating,' Charlotte complained of her former heroes.

'What else is there when you're stuck in limbo? And what can they do without their adoring circles of admirers?'

'But they are the greatest thinkers of our time,' Charlotte tried to insist.

'No, they were moderately interesting thinkers of the nineteenth century. You might say that Plato is a great thinker of our time, but those three?' Jenny shook her head decisively. 'If you ever go back, just take a look at the stuff they wrote. It's remarkably implausible at source. They were, if you like, the three greatest reductionists of the nineteenth century, but take their times away, and look what happens: they're reduced to the final reduction: food. Filling their bellies. I'm surprised Sigmund settled for the sex drive. Even a phantasmagoric orang-utan could have told him that food was the simplest common denominator. Now, where shall we go?'

'Where is there to go?' Charlotte asked.

'Oh, anywhere you please – except, of course, to the world up there. Can't get back, you know, not yet. Anywhere else, though. Where do you fancy?'

Charlotte thought for a moment.

'I like being near the sea,' she said.

'There's nothing wrong with the seaside, I suppose, except for all that water, and the way the sand gets in the sandwiches. Personally, I prefer a nice rain forest. But if that's what you like, that's what you like.'

And before she knew it, Charlotte was no longer at the lake, but walking along a shingled beach, with stones crunching under her feet, beside a grey northern sea which broke gently over the shingle, rolling the pebbles around as if it were sifting through them to look for something it had lost.

They were the only people on the beach. The only person and

orang-utan, Charlotte corrected herself. It was not a day for basking. The sky was as grey as the sea, so that at the horizon they were hardly differentiated. But it was not cold. Which was just as well, because Charlotte noticed that Jenny had changed for the occasion. The pretty floral dress was gone, and in its place Jenny was wearing a bathing suit. It was, rather, a playsuit, in the style of the thirties, with a halter neck and a short, circular skirt which just skimmed the attached knickers. Charlotte liked the colour, which was the shade of blue the sky might have been, had it been obliging. She told Jenny so, without mentioning that she was less than taken with the way it hung. The shape of an orang-utan was not the perfect one to be inside a playsuit, Charlotte thought, but, not wanting to give offence, kept her counsel.

'It *is* a fine colour,' Jenny agreed. 'I like to dress suitably.'

Here, she looked a little sternly at Charlotte, who was still wearing the skirt and cardigan in which she arrived. Which wasn't fair, Charlotte thought, because she didn't know how to appear and disappear and change clothes in the twinkling of an eye. In any case, she doubted she would have braved a bottom-skimming playsuit. She had put away body-exposing clothes more than a decade before in the name of good taste, and even though good taste was, clearly, not at a premium in Jenny Orang's world, Charlotte felt that someone had to keep up aesthetic standards.

'You don't seem to be getting very far with the FitzRoy business,' Jenny Orang said, stopping to pull off a very fetching, though not all that practical, open-toed, high-heeled mule, and tipping a tiny stone out of it.

'No,' Charlotte agreed. 'They're very nice, those three, but they don't seem very interested in my personal problems. But I'm sure FitzRoy's my ancestor.'

'So what if he is?'

'So his blood runs through my veins. And the despair I'm feeling up there is inevitable and reasonable. A matter of destiny. Nothing to be done about it, and never was. All my life was nothing because I am what I am and experience is neither here nor there. Inconsequential.'

'Consequences don't matter a fig down here. You've left that sort of thing to her up there and very wisely taken a holiday. Just relax and enjoy yourself. Never mind FitzRoy – he'd be just as dead now whatever way you cut it – if you'll excuse my little joke. I'd stay neutral on the subject of destiny, if I were you. You'd be amazed at who a person can be if they put their minds to it. Don't you find that interesting?'

'Is that all? Interesting?'

'Yes. You're not very good at speculation, are you?'

Charlotte thought about it.

'I was an idealist. Idealists don't speculate, they believe in . . . '

'Yes?'

'Things,' Charlotte said weakly. 'Reality.'

'Ahh,' Jenny said, with the very mother of a sneer on her face. 'You believed in reality. Well, down here it's just a matter of being delighted by serendipity.'

'It sounds a very improbable way of going about things.'

'Improbability is what we're all about down here. That's the difference. You normally (though that's a misnomer, if ever there was one) . . . you normally live in a world where probability holds sway. It's a very bad idea. It gives you the feeling that you know the odds. That things can turn out this way, or that way, but never the other way, because the other way doesn't have sufficient, or even any probability. Now, if you live in an improbability system, you have no idea what any outcomes might be. Anything could happen, and, of course, since it could, it does. But more important, nothing couldn't happen, and since it couldn't, it does, too. That's improbability for you.'

Charlotte closed her eyes, and wondered for a moment whether she shouldn't try to persuade her upstairs element to start taking the tablets, after all.

Charlotte still couldn't see how being mad, pleasant though it was, could alter the simple biological facts of blood and chromosomes. If she was indeed FitzRoy's descendant – and Charlotte-up-top's reading suggested that she was, to say nothing of the remarkable similiarity between their physiognomies – then she was what she was, and there was a fair chance that she had inherited her great-great-grandfather's doomed chromosome 6 or whichever it was. Holidays were all very well, but what about when they were over? Suddenly, she shivered.

'I was wondering,' Charlotte said. 'If this is all in my mind, why does it have to be so gloomy and grey? Couldn't it be a bit sunnier and hotter?'

'Now you're talking,' Jenny said enthusiastically. 'I knew you'd get the hang of it, eventually.'

And as she spoke the sun broke through what had seemed an impenetrable mountain of cloud and shone with all its might, brightening the whole scene.

'While you're at it, what about the pebbles? They're very hard to walk on in these shoes.'

Charlotte was about to suggest Jenny take her shoes off, but thought better of it, knowing how important the total look was to a sartorially minded orang. Instead, she thought sand, which, in the twinkling of an eye, appeared, in billows, smooth and bright.

'But I thought you didn't like sand,' Charlotte said.

'What I *like* is good, damp undergrowth, or nice, smooth concrete. But we're not here to please me.'

'What, exactly, are we here to do?' Charlotte asked.

'I told you. To have a very nice time. It's a pleasant enough way of inhabiting madness, don't you think? You'd rather have monsters?'

'No, definitely not. I only worry that monsters will appear, anyway.'

'No, dear. Monsters are for her up there. Not your problem, at present. You've ducked out of that, remember?'

'Doesn't seem fair,' Charlotte mused.

'God preserve me from madwomen with a conscience. It's very dull. Are you sure you want to keep on walking? Upright on two legs isn't all that easy for me, you know. Especially with these shoes. Couldn't you think up a deckchair or two?'

Charlotte apologised for being so thoughtless, and made a couple of nice, green, corporation deckchairs appear. They sat down, threw off their shoes and wiggled their toes delightedly in the sand. Charlotte looked out to sea. It was an almost Mediterranean blue now, with white froth dancing at its edges. It really was quite like a holiday.

'It's very odd, this,' Charlotte mused, staring happily out to sea. 'I thought I was supposed to be depressed.'

'No, you're not. *She's* depressed; *you're* mad. There's a difference, you know.'

'Why don't you tell me about the frock?' Charlotte suggested. 'The story we didn't have time for because tea finished.'

'The frock? It's not the main thing, you know.'

'According to you nothing's the main thing. What about the serendipity factor? How do you Jenny Orangs come to be wearing frocks and hats?'

'Oh, very well,' Jenny sighed, taking Charlotte's point. 'It's a tradition handed down to us from Jenny the First.'

'The actual first?'

'Yes. The one who arrived alive at the Zoological Gardens in 1837. Listen, what about a paddle?'

Charlotte held up her skirt and the two of them tiptoed down the hot sand into the edge of the sea. It was almost unbearably delicious. She hoped things weren't going too badly for Charlotte-up-there.

'Go on,' she encouraged Jenny, who seemed to be having just as good a time, stamping up and down in the water, making it splash everywhere.

'This is nice, isn't it? Well, Jenny the First was a very famous orang-utan indeed. Everyone came to the Zoological Gardens to see her; duchesses, thinkers, artistes, Radicals, everybody, *tout le monde*. For a while she was the talk of the town. And she was happy enough. There was plenty of attention, and although it was damned cold, compared to what she was used to, and in spite of being dragged off from her little corner of paradise, she was well looked after. A man called Hunt was in charge of her. Hunt liked animals, of course, but he became particularly devoted to Jenny. He named her, in fact. She was *his* Jenny, to Hunt. He loved her. What Jenny felt about Hunt is not recorded, though I daresay she liked him well enough. For special visitors – one of whom (and here's some serendipity for you) was Charles Darwin when he returned, a respected naturalist from the *Beagle* voyage – Hunt would take them around the back of the cage, and introduce them to Jenny, person to person, as it were, and show off his pride and joy. "Jenny," he's say, "this is Lady Muck of Suchandwhere, and she's come especially to see you. Say how-deedoo." And Jenny got quite good at bobbing something quite close to a bow, if she was in the mood. "My word," the fine ladies and gents would say, "does she understand English?" And Hunt would say, somewhat cannily, "It may well be, your Lords and Ladyships."

90

Well, word of this wonder of wonders got around, and one day the command came from the Palace. Of course, *they* couldn't be expected to go popping down to the Zoological Gardens, so Jenny, along with Hunt, was invited to tea, *chez* Their Majesties.'

'Victoria?'

'No, William and Adelaide. Though only for a matter of months. William wasn't to last much longer. Anyway, there was a good deal of fuss and commotion, and Hunt, wanting Jenny to make a good impression, had Mrs Hunt run up a fine Welsh flannel chemisette, with continuations of the same, *à la turque*. That's bloomers to you,' Jenny explained in an aside. 'And over them she wore a charming frock with a matching bonnet, so that a respectable Jenny Orang could have her audience with the Queen. The truth is that Jenny had a marked tendency to play with her genitals, and was a little careless about her bodily functions, which, naturally, was not a normal part of Court etiquette, so Hunt made sure that Mrs Hunt constructed bloomers with extra-tight elastic.'

'Wasn't the King going to meet her, too?' Charlotte asked.

'No, he wasn't very well, and anyway it was felt that children and animals were more properly Queen Adelaide's concern. Well, the great day arrived. Jenny looked very fetching in her new outfit. It was all blue with sprigged flowers dotted about, I believe (a floral tradition that us orangs, down here, and Laura Ashley, up there, have maintained in the face of cruder fashion trends over the decades). And very nice it looked, too, I understand, although the particularities of the orang figure mean, as you can see, that there is a certain lumpiness, rather than a fashion-plate sleekness. Personally, I find it most attractive. More eventful, as it were, than dull old straight, smooth lines. What do you think?'

Jenny did a splashy turn or two, so that Charlotte could judge from all angles. It was a very lumpy sight, since nowhere did Jenny have anything that could be called a waist, and she did have extremely rounded shoulders, to say nothing of a floppy sack which looked very like a giant goitre at her neckline. Charlotte tried to see Jenny with the eyes of another orang-utan and, for an instant (which was long enough), she almost succeeded.

'Very nice,' she said. 'It's just a matter of how you look at things.'

'Exactly. That's what I say. Well, Queen Adelaide (who as you know had had her share of suffering, what with putting up with William's philanderings, and *then* being so kind to the resulting offspring, of which she had none) was enchanted by Jenny. As who wouldn't be? Hunt had her on a lead, and kept it short, but Her Majesty insisted that Jenny sit by her on the royal sofa and spoke to her quite as if she were an honoured visitor from another country. Which, in a manner of speaking, she was. They took tea, and Her Majesty wasn't the least bit put out when Jenny spilled some over the royal frock – '

'Why should she be? She didn't have to wash it,' Charlotte said, her old political hackles rising.

Jenny gave her a tired look.

' – the royal frock,' she repeated. 'And then Her Majesty turned to her lady-in-waiting and said, "Do you not think that Jenny here is delightful, she quite reminds me of that enchanting native child from Tierra del Fuego who Captain FitzRoy brought to visit us." '

'Hah!' Charlotte said, pointing a triumphant forefinger at Jenny. 'Serendipity!'

'Exactly so, serendipity. You're beginning to see the way things work down here, now. Your old relative brought three natives back with him from the first voyage to Tierra del Fuego. And – once they'd been cleaned up and civilised a bit – they went to tea with the King and Queen. Anyway, that's why I'm so nicely dressed. You might say it's by royal command. An orang-utan can look at a Queen, you know,' Jenny said, and began to wander off down the beach, making great splashes with her large, flat feet, humming that she did like to be beside the seaside.

Charlotte watched her go and then turned back to the sea in which she was standing. As she did so, she heard Jenny's voice calling back above the swishing of the waves.

'Did I tell you about the Queen leaving the audience chamber and returning with a beautiful bonnet from her own wardrobe? It was a delightful summer bonnet decorated with cherries and apple blossom, and with her very own hand she took off Jenny's home-made (though nice enough) hat and put her own royal one on my ancestor's head. A lovely gesture, don't you think? Tea-time!' she called.

Charlotte turned round to see Jenny back on her deckchair, almost invisible behind the lid of an enormous hamper. She heard the tinkling of a silver spoon against good bone china.

'What happened to the Fuegians?' Charlotte asked, padding back to her deckchair, more than ready for the next bout of tea.

'She hasn't got that far yet, eh? A classic FitzRoy disaster, my dear.'

There was a snort of satisfaction from Jenny as she pulled out cups and saucers, a Thermos, plates, a good many cucumber and egg sandwiches. Charlotte spied something that looked very like a cake, before Jenny shut the lid and handed her a cup and saucer and a plate. She balanced them on her knee as Jenny did the honours with the Thermos.

'I'm still not sure if I'm thinking about the right things,' Charlotte said.

'You are incorrigible. Or are you having a little joke with me?'

'I just worry about looking at the wrong things. That I may be missing something important because I'm not looking in the right place.'

'You mean, why choose to focus the time telescope on this century, on these people, in these circumstances, rather than at anything else during the last twenty billion years? Like, why aren't you watching blue-green algae form in the old pea soup, for example? Cucumber, or egg, to begin with?'

'Yes, exactly. Egg, please.'

'The answer is: why not?'

'What kind of answer is that?'

'The only one. The answer to everything is: why not?'

'Well, it's not much of an answer to everything,' Charlotte said grumpily, biting into her sandwich and finding that Jenny was right about the sand.

'No, but then it's not much of a question, either, is it?'

'You know, I think I've forgotten what the original question was. I don't remember why I'm here exactly.'

Jenny Orang smiled as she took her first sip of tea.

'That's better. Biology and destiny. I think that's what you came to find out. Which was which and why.'

'To which you say the answer is "why not?" ' Charlotte said.

'That's not very helpful, is it? It's hardly worth the trouble of getting here. I'd like a cucumber sandwich, now, please.'

'Well, you could catch the train back,' Jenny said shuffling herself comfortably into her deckchair. 'But there isn't one. You forgot to think one up. And you've certainly missed the boat. I should just stick around and see what happens. Quite honestly, you don't have much choice.'

'But that's the point,' Charlotte said, suddenly passionate, and almost spilling her tea. 'How much choice do I have about anything? About what I am. Who I am. For fifty years I've been sleep-walking. Just being a creature of my circumstances. If there's nothing else, no way to make genuine choices, I don't want any more of it.'

'I keep *telling* you. That's a problem for her, up there,' Jenny said airily, lifting the lid of the hamper and peering inside it. 'You're getting yourself confused. All you have to do down here is relax and enjoy yourself. All that meaning of life stuff is for the half-mad; for those still clinging on to reality by their broken and bloody fingernails. You're honest-to-god-and-chromosome mad, my dear. You've made it. Enjoy.' And with a flourish worthy of a fanfare she brought out from the hamper the final item on the menu. 'Angel cake?'

Chapter 7

CAN'T UNDERSTAND IT MYSELF

———

'What do you mean by that?' said the
Caterpillar sternly. 'Explain yourself!'
'I can't explain myself, I'm afraid, sir,' said
Alice, 'because I'm not myself, you see.'
'I don't see,' said the Caterpillar.
'I'm afraid I can't put it more clearly,' Alice
replied very politely, 'for I can't understand it
myself to begin with.'

Charlotte was determined that the stories she told Matthew would not make her forget the essential inconclusiveness which she now believed was all the events of a life could be. She bore in mind, and in silence, all the time, the FitzRoy heritage which had helped to turn everything so inconsequential. That knowledge would remain in her blood, circulating around her body like a foreign body against which she had no antitoxin.

'How's the front garden getting on?' Matthew said at the beginning of one session.

'Concrete to concrete . . . The burial of guilty behaviour continues, I understand.' She smiled ruefully. 'Though it's more probably York stone, which, *mea culpa*, I've got to pay for. I haven't seen it. Julian says it's coming on nicely.'

'Still no anxieties about having your escape route blocked?'

Charlotte smiled conspiratorially at Matthew, who was looking especially baggy and rather tired this morning.

'Did I ever mention my small but very earthy *back* garden?'

'Ahh . . . ' Matthew grinned. 'You also haven't mentioned love,' he added after a minute.

'We also haven't mentioned Art,' Charlotte said, challenging him.

'Are they connected?'

'Love and Art?' She shrugged her shoulders. 'No need to get metaphysical about it, love was a much more pragmatic thing for me.'

'Was?'

'Was. I don't mean it has changed its nature. I mean there was love – perhaps – but now it isn't any more, not for me, and hasn't been for a long time. It isn't something I miss, funnily enough.'

'Tell me about when it perhaps was?' Matthew asked, as he had to.

Charlotte was willing to pass the time telling her story, feeling she had long since made herself proof against it being anything more than just a tale from the past, determined, as she was, to sever then from now.

The question Charlotte had asked Jamie just before the crash was this: 'Supposing your whole life had all been a preview, everything up to this moment, and now the foetus that would be you was asked if it wanted to come to term – to be born. What would you say?'

Charlotte knew, of course, what his answer would be. That was one of the reasons for asking it; there could never be enough reassurance.

'I'd say, "Yes, but could we come to this bit ten years ago instead of having to wait all that time to get to now?" I'm so happy with you.'

He turned and smiled at Charlotte. Her way of asking simple questions by going the most circuitous and improbable route to them was one of the reasons why Jamie loved her. It pleased him to tell her so, and he thought he loved her all the more for her inability to say simply, 'Do you love me?' He kissed the tips of his fingers and pressed them against her lips as he watched her, in profile, concentrating on the road ahead.

Charlotte's lips curved into a small smile.

'Correct answer,' she said. 'But I didn't say you could *change* anything. That's against the rules. You get what you've already got. All the stuff before now, exactly as it was.'

'Same answer,' Jamie smiled. 'I love you. But who's asking?'

'No one. That's the point, no one does ask. But, hypothetically, suppose. It doesn't matter. God, or Fred Hoyle's seeder of DNA on the planet, if you prefer.'

'Oh, the great Seeder,' Jamie grinned. 'Well, hypothetically, I'd say, "Go ahead, beam me down, I can't wait to get to the bit where I fall in love with Charlotte." '

Charlotte had settled for the answer she knew she would receive. She liked to hear him say he loved her even though of late the sounds the words made did not cause her insides to heave and her head to reel as they had the first time he said them, and for many months after. Now, they were confirmation and she let them seep into her in the ensuing silence, as if they were rays of sun gently warming her through.

It was a softer thing, now; no longer a fire suddenly leaping at her. It was more as if she had deliberately changed her clothes, put on sunglasses and tanning lotion and stepped from the cool shadows of indoors into the sunshine. Or opened a bottle of medicine and administered a dose to herself with a spoon specially kept for the purpose:

Do you love me? (Or words to that effect.)

Yes, I love you.

Charlotte had noticed then how she had lost the effect of Jamie's words in her thoughts about how they affected her. And, like a dream that you think you have dreamed before but are not sure, she wondered if she ever actually *felt* the effect of his words of love, rather than merely thought about how they did or didn't work on her. She tried to hear the words in her mind again, repeating them silently to herself in Jamie's tones as if they were freshly said, trying to squeeze out whatever power they might have had over her, but it was lost.

Jamie watched the smile fade from Charlotte's face and loved the way her features flashed her altering thoughts. An astonishing face, to be read second by second, yet retaining some mystery that denied any solution he thought he had found in her momentary changes of expression. He assumed the immediate reason for her now-faded smile was that she was concentrating on overtaking the horse box in front of them.

Charlotte pulled out and drove past the horse box. As she sped along the empty road ahead of her she watched the Land-rover and its trailer disappear behind them in the rear-view mirror and let go of her thoughts about Jamie loving her. There had been another reason for her question.

Jamie had not asked her what *her* answer would be. If he had, she would probably have lied to him, but she told herself the truth. She had asked herself that question before, many times. It was a test she had devised for herself to see how happy she was. If the answer was no, she would choose not to be born, it was clear enough how she currently felt about things. She always tried to be fair, and made a point of asking herself the question when she thought she was perfectly well contented. Each time she hoped her answer would be different, would echo Jamie's immediate response, but drunk or sober, in love or out, bored by work or engrossed in it, the answer was the same, invariable, 'No, thank you, I do not want to be born'.

And here it was again. No, thank you, I'd rather not. She heard the examiner in her head double-check.

'But you *are* happy, aren't you?'

'Yes.'

'You love Jamie, don't you, and your work is going well?'

'Yes, everything's fine.'

It was better than fine. This time in her life was exactly how she had imagined it could be when, as a child, adolescent and young woman, she had asked herself what she wanted. Now, and for the best part of two and a half years, she had everything she wanted in the way she wanted it. Work, a child, a lover, political activity. Sometimes, astonished by how things were, she checked with herself. What did she want? Nothing, she had it all. There must be something? No. It was good now. Her life was perfectly all right.

So? So nothing, so she'd rather not have been born, thank you very much.

Because of *then*? Because of the things that couldn't be changed on the road to the present, according to the rules of her game? Because of the monsters that came from back then? Charlotte supposed that was probably the reason, although there was also the unknowable business of the future, but that, too, was as much *then* as anything. The voice in her head remonstrated with her. How can *then* matter if things are right *now*, when there's plenty of time left, more time than had to be got through to get to now?

Yes, she knew all that. There was no answer. Nothing reasonable to say. She'd asked herself a question – her unborn self – and the answer came back loud and clear, not desperate, just certain: NO. NO. NO.

She was grateful for Jamie's silence. She did not want to answer her own question and either lie to him, or, telling him the truth, have to hear the hurt in his voice.

But Charlotte was not the only one who needed an amulet of words. Jamie broke the silence.

'What about you? What would you say if the great Seeder in the sky asked you?'

It was then that the green car appeared around a curve in the road. There was not enough time for Jamie to register any discomforting pause in answer to his returned question. The other car came towards them fast on the opposite side of the empty road and then, for no reason (later, they thought a small animal had run into its path – a cat, perhaps, or a rabbit), it swerved sharply into their lane, directly ahead of them. Charlotte had time to fling her arm out across the passenger seat to hold Jamie back, but that was all. She couldn't recall either of them crying out, or saying anything, and time didn't seem to slow down, as one hears it does when accidents occur, it simply ran out and came to a dead stop.

Charlotte remained fully conscious, but felt no pain in spite of being intimately implicated in the twisted metal and speared by tiny shards of broken glass. In shock, it is common to feel nothing. It's a kindness that the body does for its owner. It was, to Charlotte, as if not she, but the world, had died, and she was stuck, alive and trapped inside its inanimate corpse.

For a few long seconds, there was a pregnant silence as the engine noise died away and the exterior world seemed to hold its breath to see what would happen next. Charlotte remembered seeing dust rise up in a misty column in front of her eyes – or smoke, she couldn't say which. It disappeared into the sky, beyond the periphery of her vision, as if attracted and absorbed into the clouds overhead. Gradually, though, she became conscious of a noise, at first distant, but as she realised she was hearing it, it developed into a persistent, pitiful sound, unearthly, like the mournful wail of a Greek chorus. She recognised it, finally. There was a dog in the other car that had been badly injured – the ambulance men had to put it down when they arrived – and it was whining its distress, baying into the silence in the hope that its mistress would come to its aid, but who, Charlotte could see out of the corner of her eye, lay unresponding with her head at a strange angle on the dashboard.

Charlotte wished the dog would be silent. But the terrible yelping went on and on causing her the only distress she would later recall feeling at the time.

She lay against the steering wheel with her head half-turned towards the window on her side. She could see nothing of the wreckage except for the door of the other car which had been wrenched from its hinges and lay unattached and buckled in the middle of the otherwise empty country road.

Gradually, Charlotte understood the situation, although it was a very distant understanding that had no connection with thoughts of tragedy either for herself or other people. Only the dog expressed the horror of what had happened, and apart from its cries, there was no sound, and no movement around her.

She didn't consider why this might be, but knowing that she could not move, she waited almost calmly, without fear, without any real interest, for whatever was to happen next. Of course, the doctor told her later, the impassivity and lack of curiosity was also a merciful result of shock.

Moments, or it could have been hours, later, Charlotte became aware of someone banging on the window and pulling at the door on the driver's side. It wouldn't open. A voice shouted something to her through the glass. Charlotte heard the shout, but couldn't make out the words. And although she would recall the image of the door lying in the road, she had no memory of seeing anyone's face at the window in front of her open eyes. Then Charlotte heard the sound of a powerful engine revving up and disappearing into the distance. She didn't doubt that whoever it was had gone to get help.

It took a long time to cut her out of the car, but they gave her a shot of morphine, and she waited for them to finish, as calm and detached as before. She heard the screech of metal being sawed, but it was muted by the drug they had put into her, and untroubling.

Charlotte got her first and only sight of the wreckage as they laid her on the stretcher and carried her into the ambulance. The fronts of both cars were so concertinaed that the broken windscreens were only inches from each other. She saw the woman slumped sideways in the other car, and noticed the dog had gone silent. In the remains of her car, Jamie's shoulder was visible, but where his head should have been in relation to it, there was a tangle of metal, and though she could see a patch of something black, like the colour of his hair, it was too confused with the buckled edge of the windscreen to be certain of what, exactly, she was seeing.

The fact that he had not been taken out of the car, as she had, didn't strike her as meaningful at the time. By then she was losing consciousness. The last thing she remembered was a man's face, framed by an upturned black leather collar, coming into view, and his voice asking the man behind her head, 'Will she be all right?'

It wasn't until some days after the accident when the doctor sat on the edge of Charlotte's bed and began to speak in a low voice, that she discovered what had happened. Until then, she had used her apparent state of ignorance to stop herself from thinking, or at least from garnering any meaning from anything she knew. She put all of her life up until that time into abeyance, filing it for later, and lived entirely in the present of hazy and intermittent consciousness while they wheeled her to and from the operating theatre.

She didn't even want to know whether she was going to live. Partly this was a result of Charlotte's degree of illness; partly, she just didn't care. It seemed not to be very important.

The doctor informed Charlotte as gently as he could manage that she was the only survivor of the crash. The dog, and the woman driving the other car, died – the woman within minutes of the ambulance arriving; the dog, too, though for different reasons.

Jamie had died instantly, his cranium split almost in two by the metal window edge, but, according to the doctor, he would have died anyway from his internal injuries. Charlotte tried to give her eyes a look of agreement with the softly speaking intern when he suggested it was better that Jamie hadn't had to linger, though she was glad she had no voice to add that, for reasons other than her injuries, he might have said the same thing about herself. He was young, her doctor, and not aware of the irony Charlotte squeezed from his consoling words.

Often, after she had been officially told the results of the accident, while lying in bed in the hospital, recovering from yet another operation, Charlotte posed herself the question whether it would have been better or worse if Jamie had lived. When the doctor had suggested that it might have been a blessing that Jamie was instantly killed, he had meant, of course, a blessing for Jamie. Charlotte meant was it better for herself. There was the vague presence of guilt in this thought, the source of which she would only gradually manage to identify.

Jamie had been Charlotte's lover for over two years, and occasionally things were arranged so that they had a weekend in the country. Spending two whole nights together was a rare treat.

They had been returning from one of their weekends when the accident happened. They were tired and well sated with each other, physically exhausted, but Charlotte's driving was not called into question. It was a moment of pure misfortune, and no one was held to be responsible. But it was not as simple as putting the whole thing down to fate, and mourning for her lost lover, as the husband of the woman in the other car, presumably mourned his wife and dog.

Jamie was married, and not, of course, to Charlotte. She remembered her first thought after the doctor had left: his wife won't be very pleased with me for killing her husband. She had known nothing of their affair. And then Charlotte thought: thank God Jamie was killed, or his wife would have had to come to visit him in the men's ward just along the corridor from where his mistress was laid up. She would have been told that Jamie had not been fatally injured on the motorway back from Manchester where he was supposed to have been, but on a country road only a third of that distance from London, in quite the other direction. And with a woman driver who was not herself killed. It would have been intolerable for her, knowing Charlotte was recovering only yards away. And for Charlotte. Would Merrilyn, Charlotte wondered, making herself think the name she'd never used to Jamie, have come to my bedside and told me what she thought of me? And if Jamie had not died but recovered enough to be mobile, would she have him moved to a hospital back in London so that he couldn't visit Charlotte in his wheelchair, or limping in his carpet slippers?

There was always the possibility that she might come to see Charlotte anyway, once the circumstances of Jamie's death were known. Would the nurses let her in? But Charlotte told herself that

Jamie's widow (she now replaced *wife* in her mind with Merrilyn's new status) would not make contact. That she would use Charlotte's anonymity to mourn for her husband, and the father of her children, in the proper way. After all, the woman in the other car might, for all one knew, have been coming from, or going to an assignation with *her* lover. There was no need to delve too deeply into things that could no longer be altered.

It was partly for these reasons Charlotte came to the conclusion that Jamie's outright death was for the best. It allowed certain things to be ignored, and decent tragedy to veil the shabby revelation which the accident threatened to expose. In the light of sudden death, infidelity becomes an embarrassment, with all the shameful foolishness about it of a rich person caught shoplifting.

All these thoughts were distanced from any emotional response. She seemed to have very little in the way of emotions, beyond a generalised pity about the mess of it all. She was sad, of course, about Jamie.

And she, too, had to mourn for the father of her child. Julian was just over a year old, then. And now there would be another; a – what was it called – posthumous baby. The doctor had given her the unlikely but, he assumed, life-giving news that, incredibly, the foetus had survived the accident and the operations which had set her bones to rights. Now, if she didn't have an abortion, and she was fairly sure she wouldn't (the whole point of getting pregnant the second time was that she felt that Julian should have a sibling), the infant would be fatherless in a more precise sense than it would have been if Jamie had lived.

In retrospect, rounding off their time together, Charlotte thought that she and Jamie had been fine lovers, and good friends, too: they'd laughed together a lot. But Julian, and the new one, were to be Charlotte's children, hers alone. She had made that clear to Jamie from the moment she told him she was pregnant and wanted to have the child. He hadn't believed her, of course, but in the end she had persuaded him that she wanted to have children, and she wanted him as a lover, and they were, in fact, quite different things. Jamie could visit the child, who could even, when he was old enough, know Jamie was his father, but she didn't want support, emotional or financial. It allowed Jamie to go on loving her without having to wonder if he wanted to make his life with her, and allowed Charlotte not to wonder if she really wanted Jamie at all.

All through their time as lovers, there had been hardly any talk about him leaving his wife; Charlotte never asked it of him, and would never have done. After Julian was born, Jamie mentioned it occasionally, though with a deliberately light tone, as if it were a joke. But Charlotte always felt, for all his apparent casualness, he may have wanted her to make him choose. She wouldn't have done that, made such a demand, nor allowed such a demand to be made of her.

But the truth was, looking at it from the distance of her hospital bed, it wasn't just a matter of being independent in the abstract. Right up until the accident, Jamie had a great and hungry passion for his mistress. But it wasn't quite like that for Charlotte, not by then.

They gave each other pleasure two or three times a week, and while she knew him she had no other lovers; he was enough. But she was clear in her mind, whatever the mangled state of her body, that she had not loved the man who died, an illicit passenger, in her car. Not in the way he thought he loved her.

It was this fact, more than any other, that she did not want revealed. The wife and children who grieved for him might feel that his dying for a great, if unlawful, love made some kind of sense. A foolish thought, she knew, but human and understandable. Comfort of a curious kind. It was in the light of this that she now felt, if she felt anything, faintly ashamed of the fact that Jamie was for her a lover and a friend, and she wanted nothing more from the relationship. She had, in a sense, used him up; wasted him, perhaps, if such a notion had any meaning in the arbitrary realm of accidental death.

It was worse than that. Charlotte found herself acknowledging in the privacy of her hospital bed, that she had been getting tired of Jamie. That last weekend had been fine, as they always were, and their final conversation together in the car was, she remembered, of them speaking of love. She had not been planning to tell him at the end of the journey that she wouldn't see him again. It would not have happened for a week, or several weeks, perhaps. But Charlotte knew she had lost the edge of passion. Their affair would not have lasted very much longer.

That, more than anything, was what she didn't want Jamie's widow to find out. With Jamie dead there was no need for her to know, or for Charlotte to dwell on the other question that nudged itself to the front of her mind.

Jamie loved Charlotte with a passion, and it was for *her* passion for him early on that he loved her most. It wasn't that they didn't enjoy each other's company. They did; very much so. But enjoying someone's company is not passion. And passion, in the final analysis, was what they had while they had it, and what excited them about each other. What made him be unfaithful to his wife, and even contemplate, from time to time, giving up his marriage, was not the idea of Charlotte and him spending their days contentedly in each other's company, with a new family growing around them; but the idea of their having unlimited time to wrap themselves around each other and enjoy each other's body without interruption.

He used to say she was beautiful. He loved her body, which was firm then, and full; and he loved her face, which was not pretty, but interesting enough to make men turn their heads when she passed them on the street. Her hair was dark and thick, in those days, and her eyes a deep, almost charcoal grey of the kind Jamie claimed never to have seen before. Her features were striking. Good bones, strong shapes. She was *not* beautiful in any classical sense, but she had a face, a good one, that served her well.

On their weekends, when there was enough leisure simply to lie together, naked on the bed, Jamie would stroke Charlotte's face and stare at it for half an hour at a time. He was drinking it in, he said, so that it was part of him, and he could summon the sight of her from inside himself when she was not there. Love talk. Sexual dreamtime. What he loved most about her eyes, Charlotte knew, was the desire he saw in them, and the promise they held of how it would shortly be expressed.

Not that Charlotte ever thought there was anything wrong with that; her passion depended on his in the same way, on how he needed to touch her all the time, and how he looked at her, shamelessly adoring what he saw. Charlotte, as shamelessly, adored his adoration. She didn't believe, reviewing their two years together from her hospital bed, that what they had would have lasted the daily ordinariness of living together. It certainly would not have survived the loss of what he – and perhaps she herself – most loved: the clandestine satisfaction of their lust.

If Jamie had survived the crash, with their secret out and him, doubtless, badly injured, would she have been able to tell him that it was all over between them, or would she have found herself morally bound to an invalid she no longer wanted even when able-bodied? There was the nub of it: she *was* relieved that he was dead. It was all, from Charlotte's point of view, just as well. She feared that telling him it was over, as she was bound to do, would have triggered him into leaving his wife. And then, the death of love would have been every bit as messy and distressing a business, for all of them, his family as well as him and her, as the actual death that occurred. It would, of course, have been better if the accident had never happened, Jamie had lived, and they had quietly gone their inevitable separate ways. But she didn't think it would have turned out like that.

It had been the end of passion for her, she told Matthew. After Jamie there were no great adventures; perhaps there was something about her after his death which kept men away. Certainly, there was a wariness which must have showed, and she herself had avoided any relationship which threatened to become more than pleasant companionship and practical sex. It was as if, having the children, and Jamie dying, had been a full stop so far as desire went. She remembered their love together not with pleasure, nor regret for its loss, but with a dull and heavy heart, as if it had been something she'd been obliged to go through. And there was, always, an obscure guilt for not feeling bad about the sense she'd had of having escaped from something by his death. It was a secret betrayal; and she saw herself as a betrayer. And yet Charlotte could not feel ashamed of her disloyalty. She could tell herself that was how she was, essentially, and she didn't, a little to her surprise, really care. She had her other selves, instead: mother, scientist and active believer in the betterment of humankind.

Charlotte finished telling Matthew about love with a bleak smile.

'I suppose it does no harm to call it love,' she said. 'But it seems now to have more weight as a story about accident, doesn't it?'

'I suppose love is an accident to some people.'

'Have you ever been in love?' she asked him.

Matthew smiled.

'Do you want me to answer that?'

'Yes,' Charlotte said. 'I'm curious about you. Or are you going to hide behind your professional mask?'

'Some people prefer it.'

'I don't. I like quid pro quo.'

'OK. Never met the right man,' he said. 'Or, at least, never met the right man with the right sexual orientation.'

'You fall in love with heterosexuals?'

'Only when I can't help it. Once. It was enough. Now I go where I know I'm wanted.'

'Have you ever had a relationship with a woman?'

'Friendships. Cuddles.' He hesitated and then went on. 'The only woman I've been to bed with was married to the man I was in love with. It wasn't a success,' he said drily.

Charlotte suddenly had a vivid memory of the night he held her against him while she wept, and immediately afterwards she became aware of Matthew's shoulders under his battered corduroy jacket. They were broad and strong. She imagined them tensing while his arms held something tightly. There was a momentary twinge somewhere in the pit of her stomach, before she dropped her eyes and stared down at the coffee mug in her hands.

'Well,' Matthew broke the silence, 'we're getting up to date. Garden wrecking, love life. Too many accidents. There's just childhood left, and that'll be you sewn up.'

He was joking, but there was something of a warning beneath his light words. He was telling her he wanted the rest of the story.

'You think I'm hard?' Charlotte asked him.

'Quite hard, but not hard enough. You get points for trying. Mind you, I'd rather be your therapist than your son or daughter.'

'A judgement?' She was surprised.

He shrugged and maintained a warm smile.

'People can only do what they can do. No one does it right and everyone has their own special way, adapted to their times and circumstances, of doing it wrong. It was an observation, not a judgement. Perhaps Julian and you should talk some day.'

'What if we can't?'

'Then you can't. When I know more about how things were with you, perhaps you'll know more about how things were with him.'

'Will that help anyone?' Charlotte found herself a little alarmed.

'Not necessarily. But it might. I'm an idealist – after a fashion.'

'I think you're a spy,' she said with a small smile.

'Of course I am. Double Oh, I say! – that's me.'

She looked seriously at him.

'Do you tell Davies what I tell you?'

He shook his head and engaged her eyes.

'I write up notes,' he said. 'And Davies reads them. I don't write up our more . . . casual conversations.'

So what, she thought, it didn't matter because she hadn't told him everything. He could have death and sex and breakdown, but still she would keep the centre of her terror to herself. The *more* he needed to really understand her she had not told him about. Biology was a matter purely for her own contemplation.

Chapter 8

AND WHERE ARE YOU GOING?

———

'Where do you come from?' said the Red Queen.
'And where are you going? Look up, speak
nicely, and don't twiddle your fingers all the
time.'
Alice attended to all these directions, and
explained, as well as she could, that she had lost
her way.
'I don't know what you mean by your way,' said
the Queen: 'all the ways about here belong to
me – but why did you come out here at all?' she
added in a kinder tone. 'Curtsey while you're
thinking what to say, it saves time.'

This time she knew where she was. She had put the book down for a moment and now was back in the tiny cabin of the *Beagle* and not so disoriented as before. Apart from recognising her surroundings and the figure who lay fully dressed on his bunk, staring up at the skylight, the quality of another time, of a different space was becoming evident, so that she was half-aware now of inhabiting a dream world, wherever she happened to find herself. The pattern of inevitability, and therefore of story, was growing clear, even to the will-less eye of the dreamer. She didn't try to intercede, knowing there was no point. She was not there for the one she observed. How could she be, she was no more than a minuscule drop in the ocean of his blood?

There was not the look of grim despair on his face that she had seen that first time as he sat at his desk. Now, he stared up and to one side at the source of light, with a look of painful sadness on his face. It was as if the despair had softened, not into something less agonising, but into something larger against which he could not battle. The sadness *breathed* itself in him, bringing with it an overwhelming helplessness that was not to be fought. This was different from the look in his face when he spoke to Darwin of his terror at losing his faith. That was the fear of a man on the edge of an abyss, the moment before he toppled. But such a situation is not hopeless: it is possible to step back from an abyss, to walk away from it and try to continue one's journey. It may prove to be the case that there is no other route, but the man who walks away from the edge can hope, at that moment, there might be.

The tears that welled unattended in FitzRoy's eyes were in recognition of a failure which could not be walked away from. It was true that he had rejected the negative, terrible thoughts he'd had on that island with Darwin. He did not regard this as dishonesty, but as a reaffirmation of his faith. Now, though, it was not in his power to reject what he saw. This was something out in the world. It was the realisation of the fear he had had on the island. He could not interpret it other than what it was: a failure. His failure, certainly, and perhaps even worse if his own assessment of what he had been doing was true. He remembered back to a time of unclouded hope. He had returned from the first journey as Captain of the *Beagle* with the three natives, and had a year to prepare for the second, to finish the mapping of the South American coastline. He had other plans too, which for him ran deeper even than finding safe harbours for British vessels. He had a great experiment, which made even the King of England curious.

FitzRoy's damp eyes closed on to the scene back in England, and as they did so, she, too, found herself in an ornate room whose opulence was almost suffocating.

The girl was very short, and almost as wide as she was high, with a broad head under her severely cropped, pudding-basin, thick black hair. As a result, the charming bonnet the Queen put on her head looked, it must be said, somewhat unusual. Her Majesty, however, was delighted with it, as was Fuegia Basket, who smiled shyly under her millinery shadow.

'There,' the Queen said, stepping back. 'It looks a picture. Don't you think so, my dear?'

This last was spoken to His Majesty, who was deep in conversation with Captain FitzRoy on the other side of the room, where two other young people, both males, and of the same facial type as the girl, sat stiffly together, gloved hands folded on their laps, on an opposite sofa to the one on which William and Robert FitzRoy conversed. The King looked up, distracted at his wife's voice. Adelaide had her husband's respect for her acceptance of her situation, though not, of course, his love. But he tried at all times to be polite and pleasant to the woman who through no fault of her own could neither bear his children, nor quicken his desire.

'Beg pardon, my dear?' he said, trying to look interested. In reality, he was a little aggravated at being distracted from his discussion with the Captain, who seemed, in every way, to be a most interesting and devout young man.

'The bonnet. Don't you think it delightful on the child?'

The King looked past his wife. The round female savage did indeed have a bonnet on her head, tied at the chin (or he should say, chins) with an elegant bow. He thought he had seen it before on his consort's head.

'What? Gave it to her, did you? Very nice, m'dear, a very royal gesture.'

He returned to his conversation with the Captain about his plans for the savages.

'They have had the best part of a year in Walthamstow, Your Majesty, at an infants' school. They now read and speak a simple version of English, and have a more than elementary knowledge of the Bible as well as a grasp of the fundamentals of Christianity. In addition, they have been taught such useful mechanical and gardening skills as will serve them well on their return to their islands.'

'A splendid project, Captain. And was this at your own expense?'

'No, sir, although I did contribute to their keep. I found an equal enthusiasm for my plan in the Church Missionary Society, who agreed to pay for their tuition while they were in England. And a subscription has been organised among philanthropic Christian gentlemen and ladies to provide for their needs on their return. A Reverend Matthews will accompany us on board and stay with them, to direct the mission on the islands.'

'None the less, without you, this grand experiment could not have occurred,' His Majesty said approvingly.

FitzRoy bowed his head in modest gratitude.

'I look on it as the Lord's mission, sir. He placed these young savages in my care on the first trip to Tierra del Fuego. I am nothing but an instrument. I certainly did not have such a plan in mind when I started out. I imagined I was to do no more than fulfil the Admiralty's command to navigate the complicated coastline of the Southern Americas.'

'Well, all credit to you, and less to the Admiralty, for taking piety along with your seamanship, Captain FitzRoy. I shall make a point, when I speak next to the First Lord, of commending your excellent initiative.'

'Your Majesty,' FitzRoy whispered, all but overcome with such a compliment. 'But credit must go to these young fellows, too. They have been admirable pupils, and seem to have taken to the civilising benefits of Christianity as if they had indeed been waiting for it. It proves to me, though I hardly need proof, that the Lord is everywhere, and speaks to all hearts if they are allowed to listen. These savages threw off their ignorance and nakedness with an enthusiasm that could only have come from God's benevolence and care for all races and degrees of man.'

'Well said, young man, well said!' the King commended.

FitzRoy, who believed not at all in the transformation of species, believed fervently in the transformation of degrees of men. He saw no lack of logic in this. God's purpose was always unknown. It was not for men to make judgements about their Creator's purposes, but simply to follow the guidance He gave to their hearts and minds.

If God created some men as children, and others as the standard bearers of civilisation, He also allowed the miracle of learning about Himself to come to them through the mediation of wiser men. The great lesson for all of creation was that nothing was beyond the power of God. He might raise up or cast down, according to His will. What He did not do, FitzRoy had no doubt, was conform to laws that were not of His making. This logical absurdity was clear to FitzRoy. There could be no laws not of God's making, and what He made, He might just as easily break if He so chose. But men could not interfere with the laws. Only God could do as He wished; He whose hand controlled all things, all through time. His work was never done. He held everything together, and by His will the world turned, machines worked and mankind developed. All things and all actions existed only inasmuch and for as long as God wished them to. There was no system beyond God's plan, and no plan which was not alterable at God's whim.

It was not that Robert did not expect difficulty for the Fuegians when they got back to their islands. For the Captain of the *Beagle* the mission to civilise those regions was the very heart of the return voyage. The human seeds he brought back with him were God's will working through His servant, FitzRoy.

Jemmy Button and York Minster continued to sit quietly as the Capp'n and the Great Chief of England spoke together. They understood a little of what was said, and certainly that it was themselves, the savages, who were being spoken of. Jemmy was particularly pleased at the way the Great Chief congratulated the Capp'n, who seemed to him the very model of the handsome Christian gentleman he himself now strove to be. Jemmy wore his stiff, uncomfortable clothes with immense pride, though York found them less pleasing. York did not have the same enthusiasm for being a good Christian gentleman as Jemmy, not being partial to the rigours of school learning, and finding sitting in straight rows amidst infant English children learning his ABCs to be a humiliation for a strong young man who was a warrior, not a schoolboy.

Jemmy was different and rejoiced in being the prize pupil, taking great pleasure from the coos of approval of the lovely ladies and elegant gentlemen who came to inspect him. He loved his starched, high collar, and was never, not even when it was appropriate, to be seen without immaculate white gloves. The Reverend Matthews even suggested that Jemmy was a little too concerned with matters sartorial in the manner in which he would stop whatever he was doing to wipe the slightest spot of mud or dust from the shoes he so loved to see shining beneath him. Today, however, Jemmy felt the whole of himself to be shining, a star and a star pupil in this great centre of the civilised world. Oh, Jemmy loved being civilised, and, although he adored going about England among the real gentlemen and ladies, he was looking forward to returning to his island and, with the aid of the Reverend, building civilisation among the savages he had left behind there.

It was, in his imagination, to be the story of the Garden of Eden, all over again. They would tame the wilderness and make a garden with the seeds they would take with them, and grow delightful things to eat such as cabbages and carrots which would amaze his tribe. He, Jemmy Button, would grow the tree of knowledge for them, like God's gardener, and help them understand Christ's message that they must wear clothes, and speak English, and learn the Bible off by heart and, most of all, become good gentlemen and ladies. He had been touched by God and England (which were closely connected in Jemmy's mind) with the vocation to turn those savages into civilised beings so that His Majesty's ships would find safe harbour and a Christian welcome in those islands, where the waters and the inhabitants were so dangerous. And this safe outpost of England would exist all because of Jemmy Button's teaching. And the Reverend's, of course. York would help, too, as well as Fuegia, to whom he was now officially engaged, and who, Jemmy noticed, was looking damn lovely in the bonnet that was placed on her head by the Great Chief's woman's own hand. Yes, Fuegia would be his Eve, his Queen woman, and a great dynasty of civilised children would come from their most Christian copulations, just as soon as they landed and were united in the sight of God by the Reverend, who had explained to them that it would be better for the marriage (and therefore the nuptials, he added severely) to be delayed until after their arrival in Tierra del Fuego. Jemmy was content to be a good Christian and wait.

'You are good boys, are you not?' His Majesty bellowed at Jemmy and York, in the time-honoured way one spoke to foreigners. 'And grateful for your good fortune, what?'

Jemmy beamed a great toothy smile.

'Yessir, Your Royal, and praise be to God!' he bellowed back, thinking an equal enthusiasm required matching volume.

York grunted and nodded without quite managing a smile.

'They are all good souls, Your Majesty,' FitzRoy added quietly, wincing at the noise. 'And the Lord, in His infinite wisdom, has seen fit to elevate them to a higher rung on the great ladder of being. It is evidence of His infinite mercy.'

York, whose English was in fact rather better than Jemmy's, though he kept it to himself, wondered gloomily why the Lord's infinite mercy did not extend to putting His chosen people, inhabitants of God's own country, in a warmer climate. He hated England, always grey and damp, and even when the sun broke through the clouds, it did so weakly, because, as York knew, the sun had far to shine, all the long, hard way from his island, where the sun lived, shining joyfully and hot on the unregenerate naked bodies of his people. Soon, he knew, he would be returning, but the pleasure he felt in this was tempered by the knowledge of the months that would have to be spent in the tiny boat that rolled and rocked on the terrible waves, like the toy boats his fellow pupils in Walthamstow pushed out on the pond near to the school. But he would go through anything to get home, to be back where he belonged and to rip away the starchy noose around his neck. They thought him sullen (a word whose meaning he had taken trouble to find out). Yes. It was the right word. He did not smile as easily as Jemmy, with his eager, ready-to-please eyes and his delight in the rewards for good behaviour, not least of which was Fuegia's silent, adoring admiration for his smartness. They had his contempt, those two converts to the cold unmagical religion of this grey and dismal place, so willing to put off pleasure and accept discomfort as the Bible stories taught them. Why wait? Why not take Fuegia, do now what men were supposed to do with women? Why sit on hard seats in uncomfortable clothes in this dark, light-defying room, when you could be lazing in a tropical sun feeling the heat warm your genitals as you daydreamed the feats of athletic and sexual prowess you would soon perform?

But he had gone to England willingly with the Captain, his curiosity aroused by the strangers and his head fuzzy with the rum the sailors had secretly poured down his throat. He had not understood how far away this England was. He had been told it was an island, and he had thought it only somewhat bigger and further away from those he visited regularly on hunting and raiding trips. They said his island was called 'York Minster', and called him that, too. They had not asked what he called his island or himself. They said that it was named after a sacred place in England island. He was curious. So much newness. He went and as his own world slipped away imagined that by only a few sunrises he would arrive. By the time he realised the distances of time and space, it was too late, too far to return to where he belonged.

Fuegia stroked the satin ribbon under her chin and watched in silence the goings on. She took in everything, her eyes alert and watchful, but said nothing. She was a child hungry for understanding, but she never spoke unless a question was put to her directly. Even then, her shyness would cause her to drop her head and giggle a word or two into her chest. In spite of her squat, square shape people were delighted by Fuegia, whose face, not pretty by English standards, expressed such pleasure and interest in everything she came across.

She had missed her kin at first, as they sailed away from her island, but soon Jemmy had provided the comfort and familiarity she was lacking. Everything was so new, and Fuegia so young and open to astonishment, that she had no time for sadness. Soon the boat rang with her happy laugh, and even the toughest of the sailors treated her with the affection due to the ship's mascot. They showed her how to make extraordinary knots out of thick rope, and she learned quickly, delighted to be performing some of the tasks that these godlike creatures undertook. The cook had her help him in the galley, and she swabbed the deck with the relish of a proud young housewife.

Her admiration for Jemmy however grew quickly into adoration. He was two years older than she, with a handsome face and strong body, and, within days of them being on the ship, had taken an interest in her. But most of all she liked the look in his eyes, which, like her own, glistened with the excitement of the new, and since everything was new, they glistened all the time. She was happy and proud to become Jemmy's Christian wife in, as the Reverend said, the due course of time.

She felt less comfortable about York, whose eyes were quite different from Jemmy's. They were concealing eyes, yet not entirely effectively so. She had only to glance at his face to know that the slight smile on York's lips was designed to compensate for the cold dislike behind his eyes, which she perceived no matter how neutral he tried to keep them. And more than that was the way he looked at Fuegia when he thought she wasn't aware of it. She could have her back entirely turned to York and yet still know, uneasily, that his eyes bore into her with the angry stare of a rejected warrior.

Fuegia was very much taken with England, with the finery that was spread over the surface of things. She noted how, in the houses she visited, everything was clean and starched and proper, but that those who made things that way were kept away from company. She saw the paraphernalia of dress which required constraining mechanisms under the layers of pretty thises and soft thats to achieve the effortless-seeming essential sameness of public appearance. All this was a marvel to Fuegia, an almost godlike triumph over the natural state in which she and her people had lived in Tierra del Fuego. She did not long for the air on her breasts, or the freedom to scratch an itch in public, indeed she welcomed itches so that she might practise ignoring them. She did not want things as they really were, she had lived with that all her life until now, and was as delighted to find England and its regulation falseness as a child who enters a toyshop for the first time in its life. Her imagination was fired at the way the possible was multiplied by the denial of the actual. So, she could not respond to York's open, natural, boyish hunger for her. She far preferred the pretensions of Jemmy, with his fine clothes and new sauntering walk, and the waiting, waiting, waiting that the Christian God, in the form of Reverend Matthews, demanded instead of the seeing, wanting and taking way which had once seemed quite usual to her.

Fuegia was learning to love the joys of artifice, and wanted, more than anything, to become, one day, one of the finest and most artificial of the fine, artificial ladies she had seen. This did not mean, however, that she was not looking forward to returning home. Fuegia understood instinctively that she could never achieve her goal if she remained in England. Everyone was nice to her, but it was as a savage. If the Queen put her very own bonnet on Fuegia's head, and was, *at this very moment*, taking a ring off her finger and sliding it on Fuegia's own hand, it was because she was charmed to see them in such an unlikely setting. Fuegia knew that the bonnet did not look on her as it did on the Queen, and that the sparkle of the blue stone on her finger glittered all the more for the lack of any competing background. No, Fuegia's dreams were to take all she had learned back to where she came from, where *she* would shine among the ordinary, untouched natives who knew no more than she once had. She and Jemmy would be like precious stones among the pebbles with their English ways, their enormous knowledge of the world and their glowing Christianity. She could hardly wait to see the blue stone on her finger outshine the very sun itself when it and she, from now on inseparable, were back on the islands.

FitzRoy opened his eyes again, and the time from then to the present moment passed like a receding tide. The experiment was over, the results that very day, two years since the audience with Their Majesties, were finally known.

They had landed, Jemmy, York and Fuegia, and the Reverend Richard Matthews. All of them, including FitzRoy, Darwin and the crew had set about building a solid shelter in which to live and pray, and marking out and planting a garden. Everyone worked with a will, and continued to do so even when the native Fuegians arrived to stand at the margins of the cultivation and stare with a curiosity which had not yet become aggression.

A moment of pain and possible danger passed when Jemmy greeted his family, who had arrived with the rest. His two brothers and his mother stepped forward from the crowd and for some time simply stared at their strangely attired kinsman. Then Jemmy tried to speak to them. A few faltering words came, to be met with incomprehension before FitzRoy realised with a sinking heart that Jemmy had forgotten how to speak his own language. Gazing at him without emotion, his family turned their backs and rejoined the other natives, who continued to watch the curious activities.

Later that evening over supper, Jemmy had apologised on behalf of his uncultivated people.

'Dirty people,' he said, shaking his head, his mouth turned down in distaste. 'No clothes. Stupid savages.'

It was clear he was ashamed that his English gentlemen friends should have seen the poverty of his origins, but, more than that, he was shocked himself – having forgotten during his year in England, what he once had been. He assured the Captain and Mr Darwin that he would show the damn dirty savages the ways of civilisation. That they would learn to dress properly and to live properly, and, as soon as he had refamiliarised himself with their language, he would set about teaching them the English they would need in order to understand the word of God as it should be spoken. He was not pleased with the Reverend Matthews's attempt to learn the Fuegian language and his plan to translate the Bible. Jemmy was certain that English was the language in which God spoke.

If members of the crew had some doubts about the project, they kept it to themselves, although one or two of them (Darwin included) could not hide a smile when the crates of gifts from charitable souls in England were opened, and out came white linen – tablecloths and napkins – soup tureens, cream jugs, flower vases, fish servers, gravy boats and all the other necessities of civilised English dining.

Robert FitzRoy saw nothing strange in this. He knew these things had their role in maintaining standards of behaviour, and therefore of thought. Fuegia, too, understood their purpose, and looked forward to presiding over elegant dinners, once a suitable table had been made for dinner to occur on, and the garden had produced the proper things to eat.

FitzRoy, like a father delivering his children to their first boarding school, had left his former charges to get on with the task of settling in, once the garden was made. For ten days he sailed up the coastline, continuing his mapping, but his heart was with Jemmy and the mission, and there was not a moment when he did not wonder how God's task was getting on.

He returned to find little left of civilisation. The garden had been trampled and the fine English china smashed. The Reverend Matthews's courage failed him, and FitzRoy did not blame him for wishing to return to England with the ship.

The Captain was not without hope, however. Jemmy, still dressed like a gentleman, was not discouraged. He and Fuegia were adamant that everything would be all right. York had disappeared, it was assumed he had gone off with the other natives, but the remaining two were sure that, over time, what they had to teach would not fall on deaf ears. FitzRoy was impressed with Jemmy's patience, and believed that such faith and perseverence would be rewarded, but it was with a heavy heart that he set sail towards the north. They would pass the islands of Tierra del Fuego again in a year's time. He left Jemmy and Fuegia in God's hands, where they seemed so willing to be. And still, he consoled himself, they had encountered only difficulty, which was to be expected in the pursuit of God's work, not failure.

That was to come one year later.

FitzRoy stood with Darwin on the bridge as the *Beagle* dropped anchor in the cove where they had last waved farewell to Jemmy

Button and his newly wed wife, Fuegia Basket Button. At first nothing happened. Looking through his glass, however, FitzRoy saw a small boat with half a dozen people in it coming towards them from around the other side of the inlet. As it got closer, there was much waving and calling from the natives to their visitors. Certainly, there was no sign of Jemmy; these were the natives they had seen the first time they came to the islands, naked, innocent and godless, though friendly enough, it seemed.

It wasn't until the boat came close enough to be seen without the aid of the glass that the truth gradually dawned on FitzRoy and Darwin. One man, in a frenzy of excitement, stood up in the crowded little boat, jumping and waving his hands above his head. He was shouting, though for some time the wind carried his words away from the men on the bridge. Soon, though, there was a gasp from Darwin, followed by a groan from his companion. The wind had changed direction suddenly, and the man's bellowed words could be heard: 'Capp'n! Capp'n! Hello! It is I, Jam-ey!'

It was still impossible for a moment for the two men on the *Beagle* to believe it. The fellow who shouted and waved was stark naked, his long dark hair falling to his shoulders and matted with filth. The body was caked with grime and places of hardened mud. But the savage called to them in English and offered them a close approximation of the familiar name.

At first Robert supposed this was a student of Jemmy – a poor student who had given up his studies, certainly, but some evidence of hope, none the less. Soon, however, the native boat was close enough for hope to die.

Jemmy clambered aboard, helped by a couple of members of the crew, while the others in his boat sat silently bobbing in the swell. Robert called for a blanket to be brought and Jemmy was wrapped in it by the time he reached the bridge, but not before it was clear how emaciated he was. They took him to the Captain's cabin and watched in silence as he greedily stuffed handfuls of bread and gravy into his mouth, before giving his hosts a sudden horrified look and picking up his knife and fork to begin, with terrible control, to cut small pieces of meat and potatoes as once he had been taught.

'Jemmy,' FitzRoy asked quietly, 'what happened? Where are your clothes? What has happened to Fuegia?'

Jemmy stopped eating and looked mortified. Darwin, silent all the while, felt he did not want to hear the answer.

'Bad people. Gone,' Jemmy said, with a look like a guilty child.

'Where have they gone?'

Jemmy's English was halting, like an unused muscle. It took a long time for the full story to emerge. This was only partly because of Jemmy's loss of language: remembering that he should not talk with his mouth full, he was none the less too hungry to let the food in front of him wait until the Captain's curiosity was satisfied. He chewed carefully and swallowed before each stuttered sentence.

Two months after the *Beagle* finally set sail, York had returned from his own island, in the middle of the night. By then there was precious little left of the settlement. The seeds had died as the land they had cleared was regularly trampled by raiding parties of natives who also carried everything movable out of the hut. There was nothing Jemmy or Fuegia could do to stop them. By the time York arrived, there was nothing left except a few disintegrating clothes and a Bible that Jemmy had kept with him at all times. Even the hut had been demolished, though, in his attempt to keep civilisation going, Jemmy insisted that he and Fuegia sleep within its wrecked perimeters. They prayed now in the open air, setting up an altar each time, since to leave even the smallest sign of order was to invite the destructive jollity of his fellow Fuegians. Tearing down the hut, the garden, the altar was a regular festival. It was not vicious, more like a game.

But the game had taken its toll on Fuegia, who had lost all that was most precious to her – the things that set her apart and made her feel special. Their torn clothes were a burden to her now, they had to be washed over and over, since all they had was what they wore, and cleanliness, as Jemmy told her in English, was next to godliness. And, in any case, they were no longer decorative. What was the point of wearing rags that were not half as nice to look at as the human body beneath them? The greatest blow came when she lost her ring during a clothes-washing session in the sea. The ring the Queen of England had herself placed on her finger. After that Fuegia fell silent, and wouldn't speak in any language at all.

Jemmy and Fuegia slept in shifts, in order to keep the remnants of their lives intact during the hours of dark. York came, a thief in the night, and whispered to Fuegia as she sat disconsolately at the vacant doorway of the remains of the hut. The looming figure was familiar, although naked like the other natives. But she recognised the eyes, glinting at her, in spite of the dark. They gleamed towards her like the stars. They were the brightest thing she'd seen since she lost her ring.

York and Fuegia worked stealthily, collecting up the last of Jemmy's hold on civilisation. They took his clothes which were folded neatly at his feet, they took his shoes which, in spite of everything, he somehow managed to keep highly polished, they took his Bible. When he woke there was nothing left. And he understood immediately why.

For some time he was alone and naked. He did not miss Fuegia, his shame was too great. He did not want anyone to see him in this condition. Somehow, he knew that she had gone with York; somehow, he felt he had known all along that she would go with him. He remembered his old skills and made himself a small boat so that he could catch fish, and fed off the land as he had all his life. He did not, however, forget how to pray. Every morning and every night he praised the Lord and thanked Him for all he had. He asked God to bless his friends, the Captain and Mr Darwin – whose seasickness he wished cured – and, of course, the King of England. He also blessed Fuegia and York. He blessed everyone he could think of. While he fished or foraged, he told himself stories he remembered from the Bible, keeping them alive in his mind, and although he no longer had the means, he recollected every time he ate how he would have eaten if he had the wherewithal. He tried to keep England and what it taught him alive in his memory, and to some extent he succeeded.

One day, as he was sitting in front of his fire thinking about the times he'd had in Walthamstow, he heard a noise behind him. Until then, he had been left alone by the natives, he was no longer of interest to them now there was nothing left to destroy. When he turned around, he saw a small gathering. A young girl, a real beauty, two small children and an old man stood and watched him watching them for a moment; then the girl moved forward, and the others followed her. Soon, they were sitting around Jemmy's fire, watching the flames dance. They were a family group, although the girl's man, the father of the children, had not long before died of a wound he had received. The girl had seen Jemmy living in his desolated clearing, quiet and solitary, and something about him made her feel she would be safe with him. She took her father and the children to him.

Later, the brothers of the girl joined them, and a child of Jemmy's was born. The group lived together in some contentment, while Jemmy tried to pass on some of what he had been taught. Only the girl managed to learn the few words of English Jemmy had left, but she taught them to her children, now who sprinkled their language with odd words like 'clean', 'nice', 'teapot' and 'gloves', without any regard for what the words actually meant. At night, he told them stories from the Old Testament, as well as he could remember them, and tales of England and the English and fine living. They made all their eyes wide with wonder at the strange behaviour of the mythical white people far, far away. None of them actually believed there was any truth in Jemmy's stories, but he was revered as a story-teller of special gift, and listened to on other matters on account of it.

Gradually, it dawned on FitzRoy and Darwin that, pitiful as his condition seemed to them, Jemmy was content in his new life. He spoke of his family with the pride of any English patriarch and of his 'wife', as he called her, with a good deal of affection. And yet, these things emerged in spite of himself. Speaking to the Captain, he was ashamed of how he looked, and blamed himself for the failure of the mission.

FitzRoy suggested that Jemmy's wife and children come on board, and they were brought to the cabin, or rather, to the doorway, for there was no room for them all in the tiny room. The young woman was indeed beautiful beneath the grime, and her body, neither Englishman could help but notice, was ripe and desirable in its savage, naked way. FitzRoy, keeping his eyes low, ordered them to be given clothing immediately and they were brought back, to the relief of everyone, decked out in an array of shirts and trousers, none of which fitted, but which served the essential purpose.

The woman and her children stared sullenly at the Englishmen, who were not, as it turned out, figments of Jemmy's imagination, but real creatures who looked and behaved very much as he had described them. They were uncomfortable and frightened. If Jemmy's story was real after all, might they all not be whisked away, as he had claimed to be, to Walthamstow and made to sit at desks and learn to do reading, whatever that was? They did not like their clothes and they hated the confining spaces of the ship, which they feared at every moment was taking them away to England, where it was grey and rained and the earth was hard and nothing grew. They had loved Jemmy's stories; they did not like the reality. Reality – just the fact of it – diminished Jemmy in their eyes as they stood there, watching him smile shyly and take gifts that were handed out to him with the gratitude of one who deserved nothing. Servility was not part of their language, but they had been told of servants in England. They did not like what they saw of Jemmy and his English gentlemen.

'Jemmy,' FitzRoy said finally, forcing hope into his heart, 'will you return to England with us? You can live there, perhaps in Walthamstow, and the children will go to school and grow up to be Christian gentlemen and ladies.'

Jemmy looked at his new family and then back at his friends, FitzRoy and Darwin. Slowly, he shook his head.

'Plenty thanks, Capp'n. I stay here.'

He looked apologetic, but gave no reasons. In fact, he had seen the look of disappointment on his woman's face. He did not like the loss of the admiration she had felt for him, and knew that side by side at the infants' school in Walthamstow the admiration would be extinguished for ever. He understood that their faith in him had been cracked by his stories coming to life, and it occurred to him that he might feel the same if the vicar at the church in Walthamstow had, one day, after the Sunday service, introduced him to the Lord Jesus Christ himself.

What was more, Jemmy no longer wished for the belongings that England had to offer. He had discovered that the more things one cherished – real objects – the greater the sadness there was in losing them. Better to have nothing than to wake up one morning and find the shoes that shined from so much loving polishing had disappeared. Better to do without shoes; it was easier to think about them – easier, too, to maintain the shine with the imagination.

He would stay where he was and try to be again what he had become for his group, once the memory of the real *Beagle*, the real Englishmen had faded.

Eventually, FitzRoy had accepted Jemmy's decision. What else could he do? They had loaded the little boat with goods – food, clothing, utensils and Bibles – and waved a farewell that had FitzRoy feeling a terrible constriction in his throat. He had been genuinely fond of Jemmy, and had placed his hopes for the spreading of the word of God on him. He was desolated with the failure; it was not enough to map a continent. The crew watched in some trepidation as their Captain disappeared down to his cabin. They had seen that blackness about his face before.

As they sailed away, FitzRoy supposed he would never see or hear of Jemmy again. He was not quite correct. A long time later, word of Jemmy – or of a native who was said to be Jemmy – would reach him. Further disappointment, like bad blood, could wait, lurking in the shadows, until its time came once again.

FitzRoy lay now on his bunk at the end of that terrible day as the *Beagle* carried him away from his hopes. It was his first great failure. The first time he had been unable to realise a dearly held hope. He felt alone in the world, as if he had been abandoned by God. How else could such a disaster have happened? And if God could turn away from what FitzRoy had been sure was His own work, then FitzRoy was indeed a man alone, who without the certain aid of the Lord might come to grief in all his plans and aspirations. During his moment of doubt with Darwin he had glimpsed a lonely universe where a man was no more than a man and all guidance, all certainty fell away, but he had not *tasted* the reality of such a fear, as he did now.

He felt darkness come over him, as if his life had taken a turn and found itself in an endlessly pitch-black corridor. He could see no light, no matter how he strained his mind's eye to look towards a brighter future. And somehow, he knew, that beyond the distance he could see, at the far end of that passageway, his uncle lay in wait for him.

Chapter 9

EITHER QUESTION

---

*Alice began to get rather sleepy, and went on
saying to herself in a dreamy sort of way, 'Do
cats eat bats? Do cats eat bats?' and sometimes,
'Do bats eat cats?' for, you see, as she couldn't
answer either question, it didn't much matter
which way she put it.*

Charlotte-the-Deserter, who had taken off on her own adventure, leaving the other one to fend for herself as best she could, finished the last crumb of angel cake, which *had* been heavenly, and suggested to Jenny that it was time for a swim.

'I don't know about that,' Jenny said dubiously. 'It's not the kind of thing orangs do, you know.'

'Well, neither is talking and having tea. Come on, I insist.'

'Oh, if you insist, I suppose there's not a lot I can do about it. Don't you think you're rather taking advantage of your special status? Don't us creatures of your sick imagination have any rights?'

'No,' Charlotte said, mulling it over, 'I don't feel the slightest need to be democratic down here. Anyway, if I can imagine you swimming, I can imagine you enjoying it. So I'll make sure you have a lovely time.'

'Oh, I see, it's a benevolent dictatorship,' Jenny grumbled. 'That's the worst sort, you know. I'll probably get cramp swimming so soon after all those cucumber sandwiches and cake.'

'It's all right, I'll make sure you don't. And if you do, I'll save you.'

'Thanks a bunch,' Jenny said.

Charlotte stripped off her outer clothing, and then, thinking about it for a minute, took off her bra and pants as well.

126

'Planning a little gardening before our swim, are we?' Jenny said, rather nastily. She found the sight of naked humans a little distasteful; all that hairless skin, and so many bumps and bulges in quite the wrong places. Not a pretty sight.

Charlotte chose to ignore the uncalled-for comment of her only friend in the world, and made her way down to the sea.

After a good deal of splashing of arms and legs in their attempt to get a little distance between themselves and the shore (neither of them were natural swimmers), Charlotte and Jenny found it much more to their liking to lay flat out on their backs and simply float on the surface, 'like flotsam and jetsam', as Jenny put it.

It was quite blissful, in fact, the water buoying them up, and the heat of the sun playing over them. Charlotte half-closed her eyes and watched the way the sun's rays filtered through the drops of water on her eyelashes to make a kaleidoscope of dancing colours.

'I wonder what it must be like never to think,' she brooded lazily.

'There's nothing in the world that knows that,' Jenny said, floating nearby, the long red hair on her arms and legs wafting like an aura around her.

Charlotte lifted her head in surprise.

'But it's thinking that make us different from animals,' she said, and then remembering whose company she was keeping added: 'Lower animals, I mean.'

'As a matter of fact,' Jenny said, 'it's manners that make the difference. Manners matter most.'

'Manners?'

'Good manners,' Jenny said decisively, 'are what separate the civilised from the savage. Never, never underestimate the importance of holding your knife correctly. You will notice that I always do.'

'I had noticed that,' Charlotte agreed, a little bemused. 'But I thought it more interesting than important.'

'You human beings always think that thinking gives you the edge over the natural world. But I have to tell you that there's no species alive in the world which doesn't believe the same thing about themselves.'

'I hate to have to contradict you, but lesser species do *not* think. They don't have the higher brain centres to think with.'

Jenny shook her head sadly from side to side, but then stopped as water seeped into her ears.

'That's what they *all* think, dear. From jellyfish to gorilla. "We think, therefore we are the bee's knees." '

'Jellyfish can't think that. They can't think anything.'

'That's what they think about you. Listen, a three-toed sloth moves very, very slowly compared to a human being. But do you think *it* thinks it's moving slowly? Of course not, it thinks it's moving at the right pace, and everything else moves very, very fast. See? It's the same with thinking. Everyone thinks they think and everyone else thinks the others don't. Human beings think of building cities and computers and jellyfish don't. They think of other things and you don't appreciate what they think about, that's all. You don't suppose the jellyfish are all thinking "Oh, those clever humans with their cities, we wish we'd thought of them", do you, because what would wet, floppy things like that want with cities even if they saw any? And don't go on about having big brains, because that's just a human view of what does the thinking.'

Charlotte was having too nice a time to get very upset with this, but she was puzzled.

'So everything is equal?' she asked. 'Amoeba and astrophysicist?'

'No, dear, everything is not equal, because jellyfish do not have decent table manners.'

'That's objectively important? Table manners are the answer to it all? It's ridiculous.'

'I'm afraid it's true. It's about distance, you see. Please-and-thank-you, and pass-the-butter-if-it's-no-trouble, create a distinction between you and me. A jellyfish would just tread on you to get to the butter, mark my words. Politeness means that you're you and I'm me and *then* we're in a position to have a useful conversation. Which is why it's such a pity that they stopped having those splendid tea-parties at the Zoo, just as the chimps were beginning to get the hang of civilisation. Taught them to paint, instead,' Jenny said contemptuously. 'Art and allied *creative* pursuits belong in the most primitive part of the brain. Dumb, dumb, dumb!'

'Well,' said Charlotte, still unconvinced but not wishing to spoil her pleasurable float with argument, 'thank you for explaining it to me.'

'You're welcome, and have a nice day.'

They floated on in a resumed silence.

'I rather envy FitzRoy,' Charlotte said after a little while.

'You do?' Jenny replied. 'I thought he was your nemesis?'

'It's his simple-mindedness I envy. His faith.'

'Funny thing to say about someone who ended up the way he did.'

'Yes . . .' murmured Charlotte, choosing to leave that little detail aside for the time being.

She couldn't help but be envious of FitzRoy's simple thoughts, aching, as she had up there, for the certainty she had lost in the perfectibility of the human condition. To have faith, to simply *believe*, seemed to Charlotte to be a secret garden to which she had lost the key.

'Certainty is a very dangerous thing,' Jenny said. 'I'd treat it with great scepticism, if I were you. I'm afraid fear and doubt are the stuff that survival is made of. Fear and doubt, and a capacity to organise others. Darwin's the one to envy; a very satisfactory combination of timidity and temerity. He's your man.'

'He was amiable and good-hearted,' Charlotte agreed. 'But I don't see what makes him all that special. He was fortunate enough to have a good idea at the right time, just through sheer luck. Luck is the thing about Darwin, I'd say.'

'Well, don't say. Don't forget his belly-ache. Never underestimate a man with a bad belly-ache. You're right, I do like this swimming stuff. Thank you, it's really very pleasant.'

Charlotte and Jenny stopped talking and concentrated on the pleasure of bobbing weightlessly on the gentle motion of the sea, their legs and arms wide, like starfish.

Soon, though, the peace was interrupted.

'Damn!' said Jenny as the sound of splashing oars and argument broke into her rain-forest reveries. 'I do wish you would keep them out of it. We don't need them, you know. Haven't they caused enough trouble up there? You're really not concentrating on not concentrating.'

The boat approached them, with Sigmund pulling on the oars and grunting with each stroke while Karl reclined at the back and Charles shouted, 'Ahoy there! Ahoy there!' at the two bodies floating belly up in the water.

'Oh, I say,' Charles dropped his voice and went very red. 'She's
. . . got no clothes on. Sigmund, row back the other way.'

'Don't you dare,' Karl said. 'Keep going in the direction of
dinner.'

Sigmund, who had his back to Jenny and Charlotte, continued to
pull towards them.

'It is perfectly normal to fantasise about the naked bodies of the
other sex, Charles,' he said soothingly.

'The monkey is wearing a bathing suit,' Karl said, turning to look.
'A blue one.'

'That, my friend, is not such a normal fantasy,' Sigmund told him
in an ominous tone. 'Not that I'm saying it's wrong,' he hastened to
add. 'Only that if you put yourself totally in my hands, I'm
sure I can help you.'

'No, really,' Charles explained, still pink. 'It's objectively true.'

'Hah!' said Sigmund and Karl simultaneously. 'What do you
know about reality?'

Then they turned to each other and added: 'And what do *you* know
about reality?'

Luckily, they had come close enough to Jenny and Charlotte for
Sigmund to observe that what each of his fellow travellers had
observed was the case, and for Karl to remember the urgent mission
they were on.

'Excuse me,' Karl shouted to the two swimmers, while Charles
averted his eyes. 'We were wondering about supper.'

'Don't you three ever think about anything apart from your
stomachs?' Charlotte asked, annoyed at the interruption. She was
surprised that creatures of her imagination (Jenny included) should
have such vivid appetites.

'If you had my trouble,' Charles sighed, still looking discreetly
away, 'you wouldn't be able to think about much else. You have no
idea of the agony I've had to put up with . . .'

'A man's belly needs to be full if he is to achieve great thoughts,'
Karl explained.

'Great flatulence, more like,' Jenny muttered under her breath.
'For God's sake, think up something for them to eat so they'll leave us
in peace,' she told Charlotte.

Charlotte waved her hand towards the shore.

'There's a hamper of food – yes, and wine,' she added as Karl opened his mouth to speak. 'It's by the deckchairs. I've just refilled it. Go and help yourselves.'

The three men headed towards the shore in great good humour. As they landed they could be heard to join together in a boisterous chorus of the 'Red Flag' with Karl singing the words, Sigmund providing the 'rum te tum tum rum te tums' of the rhythm section, and Charles doing a very pleasing descant.

'I wish you'd find something for them to do,' Jenny said. 'They're getting to be an awful nuisance. I think it's very selfish of her up there to lumber us with the useless leftovers of her world.'

'But what can they do? They were great thinkers. They didn't *do* anything except think, and there doesn't seem to be much call for that down here.'

'If they're great thinkers then I'm not surprised you dropped by. Among us orang-utans great thinkers are required to produce great thoughts; otherwise they don't get a certificate.'

'Well, they tried,' Charlotte said generously.

Marx, Freud and Darwin had settled on the sand, and were happily eating and drinking again.

'It's extraordinary the way that woman goes on about Robert FitzRoy. It's pointless. The fact is he was a religious bigot, and that was that. Even what happened to those poor natives didn't convince FitzRoy that mankind wasn't a special case in nature. I've never met a man more immune to the significance of his own failure,' Charles said, shaking his head so that his long beard swept from side to side across his chest. 'You only had to look at what happened in Tierra del Fuego and then see that orang-utan in the Zoological Gardens to know where man belongs in the scheme of things.'

'FitzRoy was a prisoner of his class and period. He had no choice but to conform to the current ideology,' Karl mumbled from his horizontal position on the sand.

'Well, *I* saw things differently,' Charles insisted.

'You had the advantage of coming from a long line of Nonconformists. Not,' Karl added hurriedly, 'that they were anything more than a bunch of liberals.' He spat the word at Charles. 'You know what your grandfather called nonconformism? "A feather bed to catch a falling Christian." Good man, Erasmus. But even with your advantage over most of your class, you chose to spend your time belly-aching in bed about your upset stomach and let others do the argumenting for you.'

'I was a *martyr* to hereditary weakness of the stomach,' Charles insisted, cutting himself a hunk of roast beef.

'Psychosomatic,' Sigmund, who was repeatedly running sand through the fingers of one hand while gnawing on a chicken wing with the other, explained. 'Your mother died of a stomach disorder when you were very young, is that not so? Naturally, you internalised her absence by taking on her –'

'He was a scaredy-cat,' Karl said, sitting up and waving a sandfly away from his face. 'Left all the revolutionary work to his friends, while he stayed home and groaned on the sofa. But you didn't mind taking the credit once Hooker and Huxley had smoothed the way for you.'

Charles was very offended.

'Neither of you can hope to know what I suffered. The agony . . . the terror.'

'Terror of being disapproved of by the rich and famous people you so much wanted for your friends. What happened when Lyell refused to endorse evolution? You sulked. What happened when the Radicals claimed your theory as justification for social change? You denied everything and pulled the covers over your head.'

Sigmund nodded sagely and waved his chicken bone to assert his point. 'Clearly the desire for approval was a symptom of the trauma of losing the primary parent so early in life.'

'Simple cowardice,' Karl said, snatching the bone from Sigmund and flinging it over his shoulder. 'Lack of guts. That's all that was wrong with your stomach. Same as this Charlotte woman. I've got no time for her nonsense. She hasn't got the stamina to be a revolutionary, so what does she do? Flies off to cloud-cuckoo-land, and has the unmitigated cheek to banish us here, too. As if it was our fault that things went wrong.'

Sigmund looked daggers at Karl for taking away his bone, and then with a challenging look on his face, brought another wing out of the picnic basket and began ostentatiously to chew on it.

'Revolutionary!' Sigmund sneered, poking the eaten end of his bone very close to Karl's face. 'Political idealism is always related to emotional deprivation which results in aggression towards authority . . .'

'Oh, yes, thank you very much,' Karl whined. 'Of course, *you* know everything. I provided intellectual tools for people with a social conscience to work for justice. There's nothing neurotic about that. You, what did you do? Sat around and thought about sex. And then you made people lie on couches and tell you about their willies. Oh, very useful. You gave the middle classes a chance to obsess about their petty psychic discomforts when they should have been out there working for the international brotherhood of man. You did more to prevent the revolution than all the capitalists in China.' Sigmund raised an eyebrow at this, but let it pass, since Karl was obviously working himself up into a passion. 'You, you are nothing more than a diverter of energies . . . you, sex maniac . . . you, pawn of the forces of repression . . . you, sop to the self-seeking bourgeoisie . . . you Viennese idiot!'

Sigmund was not going to stand for this.

'Sticks and stones . . .' he chanted. 'Mr World Communism! Mr Historical Necessity! Who got it *all* wrong, Mr Clever Dick? Tell me that? What did you do for the world? Your beloved proletariat spends half a century being shipped off to collective farms, and queuing up for bread until finally the poor misguided fools can't stand it any more and your pathetic socialist revolution collapses like a house of cards. And don't tell me that wasn't what you meant when you called for the dictatorship of the proletariat, because that's what happened. And it's your fault. You were just *wrong*. You don't know the first thing about people, you . . . polymorphously perverse retard!'

'Yes, it was true there were some things – *some* things – I was not completely right about,' Karl admitted in a low growl. 'But everything would have been all right if history had not got confused. How was I to know that damn fool Stalin would come along?'

'Even if he hadn't, what did you have to offer the world? Do you remember what you said life would be like after the revolution? "Man will be free to hunt in the morning and fish in the afternoon." That was what you had to offer your masses. All you offered in the end was roast Bambi in the place of religion as the opium of the people.'

133

'And what is wrong with a good day's hunting and fishing?' Karl said, jutting his chin out.

'You had the human race completely wrong. Don't you understand that as long as the unconscious remains unexamined, there's no point in trying to better the world. The monsters have to be dealt with first. Otherwise they become embodied and stalk the earth. There is no earthly paradise without psychoanalysis. That is what I, the Viennese idiot, showed the world.'

'Well, I don't mean to be rude,' Charles interpolated. 'But, quite honestly, neither of you seem to have grasped the point that what we are is determined by evolutionary history . . .'

Karl and Sigmund, each puffed up like a pair of fighting cocks, turned to stare at Charles for a long moment.

'Shut up!' they bellowed in unison.

'Oh no,' Charles groaned, clutching at his stomach. 'Now look what you've done. I think . . . yes, I'm sure . . . I'm going to be sick . . .'

Chapter 10

A BOTTLE MARKED 'POISON'

. . . if you drink from a bottle marked 'poison',
it is almost certain to disagree with you, sooner
or later.

'So what have you been up to, Mother?' Julian asked, eyeing with approval the empty paper cup which had contained yellow pills Charlotte had thoughtfully left in view on the table in front of her chair. She had little fondness for Julian, but disliked lying to him. She much preferred to let his own eyes deceive him. In fact, the pills were in her handbag, waiting to be added to her collection in the drawer of her bedside locker.

'Nothing much. I see the therapist,' she said, and cast around for something to add. 'And relax. I've been doing a bit of reading.'

She had also left *Mansfield Park* on the table. He turned his head sideways.

'Jane Austen. Just the job.'

'Why?' Charlotte asked, knowing he had never read her, nor anything else for that matter not officially sanctioned by the thrusting young men's magazine he read in order to find out what 'people' were up to.

'Fine writer,' Julian said, unabashed. 'And reading takes one's mind off things.'

He failed to notice that, had Charlotte's mind been taken off 'things' by *Mansfield Park*, his last statement would have put it right back on them. But Charlotte was determined to offer the appearance of compliance to all comers.

This surprised her rather, because if you couldn't be offensive to an unloved son when you were in the madhouse and licensed, as it were, to misbehave, when could you? It was, she recognised, a lost opportunity, and she wondered a little about why she was letting it go.

'Have you been getting out at all?' Julian asked.

'Sometimes I walk up to the little park.'

'That's good,' her son said, who walked nowhere, ever. 'You know, you ought to get out more, you're looking a bit pale.'

Like a withered plant, Charlotte thought. Such concern. And from *Julian*. But she knew that her health was uppermost in his thoughts these days because he'd had a nasty shock discovering that what was usually uppermost in his thoughts – *his* well-being – was more than somewhat dependent on his mother being well in body and mind. Especially mind. Charlotte suspected, however, that apart from his visits to check up on her, he was also investigating institutions that kept inconvenient mothers out of harm's way. He must have had yet another fright when he found out the cost of fostering out unwanted parents.

Things, as he frequently told her, these days, were not what they were. To which Charlotte replied with a resounding, 'Good!', though under her breath, of course, on account of her policy of meek behaviour.

Julian did not usually stay for longer than necessary, to the relief of them both. He would give her a rundown of his busy life, but Charlotte only got an impression of brilliant sales in the face of a sticky market (which she assumed meant he wasn't making anything like the money he thought he was entitled to), parties, theatre and art gallery visits (which were always 'openings' to which he was invited, never just because he was interested), and the purchase of clothes (whose only notable characteristics were the label in the collar and the exorbitant cost).

Sometimes, in the intermittent silences between them she would toy with the idea that he was, in reality, a saint, going about the world doing good and thinking wise and important thoughts, while concealing himself in a cloud of disapprobation, but she couldn't make it live. He was a little shit, and that was that. What would his great-great-great-grandfather think of such a descendant? Not much. Bad blood, he'd say. Charlotte couldn't help but agree with that. Bad blood, all right.

Today, however, he seemed to have something on his mind. He fingered the spine of *Mansfield Park* as he spoke.

'I was at your house today.'

'Oh?'

'I went to see how the gardeners were doing, and I just popped in to see that everything was all right.'

'Thank you,' Charlotte said, automatically, not caring whether it was or not.

'I found something.'

With a reticence which was most unlike his normal manner, he handed her a piece of paper. It was yellowed and crisp with age.

'I found it behind the dresser in the kitchen. I'd knocked over that bowl of spare keys you keep there, and they fell behind it. That was there when I pulled the dresser out.'

He spoke unusually quietly, and then waited for Charlotte to look at the paper and recognise it for what it was. For a moment she didn't understand what she was reading. There was just a date and a couple of sentences.

9.11.65. I can get free this weekend. I'll come to your place 9 a.m. Saturday.

It was signed: *I love you – Jamie.*

After a moment, Charlotte looked up at her son.

'He was my father, wasn't he?'

'Yes. I told you he was called Jamie.'

'And that's all you ever told me.'

'That was all there was to know. You saw him once or twice when you were a baby, but we . . . stopped seeing each other after I got pregnant with Miranda. And then he died.'

'I've never seen his handwriting before.'

'I've told you, Jamie was your *biological* father. There isn't any more. I hardly knew him.'

'Yes, I know, your baby-maker. Your stud. But that note sounds as if you knew him quite well. It's dated over a year before I was born.'

'He was a trades union activist,' Charlotte said in the neutral voice of a court reporter. 'A Scot. I met him at a conference. He died in a car crash just before Miranda was born. There really isn't anything else. We wouldn't have got married. We didn't believe in that kind of thing. Does that help anything?'

137

Julian was silent for a moment.

'What you said at Christmas – about never having liked me. It was true, wasn't it?'

'Julian,' Charlotte was alarmed at her son's newfound desire for frankness. She began to realise how much his shallowness had suited her all these years. 'I wasn't well, even then.'

'No, it had nothing to do with madness. You meant it. I know that. Do you think I didn't always know it? How could I help knowing, when there wasn't ever anything I did, or was interested in that you approved of? I was good at arithmetic, do you remember? *Very* good, as a matter of fact. But you didn't think arithmetic was important. It wasn't politically concerned enough for you. Anyway, how often were you there to notice anything about me, or Miranda?' Suddenly, speech came to him like a flooding lake, all the former boundaries between one thing and another disappearing. 'You went to demos and political meetings. Evenings, weekends. You dashed in and out as if saving the world wasn't just more important than your kids, but more interesting, too. Do you remember when you got into the Women's Movement? You used to lecture me on what was wrong with me because I was male. Yes, I know you called it "explaining" and teaching, but what you were really doing was telling me I was a piece of shit. Remember when you used to go to that feminist bookshop and you and Miranda went inside, and I had to wait out *on the street* because, although I was only nine, they didn't allow males in? Do you remember all that?'

She stared at him. Of course, she didn't remember it; not the way Julian did. But this new Julian astonished her; it was as if some spell had been broken, a princess kissed and come alive. Now he was shouting his rage at her.

'I remember it, Mother. And what it felt like to be told I had no father worth knowing about, and that my mother didn't think I was worth spending time with. And the funny thing is: you despise *me*, because I don't *care* about people I don't know, and because I make money and enjoy spending it. Well, you're right about me. I turned away from you, and everything you were, Mother, because I was *dying* of misery. And I *like* what I am. I like being successful. I like being a rich young man with a portable telephone, instead of being an unwanted little boy standing outside a feminist bookshop. And if I

138

lose my Porsche, I'm going to do everything in my power to get it back again. Do you hear me?'

While he shouted his pale cheeks flushed red, and his thin lips tightened the better to spit out his anger, but, pausing now to catch his breath and turning away from Charlotte in his rage, something happened to his eyes, so that when he turned back to face her, they had dimmed and lost their fire. The tension in his lips disappeared as he let his facial muscles go, like a runner might, seeing the finish line and realising he has no chance of winning. He pulled at his waistcoat, and tried to impose some order on himself.

'Julian,' Charlotte began, but stopped. She had no idea how to go on. She didn't know what to say to the unknown young man who had emerged in front of her, but who was already disappearing before her eyes into the dull, bored face of someone all too well known. She felt relief as he snapped back into himself, and spoke to her as if the previous few moments had never existed.

'I must go. Got a party to get ready for.'

He swivelled on his well-cared-for heels and walked away.

Charlotte was left alone, grateful that, after all, she would not have to reconsider the nature of her son, nor the reasons why he was everything she hated. She looked down at her closed fist and slowly spread her fingers. Jamie's note from twenty-five years ago lay crumpled on her palm. An assignation a quarter of a century old. 'I love you', it had said. Charlotte tried to feel something about this, but was not surprised to find herself feeling nothing at all, except relief that she was being left alone again. She thought there was no point in keeping the old piece of paper, which, in any case, existed only because of accident, not because it had been cherished. But when she got up to throw it into the wastepaper basket she found herself walking past it, out into the hall and down to her ward. She slipped Jamie's long-lost note in the back of her bedside drawer to live with the secreted pills. As far as she could see they belonged together, because, though she was keeping them, she had no notion what she was keeping either for.

Charlotte got up and went into the little patients' kitchen to make herself a cup of coffee before she went for her session with Matthew. Matthew came in after a few moments, and she realised he must have seen her and Julian together.

'All right?' he asked carefully.

'Yes,' she said, sipping her coffee. 'Just a little family disagreement.'

'It happens in the best of them,' Matthew said.

She heard herself snap, 'How would you know?' and was appalled to hear herself so cruel and angry. Matthew just pursed his lips and offered her an exaggeratedly camp 'Ohhhh!'

'I'm sorry,' she said, ashamed.

'Not too sorry, I hope.' He grinned. 'That's the liveliest I've ever seen you.'

'Want to talk?' Matthew asked when they had settled into their opposite chairs in his office.

'Not about Julian. I was a bad mother. He's right. What else is there to say?'

'Well, let me see, where were we up to. It seems to me it's time for the childhood . . .'

She had known that he would want her to go further back, beyond the deaths of the Marxist dream and her daughter, and beyond the ambiguous loss of Jamie. She might have remained silent, but she found herself wanting to hear what she had to say about her beginnings.

Neither Charlotte's political idealism, nor her later genetic obsessions had quite extinguished a special piece of knowledge she had possessed from an early age. For all her socialist and scientific preoccupations, Charlotte had long been well aware that the individual was a reality, and personal history a fact.

She was nine when she first understood that destiny was not merely a word much bandied about in fairy-tale and fable. It was her teacher, Mr Styles, who had put her on the right track. With a small cough he announced the beginning of a biology lesson.

'We are going to talk about – reproduction,' he explained, the last word falling short from his lips, so that it barely reached the ears of the waiting class of children. 'Reproduction is the process by which babies are made.'

Charlotte watched his tiny, rosebud mouth contract so that his lips were pushed out, away from the rest of his face, as if they wished to dissociate themselves from the words that formed behind them. After a few giggles from some boys in the back and a general shuffling of chairs, the class settled, ready to listen to what it was Mr Styles's distasteful duty to tell them.

'You will remember how I told you last week that every living thing is made up of millions of tiny cells. Well, every living thing begins as just one single fertilised cell in its mother's body.'

It took a moment before Charlotte realised that by 'every living thing', Mr Styles meant her, too; but once she did, the rest of the lesson was lost in her wonder at the thought. She ignored the bit about in her mother's body, and missed all the stuff about the egg and the sperm meeting, and the subsequent division of the cell into more and more cells, until, finally, a rabbit emerged.

Mr Styles's thin, particular lips returned to their normally fastidious position, and his hand ran over his shiny Brylcreemed cap of hair, as if he feared that, in the telling of his tale, a strand might have strayed out of place, or his side parting become kinked.

At break Charlotte stayed behind to ask Mr Styles how big it was.

'How big is what?' he asked distractedly, having put the whole unpleasant subject out of his mind.

'The cell. The one everyone is to begin with.'

'Oh. Not big. Small. So small you can't see it except with a special microscope,' he told her, shuffling his books together, more than ready for his tea and biscuits down in the staffroom. He was relieved that that had been the only supplementary question he'd been required to answer.

Charlotte had not been able to imagine anything so small you couldn't see it, and was troubled; but, as it so happened, that same week her father gave her a fine gold chain to wear round her neck, with a single seed-pearl held between two of the minute links at her throat. The pearl was tiny, barely bigger than a pinhead, and more oval than round, though not quite oval either. It lay on Charlotte's finger, a milky, iridescent white, that was as near to transparent as it could be without actually being so, which made it to Charlotte's eyes, magical. Since it was the smallest, most delicate, strangest thing she had ever seen, Charlotte was reminded of the mysterious single cell she had once been, but until now, in spite of Herculean efforts over several days, was unable to imagine.

She gazed at the seed-pearl as if it were herself, nine years and nine

141

months before, with all the wonder of a physicist discovering the origins of the universe.

'This is for you,' her father said, taking the chain from her hand and fastening it around her neck. 'For my girl.'

The part of the chain that had dangled loosely from her finger was cold for a second against the back and sides of her neck. It fitted her perfectly; the seed-pearl nestling in the dip between the two prominent bones where her throat and chest met.

'There. You look lovely in it, darling,' he smiled, making a bunch of tiny lines appear at the edge of his eyes. 'Do you like it?'

'Yes,' Charlotte said. 'It's beautiful. Thank you, Daddy.'

It was then that he told her he wouldn't be coming to see her any more.

'There are reasons,' he said hesitantly, as if half in mind to tell her. Then he looked more decisive. 'But I can't explain them to you. You're too young to understand. Perhaps, one day, we can meet. When you're older . . . and I can tell you . . .'

Charlotte's thumb and forefinger tightened their grip around the seed-pearl at her throat. She misunderstood. When he said he couldn't see her any more, she thought it meant he intended to come round to see her mother when Charlotte was out.

'Don't you like me any more?' she asked.

'Of course I do, darling,' he said, squatting down beside her and taking her in his arms. 'I love you with all my heart, but I can't come here any more.'

Charlotte realised that he wasn't going to see either of them again. She did not know what they had done wrong, but she remembered times when she'd heard her mother shouting at him, saying things that made him raise his voice, and she thought that might have something to do with it. She did not doubt that he meant what he said, and that she would never see him again. She had, in a curious way, been expecting it, though she hadn't known it consciously.

She stood quietly, with her hand covering the seed-pearl at her throat and remembered something from years before, when she had been very small.

There had been monsters in Charlotte's life, always. All through her childhood, only too imaginable horrors lurked under beds, around corners, inside cupboards, behind the noise of the flushing toilet. She battled nightly against a monstrous army of invisible demons, sucking in her fear to make a tight, hard ball in the pit of her stomach, and waited, trembling, for their attack. The terror was that they never did. They stayed hidden and relied on her knowledge of their existence to do their work for them. Sometimes, unable to bear the fear any longer, she would open the cupboard, look under the bed, make herself turn the lethal corner. But the fact that they were never there only proved to Charlotte their cunning, and the invincibility of their special powers of which she had none. She was always too small, too slow, too tied to ordinariness to overcome them. It seemed unjust that she should be faced with such powerful adversaries.

Sometimes, though, they did break cover, but always in disguise and when she wasn't expecting them. One Sunday evening, when she was four years old and still small enough to be held in the crook of his arm, Charlotte was on a bus with her father. The light was beginning to fade, and he was taking her home, back to her mother, after a day out together, and telling Charlotte a long, funny story that he had told her a hundred times before but which always made her laugh and wriggle with the nonsense of it. They were, looking back, a picture of mutual devotion.

A tramp who had come into enough money to lash out on a bus fare sat opposite them, large, dishevelled and mumbling drunk. His moment in her life came back to her suddenly, now that her father was leaving for good, as bright as an image from a difficult film seen too young, but now remembered with a new understanding. His face was grey with ingrained grime, like a risen ghost complete with ashes, and his tattered clothes were stained beyond guessing their original colour or pattern, smelling of God only knew what. For a while everyone on the bus ignored him, as people do in public when the improper suddenly comes into view, and he contented himself with singing something tuneless under his breath, and occasional mutterings that were inwardly directed. But, although Charlotte took her cue from the rest of the passengers, and concentrated on trying to annoy her father by leaping ahead in the story he was attempting to tell her (which was also part of the game), she was all the time aware of the dirty, drunken, dangerous presence opposite her, and, as if a cupboard in a dark room had creaked open a crack and threatened her with its contents, she kept him cautiously in her peripheral vision.

Her fears, as she had always feared, and would always fear, were not unfounded. Suddenly, he shook himself as if waking from a bad dream and lurched towards her across the gangway with a malevolent look in his eye, so close that Charlotte could smell the methylated spirits on his breath.

'You love your daddy, do you?' he slurred, his tone vicious and mean.

She stared at him hovering above her, and curled her fingers tightly around her father's arm. She wanted to look at him for reassurance, but found she couldn't look away from the drunk's contemptuous eyes.

'Yes,' he sneered. 'Go on, love him. Love him all you like. But you mark my words, girly, he'll leave you. You think he loves you, but one day off he'll go and you won't see him for dust. Mark my words, I know.'

He prodded the air between them with his blackened wand of a finger. Like a curse. Like a witch-woman in the grip of a vision.

Several women on the bus clicked their tongues and muttered to each other. The conductor stepped up from the platform and moved close to him, hanging from the strap, warning, 'That's enough from you, mate. Sit down, and don't bother the passengers or I'll put you off the bus.'

Charlotte's father put his arm around her and hugged her close, but she still couldn't take her eyes off the man, who turned his head for a moment to snort at the conductor, before slumping back into his seat opposite.

'I paid my fucking fare. I've got as much right . . .' he mumbled.

'Take no notice,' her father said. 'He's just had too much to drink.'

'You listen to me, little girl,' the drunk insisted, leaning forward so that his eyes, dead as they were, burned icily into Charlotte's. 'I know what I'm talking about. He's no good. He'll make you promises, but it's all lies. He'll bugger off, I'm *telling* you.'

They had got off at the next stop, although it wasn't theirs.

Charlotte had finally met one of her monsters and she knew why it was that she had always to avoid confronting them. Better to live with the fear than open the cupboard and come face to face with one. They knew things, those creatures who lurked in the dark, threatening her. They knew *what there was to be frightened of*, and instead of leaving you in peace, letting you imagine the *everything-will-be-all-right* that people do if left to their own thoughts, they tell you the worst, given half a chance.

Her father tried to reassure her, saying the drink made him talk like that and she wasn't to take any notice. But nothing her father said made any difference because Charlotte knew that the drunk had spoken the truth. He had the truth draped about him like a cloak. It wasn't drink that made him say those things, or if it was, it only made him say what he knew about the future, about the way things really were. She'd never since believed anyone as much as she believed that tramp.

There was another reason why he was so convincing: he looked into her four-year-old eyes and, instead of treating her like a child, confronted her with a terrible, unthinkable truth. And, in spite of this menacing manner, and the frightening thing he had to say, Charlotte felt, as well as scared, *respected* in a curious way, as if it were the first time that anyone had treated her like a person who had a right to know about matters that affected her.

The drunken tramp had thrown her into the isolation of her own particular life. It was her first intimation. He spoke directly to her, giving her no quarter, softening nothing, and presented her with a future which, good or not, was hers alone. The fact that she also perceived his words as mysterious soothsaying was almost incidental to the feeling she had, for the first time in her existence, that there was a life which she, and only she, would have to go through.

Even so, she *did* believe his prophecy would come about, and she did not believe the comforting words of her father.

She didn't know why the drunk's words had sounded so true to her. But at that moment on the bus, she had simply heard the voice of truth and knew it to be what it was. Perhaps a part of her had already understood something that chimed with what the drunk said. She had never thought there was anything false about her father's love as it was directed to her then, but she supposed, looking back on it, there were clues enough in the fact that he did not live with her and her mother to signal danger once she had been alerted. And there was something about her father's eyes.

145

'Charlotte?' her father said, unable to bear her silence any longer.

She looked up at him and blinked the tramp away.

'The necklace?' she asked. 'Can I keep it?'

A look of disappointment filled in the creases around his eyes.

'Yes, of course,' he said, standing up again. 'It's yours to keep. From me. I got it because it is beautiful, and it reminded me of you.'

And that was what Charlotte thought, too: it was like her, or what she once had been.

She kept it on at night, fingering it in the dark to help her in her task of imagining herself an unimaginable single cell, so tiny, so singular, invisible in a place where no light shone. At first, she tried to picture all of her, head to toes, within the diminutive compass of the cell, but, like the modern biologist she became, she dismissed the notion of a homunculus as ridiculous.

When she was lying in bed, in the dark, she had no body, she was only her thoughts, her *self*. That was how she finally came to picture her single-celled entry into the world.

The tiny globule contained all that Charlotte was, the thing she felt herself to be when the lights were out and there were no places, no people, no things, and no future that was suddenly subject to alteration. It was, she discovered to her surprise, an existence not of smallness, but of immense size. As soon as she managed to find the single cell in her imagination, and herself within it, she discovered herself to be everything, an unbounded creature, suspended in an infinitely large and inky black space. Charlotte had never imagined such vastness. It frightened her to think that she had once been all alone in a place of such immensity. Had she been frightened, then, she wondered? Had she been lonely? What had she thought about?

It occurred to her that she could have had no memories because nothing had happened to her yet. Well, the sperm had fertilised the egg (she had picked up that bit of information in the playground after the lesson), but the sperm wasn't *her* and neither was the egg. The sperm and the egg were before her, so if it happened, and how it happened, was nothing to do with her, because she hadn't existed. And if there was no *before, after* was nothing she could have known about at the time, either, therefore there could have been not only no memories, but no expectations, and therefore no thought at all. For what could be thought that didn't require memory or expectation?

Apart from the soothsaying tramp whose words she had blanked out until it happened, Charlotte had not known what was going to happen in her life that day her father gave her the seed-pearl, even though she was nine, and filled with thoughts. She couldn't have guessed that she would never see him again. So how could a seed-pearl of a thing, in a sealed universe where nothing had happened and nothing was known, know anything about *next*?

What had it been like, then, when there was nothing she could think, and all she could know was that she was, and that didn't seem like much to know all on its own? She felt pity for the single cell which was, and would become Charlotte, which hadn't even got a name to call itself by, and though larger in a special way than anything she could imagine, knew nothing. She felt a fellowship, a sense of responsibility for the immeasurably small, peculiarly huge, glowing, milky white thing which was her, but wasn't, which was almost nothing and had no choice.

This was Charlotte's introduction to the facts of life. Not the messy, biological procedure that caused life to come into being, but the *facts*, the hard reality of life. What she understood from the series of biology lessons dealing with reproduction, which Mr Styles so much wished he didn't have to teach, was that she was her own particular self with her own particular built-in set of circumstances which would never, could never, alter. The tramp had also told her that, in his way, but she had forgotten. The facts of her life – her father was her father, her mother, her mother – would not change, even though a lifetime of events might – *would* – happen to her. She would carry her original circumstances with her wherever she went, whoever she became through the living of life. And she also understood that although once, before memory, she had not been herself, or only in an essential way that she could only half-grasp when she tried very hard, even then the die had been cast.

Somewhere between the time when she had no name and no circumstances, and later, though she didn't know how much later, she had settled into the inevitability of her life. As that life began to twist and turn, apparently without her willing it to, it was both terrible and thrilling to know what she had learned; to see the

147

pattern, and to know that it was immutable, yet at the same time subject to the accidents of others and the future. It made her feel on the one hand helpless, adrift on a sea of destiny; and on the other comforted by the thought that in some most important way, it wasn't, any of it, really her fault.

But the real import of that single cell, which was half her mother and half her father, though uniquely herself, was yet to be revealed to Charlotte. She had still more to learn about destiny.

Charlotte wore the seed-pearl necklace for a month after her father had given it to her, without taking it off. Then she undid it, wrapped it in its original tissue paper, and never wore it again. Her father didn't keep his word. She never did see him again after that day.

For years, Charlotte couldn't ask her mother why her father had stopped seeing her, because Annie refused to speak about him. As far as she knew, her mother never mentioned her father's name for the rest of her life. It was forbidden. When she did finally speak of him to her daughter, he was referred to only as *him* or Charlotte's father. She had, of course, to mention his surname frequently, since she had taken it by deed poll as her own, but the name was never used with reference to him.

Charlotte suspected that it was her mother who was largely responsible for her father's continued silence. She wanted very badly not to believe that he had never tried to contact his daughter again. Had Annie intercepted his letters and phone calls, she wondered, or was it simply that he couldn't face having to run the gauntlet of her mother's hatred to get to Charlotte?

Charlotte developed her own anger at her abandonment, but it was never expressed beyond the putting away of the necklace. She didn't hate the necklace because it held such a weighty secret about herself, but she would not wear it. So, like her mother, Charlotte kept her silence.

Charlotte lived lovelessly with her remaining parent. It was a mutual lack of feeling. Nothing was ever said or done. There was no simple deprivation, no palpable cruelty. Annie cared for her daughter's physical requirements, and worked hard to ensure that she had what she needed materially, but there was an absence of what might be

148

thought of as normal affection on both sides. It was never talked about, but both of them knew that all their relationship consisted of was a sense of duty to each other. If it was sad, they were both used to the situation – whatever should have happened to mother and child in Charlotte's early years, simply had not occurred. A powerful emotional bond had not been formed. Neither Annie nor Charlotte knew the reason for this, nor did they bother to analyse it much since both suspected there might be no reason at all, beyond the unspoken fact that the focus of each of their emotional lives had been the regular though infrequent visits of Charlotte's father, and in his unbroken absence the truth of their weak linkage became obvious. If it had been different each could have turned to the other for comfort; yet, Charlotte came to think, it would not necessarily have been healthier. More and more, as Charlotte's interest focused increasingly on biology, she came to see her mother as little more than the provider of half her genes. It was a vital role, but, as she read in a book on animal behaviour, not necessarily an emotional one. As her biologist's eye view developed, the lack of love between her mother and herself came to make perfectly sound sense.

Long before the sociobiologists went into print, Charlotte came up with the notion that it was the genes, and not the people who carried them, which were the motive force of existence. Annie's genes (not Annie herself – no more than a vehicle for her genes) demanded that Charlotte be nurtured so that she should maintain their existence. This accounted for maternal concern well enough, and did not require emotional bonds as a necessity. Guilt – her mother's and her own – disappeared as absurdly irrelevant in this picture of the world. No need to feel bad about lacking feeling when it was clearly nothing more than an invention of the sentimentally unscientific.

Her father's absence, of course, also came to make perfect sense, as her studies into genetics deepened. Sperm being plentiful in supply – cheap, the sociobiologists would say, as opposed to her mother's expensive single investment – there was no percentage in the male hanging around taking care of it. Better to be off and passing on more of his genes among the next generation. It was not until years later that she read the startling texts that did the arithmetic on her interesting ideas, but she did not need the sums; her own life experience confirmed what they had to say. Charlotte's world had meshed so well with the implications of behaviourism that she had no choice but to see the world in that light. Reduced, yet understandable.

It was seven years before the subject of Charlotte's father came up between her and her mother. When it did, not long after Crick and Watson cracked the genetic code, Charlotte had already discovered too much about her forthcoming profession not to know what it might mean for her own life.

Sitting in her chair opposite the patient Matthew, Charlotte havered between remembering and resistance. The remembering, she suspected, was necessary, but she hardly felt strong enough. The point of it seemed to elude her. Why did she have to go through the difficulty of recollecting? And even if she did make the journey back through her past, there remained always the thing she could do nothing about, that no one could do anything about. If remembering was an explanation of who she had turned out to be, and therefore in some way useful to her, wouldn't she always be defeated by the simple fact that she was who she was? A person might be able to understand away the pain of their life, but what was to be done about the blood, the biological history, which was already in her before she even took her first breath? Look at it as history, or see it as biology, what was there to be done about a pattern that lived inside every cell of her body? It was too much, and she was too tired. But, Charlotte thought, staring at the rain which had begun a deluge outside the window, causing the afternoon to blacken, she had continued to tell Matthew her story, and so she supposed she must want to do the telling.

After school one day, just before she was due to take her O levels, Annie greeted Charlotte at the door. It was not usual, and Charlotte saw a strangeness in her mother's eyes that she couldn't define.

'I've got something to tell you,' Annie said, leading her daughter into the kitchen. 'Sit down.'

Charlotte sat, knowing something bad was on its way. She still had her school-bag over her shoulder, so that she had to lean forward on the kitchen chair, making her seem more eager than she felt to hear the news her mother was about to tell her. Somehow, she knew who it would be about.

'Your father's dead, Charlotte,' Annie said, her voice as dry as dust.

For a moment Charlotte thought that was all there was going to be: an announcement, and then getting on with life as if nothing out of the ordinary had happened. But Annie had been thinking hard about it since she received the phone call, and had made a decision.

'You've got a right to know about him,' she paused for a moment as if choosing between alternative ways of beginning. 'Your father and I weren't married.'

Charlotte put the information about her father being dead into a waiting area of her brain. For the moment, she needed all her attention to listen to her mother.

'I took his name so that you would have it on the birth certificate. Mother and father with the same name – so long as you didn't look too carefully where it described me as a "spinster". He was married to someone else. Someone more his kind.' A bitterness, like bile, entered Annie's voice. 'We started our affair in the hotel where your father came with her for a holiday by the sea. He was rich and handsome. You remember how he was handsome, don't you?'

Charlotte nodded, remembering well her father's fine face, all angles and shadows, and the remarkably long sharp nose he jokingly called his beak, which he teased Charlotte for having inherited.

'It happened while his wife had her afternoon naps. She was too well-bred not to have an afternoon nap. He booked another room on a different floor without her knowing, where we could spend the afternoon together. I was free after lunch, you see.' Her features contracted in disgust and rage. 'I worked in the hotel. As a *chambermaid*.'

Part of Charlotte wished her mother would stop. These were things she didn't want to know. A story she wished she hadn't heard. But she couldn't get up and leave the room. She couldn't stop listening as her mother now collected herself a little and continued.

'I fell for him, of course. And by the time he left, I'd fallen for you, too. He'd gone by then, back to his everyday life. He bought me a gold bracelet when he left. There wasn't any question of seeing him again. I was a holiday fling, nothing more. I got his address from the signing-in book in reception and I phoned him once I was sure. I'll say this for him, he didn't try and put me off, or get out of it. He told me he would make arrangements, and before the month was out I got a letter with some cash and a set of keys in the envelope. He'd rented this flat. Yes, *this* flat. I was to live here and bring you up. He wasn't in love with me, I knew that, but it was the sex. For a while, he couldn't leave me alone, once he had me nearby and safely hidden away. His wife wasn't brought up to give a man pleasure. He looked after me, gave me money and came round whenever he could get free. I saw him two or three times a week. I realised soon enough that he wasn't going to marry me. He had a sense of duty, your father, but when it came to choosing between his duty to the woman he was already married to, and the woman who'd had his baby, he stuck with her. What was I supposed to do? I had a small baby, and I couldn't earn enough to keep us. I had to settle for being his bit on the side, secreted away. This is one Cinderella who never married her Prince.'

Charlotte waited through all these words to hear something that concerned her. Annie, who had been talking to the table-top, her eyes down, on the past, looked up then, and seemed to sense Charlotte's need. She gave her what she could.

'He loved *you*, of course. You were why he went on coming. After a couple of years he'd had enough of me. Sex doesn't last for ever, don't ever let anyone tell you it does. But you were his only child. *She* couldn't, or wouldn't, have any. I became just a nanny he kept to look after you. I knew that. He gave me money so that I didn't have to work. I was to stay with you, bring you up. First I was his secret love, hidden, like a proper princess in a tower, and then I went back to being not much more than the chambermaid I'd been to start with. I took to reading and educated myself that way a bit. It wasn't that I was trying to better myself, I just didn't have anything to do. So I know more than I used to, but it hasn't been much use to me. I could have gone out and got myself a job, but I thought, why should I? Why should I bother, and why should I give him the chance to be pleased I was making something of myself? I knew he felt guilty about me. And so he should have. I wasn't going to let him off that easily.'

Annie's breath came fast, as if she were expelling puffs of smoking poison. She was quiet for a moment, and then she got on with the story she had to tell, almost doggedly.

152

'He stopped coming because *she* found out about us. Duty again, you see. He had to make a decision. She was the wronged one, so he decided it was his duty to stay with her. She didn't have children, and she couldn't stand the idea of his loving a child who wasn't hers. I don't think she cared much about me. I suppose she knew that I wasn't important. She made him swear not to see you again. And naturally the man of honour kept his word. I think it broke his heart though, I think that was why . . . It certainly wasn't that he was missing me. It turned out she only kept him another seven years. She got seven more years and I got a wasted lifetime. But he loved you all right, and made sure you had everything a child could want, sending you to a good school. You frightened him, though. Part of him was relieved, I think, to be made to put you out of his mind. I knew what it was; he mentioned it back in the days of our affair. He hadn't minded not having children, he said, because he was worried about passing his heritage on. He felt he was doomed, you see. Cursed by some family curse – I never found out what it was.'

Charlotte's eyes widened at the sudden melodrama. Annie gave out a laugh before she went on to explain.

'He was a bastard, I think. He didn't speak about it much. But there was something fancy in his background. Funny really, you were just another bastard in a line of classy bastards, not that that made *me* feel any more respectable. It was all right for men of good families to have bastards, but the poor cow who has them for them is just another slag. It wasn't *my* blood in you that interested your father, it was his. There was something in the blood, he believed. Sometimes he got into terrible tempers and then black depressions. He was convinced he'd come to a sticky end.'

Charlotte hadn't moved, but she began to feel dizzy and nauseous. She tried to ask her mother to stop, but her mouth was full of the bad-tasting stuff that comes up before you're sick, as if her mother's bile had transferred itself to her body. She didn't dare say anything, and she couldn't move.

'It turned out he was right, or he made himself right. That's what happened. He did it last week. Cut his throat, his solicitor told me. But he's made provision for you. Your education's taken care of and

153

there'll be a bit of money when you're older. I suppose you could say you were born with a silver spoon in your mouth.'

Annie finished her tale with a laugh that died as soon as it hit the air. Charlotte was astonished to see a tear roll down one of her mother's cheeks.

Somehow, Charlotte understood that Annie had told her this story in the way she did, out of hatred for her father more than for her. Or rather, the hatred and resentment Annie felt for her daughter belonged really to the man who had imprisoned her will so long ago. Charlotte did not receive the hatred as a personal thing, but the story itself entered her mind and heart and lived there, unalterable.

It was then that Charlotte's unique destiny began to take on a specific shape. The excitement Charlotte felt, as a fledgling scientist, when Crick and Watson discovered the actual shape of the DNA molecule, was muted by the hint of a genetic destiny for herself. The double helix was as elegant a solution to the mystery of life itself as anyone could have hoped for, but to Charlotte it had none of the power of cursed blood and a knife drawing a necklace of death across the throat.

She coped with the paradox of blood versus biological science by allowing two separate strands to develop. Charlotte kept her concerns about having bad blood for her inner life, while outwardly she moved through the academic stages that would enable her to become a working scientist, and developed her political idealism. None the less, her fears about her own tainted heritage did not disappear, and however down-to-earth her biological activities, the other thing was always somewhere in the back of her mind.

From the age of sixteen, Charlotte took on a dual existence, and more and more the two Charlottes colluded to keep their mutual existence going. The one who knew about her doomed blood curled up and slept – or if not slept, at least played possum – while the other, practical and outgoing enough, and concerned with biology, not as destiny but as science, carried her sleeping self about the world carefully, so as not to jog her into wakefulness. It sung her lullabies of scientific objectivity and the innate goodness of the human race. Everything that tended to warmth and goodness in her lived for political justice and scientific progress. Not enough remained for her private self to be much more than an emotional vacuum. It was not to be until many years later, when the politics had collapsed and her child died, that another Charlotte woke and demanded her right to be heard.

Chapter 11

NOTHING WHATEVER

'What do you know about this business?' the
King said to Alice.
'Nothing,' said Alice.
'Nothing whatever?' *persisted the King.*
'Nothing whatever,' said Alice.
'That's very important,' the King said, turning
to the jury.

She recognised the sound immediately. It had the comforting rhythm of a childhood nursery rhyme of the kind her father – once or twice – stayed long enough to tell. Soothing, repetitive and with a tempo akin to a living pulse. Only the sudden sound of the book falling from her lap jarred the regular rhythm in her ears.

He was the only one in the railway carriage, apart from her own invisible presence. She didn't recognise him at first. She saw a grey-haired, elderly gentleman in a frock coat, a Victorian down to the neat white spats covering his boots. He stared out at the passing scenery but it was clear he wasn't seeing it. The grey eyes gave him away, and then the nose, not so beaky now in the ageing face, more settled, somehow, classical rather than a sharp protuberance. And the eyes themselves had lost their gleam, the grey no longer startled, having grown dimmer over the years. It was a distinguished face, but clouded and troubled. Much more like her own, now. Before, their similarity had been marked by those particular FitzRoy features, but now the whole saddened visage looked familiar. She would have recognised him sooner but for the civilian clothes, which also detracted from the stiff nobility he had once had in his rigid naval uniform. He still was not exactly ordinary, but some light had left him, and a deep tiredness had replaced the youthful alertness.

He felt old. Much older than his fifty-five years. And he *was* tired: finding this journey back to London interminable. The thought brought a sour smile to his lips. A man who had three times travelled the oceans to the end of the world and back again was exhausted by a visit to Oxford. He ached to be home, where Maria would provide the comfort and reassurance he so desperately needed. He grimly envied Darwin his dyspepsia, which kept him reclining on his couch at Down House, while younger, fiercer men battled on his behalf. FitzRoy's belly was robust, it was his mind that gave him trouble, but it was an invisible ailment, not one that allowed him to count himself an invalid entitled to avoid difficult situations.

He tried to comfort himself with the thought that he, at least, had continued to fight his own battles for what he believed in, but his present misery was close to overwhelming; there was no comfort at hand.

The dim grey eyes clouded even more as tears filmed their surface, threatening to overflow. Such a public display of emotion was unthinkable, even alone in the carriage, and with all his might he forced them back. He was, he felt, as far as it was possible to be from the brave young man who, in the name of God and decency and the proper order of things, had willingly faced all the dangers of an alien world and uncharted waters. Now, he was defeated and brought close to open weeping by the derision of those whom once he would have held in contempt. A dreadful sadness and a bitter taste of defeat filled him, not just for the present moment, but for his whole existence, and he found it hard even to breathe. Only a vestigial sense of duty and the thought of Maria prevented him from wishing himself dead.

For the past twenty years failure had dogged him, and when he tried to account for it he could not help but feel it was his destiny stalking him, rather than mere misfortune, or even poor judgement. It was as if his life spun purposefully beyond his control. Sometimes he even thought he heard its malevolent, ghostly laugh behind his shoulder. And yet, it had seemed to him at the time of his return from the second voyage on the *Beagle*, that he had overcome the greatest of dangers it was possible to confront.

As he set foot on English soil again, nearly twenty-five years before, he had feared that his life would spin slowly and inexorably out of control, so endangered were his defences. It was as if that walk with Darwin on the tiny Galapagos island, and the pathetic fiasco of his Fuegian experiment were twin prongs of the Devil's pitchfork. The third prong, of course, he carried always in his blood. Now, the implement began to look hideously dangerous. A hairline crack had opened up in the solid rock of FitzRoy's faith which, ignore it as he tried, threatened to engulf his belief. And what else did he have to keep him safe from the danger of insanity?

It had been Mary who secured him for God's party and gave him back the narrow, straight road of his life. Although he had not mentioned her once during the five years aboard the *Beagle*, FitzRoy had married Mary just three weeks after landing back in England. Darwin had assumed his Captain had kept his romance to himself, but the truth was that Mary was a cousin whom he had known only distantly when he left. The hasty marriage had come about as a result of FitzRoy's certainty, on meeting her again, that she had the strength and faith to re-secure his own.

She was a beautiful young woman, of that there was no doubt, but it was her mind, as resolute as her face was handsome, which won FitzRoy's heart. The severity of her belief in the absolute truth of the Bible was equal in fervour to Robert FitzRoy's pride. They made a true partnership, a perfectly matched pair; ramrod straight in thought and bearing, fine-featured, formal twins devoted to propriety in appearance, word and deed. The beauty of her face had turned FitzRoy's head far less than the beauty of her conviction.

It was she who encouraged him, to Darwin's fury, to append the essay on faith in the biblical account of the creation to his part of *The Narrative of the Voyage of the Beagle*. *A Very Few Remarks with Reference to the Deluge*, as Mary suggested he call it, reaffirmed his faith, rejecting, for the benefit of young sailors who might chance to doubt, all thoughts of a secular creation. He admonished Voltaire for turning young minds, and advised the learning by heart of Genesis, in which everything was explained to the satisfaction of all but followers of the devil.

But from time to time that tiny fissure in his mind tripped FitzRoy up, and it was Mary – undoubtedly a gift of the Lord to a troubled soul – who provided a bulwark against his fears. She did not confuse reality by debating the truth which was so simply evident to her.

Soon after they had married, she had entered his study and found him at his desk, his piercing eyes staring at the far wall but focused beyond it, as if seeing some horror that even wilful blindness could not save him from. She did not ask him what the matter was, and she would never know exactly what monsters her husband lived with. She understood, however, that such a look sprang from a dark place, and that all shadows in this world were subject to the lightening power of faith. She left the study for a moment, and returned with a Bible, which she placed gently in her husband's hands, causing him to look up, surprised to find his wife in the room.

'Read to me from Exodus, Robert. Read to me of God calling to Moses from the burning bush, and His promise to deliver the children of Israel.'

Robert's face cleared as he read to his silent, smiling wife of the fiery bush which was not consumed, of God's demand for faith, of obligation, of the burden and renewed sense of purpose that Moses received from the Lord. When he had finished, Mary smiled and kissed her husband gently on the cheek.

'Thank you, my dear,' she said, and quietly left the room.

The tempest subsided in the landlocked sea captain, and he thanked God for the strength he had received through the medium of his wife.

But still she had not been enough, FitzRoy thought, staring into the darkness of the passing countryside through the train window. She had shored up his faith, but she could not prevent shame and absurdity from stalking him, as if his secret, unexpressed doubts and fears took another belligerent form, refusing to leave him alone, or as if the Devil himself blew winds of disaster in his direction. Disgrace, recognising its home, haunted FitzRoy, so that he could go nowhere and do nothing without it making its presence felt.

Everything he had done with his life had turned sour, although each stage in his career had seemed nothing more than what might be expected of a well-born young aristocrat with a strong sense of duty. He recalled with horribly fresh pain that made him wince, each disaster.

His election as an MP should have been a mere formality; the heroic young naval commander taking his rightful place in the governing of his nation. Instead, he had become the laughing stock of London as his internal tempest swirled simple pride and dignity into ridicule. A rival Tory candidate for the safe Durham seat and a good deal of innuendo caused what should have been the simple business of electing one of God's chosen Tories to become a bear fight with duels arranged and accusations of cowardice to ring in FitzRoy's ear. The quiet advice from Mary came to nothing as hurt pride and outrage overtook all thoughts of politic behaviour until, finally, the shameful day had come when FitzRoy's friends were obliged to drag him away from further damaging his rival, whom he had felled with a furled umbrella outside his own club. FitzRoy could still hear the sound of sniggering all these years later, and even his good and useful conduct as an elected member of Parliament did not make up for the shame he still felt.

But if hotheaded, unseemly behaviour might be forgiven, even by his disapproving middle-aged self, failure on the grand scale as Colonial Governor of New Zealand was a stain which could never be removed.

No one questioned the fact that his task of mediating between the savage Maoris and the equally savage white settlers was fiendishly delicate. No one, that is, except Robert himself, who set about making momentous decisions with a confidence that only one convinced of his nearness to God could have had. His refusal to institute criminal proceedings against the Maoris who had massacred white men; his unilateral decision to turn debentures into legal tender; his public abuse of the anti-Maori Jeringham Wakefield; all these acts finally provoked questions in Parliament as to his competence, and petitions against him by the settlers. But in the end his recall had more to do with his arrogance in taking action before informing the home government, than with the decisions them-selves. He remained steadfast in his belief that he had been deeply and irreparably injured, and even now he was unable to feel anything but aggrieved at his treatment. His disgrace could not have been more public. *The Times* and the *Morning Chronicle* ran damning articles about the Governor who, they suggested, was running the colony as a wealthy, arrogant young man might run his life. Yet all along, *all along*, he had only acted according to his conscience and his

160

sense of what was right. What point was there in getting permission for his actions when he had already judged them the best, the only ones possible?

He returned to England with Mary and his three children, utterly discredited, his political career in tatters, still unable to understand what it was, apart from malice and a cursed bloodline, that had gone wrong.

His faith, however, with Mary's help, had held him fast. He did not sink into the despair that had grasped at him before he had her to keep him safe. He returned to his interest in the sea, testing steam-driven ships for the government.

FitzRoy approached in his memory the terrible decade of the fifties. He had hoped the train might deliver him to London before he had time to recall the past, dismal decade.

He remembered the loss of Mary, and then his only daughter with a stoicism of which Mary herself would have been proud. But there was a dull pain; a recognition that wives and children died, and it was God's will, did not assuage the private sense of loss. Mary, he had no doubt, would have been happy to know he had remarried two years later. It was for such practical understanding that FitzRoy missed her most. His new wife, another, more distant cousin this time, was Maria, not Mary, and the similarity did not end there. He could count himself an extraordinarily fortunate man to have found a second wife as devout and devoted as the first.

And there was a new appointment, as dear to his heart as anything he could imagine. The Royal Society had recommended to the Board of Trade that a Meteorological Department be set up and that FitzRoy should be in charge as Meteorological Statist. He grasped at the opportunity to make life safer for men at sea by collating information, and issuing informed guesses as to the coming winds and weather in specified areas. He might have seen in his fortune at finding a new wife and function dear to his heart, an end to the cycle of his misery; the failure and the fears. And yet, as if the Devil gave only to inflict more pain, the failures and the fears seemed to conglomerate in the final year of the decade.

That he was doing good work there was no doubt. Lives were saved by knowing a storm was approaching a fishing area. It was true that he was not always correct: sometimes a predicted storm failed to happen, or one blew up suddenly of which he gave no warning. But it was *better*. The fishermen and sailors wrote to tell him so. And although it was true that he was ignoring the true nature of his job, which was simply to compile statistics about weather, there could be no doubt that foretelling the weather, and issuing barometers to seafaring communities, was by far the most important work he could have done. He was unhappy with the word 'foretelling'. It sounded too much like magic, whereas what he was trying to do was extrapolate *scientifically* from given data. He invented a new phrase – *weather forecasting* – and persuaded *The Times* to publish for the first time ever a daily assessment of the coming weather.

That he was not being unreasonably optimistic about his success was proved one Sunday, when Maria and Robert were still at church and their young daughter answered a knock at the door. An equerry sent by Queen Victoria asked if her father would oblige with a forecast for the following day, since Her Majesty was planning a trip to the Isle of Wight and wished to know if the seas would be calm enough for the journey.

Why should he not assume that the darkness of his life was moving away, like a storm disappearing into the distance? Because he was FitzRoy, nephew of Castlereagh, the madman and suicide. Because failure waited gleefully around corners to trip him as he strode confidently again, his head held high.

There were complaints about his activities. He was dabbing in his *forecasting*, some said at the Board of Trade, at the expense of the proper task of accumulating information. He was, simply, not doing what he had been appointed to do, but something of his own devising which was of doubtful scientific provenance. FitzRoy was unmoved by the criticism, at least in the sense that he refused to change his ways, knowing himself to be right. But the sour taste of things going wrong was beginning to rise in his gorge when Sulivan, his one-time junior aboard the *Beagle*, was given the post of Chief Naval Officer in the Board of Trade's Maritime Department, and Fitzroy, who by all that was just should have got the job, was passed over.

Then reports began to come in about a massacre of missionaries in Tierra del Fuegio. Jemmy Button had been found, still with a modicum of English, and a mission was sent, as it had been so many years before. This time, however, it didn't simply not work, it cost the lives of seven men, and most dreadful, there was a single survivor who suggested that Jemmy Button had taken the lead in the murder of the white men, aggrieved at not receiving enough gifts from them. It was not absolutely certain that he was involved, but there was no doubt that a son of his – one Billy Button – was part of the stone-throwing party.

The bitter-tasting stuff rose higher in FitzRoy's throat. He did not want to be reminded of the inexplicable failure of God's work, and certainly not in such a personal way. Jemmy, it seemed, had reverted to a state more savage than FitzRoy had first found him. And worse, worrying him at the back of his mind, was another notion, almost the opposite. If the story was true, about his taking revenge for not receiving the presents he felt were his due, then it was Jemmy's greed for the things the white man had shown him, and which he expected to be given, which had caused his murderous attack. And the benefits of civilisation, not the handicaps of savagery were the source of his hideous behaviour.

The final, and most terrible blow in 1859 came in the same month of November as the story of the massacre appeared in the press. Again, FitzRoy couldn't help but see that he had played a part in it coming about. Charles Darwin, the callow young man who by accident he had chosen as his dining companion, published his *Origin of Species*. There, as proof, were the accounts of the finches he had collected in the Galapagos, and the tortoises they had sat upon, with differently shaped shells according to which island they inhabited. The evidence, at least in part, and certainly the germ of the idea for what Darwin called 'natural selection' had been provided as a direct result of his voyge on the *Beagle*.

FitzRoy had thought himself the Lord's instrument in bringing civilisation to the Fuegians, yet His work had not, in the end, been done. And now it turned out that God's servant had enabled the least godly theory of mankind's origins to see the light of day. Not light, FitzRoy thought, staring into the blackness of the night-time countryside as it swept past him. There was no light to be shed from such a spiritually bereft source. It was the Devil's work. And how could it have been that FitzRoy had been the one to give the Devil his voice? He knew, of course, that evil stalked the earth, and that Satan dressed himself in divine disguises, the better to fool man into doing

163

his desperate work. So had he been a tool of the Devil, all along? Had he been tricked into doing the work of the Prince of Darkness?

It was a conclusion he could not avoid. Without him Jemmy would have remained the simple, good-hearted savage he was when they first met him. Without him Charles Darwin would have stayed home, taken an easy living in the Church, and contented himself with collecting beetles. He saw himself at the centre of a terrible web of evil; if not the spinner, then the errand boy of the manufacturer of the silk.

He had prayed for guidance; for a way to repair the damage he had unwittingly done. The theory of evolution had caught hold of the public imagination and was being spread by clever, plausible men like Thomas Huxley, a notorious and open atheist, who found no shame in describing himself as 'Darwin's bulldog'. There was nothing he could do, now, about Jemmy Button having been lost for God's glory, but he could stand up and show that the Lord had a bulldog of his own.

But Huxley was a young, clever firebrand, not a tired, almost defeated fifty-five-year-old with no more than the embers of his intellect still aglow. FitzRoy knew himself to be dogged, but no bulldog. Even so, reparation had to be made, and perhaps age would count against youthful energy.

He wrote letters to *The Times*, signed *Senex*, ridiculing the notion that flint tools found on the banks of the Somme were remnants of Palaeolithic man. They were, he had explained, simply left by wandering tribes who had lost their civilisation. He had been pleased with the scorn he had poured on those who believed in the great age of man. 'In what difficulties do not those involve themselves who contend for a far greater antiquity of mankind than the learned and wise have derived from Scripture and the best tradition!' Faith, he had insisted, was so simple and, therefore, so true. Yet, he had not been listened to. And the sound of contemptuous laughter was clear behind the dismissive letters which followed his.

Now, after his visit to Oxford, all the fight had drained from him. Perhaps, he thought, he was no use to God. Better, perhaps, if he kept silent. He had been deeply humiliated at Oxford; all the more so because once again he had lost control. He had not travelled to the meeting of the British Association for the Advancement of Science

164

with the purpose of defending the Creator's honour. He was there on Friday to give a paper on British storms. It went well enough, though it caused no excitement. He had stayed for the following day's meeting, but the audience this time was not the small polite collection of fellow scientists. The rabble had arrived, and the venue actually had to be changed because the hall could not accommodate the crowd. Hundreds of students and ladies of fashion turned up to watch Huxley debate with Oxford's Bishop Wilberforce. It was, FitzRoy noted as he sat quietly amid the chattering throng, a sign of how low public standards had sunk that all over the room people were referring to the Bible-believing Bishop as *Soapy Sam*. There was no respect left, and it was Darwin and his heretical theory which encouraged mere students to feel they might openly joke about their betters.

FitzRoy hardly heard the debate. Partly, this was because the noise of the audience – actually cat-calling and hooting – was too great to make out much of what was said. But it was also that FitzRoy's mind was too distressed to take in the words of either side. Words, he knew, even fiendishly clever words, were not the point. Faith was what mattered, and there was nothing to debate about belief. A particular exchange between the Bishop and Huxley caused something close to a riot, young men jumping up and down and waving their arms about, women fainting. Disgraceful behaviour; but FitzRoy missed the actual interchange because he had been thinking about what his own contribution was to be on God's behalf. Finally, when things had quietened down a little, FitzRoy stood, and gained the floor.

He profoundly regretted, he said with all the quiet dignity he could muster, that Mr Darwin's book had been published, and he rejected any notion that it was a logical arrangement of facts, as Huxley had suggested. He told the meeting that he had often expostulated with his former companion on the *Beagle* for considering views which were contradictory to the first chapter of Genesis.

He was getting into his stride and feeling that he had injected some propriety into the debate, when a chant began to rise from the back of the hall. 'Monkeys! Monkeys! Monkeys!' the young men jeered, and finally drowned out FitzRoy's words as the cry was taken up all around the room. FitzRoy threw dignity to the wind as his rage at being silenced by a rabble overcame him. He picked up the large Bible he had brought with him to quote from, and, with both hands, hoisted it over his head. He would not be silenced, God would not be silenced. He held the book aloft with one hand now and bellowed over the collective derision of the crowd: 'The Book! The Book! The Book!' to counterbalance the derisive cry of 'Monkeys!' He did not realise that, as he shouted, tears of fury came to his eyes and that he looked for all the world like a madman prophesying doom. After a few moments the young men began with delight to alter their own chant to 'The Book! The Book!' and pointed their fingers towards FitzRoy in contemptuous rhythm, as he seemed now to be joining in with *them*. All round the room people whom he respected, important people, tried to hide their smiles as pandemonium reigned. FitzRoy had made himself a laughing stock not only among the ignorant students, but among his peers as well. His voice was drowned by the crowd aping him, and he could not stop it happening. Finally defeated, he let the Bible fall to his side, and dropped back on to his seat in a terrible confusion of shame, while the meeting settled back into a semblance of order and continued as if he had never stood to voice the truth of God.

Now, there was nothing left but to get back to his home and his wife and receive the comfort and reassurance that only she, it seemed, out of all the world, was able to give him. He would tell her that he had done his best but that the world had derided him. He would tell her that he was no longer fit for this world which threw the evident, immortal truths aside in favour of dismal notions of a blind, uncaring, motiveless force which made human beings little more than talking animals. She would press his aching head to her bosom and call his enemies God's enemies and their ideas 'shameful'. She would tell him he was right to stand up for the truth, and that it was they, the Huxleys and the rabble-rousers, who would suffer the pains of eternal hell for their atheistic beliefs.

But as the train approached the city, FitzRoy knew that, although he longed for her comforting words, he would never shake off the humiliation of that day, and that he would feel as isolated and alone, for all her presence, as if he were still despairing in his tiny cabin on the *Beagle* with nothing but the empty greyness of the sea surrounding him.

Chapter 12

ONLY A SORT OF THING

———

'. . . if he left off dreaming about you, where do
you suppose you'd be?'
'Where I am now, of course,' said Alice.
'Not you!' Tweedledee retorted contemptuously.
'You'd be nowhere. Why, you're only a sort of
thing in his dream!'
'If that there King was to wake,' added
Tweedledum, 'you'd go out bang! – just like a
candle!'
'I shouldn't!' Alice exclaimed indignantly.
'Besides, if I'm only a sort of thing in his dream,
what are you, I should like to know?'
'Ditto,' said Tweedledum.
'Ditto, ditto!' cried Tweedledee.

The monsters Charlotte had known as a child had never gone away. She believed this was because they were really there, huddling in dark places, threatening her with their reality. The trick was to keep the cupboard locked and never to look under the bed or turn unexplored corners. She was sure of this now. Don't look.

But it didn't always work. Sometimes, whatever efforts one might make to keep safe from them, they burst from their hiding places and, on buses, and on empty country roads – or in gardens – told her that her worst fears were more than mere imagination.

All she had done with Matthew was chart the progress of the monsters. She didn't feel that she had understood them, or exorcised them, or achieved any of the other results which were supposed to be the denouement of two semi-strangers sitting alone together in a room unravelling the past. There had been no untangling. She was mad and depressed when she entered the hospital; now, she was merely depressed. When she asked herself if this was an improvement, her answer was equivocal. She supposed that there had been a progression of a sort: any lessening of a number was a progression. But then so would an increase have been. If she had made progress then, it was of an entirely neutral kind. But when she demanded further, she was obliged to admit that in her heart of hearts she would, if given the choice, prefer madness to depression. No one, she realised, had asked her which aspect of her illness she wanted to be rid of, and now it struck her as strange that it should be assumed she would rather be depressed than mad.

It was true that she had felt a hideous shame at her activity in the front garden – but only after the diazepam had been administered. And there was a sense in which she regarded shame as an acceptable alternative to misery. Of course, she could have taken her tablets instead of secreting them in her locker drawer if she was so eager to slough off the depression; they might have worked. But it was the *principle* of the thing which annoyed her; the fact that *no one had asked her* what she preferred. Just as no one had asked her, while a single, undivided, but fertilised cell whether she wanted to be born or not. This lack of consultation made her quite beside herself with anger when she thought about it. She wished to be consulted about things which concerned her so closely. She felt lumbered with a *fait accompli*, and somehow, illogically, it wasn't only Matthew she blamed for taking her madness and leaving just depression in its place, but she couldn't say who this other one was. And this was why she didn't voice her complaint to Matthew; she didn't want to expose to him her sense of something going on which not only he, but she, too, knew nothing about.

She also didn't want to take Matthew to task because she had fallen in love with him. It had sneaked up on her, this love, making itself known only in momentary flashes as she noticed herself concentrating, when she was alone, on the memory of him holding her through her weeping, and on re-creating in her mind a particular expression she had seen on his face, or the shape of his hands, clasped together in his lap as they talked. As if she were concocting a special meal, she would build the image bit by bit into the desired form, and then feast on her finished work, holding it before her and gazing on it for long periods, until she became conscious of how she had spent the past half-hour, or even hour, and then, flustered, forced the picture to disperse. Her static fantasies became a fixation over the weeks, until she was spending a great deal of her time with Matthew's ghostly arm around her, and his face, hands, shoulders, thighs floating before her apparently unseeing eyes. There was enormous comfort and pleasure in the sight of him, real or conjured. He was a kind of pacifying drug she took at regular intervals, but she managed for a long time to keep the meaning from her conscious thoughts. When she could no longer avoid the fact that she was powerfully attracted to him (which was how she put it to herself, love being an unacceptable word) she was embarrassed. Was there anything sillier than an almost-fifty-year-old woman falling in love with a gay therapist? Charlotte did not like to think of herself as silly, certainly not in the emotional attachment department, so she tried to force herself not to think about Matthew. It didn't work. Her mind was as addicted to creating images of him and gazing on them as it would have been if she had been injecting herself with morphine during the past four weeks.

So it was not the case that she had been deprived of madness and left only with melancholia; addiction had replaced the madness, and, again, she would rather not have made the trade.

Matthew, of course, would have called it 'transference', a word designed to release the sufferer from the sense of her own foolishness by allowing it to be part of an inevitable and necessary process in the healing of the mind by psychotherapeutic techniques. But such an alibi would only have made her feel even more ridiculous: conforming to a theory for which she had no respect was a demeaning vision of herself she rejected out of hand.

While she was in the hospital, Charlotte managed to keep her burgeoning obsession to herself. The easy and amiable sessions with Matthew continued almost as if it was only the man she created in her mind with whom she was in love. She found it peculiarly easy, facing him across the room, to be rational and reasonable. Certainly, Matthew had no evidence that she had fallen in love with him. She was content to yearn only to touch and be held by the Matthew-of-her-mind. With the real man she managed to maintain a distant friendliness, although he expressed his warmth quite physically, pressing her hand between his two when she left a session, and smiling with an almost enticing affection. She decided she must not pay much attention to his manner, although each touch and each smile was automatically added to the store of her invented images of him, to be remembered at her leisure.

'How do you feel about going home?' Matthew asked her one Monday morning.

She was a bit surprised, although it had all along been said that she should return home as soon as she had been stabilised.

'I'm cured, then?'

Matthew laughed.

'Like a kipper,' he said. 'You'd stay on the antidepressants and come and see me once a week, but we think you'd benefit from getting back to normal life. Gradually, of course.'

'Not back to work?'

'Best to see how you go. In a couple of weeks or so if you're feeling up to it.'

'Dr Davies approves, does he?'

'It's all part of the Davies master plan. Very dangerous to stay too long in hospital. One's liable to get too attached to someone else washing the sheets. It's not good for a person's sense of independence.'

'You should tell that to most of the married men in the country. Is independence such a prize?'

'Freedom matters,' Matthew said.

'Like the freedom to destroy one's own garden?'

'Yes, so long as it doesn't frighten the horses.'

'I certainly frightened the horses, didn't I?' Charlotte said, with a satisfied smile on her face.

Matthew nodded solemnly.

'Terrified them. What about it? Home?'

Charlotte suppressed the panic which was threatening to rise in her.

'So I'm not mad any more?'

'It's not a serious description of a person's state.'

'No, but supposing for all that it exists, supposing madness could be a place where one could consign the disappointments and fear so that it was possible to get on with getting on with things?'

'Send them packing, you mean? A sort of holiday camp for the distressed and discarded?'

'Yes.'

Charlotte could not have said why she came up with such a notion.

'Sounds like Wonderland to me. Nice idea, though. Pity life doesn't work like that.'

'It could do. I mean, you only have to invent a new basis for psychology.'

'That's all, huh?'

'Listen,' Charlotte said, feeling inspired now. 'You throw out the premise that mental health depends on an integrated personality. Supposing you saw the mind more like a colony of separate personalities for different circumstances and people. Why not let different personalities lead different lives? I don't see what's to be done about past trauma except to organise oneself effectively.'

'Oneselves,' Matthew corrected.

'Exactly.'

'But since they're all part of the same person, what if they all want to do much the same thing?'

'They can, but if they want different things, they can go their own separate ways. That way you wouldn't step on your own toes.'

'Well, it's an interesting thought, but we *were* talking about you leaving the hospital. All of you, I mean, leaving.'

Charlotte let go of her procrastination.

'Why not?' she said. 'You've had my life story. There's nothing else for us to talk about, and I can swallow pills anywhere.'

'I told you I'll see you every week. And I don't have any real evidence for it, but I've got a feeling that there is something else to talk about. I don't know what it is, but I don't think you've quite finished your story.'

Charlotte refused to let her face show surprise or recognition at what he said. If she was in love with the Matthew she carried away with her, it did not seem to her to require her to tell him everything. She would leave, and even continue to have meetings with him, perhaps, but she would not tell him about her fears of being a FitzRoy, nor about the fact that she was not taking her tablets. Love, of the kind she was gripped by, did not require disclosure.

She was anxious about going home. About the uncertainty of being

171

back in that house and in her life. She knew she would carry her despair back with her. But why should she not feel depressed in the comfort of her own home? She thought, without very much evidence, that she could prevent another occurrence of really crazy behaviour. It seemed to her, now, in spite of her fantasy of split personalities, to be a matter of will, although she couldn't remember any sense of choice about the episode in the garden. Still, she was forewarned now, and that was a difference.

'All right,' she said decisively. 'I'll go home.'

It was only once she'd left Matthew that the awfulness of separation from him came into her mind. She told herself that being at home would not prevent her from conjuring him up. The imagination shouldn't need proximity to reality as building material for the fantasies it made. But, none the less, she felt quite distraught at the idea of being separated from him. It was as if she was happy to let his reality be, and settle for his inhabiting her mind, but only so long as he was actually within reaching distance. She knew that mere images would not be enough if he were physically too far away. Their continued once-a-week meetings would not be enough, she sensed. She needed to feel he was close by, in the flesh, that she might bump into him in the corridor at any time. She did not want to know for certain that for six days there would be absolutely no chance of contact with him. But to refuse to leave would arouse suspicions about her condition, and still, there was something she had to protect which was even more important than her desire for Matthew. So she did not run back into his office and tell him she had changed her mind, she wanted to stay after all. In any case, there was a task to be done; something which had gradually been growing in her mind, and it could only be done once she was discharged from hospital and back at work.

Julian brought her home from the hospital. He was his old self again; flashy and superficial. There was not even a glimmer of the unhappy, unloved little boy whose emergence had so startled her in the hospital. Only for a moment did mother's and son's eyes meet, as he took up her suitcase from the bed, and for an instant she saw in them a warning not to bring up the momentary pain he had allowed to show.

172

There was no need for him to worry; Charlotte wanted to remember that less than she wanted to be reminded about her naked gardening exploits.

However, this last recollection was unavoidable, since in order to get to the warm, dark safety of her sitting-room, it was necessary to cross the front garden, and, moreover, to acknowledge it, because a woman gardener (she supposed from the wellington boots and the ruddy complexion), was crouched beside a Yucca as tall as a small tree, and looked up expectantly at her arrival.

'Well, what do you think, Mother?' Julian asked, as if he had arranged a banquet for her return and wanted her to be delighted by the spread.

Charlotte walked through the gate Julian was holding open, and stepped gingerly on to a rough, well-weathered square of York stone. For a moment, all she could see was the devastation of felled shrubs barring her way to her front door. She forced herself to look at what was there and not at what her memory tricked her with.

A triumph of cool design confronted her. Gravel and paving stones replaced the grass, and the plant life consisted of no more than an isolated scattering of spiky Yucca and palm trees. She could think of very few other designs that would be more inappropriate in a suburban front garden.

'Um, very nice,' Charlotte said, with a vague smile towards the gardening lady, who was looking expectantly at her.

'The plants were chosen for their sculptural qualities. They work nicely against the flatness of the paving, don't you think?' she explained.

'Oh, yes,' Charlotte agreed, dying to get inside her house, 'very sculptural. But will that palm tree be all right in the winter?'

'*Cordyline australis*,' the gardener said decisively. 'It's very hardy even though it looks exotic, and none of the plants need any attention.'

If they had, Charlotte thought, there were so few that caring for them would take less time than it took to make a cup of tea. This kind of garden designing was like laying a carpet, when it was done it was done. And, she realised, if she should ever take it into her head to damage the plants, their sharp-edged leaves and serrated edges would lacerate her hands long before she managed to do them any

173

harm. Was it deliberate, she wondered? Had Julian given them a brief only to include plants which protected themselves from the destructive urges of mad middle-aged women?

Never mind, it didn't matter. Charlotte crossed to the front door smiling an appreciative thank-you at the gardener, who seemed pleased enough with her reaction. En route, she noticed a net curtain twitching in the neighbour's downstairs window. She tried to look as sane as she could to reassure her.

Once Julian had brought her bag in and made sure Charlotte's pills were beside her bed where she could not forget them, he took his leave, having an important engagement.

'You'll be all right, will you?' he said.

'Yes. Don't worry. I'm fine.'

And, apart from the gardening lady, who still had to put finishing touches to the garden, she was left alone in her house, to wander and reacquaint herself with it.

In spite of Matthew's suggestion that she wait for a couple of weeks, Charlotte turned up for work the following day. Most people at the laboratory thought it too early, but they assumed that Charlotte needed the distraction of work to take her mind off the tragedy of her daughter and her own breakdown. In fact, it was a more positive act than that; getting back to the laboratory was something she wanted very badly.

The death of Miranda, and the confirmation of the FitzRoy book, had caused Charlotte's mind to spiral down towards the microscopic world of blood and inheritance, and the laboratory now seemed the only place where real answers to her questions might be found.

So much of FitzRoy's story, his *character*, chimed in with details of her past she was more or less convinced by the time she had finished her first reading of the book, and when she looked at the pictures of FitzRoy young and old, and also of Castlereagh, she could no longer doubt that she was a FitzRoy. The physical evidence was compelling – the grey eyes, the sharp nose, the receded chin. They were all present in her, and, she could see, to some extent in both Julian and Miranda. She couldn't deny that they must have those chromosomes in common, but it was other, less evident chromosomes which gripped her mind.

On the surface, going back to work seemed to have been

successful, though her colleagues thought they noticed some change in her. She was rather more withdrawn than before, quite reserved, secretive, some would have said, and she was staying on late.

When they passed the glass door of her laboratory on their way home, Charlotte could be seen, still in her white coat, on her stool, engrossed in what was on the bench in front of her. When she noticed the movement outside her door from the corner of her eye, Charlotte would look up and nod absent-mindedly as they waved a goodnight to her. There was, perhaps, something slightly furtive about the look on her face at times like these, and other moments, when she realised she was being overlooked. Her colleagues were not alarmed, they merely agreed when one of them casually mentioned over coffee that Charlotte was quieter than usual, but they put it down to her bereavement and left it at that.

The lab, near Regent's Park, was a centre for genetic research, which, as well as working on projects for drug companies, provided a service for the medical profession and the police. Charlotte analysed chromosomal data for doctors and detectives, but now she was working on a project of her own. It was this private investigation which kept her in the lab long after the others had hung up their white coats and gone home.

On her first day back at work Charlotte had waited until the lab was empty, then rolled up her left sleeve and taken a blood sample from herself. She labelled the test tube carefully and placed it in the centrifuge with the other samples to be prepared for testing.

Charlotte treated her private sample like the rest of the batch. Her separated serum was stained and subjected to electrophoresis, and the result was a graph-like photograph, showing various sequences of amino acids. In addition, she prepared a karyotype, a picture of the chromosomes of a single nucleus, separated and paired by shape to show the full complement of forty-six, half that had come to her from her father's sex cell, and half from her mother's.

For a week, night after night, Charlotte shone her fluorescent lamp on the electrophoresis pictures and the karyotype she had made, and pored over these special images of herself for hours on end. She was convinced (though irrationally rather than scientifically) that there was something to be found, if only she looked at them hard enough.

The twenty-three pairs of chromosomes on the karyotype were

complete, and she knew the various amino acids on the electro-phoresis pictures accounted for everything she was, once everything she had experienced had been subtracted. Each amino acid the DNA coded for added something to the individual she was, though precisely how was still a matter of speculation. But although there was undoubtedly a complete message staring her in the face, she couldn't interpret it, because she didn't know (and no one knew, so far) enough of the genetic language. As to finding the precise site of the particular mental characteristic that had led her FitzRoy predecessors to despair and suicide, the search was hopeless. Even supposing the suggestion that congenital depression might be coded for on chromosome 6 was correct, there was no way of discerning which sequence of nucleotides translated into the specific trait she was looking for. And for all she knew, that particular sequence had not been passed on to her. For most of the length of most of the chromosome it was like looking for a meaningful message in an infinitely long tickertape produced by a monkey on a typewriter with only four keys. Not only was she looking for a needle in a haystack, she didn't know which haystack, and the needle she was looking for might not even be there.

But Charlotte continued to look, all the same, at the maggoty pairs of chromosomes, and felt that, if she only looked carefully enough, with the right kind of attention, she would know what she was seeing and what, therefore, she really was. It was more a form of compulsive meditation than a process of analysis.

Phenotype is the name given to the physical expression of genetic instructions. Charlotte kept a mirror in the drawer of her bench which she took out and propped up on her desk while she was examining her gene photographs. What she saw in her mirror, when she lifted her eyes from the karyotype and the electrophoresis print, was the expression of the contents of the original single cell which had been Charlotte's beginning and had divided and replicated, so that every part of her carried its instructions. Her face, her colouring, her eyes, her hair – but also other things that could not so clearly be seen.

The mirror showed her all that could be known for certain. A face looking its age; strong features but in a less precise outline than when she was young, with the flesh surrounding her cheek and jaw bones softened and losing its defining tone. There were lines under and at the corner of those now alarmingly grey eyes, and a pair of long parentheses bracketed her mouth, from the edges of her long, narrow nose almost down to her chin. Her hair was steely grey, but wiry and wilful so that by the end of the day much of it had escaped from the tightly pulled back style she created each morning. She looked into the mirror and saw a woman who had been transformed from a strikingly good-looking girl into a middle-aged woman who might still have been called handsome were it not for the weariness that curtained her features and made them sag more than the years required. Charlotte did not mind the signs of age. She noted them, but they did not concern her at the moment. She saw what she expected, what anyone might expect from the reflection of an almost-fifty-year-old face. All of it, the former youth, and the rate of ageing, was controlled by the genes hidden in the chromosomes she stared down at for a moment. None of it told her anything, except for the grey eyes and the nose. Those recognisable FitzRoy features connected her genetically to the past she feared. They were inescapable proofs that she was subject to the laws of genetic inheritance, just as Robert FitzRoy's reflection told him what he needed and feared to know about his relation to his uncle.

Increasingly, it was Charlotte's silent, self-obsessed belief that she had been doomed from the moment she was born. From before that moment, in fact. Her doom, if it was true, could be traced back (with the benefit of hindsight and an informed guess on the basis of those grey eyes and aquiline nose) to 1769 at least. But if *that* were true it could just as well have gone back to millennia before that first known date: to a suicidally depressed protozoan, perhaps, she told herself with the remnants of a grim humour.

What she *was*, of course, was not entirely dependent on her parents' contributions, because accident also played a part. She was not half of each in any simple way, she knew, but someone quite else who had been caused by the mixing of what she had received. What she was had everything to do with the twenty-three pairs of chromosomes she gazed at, but ruled always by the chaotic dance of chance. Which made the photograph she gazed at useless, uninterpretable. It told her only that she did not have certain conditions, no Down's syndrome, no Turner's, nor Klinefelter's disease. But she knew these things already. It could not tell her what she most wanted

177

to know. It could not alleviate the fear she had for herself because she did not know if what she feared belonged to her heredity and, if it did, she had no way of knowing which part of which chromosome would contain it. The pictures she had made of her innermost self were, in reality, useless as a practical aid, and the sense of inevitable doom went on increasing in spite of the hours she spent staring at the evidence.

But she could not stop, she could not make herself put the pictures away and get on with thinking about something else. For Charlotte, at this point, there *was* nothing else to think about; everything else – politics, family, love – had crumbled or died. She looked down at her photographs like a crazed palmist who had become fixated on the message etched into the centre of her upturned hand. Somewhere in there was the truth, a pattern, an explanation, the story of Charlotte's future and history's past, so she looked and looked until her eyes began to tear with the effort, and her brain began to scramble at being so focused on the rectangular message from which it could derive no certain meaning.

At home, she built pictures of Matthew as unreal and unfathomable as those she had made at work. Quietly she despaired of her love for him, which seemed to have gained an obsessive life of its own. But at work she had become self-centred in the most precise sense, passing through the whole image of herself in the mirror, downwards to the smallest components of her being. She tried to travel inwards, from the surface of her skin; from flesh, to blood, to the very nuclei of the cells, and then beyond, to unfathomable, unseeable regions which, in the present state of knowledge, gave up their secrets only to the mad.

But it seemed she was not mad enough any longer. She achieved no more than a private desperation. Perhaps, Charlotte mused, it had been too *reasonable* a search. There was too much logic about it; she was looking for an answer, and she was looking in at least one of the right places. She only did not find what she was after because the code had not been cracked.

In a way, her increasing passion for Matthew had the real mark of madness about it: a hopeless longing for a man who was certain not to reciprocate her feelings. For a week or so after getting home from the hospital, her days were filled with the obsessive minutiae of chromosomal reality, and her nights with the frustrated fantasies of emotional unreality. A balanced sort of life, she thought bitterly, when occasionally she stepped back and considered how she was getting on. She wondered, with remarkably little fear, how long it would be before she fell flat on her face.

The tumble occurred at the beginning of the following week, on the day she was supposed to return to the hospital for a session with Matthew. She got up and was ready to leave at the right time, and it seemed to her that she had the intention of keeping her appointment. In fact, once she had put on her coat, she sat down at the living-room table with notepaper and pen and wrote a declaration of love to Matthew. She explained how images of him had grown and taken hold of her mind, and how now she spent most of her spare time imagining the possibility of them coming together, in spite of all the obvious difficulties of sexual preference and the lack, on her part, of youth and beauty. She said she knew that, in reality, he could not love her, but none the less, she could not put him out of her mind. She would not see him again in his capacity as therapist, but she begged him to meet with her. He had once slept with a woman, he had told her, even though it was because of his love for her husband; now she was pleading with him – 'on her knees', she wrote – simply to give her the chance to hold him, to caress him as she did in her fantasies. It was all she asked; she was not demanding he love her in return, only that she be allowed to lie with him and feel his arms around her.

Charlotte took the letter to the hospital and handed it in at reception, asking that it be delivered to Matthew immediately. Then she returned home and sat for the rest of the day, still in her overcoat, in her armchair in the living-room. She stared out of the window at the tall Yucca, which was directly in her line of vision, and gave it such complete attention that the letter, and Matthew's reaction to it, were utterly banished from her mind. She managed to sit through the afternoon without the slightest sense that she was waiting for something to happen. It was the first really peaceful day she had had for a very long time.

Chapter 13

JUST WHAT I CHOOSE IT TO MEAN

———

'When I use a word,' Humpty Dumpty said in a
rather scornful tone,
'it means just what I choose it to mean – neither
more nor less.'
'The question is,' said Alice, 'whether you can
make words mean so
many different things.'
'The question is,' said Humpty Dumpty, 'which
is to be the master –
that's all.'

By the time Charlotte-the-Crazed joined the three men back on the beach they had finished every crumb of food and drop of wine she had imagined in the hamper for them and were dozing in the early evening sun.

She had left Jenny to continue floating, happy in the knowledge that she had added yet another pleasurable activity to the repertoire of fantasised orang-utans everywhere. She wanted to have a word with Charles without Jenny's dismissive presence, and possibly, if there was time (and why wouldn't there be?), a chat with Karl about why his plans hadn't seemed to work out in the way all his well-wishers had hoped. She wasn't quite sure about Sigmund; she thought that logically, she must want to speak to him, since he was here in her imaginings with her, but she couldn't think for the life of her of anything she wanted to say to him. It struck her, though, that not having anything to say to him was perhaps the point she wanted to make.

It all looked a bit academic as she padded up from the shore. Each of the monuments to nineteenth-century thought and twentieth-century activity was fast asleep and snoring rather loudly. Charles was more fitful than the others as he moaned and groaned about his phantom stomach-ache even in his sleep. Charlotte took the opportunity to pull her clothes on, and then sat down next to Charles, on the sand.

Charles opened his eyes very slightly as Charlotte's shadow fell across his face.

'Emma,' he whimpered. 'Is that you? I've such a pain, my dear. Insufferable pain . . . Emma . . .'

He opened his eyes and for a moment Charlotte saw real sadness in them as he realised it was not Emma beside him, and that it never would be again. Emma, with her rock-solid love of religion and her husband, had been sure that they would be together through all eternity, in spite of Charles's scepticism and downright ungodly ideas. And Charles, hardly believing, yet hoping she might be right, had held on to the image of being reunited with Emma in an afterlife he no longer credited. But she had been wrong. Wherever she was, or was not, it was not beside her husband. And if, as now seemed to be the case, the afterlife was nothing more nor less than being invited on holiday with the mad, Emma had not been required to attend. Which was what she had done all her long married life to Charles. Attend him, lovingly, selflessly, even with humour. It was unjust that she should not be part of the outing.

'I suppose you couldn't rustle up Emma?' Charles asked, opening his eyes and sitting up. 'I'm not used to being so knocked up without her beside me.'

Charlotte was not sympathetic.

'I think she deserves a rest. All your wives do. Anyway, I want to talk to you.'

Charles shook his head. The mad are so self-centred, he thought.

'Well, what do you want to talk about?' he said, grimacing as a particularly painful spasm cut through his guts.

'Heredity.'

'Oh, but I don't know anything about that. All that genetic stuff was after my time. Damn shame, because it would have clinched the argument. I never could work out what the *mechanism* of natural selection was. I just used the idea of breeding and took it to its logical conclusion. Fancy pigeons, that sort of thing.'

'I know,' Charlotte said severely, 'the random mutations from which nature selects what's useful and breeds from, while the rest go to the wall.'

'Yes, quite. Accident and happenstance.'

'Selection doesn't sound like accident.'

'Mmm. Badly chosen word. But language is so difficult.'

'Weren't you terrified by the idea?'

'It was a beautiful idea. Perfectly simple. The most elegant solution to the development of species. It beat FitzRoy's superstitious god stuff into a cocked hat. Do you know what rubbish that man spouted? And stuck on the end of *my* narrative of the *Beagle* voyage. He began his splendid essay by saying how much anxiety he had suffered during the voyage as a result of being disposed to doubt, if not disbelieve, the inspired history written by Moses. Hah! Never in the history of doubting did a man doubt for as short a moment as FitzRoy.'

'Hear! Hear!' mumbled Karl, who had woken in a rather amiable haze at their voices. 'Down with doubt! Up with Moses! Working-class boy, you know. Did well for himself.' And he waved a rather feeble fist in the air.

Charles ignored the interruption.

'And, my fine Captain went on, much of his uneasiness was caused by reading Voltaire.'

'Mmmm . . . that'll do it every time,' Karl rumbled. 'Down with Voltaire! Up with Moses! What's next?'

'Me. I'm the friend to whom he admits doubts about the Galapagos landscape being the result of the forty days' flood, and therefore questioned the biblical explanation of the creation.'

'You devil, Darwin! You doubt-maker! You corrupter of men!'

'So his error, he says, was in not studying the Bible hard enough. But once he did, he understood that when Moses says a day in Genesis, he means a day, twenty-four good old hours, and that's that. You see, vegetation was produced on the third day, according to Genesis –'

'Correct,' snapped Karl from his prone position. 'Proceed.'

'– but since the sun and the moon were not created until the *fourth* day, a day could not be much more than a day, and certainly not an *age* (and therefore no time for newfangled geological theories to work), because how could the vegetable world be nourished without the warmth provided by the sun? Ergo, a day is a day. And therefore all things came into being within the first seven days and there could not possibly have been time for fossils to be deposited by natural causes. God just put them there to tease us!'

'By Christ, sir, the man's got a point.'

'No, but you haven't heard the best, Karl. Why is it that no megalosauri or iguanadons exist in the present?'

'I don't know, Charles, why is that?'

'I remember this bit off by heart. Listen: "As the creatures approached the ark, might it not have been easy to admit some, perhaps the young and the small, while the old and the large were excluded?" And there you have it, comrades! There are no dinosaurs today because they were too big to get into the ark.'

'Charming, charming,' murmured Karl and closed his eyes again.

'Stupid, stupid,' Charles said with a rising anger. 'He was too stupid not to believe. He *refused* to think.'

Charlotte defended her putative ancestor.

'But who *would* want to believe there was nothing out there which *cared* about us one way or another? Didn't the idea that the human race was the result of an aimless process bother you? That we're nothing but the end product of millions of accidents.'

Charles looked bemused.

'It was a *beautiful* idea,' he repeated. 'And it was right. What more could any scientist want?'

'Something that cared about what was being created?'

Suddenly, a cloud seemed to pass over Charles's face, making his open amiability disappear.

'No,' he said bitterly. 'If friend FitzRoy had turned out to be right, and there was a God in the heavens who made everything, it would only have meant that we were the playthings of an evil intelligence. They wanted me to believe that there was a heavenly purpose in suffering. I watched my lovely Annie die, slowly, inevitably. Ten years old. A treasure. Her existence only made the world a better place. And yet she suffered terribly and died. If there was a God, I would curse him for his cruelty. There was no purpose in her death, and if it was intended it could only have been intended by a malevolent force. The only solution to such a pointless loss is accident, in a universe which is governed only by the laws of blind, purposeless nature. And I showed it to be so.'

He had tears in his eyes now at the memory of Annie, but there was raging anger in his face at the mere idea of a responsible being in which he claimed not to believe.

'But so many children died then,' Charlotte said. 'FitzRoy's first wife and only daughter died, too.'

'Yes, and Huxley's wife and child, and Hooker's, my own son's wife, too . . . and do you suppose that because so many died, the ones who survived merely shrugged their shoulders, "Oh, well, there goes another one". If you think that, you are foolish, as well as mad. To lose a loved wife, a beloved child. To watch Annie's life slip away and remember all the while how she laughed and played and clung around my neck. Do you think one gets used to death?'

Charlotte thought of her own numbness when Miranda died. She wished she could have wept into eternity for her as Charles did for his daughter.

'That was the final split with FitzRoy,' Charles continued. 'He came to lunch at Down not long after his girl died. Of course, we had grown far apart by then on account of his Bible-thumping. But he sat at my table and told me that his faith in God comforted him in his loss. His daughter and his wife before her were taken by God, and he believed it must be for the best, just as, he said to me, it must have been when the Lord took Annie to his bosom. I couldn't speak for the anger, but when I finally found my voice, I damned him and his God to hell. And I still do. Of course, Emma was terribly upset and bustled around trying to smooth things over. But FitzRoy and his godly new wife puffed themselves up like diseased toads with outrage. Not at their God for killing innocent children, but at me for blaspheming. I was a mild enough man, but I cannot abide fools. I put up with FitzRoy's nonsense for years aboard ship. I even felt sorry for the struggle he had to keep his nonsensical beliefs intact in the face of all the facts. But this was too much. I'm sorry for his pain and his wretched end, but frankly, he brought it on himself. We never spoke again. We had nothing to say to each other.'

'And nature – why don't you feel anger about nature taking the children away?'

'Nature is blind. Life is hard and cruel but there are no deliberate acts. It is what it is. Accident.'

'Which is where I come in,' a voice to the left of Charlotte said.

Karl had been listening with his eyes closed.

'I wanted to shape the great accident we are into something purposeful, but humanly purposeful.'

'Yes,' Charlotte said, 'I did, too. You did leave something of a vacuum, Charles, a terrible well of despair. And, I grant you, Karl, you tried to fill it. You reinvented hope.'

'A spurious hope,' said Sigmund who had also woken. 'Such theory, such grand plans. Very attractive, of course, but all you did, Karl, was replace the hole religion left with the same thing under another name.'

Karl had been mellowed by his nap.

'I only wanted things to be nice. What could be wrong with giving those who had nothing, a sense of destiny? Charles may have dismissed God, but the poor and helpless were none the better for it. Religion turned them into willing slaves, but in no time at all the capitalists had appropriated the theory of evolution to turn them into wage slaves. How could it be wrong to offer a theory that the poor would inherit the earth without having to die first?'

'Because it was hot air. Because it didn't work. You were also appropriated; it was in your name the poor were starved and killed and deprived of the most elementary right to think for themselves,' Sigmund said, more in sorrow than in anger.

'But who was more theoretical than you?' Charlotte asked the Viennese gentleman. 'There's not one iota of what you said which was provable, and anyway what use is it to the underprivileged to know that they wished to have sex with one parent and kill the other? How was that supposed to help? You know,' she went on thoughtfully, almost to herself, 'I don't think any of you are of any lasting importance. I mean, in the end, none of you really improved anything very much. You could say, it's astonishing how little effect you've had. The poor are still poor, the confused are still confused, and science has provided no more comfort or certainty than religion did. The only theory that hasn't been tried yet is the theory that there's no theory at all, and we've all just got to get on with it as best we can.'

185

'Well, you're a fine one to talk,' Sigmund said. 'You are mad, you know, and wandering about in a non-existent space of your own imaginings talking to orang-utans. If that's what you call getting on with it, then I'm a monkey's uncle.'

'No, I didn't mean me. I'm as redundant as the rest of you. That's why we're here, I suppose. Out of harm's way. I can't see how any of us could be any use to Charlotte-up-there. She will just have to manage on her own.'

And with that thought, Charlotte-the-Evasive let go of all attempts to make sense of anything and lay back, comfortably, in the arms of irrelevance.

Chapter 14

A THICK BLACK CLOUD

'. . . It's getting as dark as it can.'
'And darker,' said Tweedledee.
It was getting dark so suddenly that Alice
thought there must be a thunderstorm coming
on. 'What a thick black cloud that is!' she said.
'And how fast it comes! Why, I do believe it's got
wings!'

The light was as gloomy as it had been on her first encounter with her ancestor, when the dream sea had caused the walls to creak and the floor to rock. Now, the floor and the walls were silent and still. She had come to the end of the FitzRoy biography.

This time, although the day was just beginning to break as before, she was not at sea, but in a large sombre bedroom filled with looming furniture. In the dim light she could make out heavy, dark-red velvet draperies at the windows and around a double bed in which two figures lay. Or rather, he sat, while the other lay. He was in a white nightshirt, done up to the neck, as if this was the nearest he could get in bed to formal sartorial correctness. He was awake, his body stiff and alert, but his face was masklike; so static that she felt alarmed when she saw it, and would have tried to waken the sleeping figure next to him if she hadn't already understood that she could have no effect in this world; that her position was no more than that of a ghostly witness. A Cassandra in reverse.

With the dawn beginning to break, Robert FitzRoy was sitting up in bed, as he had sat the whole night through, propped on his pillows, his eyes wide open, keeping watch over the still form of his wife

187

beside him. He thought, 'Look how my Maria sleeps; so weary. Exhausted from too much anxiety. And for too long. Too long.'

But even while her body gained relief in suspended consciousness, he saw how her cares continued to bedevil her. Apprehension was etched into her flesh. Deep furrows of concern ran beside the turned-down corners of her mouth, and worry made vertical tracks between her eyebrows in spite of the profundity of her sleep. He thanked God that her body, at least, could find repose.

Last night she could no longer continue to listen to his ravings, and said, with the utmost gentleness, that she had to go to bed so that she might give better attention to his thoughts in the morning. He allowed her words, her tone of voice to resonate in his head.

'. . . so that I might give better attention to your thoughts in the morning, dearest.'

He was ashamed that she should have had to beg him for rest. In any case, his wild thoughts were not for her; she should not have had to bear the burden of them. They were intolerable, even to himself.

For many weeks he had been incapable of controlling his thoughts. He had lost the capacity to think. His mind was subject, now, to what it should have regulated; thoughts rioted, babbling recklessly, rampaging in his head. Coherence had been defeated, like a country, once civilised, but overrun with savages who scrambled over the remains and wreaked havoc where once an architected order had prevailed. He was, finally, overcome. He was finished.

And even when the tumbling, frenetic thoughts exhausted themselves, as at last, in the early hours of this sleepless night, they had, he did not have the strength to continue. The savages might sleep, but the ruins they had left were too profoundly damaged. He did not have the capacity to reconstruct the landscape of his mind, stone by weighty stone, into the semblance of a place which might be lived in once again with dignity and purpose. There was no dignity, no purpose left. What, in any case, would be the point of such an effort? Even as he tried to imagine a simple city of lucidity rising out of the ruins – a modest town without unreasonable cathedrals or palaces –the savages stirred in their sleep, excited, even in their weariness, at the chance to dismantle anew even the smallest signs of civilisation. Why heave stone upon stone, only to watch them torn down with shouts of glee by the marauders? He had tried and failed too often. He could not begin once again. Let it go. He also wanted to sleep.

With each failure – the return of the Fuegians, the nonsense of his election duel, the recall from New Zealand, the crowd shouting him down as he held the Holy Bible aloft in Oxford – depression had overcome him. Yet each time, eventually, he had won out against it. Now, it was as if all his reserves were used up. Perhaps one needed youth to struggle against despair. Finally, the entire nation was laughing at him.

The Times itself had turned against him, and, with a humour infinitely more cutting than an angry rebuke, had published a leader making heavy fun of the regular failure of FitzRoy's weather forecasts in its own pages to predict the coming weather. They did not even take the failure seriously. Perhaps that was the worst thing. Weather was unimportant, they thought. A matter only of needing to put on galoshes for an afternoon walk, or avoid the annoyance of taking an unnecessary umbrella. They were fools, FitzRoy knew. He had more letters than he could count from those to whom the weather really mattered: sailors, fishermen who were grateful for his life-saving forecasts. Yet, the daily weather forecast had been wrong often enough for it to become the subject of national levity, and finding someone to laugh at was all the public were interested in.

FitzRoy remembered the pebbles on the shore and how, when he had tried to map a coastline, they had overcome his mind with the terror of the uncertainty of what he was doing. It was the same now. He might correlate wind and barometic pressure, observe cloud formation and make informed guesses as to what they might mean, *but something was missing*. Some vital factor which he knew nothing about seemed to upset his co-ordinated data and make nonsense of his predictions. It was as if there were a wilful demon blowing all his indicators to the four corners of the earth, purely to discomfort him. One day, of course, weather systems would be understood, and predictions would be made for specific areas, weeks and months ahead. The world would be a better, safer place. But no one would remember FitzRoy, struggling with his figures and charts to understand and improve the world before its time. He knew that he had saved possibly hundreds of lives of men who had found safe harbours before a predicted storm had hit their ship. Yes, *saved lives*.

And what had Charles Darwin done? Had he saved lives, or improved the world in any way? What had he done to be fêted up and down the country by young scientists? Why should he be remembered, as FitzRoy knew he would be? He had stolen faith from the world. He had deprived the world of the loving care of an infinitely good Creator, and put damned monkeys in His place. And for that he was honoured, while FitzRoy was mocked.

Now, it seemed to him that he had tried enough. Over and over in his life, since he was seventeen, he had striven for reason, for faith, for continuance, while hordes of unreason rushed in his ears, pulsing and surging around the casing of his brain, searching for ways to seep through and drown out his efforts. The blood; it was the blood, of course. His blood had always been at variance with his will. It mocked his struggles against it, its confidence supreme, for who can vanquish their own blood? It was always certain that he should drown in it.

And now he had no fight left in him; at sixty, he was old, and more weary than he had ever imagined it possible to be. He was the laughing stock of all those whom he wished to be acknowledged by. Even his wife, in her gentle way, begged for his silence. It was enough. The fight was finished. Let blood's will be done.

Even so, he did want Maria to know, as God knew, that he had done what he could to overcome the misfortune of his fate. Yesterday, he thought that to be a joke in *The Times*, and therefore to all the men who mattered in the nation, was the final straw. But it was no longer important in this daybreak. He did not care any longer what opinion the world might have of him. Let them laugh as if he were a buffoon. And posterity was nothing to him now; a mere phantom prattling foolishly about what it could not know. None of that mattered in this final dawn.

'But, Maria,' he whispered towards his sleeping wife, 'I would have you know I did not give up until there was no longer any choice left to me.'

He prayed that she would understand that much, after he had gone, when this day, of which he was still part as it dawned, began to lose the light, as it would, without him.

For sixty years of days, he had witnessed the dark approaching. Today, he would not see the sun set, though it would, of course, it

190

would, nevertheless. He wanted no more than that, in his absence, in tomorrow's dawn, Maria would wake and know that he had done battle with his demons and his fate, and if, finally, he had lost, it had been an honourable struggle.

That struggle seemed to him now to have both begun and been irrevocably lost with a meeting with one of the most personable young men he had ever come across, but who was to dog his life and mind for ever after, like a jeering monkey. His knowledge of phrenology had warned him that the shape of Darwin's nose did not bode well, though he had thought (how wrongly) it indicated a lack of persistence. He had overridden his own doubt in the face of the young man's charm. FitzRoy's failure of judgement that day, thirty-five years before, set the seal on the doom which the death of his uncle had foretold. His torments thereafter were not solely the result of his unhappy heritage, but also God's punishment for opening the door to the seemingly innocuous boy who was to pursue the Devil's work with such terrible efficacy – and with the helping hand of Robert FitzRoy.

Maria made a small sound, a tiny moan, and for a moment FitzRoy thought she might be about to wake. He was looking down at her still, although he had been seeing only his own recollections. He thought he saw her eyelashes flutter, but, as if she knew this day was one to postpone for as long as possible, she turned on to her side and managed to sink back to the depths of sleep. FitzRoy was glad she would stay safe for a while longer from the growing brightness of the rising sun.

These last few hours of the night, and of his life, had been the first for many weeks when he had not been agitated and anguished to an intolerable degree. Indeed, it was years since anxiety had moved permanently in with him. Perhaps for all his life he had lived with an ever-present fear of failing in his duties; and then when failure became a habit, rather than a mere threat, there was the constant, minute by minute shame of living with his all too public disgraces. It was only that it had all got so much worse in the last months; the anxiety spilling over to his physical self, to his every jerking, undirected movement; his stuttering, half-finished, never-finished sentences. He was like a man with a nervous tic, seeing himself in the glass, knowing how others were seeing him, and yet being unable to control himself.

191

But, during this night, a physical peace at least had settled over him. He could not have sat so still for so many hours if he had not the assurance of a mind finally made up.

This notion, that FitzRoy had *at last* made up his mind, might have surprised those who had known him through his life. Was there ever a man whose mind was so utterly made up, all along, about whatever activity or issue was to hand? There were those for whom the mere sound of the name *FitzRoy* meant stubborn, self-righteous determination. His unswerving faith in himself and what he held to be the truth, was what made him such an awkward enigma for more pragmatic men. He was, many people felt, the most noble and the silliest of creatures. And there were those, too, who in truth envied him a little for the certainty which allowed him to live with paradoxes which might make others morally fidgety.

He had no doubts about the manner of his death. Soon the maid would come, although, since it was Sunday, it would be later than usual. Around eight-thirty, perhaps. When she drew the curtains back to let in the full light of the morning, he would kiss his rousing wife a gentle, unalarming good-morning, which would serve too as farewell, and go as usual to his dressing-room where, without fuss or drama, he would, in the manner of his uncle, submit to his fate and sever his carotid artery to put an end to his life. He did not worry that his resolve would fail at the last moment, or that squeamishness would make him botch the job. He had his uncle's tenacious and efficient example to follow. He was no Stokes. He knew that, in this at least, he would not fall short of his own expectations.

Maria moaned again, and this time opened her eyes.

'Is it morning already?' she asked, seeing her husband wide awake beside her. Her voice was hesitant, doubting that a day could begin in such darkness, hoping that it had not.

'No, my dear, not yet,' he whispered, as if there were someone sleeping whom he did not wish to wake. 'Go back to sleep. There's time still.'

She smiled slightly at him, but even as she did so her eyelids fluttered closed, grateful not to have to see the anguish in his expression.

He felt like a skeleton, as if despair had eaten away his flesh and left him with nothing but bare bone. The acid had corroded his soul. He was no less a believer than he had ever been, and yet he had to commit the most sacrilegious of acts. Somehow, he felt that God would forgive him. God would understand the burden he had carried all his life and allow him to ease himself out of his existence. He trusted with a final, absolute trust in the goodness of God to take pity on his tormented soul and forgive him his ultimate trespass. God knew he had tried and God knew he was without further resources.

FitzRoy raised his hand to find the pulse that beat in his neck. As he did so he heard the front door open and close, indicating the arrival of the maid. He began to count softly to himself as the light footsteps climbing the stairs synchronised with the final throbs of life beneath his fingertip.

Chapter 15

OFF WITH HER HEAD

_____

'Let the jury consider their verdict,' the King
said, for about the twentieth time that day.
'No, no!' said the Queen. 'Sentence first –
verdict afterwards.'
'Stuff and nonsense!' said Alice loudly. 'The idea
of having the sentence first!'
'Hold your tongue!' said the Queen, turning
purple.
'I won't!' said Alice.
'Off with her head!' the Queen shouted at the
top of her voice.

Charlotte had spent the whole day sitting in her living-room chair since returning from the hospital to deliver her letter to Matthew. She had done nothing more than watch the rain-soaked morning and afternoon disappear into the half-light of dusk. If each nerve ending was alert and waiting every second for the telephone or doorbell to ring, Charlotte was not conscious of it. And yet, now the light had finally failed, there was a terrible heaviness around her heart. And if she did not call it disappointment, it was only because she refused to allow herself to know what her own expectations had been. But the lack of a response from Matthew, by the end of the day, felt to her exactly like the end of hope and she understood, even if she wouldn't quite acknowledge it, that during every moment of her vigil in the armchair some part of her had been tense with waiting for Matthew to get in touch. The silence, combined now with the loss of light, was deadly.

She decided, around the time she used to get the children ready for sleep when they were five or six, that in a moment she would run herself a bath and get into bed. She admitted at last that nothing would happen now; there was nothing to wait for. Matthew would not phone or arrive on the doorstep, and she couldn't bear to remain awake and feel the shame of her unwanted confession of hopelessly inappropriate love.

Letting hope go and releasing the tension caused her to feel monumentally tired, as if the putting down of the burden she had carried actually increased the weight on her. Nothing, she knew, was more dangerous than hopelessness. Yet, the idea of danger confused her. If she did not care about herself, what danger could there be? She knew, however, as she had known all along since the beginning of her breakdown that something – though she still didn't understand what – depended on her remaining apparently normal and in control. She felt oddly alarmed that writing the letter might have compromised the thing she was protecting by proving her to be unstable. Her own shame at the revelation she had made to Matthew was joined by the fear that she might have put in jeopardy whatever it was she was fronting for. But that idea infuriated her, not only because she didn't know what it was that demanded her sane and sensible, but also because of the burden itself. She longed to feel unobligated. She wanted oblivion; to wrap herself in tissue paper and tuck herself away in the dark at the back of a drawer. In the meantime, the best she could manage for herself without betraying whatever it was she was looking out for, was a bath and an early night.

The doorbell rang just as she was about to rouse herself and go to the bathroom. Almost before the sound reached her ears, her heart began to pound and her nerve endings burned as if electrified by the signal they had still not really given up waiting for. She was so overwhelmed by the rush of adrenalin that, for a moment, she couldn't move. And then, in panic, realising that all the lights were off, and Matthew would leave any second, supposing her out, she propelled herself from the chair and raced blindly for the door. She did not give herself time to consider what Matthew might have to say to her, or even what she would say to him once they were face to face. All she knew was that *now* something was happening in her life. That what had seemed to have stopped for ever was alive again and she was once again (after so long) back in the world of feeling and hope. Expectation rushed through her, chasing her blood along its channels, pressing on her heart and brain as she reached the door and pulled it open.

But it was not Matthew, after all.

Charlotte did not recognise the young woman who smiled nervously at her from the front step. All she felt was the terrible energy flowing through her, but which suddenly was without purpose. She thought for a moment that she might die from the power of her disappointed hope.

She stared at the wrong face in front of her, unable to speak, or even think.

'Hello,' the girl said, a surprised look on her face at the ferocity of Charlotte's stare. 'Is this a bad time?'

Charlotte tried to get a hold on herself and pushed her misery down, back down, where it habitually lived. She concentrated on her unknown visitor. Was she selling something, Charlotte wondered? But the girl was too well dressed for that, and who wore such a hat when selling things door to door? It was the hat which nudged Charlotte's memory.

'You're . . .' Charlotte began, perplexed, before realising that she couldn't remember the name. Perhaps she had never known it.

'Elaine,' the young woman said. 'We met at Miranda's . . . I came here after the . . . when Miranda died.'

It came back to Charlotte, now. This was the girl who was all eyes and elegant hairstyle under a very similar hat, who had tried, tongue-tied as she was now, to express something like grief at Miranda's death. Not grief, she recalled, condolences. This was the one who felt it was proper to say something and had said it so badly. Whom Charlotte had snapped at about greed. There was the designer suit (a different one from the funeral) and the impeccably drawn red lips. What did she want? Had she left something behind? If so, it was a long time before she had missed it. Charlotte raised her eyebrows in a question.

'Yes, I don't think I caught your name. What can I. . . ?'

'Could I come in, Mrs FitzRoy?'

Charlotte was certain that this girl would call all women 'Ms', except for those who were mothers of people of her own generation. In reality, even these liberated ones needed the security of married parents.

'Oh, yes,' Charlotte said reluctantly, but stepped aside automatically to make room.

In the hallway, there was a moment when both just stood face to face without either moving or speaking. Eventually, Elaine felt it was necessary for her to explain herself. She was rather surprised, it seemed, that Charlotte didn't immediately know why she had come. Something else that was expected of the parental generation; they should *know* what was on the children's minds. Charlotte, from the look of bafflement on her face, clearly didn't.

'I wanted to talk to you, Mrs FitzRoy.'

'You can call me Charlotte,' Charlotte said, allowing her bafflement to push thoughts of Matthew's silence out of her mind. 'You'd better come in.'

'I'm sorry, were you on your way out?'

Charlotte looked down at herself and realised she still had her coat on from the morning trip to the hospital. She shook it off and threw it over the banister.

'No, it's all right . . . I've just got back.'

She led Elaine into the living-room, and turned on the main, overhead light. Charlotte sat down in her chair and indicated the sofa, hoping Elaine would stop standing in the middle of the room, looking speechless. Whatever was the matter with the girl?

'Mrs FitzRoy . . . Charlotte,' Elaine began, and came to a halt.

'Yes?' Charlotte leaned forward. It was obviously not a matter of something left behind, but what it could be, Charlotte could not possibly imagine. 'What is it, dear?'

The *dear* seemed to do it. Elaine's jaw visibly loosened.

'I wanted to come and see you . . .' she said.

Charlotte waited with bated breath. When was she going to get her bath and the infantile early night?

'. . . to talk to you.'

Nothing else happened.

'What did you want to talk to me *about*?' Charlotte said with a creditable attempt at patience.

'When you spoke to me at the . . .'

'Funeral.' Why was the girl unable to use the word?

'Yes. When you spoke to me then . . .'

'Yes, I'm sorry. I was a bit rude. I'm afraid I was rather upset. I had no right to take it out on you.'

Perhaps that would do it. Would she go now, and let Charlotte get on with putting herself down for the night?

'No, no, you don't understand. It wasn't rude at all. It was . . . I've been thinking about what you said. About how we were wasting ourselves . . .'

Had she said that? Charlotte wondered.

'. . . and our greediness. You were right. I didn't realise at the time, but . . . things have happened, and it came back to me, what you said. It was true. I wanted to come and talk to you. I know I've got a bit of a cheek, just coming here like this, but I hoped you wouldn't mind.'

'Well, no,' Charlotte said cautiously. She most certainly did mind. 'But I don't see what . . .'

'I can't talk to my mother. We don't talk about anything, I don't think we ever have, really. I mean, when I was eleven, she just gave me a book on the facts of life and left it at that. She never sat down and spoke to me about it.'

Charlotte was utterly confused, and not a little alarmed. Was this over-dressed young woman going to relate her entire life story?

'You aren't asking me to tell you about the birds and the bees, are you? Surely you must have picked it up by now?'

Charlotte was sorry she had not held her tongue. A large droplet appeared in the inner corner of Elaine's left eye, threatening to make a dreadful mess of her black eyeliner if it spilled down her cheek. Charlotte dove for the box of tissues she kept by her chair for her late-night crying sessions and handed them across to Elaine, who took one and dabbed skilfully at her eye. A disaster had been averted, but Charlotte told herself to proceed with a good deal more caution, although why she had to proceed at all was still beyond her comprehension.

'I'd better make a cup of tea,' she said, yielding to the inevitable. 'It'll make us both feel better.'

Elaine mumbled a mucousy, 'Thanks', from behind the damp paper handkerchief, as Charlotte escaped into the kitchen.

She filled the kettle, and then, remembering how Miranda's

sophistication prevented her from drinking tea, she called, 'Or would you rather have coffee?'

'Well, actually, do you have any hot chocolate? If it's no trouble.'

In a bottle or a feeding cup? Charlotte wondered. Things were more serious than she had supposed. Why the hell didn't the girl's own mother give her hot chocolate? Gritting her teeth, she turned the kettle off, put a pan of milk on the stove, and arranged half a dozen chocolate biscuits, left over from before her admission to hospital, on a plate. Charlotte had to stop herself from taking Miranda's old Smarties mug from the cupboard. That was going too far. She put properly grown-up cups and saucers firmly on the tray in an attempt to set limits on the current, unlooked-for encounter.

'What do you do?' Charlotte asked Elaine as she sipped her hot chocolate. There was something bizarre about her sitting there taking comfort from the childhood drink while still wearing her hat. Did she ever take it off?

'I'm the fashion editor of *Herself*. It's a glossy magazine for the younger woman junior executive. It caters for women who are reaching the middleish rungs of the career ladder and haven't decided yet whether to continue or have children. You know, late twenties, own flat, a couple of recreational lovers and someone waiting in the wings to whisk them off to suburbia to make babies and quiches, but they won't wait for ever, sort of thing.'

Charlotte didn't know.

'And do you help them make up their minds?'

'We run lots of articles about the psychological tensions between having fun and having a family. But we tend to come down firmly on the side of being settled. In the end, it's what most women want. Not too soon, of course, but eventually, and before it's too late. You know, the biological time-bomb?'

'I believe I've heard of it. And you're in charge of what to wear? Do you show clothes for fun or family?'

'I try to achieve a good balance. You know, sharp suits for work, but also feminine enough for having lunch with women friends when the children are off at school and hubby's at work. Miranda was very good at making clothes look glamorous but not impossible. It's quite a talent, Mrs FitzRoy.'

Charlotte took this tribute to her late daughter in the spirit in

199

which it was intended, noting that she had become Mrs FitzRoy once again.

'Thank you. It's nice to know that she was appreciated.'

Since she began talking about the magazine, Elaine had taken on the bright look of someone selling a concept. It was her usual daily manner, Charlotte supposed. Now, though, her manner changed. Her eyes became slightly less wide, her elegantly crossed legs seemed a little more haphazardly placed. She changed her grip on the cup from holding it by the handle with little finger prettily raised, to clasping it with both hands as if she were cuddling it.

'But there's more to life, Charlotte, and we only get one chance to get it right. That's what you were trying to tell me, wasn't it?'

Charlotte had no recollection of trying to tell anyone anything on the day of her daughter's funeral. She was about to say so, baldly, but was stopped by the look of great intensity and need which had come into Elaine's eyes as she leaned forward in case she might miss the answer.

'More to life than a career and a family?' She tried to take the question seriously. 'Well . . .' She couldn't think for the moment what the more might be.

'Yes,' Elaine broke in excitedly. 'I couldn't see it then, when you spoke to me. And yet, in a way, I knew you were telling me something more important than anything in my life. You understand so much. You've been through it and suffered for all of us who don't understand.'

'Pardon?' Charlotte said, feeling that something had gone seriously wrong with reality.

Elaine had eased off her high-heeled shoes as she spoke, and swung her legs on to the sofa, curling them up beside her. The great black eyes became magnified by the film of tears that now welled up. No delicate droplet in the corner, this time; the whole dam looked like it was about to burst. Charlotte felt she was a passenger in a car passing over the dam, and that it was not going to get across in time to miss the deluge.

'You know, the way you wear your hair is so wonderful,' Elaine said, inconsequentially, the dam drying up instantly as a new fashion notion popped into her head.

Charlotte wasn't aware of wearing her hair at all. It was just stuck to her head like hair was supposed to be, and currently hung down, hairpinless, grey and frizzy, around her shoulders.

'It's such an affirmation of what you are,' Elaine eulogised. 'The greyness and leaving it loose and *sauvage* like that. It's a real statement of how you demand to be seen. I wonder,' she added thoughtfully, almost to herself, 'if Martin could dye mine to that colour . . .'

'I didn't quite understand what you were saying about my suffering,' Charlotte ventured into the silence created by Elaine's thoughts about the new vogue for dyed grey hair.

Elaine returned to the moment, putting away, for the time being, her burgeoning ideas on colours and styles to be worn with *le nouveau gris*.

'Oh, *yes*. When I heard about you, about what happened to you . . .' Elaine was lost for words again, but only momentarily. 'It was incredible the way it coincided with my relationship ending. But, of course, I know that it wasn't coincidence at all. It was as if you were calling out – explaining something to me.'

'I was?'

'Yes, I knew it the moment I heard. Oh, I don't mean you deliberately called out to *me*. I wouldn't be that arrogant. But I felt your message as if it was for me. I know I was just an irrelevant stranger in your life, but you did speak to me at the . . . funeral. You made a connection between us.'

'You heard what from whom?' Charlotte asked, ignoring, for the moment, the matter of the alleged connection between them.

'About your breakdown. From a friend who also happens to be a friend of Julian's. And it was so clear. It was like it was meant. That it was a message, because I didn't know Robbie knew Julian, but I was saying to him over drinks about how I had to find someone to replace Miranda's particular *je ne sais quoi*, and then he told me about you and what had happened and so on. It just hit me like a ton of bricks. It came to me, in that moment, like a thunderclap, and I remembered what you had said to me. Every word, as if you had engraved it on to my heart. In fact, Robbie thought I was pregnant or something, because I looked as if I was going to faint, he said. Anyway, I asked him to arrange a lunch with Julian and, oh, I don't know, my whole life changed . . .'

201

'*Julian* changed your life? My son, Julian?' Charlotte asked, astonished at the idea.

'Well, it was you, really. You made Julian, after all, and also you really got me thinking, once Robbie told me what had happened to you. But, yes, meeting Julian is the most wonderful thing that ever happened to me.'

Well, everyone to their taste, Charlotte thought. He certainly wasn't the most wonderful thing that had happened to *her*.

'So, you're having an affair with my son. I still don't quite see what my . . . breakdown has to do with it. Why did you come to see me? Do you want my blessing or something?'

'Oh, I'd love that. It would mean so much to me. But it's not an affair, it's much more special than that. I messed around having affairs with lots of men, Charlotte, but, believe me, this is something different. This is life-changing.'

'You mean you're taking your magazine's advice and giving up a career for domestic life?'

'Oh,' Elaine blushed beneath her blusher. 'I wouldn't dare think like that, yet. But, perhaps . . .'

'I still don't quite see where my suffering comes into all this. There seems to be a bit of a gap between the thunderclap of enlightenment and the bliss of meeting my son, which I can't grasp.'

'Oh, yes. Gosh, so much has happened, I get overwhelmed by it all. By the amazingness of everything. I'm not being very clear, am I?' Elaine said excitedly.

Charlotte thought she was making herself perfectly clear about the amazingness of everything, but had a little more trouble making sense.

'Why don't you take a deep breath and try taking it a little slower?'

Elaine smiled a little girl smile, charmed by her own muddle-headedness.

'It was that you had this terrible breakdown; you'd been right down there, you know, to the depths . . .'

Charlotte found herself wanting to say that *she* was up here, it was the other one who was down there, and she was pretty sure who was having the most fun. But as soon as she thought it, she lost its meaning. She said nothing, but continued to listen.

'. . . You *know* what mental suffering is. And you came back. You got through it and came back with this astonishing wisdom.'

'Which astonishing wisdom?' Charlotte asked, astonished.

'The way you are now, for example. How you sit so still and understand. Your silence screams your strength and wisdom. And your breakdown was such an example to me. There I was, crying my eyes out over Jake, my lover, being such a bastard, and I thought I was in love with him, and feeling that my life was over, you know? And suddenly I'm confronted with this story of you, *really* suffering, and yet coming through it with such inner strength. It made me ashamed. And then I had lunch with Julian and, God, it was like . . .'

'. . . a thunderclap?' Charlotte suggested helpfully, trying very hard to see her son as such.

'Yes, absolutely. You see, you understand so well. It was like chemicals meeting in a test-tube. We were in love as soon as we sat down, I think. For me it was the way you shined through him, as if you were in his head, looking after us and making us realise how right we were for each other. Julian said he had thought exactly the same thing, after I told him how I felt.'

Charlotte was not surprised to hear that Julian had waited for Elaine to tell him what to say. It seemed there was little her go-getting only remaining offspring wouldn't do to bed a pretty girl. But at the moment this worried her less than the notion that she had been through the fires of hell and come back a sage. More like an onion, it felt to Charlotte; one whose layers had been scattered far and wide.

The extraordinary imposition of wisdom this silly girl placed on her was very distressing to Charlotte. She felt so empty, so drained; devoid of something that was essential to her which was not just Matthew's non-response to her declaration of love, but was some part of *her* which she suddenly understood had gone missing. And this idiotic girl in a foolish hat was turning her into, who? Mother Teresa? Mother Earth? Mother of God! Charlotte thought, please make her go away.

Charlotte felt her throat constrict with the effort of not screaming, not silently but really rather loudly, at Elaine, sitting there with a simpering devotional look on her face: 'Go away! Leave me alone! Have you any idea how dismal I feel? Have you any idea how little I care about your tedious emotional life and the fact you're fucking my son? Have you any idea that I am nothing but a shell of a human being? And you come here, as if you've taken possession of me and demand attention for your silly, self-important self.'

She said nothing.

'I understand your silence,' Elaine said in a hushed, meaningful voice. 'I know words aren't adequate for what you've been through and what you are now. Or for what you want me to understand. God, when I think of the time I've wasted, writing *words*, wasting them on superficialities . . .'

She'd better watch it, Charlotte thought. Julian won't want an ex-fashion editor turned saint for his – what did he call them? – babe. That wouldn't amuse him at all.

'Look,' Charlotte managed to squeeze through the lump of rage in her throat, 'I'm feeling rather tired. I'd like to be alone, if you don't mind. It was nice of you to come. But I wouldn't be in too much of a rush to give up your job, if I were you.'

'Of course, I'm so sorry. You must have so much to think about. I do see what you mean about the job. It's important to take things slowly, isn't it? Just rushing into things is what I've always done. But I've got to prepare myself, haven't I? I've spent so much of my life being greedy, now I'm being greedy for change. I know I've got a lot of work to do on myself, Charlotte. I'm going to do this right and I know I can do it, if I have your help.'

She slipped her stockinged feet back into her shoes and straightened her clothes.

'Thank you so much, Charlotte,' she said, planting a scarlet kiss on Charlotte's cheek. 'Thank you for your encouragement. Please don't get up. I can see myself out.'

'It was nothing,' Charlotte said, watching Elaine disappear at last out through the living-room door.

Now, finally, she was free, but as soon as the front door had shut on her astonishing visitor, the last vestige of whatever it was she needed to keep on carrying on disappeared. The surge of hope at the ringing of the doorbell, and the shattering disappointment which had replaced it when she opened the door, had drained her. She was ruined, entirely used up. An aching emptiness scratched around the perimeter of her mind, like a famished cat, determined to be let in. There was no more keeping it away.

I don't want any more of it, Charlotte thought, switching off the living-room light and all expectation, and took herself off to bed. She could no longer be bothered with a bath. She could no longer be bothered with anything. The visit from Elaine and Matthew's silence had emptied her. She had actually felt the last reserve of courage drain away as the girl poured out her self-regarding adulation for Charlotte's strength and wisdom. She was left bare by foolishness, by lost-and-found memories of seed-pearls and tramps from long ago, by the absence of ordinary feeling for anyone connected to her, and for absurdly concocted affections which could only give her shame at her own stupidity.

She felt evacuated. Ruined: utterly deserted. Abandoned. Though by what she was not sure. It was not just by Matthew's rejection, nor the fact that there was no one else in her life whom she cared enough about to want to be with. A great deprivation welled up in her, and the sturdy middle-aged woman began to crack apart as the unfulfilled needs of a monstrous, raging, unloved child welled up and finally took over Charlotte's space in the world.

She would not have had it so. She would have preferred to live quietly inside her official depression, moving slowly, as if under water; taking to her bed when the sun set; going no further in a day than her living-room. She knew the value of what she could have had: the right to languish in the arms of an authorised mental incapacity. Why could she not settle for that? What was wrong with giving her brain a rest, with lying fallow and waiting for the energy of mental health to grow back like new pasture?

But it was too late to battle with herself. She could not carry on in any form. She lay on her bed in the dark, curled up, knees to chest, too miserable even to take off her clothes and get into her nightdress. All she could do was hug herself in a hopeless attempt to keep herself from flying apart. But the awfulness was already overwhelming her.

'I'm not well,' she whispered, terrified that she might overhear herself. 'Why won't someone help me? Why isn't someone here? I *need* you.'

By reaching out and lifting the phone, Charlotte could have had someone there. Her GP would have arrived and diagnosed a relapse into crisis. Julian would, with reluctance, have come round and ground his teeth at the further disaster he had been dreading, phoned the GP and barked at him to get here fast and diagnose . . . Jackie, from the lab, would, perhaps, sensing a surprising but urgent need, have left the washing-up and bathing the baby to her husband and rushed round to provide practical assistance . . . Help was on the end of the telephone. It had nothing to do with what Charlotte wanted.

Charlotte was getting lost in a chromosomal predisposition; adrift in the convoluted grey matter which received too little of something or other (or too much) and turned into the formless mess of despair. Somewhere, in some part of every cell of her body, something was (or was not) there, as it had (or had not) been there in her father's cells, and in all those FitzRoys going back and back, and it dragged her down, as it had them, into the dismal depths where no rays of light were strong enough to break through.

She could not do without what she was missing, whatever that was. The deprived child could not survive the biochemical accident on her own. Charlotte could identify the qualities that had disappeared since the day she had wrecked her front garden. They added up, virtually, to an entire person, who had decamped, leaving her alone with the pathetic little creature who could never rise above the murky waters of her genetic destiny. All her strength was gone. A strong, lively, argumentative, humorous being had packed its bags and gone on holiday, or worse, left for good. It was Charlotte's survivor – the one who laughed, made snap judgements, watched the absurd dance of life from a healthy distance, and poured wine over the head of her son with relish. She had signalled her departure by stripping herself and the garden naked in a kind of farewell performance, before heading off for far-flung places where the dragging weight of the deprived child could not pull her down. The abandoned infant was abandoned once again, and there was nothing Charlotte could do any longer but remember the energy and strength that was lost.

Charlotte opened the drawer in her bedside table and fumbled around in the dark until her fingers found the small knot of tissue paper right at the back. She took it out and turned on the light, untwisting the tissue for the first time since she was a child. The seed-pearl lay nestled on top of the coiled silver chain, just as she had last seen it, so many years ago. In spite of the decades and her changing, ageing life, it looked exactly as she remembered it. It did not seem less significant now that she knew better what it was, and how it was different from the single cell she had once been, about which she understood so much more. Still, it glowed minutely in the palm of her hand, and still, she felt a catch in her throat at the memory of what it had meant to her; at the enormity of what she started out with: so much for something so small.

There was terror, too, in the knowledge of how the original seed-pearl of herself had proliferated, with its terrible burden of destiny, dividing and splitting, but retaining its dreadful message, through everything that was her. She did not exist apart from the daughter cells of the original seed-pearl, and the part of her which she knew, now, was *other*, her saving grace, had flown away, fleeing the wreckage, survivor that it was.

She had thought her destiny settled when she first understood about the way in which circumstances are unalterable from so very early on, but she had not been entirely right. That other Charlotte, the tough, laughing one, had come along, too, for the ride. She must also, Charlotte supposed, have been decreed in the message of the first cell. Charlotte had not taken her into account; how could she have known? But if the despairing one had stuck around, fulfilling its miserable self, why had the survivor been less tethered to her? How could she have broken free and left her to her fate? But perhaps that, too, was written in the chromosomes, and the nature of survival, after all, is knowing how to get out while the getting is good.

'But what about me?' Charlotte wailed into the darkness of her bedroom. 'What am I to do?'

But the wailing only sapped her strength a little more.

Charlotte FitzRoy, curled foetally inside her disordered bedding, had reached the inevitable conclusion to which her chemical imbalance pointed. Once arrived at, it had the simplicity and authority of all perfect arguments. The storminess of dispute had reached its still point of certainty. A calm settled over her. She was no longer lost, but in the only place it was possible for a deserted child, hopelessly ill-equipped for the task of practical living, to be.

And, as it often appears to do when a correct solution seems to have been arrived at, life concurred with her conclusion. Only the night before Julian had delivered a full bottle of tablets he had picked up from the doctor. He was meticulous about not allowing her diminished supply to get too low. Not only did the bottle next to her bed positively bulge with the means to redress biology's error, but pulling out the drawer to find the seed-pearl had caused the envelope containing all the pills she had secreted during her stay in the hospital to roll forward from the back and become visible. It was not, it turned out, a matter of *not* taking the tablets, as Charlotte had thought (unsurprising that an abandoned child should have made a mistake), but a matter of taking *enough* of them to make the problem disappear.

Charlotte got up slowly and pulling a blanket around her, went to the bathroom to fill her bedside glass with water. As she turned on the tap she glanced at the mirror above the sink. It seemed to her that the creased face and dim eyes set in an aura of crinkled grey hair was no more than a mask. She could see quite clearly, behind the transparent, apparent face, the real image of herself: dark-haired, wide-eyed, smooth-cheeked, not a day over three years old; far too young to be left alone, far too young to manage what could only be dealt with by the adult who should have been in charge of her. The mask smiled reassuringly at the child with the trusting eyes behind it, and Charlotte FitzRoy, descendant of all those FitzRoys, took her glass of water back to the bedroom where the obvious solution waited.

It was Jackie, from the lab, who found Charlotte the next morning. She had been worried by Charlotte's absence from work the previous day, and then when she hadn't turned up that morning and didn't answer the phone, Jackie decided to go and see if everything was all right. Somehow, she felt it wasn't. Of course, she knew that Charlotte had been ill.

She rang the bell and then banged on the door, but got no reply. Round the back of the house she found the kitchen window open and climbed through it, wondering, as she did so, why it was that she couldn't assume, like other people, that everything was probably all right. She concluded that some people were worriers and she was one, and it was much easier to break into someone's house and find out for sure they were all right, than to spend the day worrying. She acknowledged that her need to assuage anxiety caused numerous unnecessary visits to the doctor with her baby, and a continual smug look on the face of her husband when all turned out to be well. But she was what she was, and she was sure Charlotte would forgive her for climbing through her window while she was out shopping or feeding the birds in the park, which, Jackie was sure, was what Charlotte was doing. Almost sure, anyway.

She wandered through the downstairs of the house, conducting a cooing search, calling out Charlotte's name before moving on to the next room, and then finally climbing the stairs.

She was surprised at how unsurprised she was at finding Charlotte unconscious in bed with an empty bottle of pills beside her. She was more surprised when checking for a pulse (Jackie, being a very practical worrier, had done a First Aid course with the St John Ambulance Brigade) to have found one; very faint, of course, but definitely there. She dialled 999, impressed at the quality of a heart which persisted so stubbornly against all its owner could do to stop it. Jackie remembered a houseplant she had been given by her mother-in-law. She had hated it, although she had nothing against plants as such, and somehow managed not to water it for months. Every day she looked at it, noting with an almost vicious satisfaction how it had drooped a little more. Then, one day, deciding it was dead at last, she put it outside the front door, to be taken away with the rubbish. It rained overnight, and by the time the dustcart came, the wretched thing had straightened itself up and was glowing with life and strength. Naturally, the dustmen left it where it was and Jackie was obliged to bring it indoors and admit defeat. She watered it regularly and now no one came to the house without remarking on what a wonderful specimen it was. Jackie still hated the thing, but she knew when she was beaten. She supposed it was much the same with the human heart as it was with houseplants, given half a chance.

The ambulance arrived, and Charlotte was borne away to be saved for another day.

The doctor on duty in Accident and Emergency also remarked on Charlotte's amazing powers of survival. No one who had taken so many pills and not been found for so long, should have stayed alive. The woman who found her ought to have found a corpse. But the doctor had been a doctor for long enough to know that, when it came to the human body, surprises were not all that uncommon. He was not entirely averse to the proposition that something more than biology accounted for the behaviour of the somatic system. Not that he was inclined towards mysticism or anything, but he was prepared to acknowledge that there were unexplained *events* sometimes – unexpected remissions, curiously unnecessary deaths, strange results from apparently inert substances. It was, he was sure, mysterious only because science had not yet identified the component which explained the connection between body and mind. There were clues, however, in the studies done of placebo effect, and the endorphin production of the brain. He was satisfied that a physically based explanation would eventually be found.

Whatever the reason, Charlotte was alive, though barely, and she most certainly shouldn't have been. Doctors and nurses work with a will on the most improbably small indications of life, for each loss is a personal one, no matter how superficially hardened they might have become to death. Charlotte offered a challenge and they did everything they could to build on her own determination to survive.

'But isn't it strange,' a nurse asked the doctor when they had sent Charlotte up to intensive care. 'That someone who tried to kill herself should have such a will to live?'

The doctor agreed that it was strange, though he'd seen it before.

'Perhaps only a part of a person wants to die; perhaps another part wants to go on living,' he suggested.

'What part would that be?' the nurse asked.

'I don't know, but if I did, I'd bottle it, stick a label on it, saying "Drink me", and make it freely available on the NHS.'

'Only to people with exemptions from prescription charges,' the nurse smiled.

The doctor just had time to smile an acknowledging grimace back, before the next emergency was wheeled in, and, business before speculation, there was another repair job to be done.

Chapter 16

I'VE MADE UP MY MIND

---

*'. . . I've made up my mind about it; if I'm
Mabel, I'll stay down here! It'll be no use their
putting their heads down and saying "Come up
again, dear!" I shall only look up and say "Who
am I then? Tell me that first, and then, if I like
being that person, I'll come up: if not, I'll stay
down here till I'm somebody else".'*

'You've got trouble!' Jenny's voice suddenly pealed through the
peace and quiet of blue skies, soft sands, gentle waves and balmy
winds.

The three elderly gentlemen had dropped off to sleep again, and
Charlotte herself was dozing happily. At the sound of Jenny's voice
she opened her eyes and looked out to sea, where the orang-utan was
still bobbing in the water.

'Trouble? What kind of trouble?' she called, not pleased at being
distracted. She was enjoying the holiday idleness which madness had
turned out to be.

'The worst kind. *Big* trouble!' Jenny shouted, rolling over and
starting to swim, doggy-paddle, towards the shore.

Charlotte looked around to see if she could spot the trouble Jenny
mentioned and seeing none, watched the orang-utan puffing her way
to the beach. Jenny finally reached her depth, long red hair matted
and dripping, and found her footing in the shallow edge of the sea to
pant up the beach. She stepped wetly over the sleeping figures on the
sand, and flopped down in the deckchair.

'I didn't think trouble happened here,' Charlotte said. 'I thought
all that happened here was sun, sand and serendipity.'

'It's not *here* where the trouble is,' Jenny replied, pleased to have the answer to yet another riddle. 'It's there.'

'Where?'

'There. Where you come from. It's her. Charlotte. You know, the one who isn't mad.'

'What's happened?' Charlotte asked, alarmed now, as well as exasperated.

'Overdose. Enough to kill the both of you. How are you feeling?' Jenny asked with all the curiosity of a big-brained ape.

'Christ!' Charlotte breathed, and struggled up from the sand.

'Yes, it's a bit of a nuisance, isn't it? They can't be trusted up there. And just when you're beginning to enjoy yourself. Isn't that always the way?'

She shook her head in sympathy as well as trying to clear her ears of water.

'But what will happen to me?' Charlotte asked, dumbfounded, and at a loss to know what to do now that she had stood up.

'Well, my dear, she's supposed to be holding the fort up there for you. And here – well, here is just a playground for your mad imagination. Dead people don't have an imagination, you know. We all go *pouff* if she dies. We burst like a soap bubble. And there won't be so much as a hole left in the space that we vacate. A shame really.'

'But what can I do?' Charlotte asked, distracted.

She was, in truth, rather more concerned about her sunny, seaside, underground world going *pouff* than about her substantial self's imminent death.

'I'd have a word with her if I were you.'

'What good will that do if she's taken the overdose already? And anyway, *how* do I have a word with her?'

'The human spirit is a remarkably funny thing. It has a definite tendency to want to stick around, given even half an excuse. Maybe you can think of something. As to how, well, use your imagination – it's practically all you've got left.' Jenny chuckled at her dualist joke. 'By the way, are you beginning to feel a little faded? I can't be sure, but I have the funniest feeling that I'm not entirely all here . . .'

Certainly, everything seemed to be getting faint. The snores of the three sleepers faded as in the increasing gloom Charlotte turned to look at the sea. It was no longer blue, but a murky greyish green, and the surface foamed with what appeared to be a thick carpet of incoming effluent. The sky was cloud-struck. A dark shadow rolled in from the horizon. In fact, the fog had grown so thick, even in the last few seconds, that Charlotte, looking about her in every direction, could now only see a few inches in front of her: Jenny, the elderly gentlemen, the deckchairs, the hamper, indeed, the whole beach seemed to have vanished. Charlotte looked down at her feet, as if to check that they were still there, and saw she was standing, not on sand, but a marble floor, and tiptoeing cautiously through the fog, she saw immediately in front of her a very small door complete with a tiny handle and keyhole. She seemed to be at one end of a corridor.

The door, small as it was, at least held the promise of something behind it, whereas there was nothing left of the underground world except for a few inches around Charlotte herself, which even as she stood there seemed to be contracting even further. She did the only thing it was possible to do and knelt down at the door, cautiously putting one eye to the keyhole. She felt a cold circle of brass around her eye socket, but saw nothing. The swirling greyness seemed as thick and impenetrable on the other side of the door as her own.

'Are you there? Are you there?' she called into the absence. She didn't know who she was calling; Jenny, she supposed, her only friend, but anyone would have done.

For an alarmingly long moment, there was silence. Then she heard something.

'Are you talking to me?' a familiar voice said.

Or rather it was almost a familiar voice, but higher, weaker, more childlike than the one it reminded her of. And there was another sound: a kind of singing in the background, a soprano chorus singing a lilting, sad-sounding song that was nearly, but not quite, a tune.

'Charlotte? Is that you?' Charlotte asked, putting her mouth to the keyhole. She paused for a moment while it crossed her mind that Jenny was indubitably right: she was quite, quite mad.

'Yes,' the inconsequential little voice answered. 'Who are you?'

'Me. This is me,' Charlotte said. 'What's that singing sound?'

'Don't know. Can't hear it,' the childlike voice said, unconcerned. 'Who's me?'

'Me. You. Us.'

Charlotte, having poured pronouns through the keyhole, put her eye back there, but, before she could focus, received an answer not from the other side of the door, but from the disembodied voice of Jenny.

'That's the sound of your blood singing in your ears. Listen carefully,' she said helpfully. 'It's singing: "bad blood will out . . . bad blood will out . . ." It's like "London's Burning"; it's a round. I suppose that's on account of the fact that the blood circulates *round* the body, but it's not much of a lyric, if you ask me – too repetitive for one thing, and the tune leaves a little to be desired. Still, with all that poison in it, one can't expect too much.'

Charlotte's vision had cleared by now, and she found herself staring at a large grey pupil which peered at her from the other side of the keyhole. She was, she realised with a shiver, looking herself in the eye.

'Charlotte,' Charlotte said to the eye, 'stand back a bit, let me see you.'

The eye diminished in size as it retreated. A face appeared around it with a bewildered expression. It was not Charlotte. Or rather it was not the same Charlotte as the one on the mad side of the door. This one, through the keyhole, was an infant. She had the same look of alarm as children do when woken from a disturbing dream, before they are fully back in reality.

'I don't understand what's happening,' she said, in a frightened voice.

'You've taken an overdose, you idiot!' Charlotte exploded at her. 'I trusted you to take care of things, not make a complete mess of them. Not kill us.'

Charlotte could see that the Charlotte through the keyhole was beginning to recollect. It was coming back to her. A sad, disappointed look came into her eyes, but there was stubbornness there, too.

'I didn't like being on my own. I didn't like being left,' the baby Charlotte said. 'There was no one to look after me.'

'You're not a baby, you're the same age as me.'

But as she spoke Charlotte could see with her own single eye that this was not the case. The look of obstinacy on the child's face increased.

'I'm too young to manage on my own. I don't understand about things and I get frightened and everything was very difficult. I *am* a baby. *You're* the grown-up, and you went away.' This was an outright accusation. 'You can't expect me to cope with everything all by myself.'

And with that the little girl sat cross-legged on the ground and stuck her thumb firmly in her mouth.

Charlotte felt very much like doing the same thing, but there was an emergency to be dealt with; only one of her could sulk if they were to survive. The barrier of the keyhole was unsatisfactory, but it occurred to her that the separation was a necessary one. She thought of positive and negative particles colliding in quantum space and exploding into non-existence, and decided not to try the door handle.

'Listen to me,' Charlotte said carefully. 'The one who couldn't cope up there was *me*, not you. *I* was the one who went mad. You only feel like a child. You're not really. You're the one that gets on with things. The one that brushes our teeth every morning, and gets us dressed without having to think about it. It's *me* that takes all the clothes off again and runs about destroying the garden. That's why I went off – if I'd stayed we'd have been locked up. This way, you can potter on, and I can be as mad as I please down here, out of harm's way.'

'But why should you have all the fun?' the little one demanded

'I'm sorry, but you don't *have* fun. It's just not what you do.'

'Well, I protest! And I have protested. I don't care if we die. And I'm glad of it. So there!'

'You don't have to die. Just hold on.'

'No, I've made up my mind,' young Charlotte said firmly. 'I'm definitely going to die. Right now. Here I go: dying, dying . . .'

Charlotte-the-Mad felt panic threatening; a dangerous turbulence like rising water was beginning to engulf her. Perhaps this was the beginning of the death process. How could she know?

'You can't make up your mind for both of us,' she pleaded.

'Oh, yes I can. You can decide to go mad without asking me, I can decide we'll be dead. I don't care about being alive. It's boring and I don't like anyone. Dying, dying . . .'

'You like me,' Charlotte wheedled.

'I *did* like you. You were the only one who could make me laugh, sometimes, and everything didn't seem so *serious* when you were around, but you left and then there was nothing but very, very serious, and no laughter to be had at all. Is that what you'd call a fair distribution of fun?'

'No, it isn't. I can see that. But fairness hasn't got anything to do with it. There's a bit of you – a bit of us – who's abandoned, a hopeless child, and there always will be. She's always going to be miserable, but the rest of you can manage. You just have to get on with it.'

'But there wasn't anyone to comfort her, once you'd gone. You were the only one who knew about her, and then she was frightened and there was no one else there to be kind to her. That was all she needed. Someone, you know, to let her have a good cry every now and then, and jiggle her and hold her. I can't do that. I can only manage if I don't know about the rest of us.'

Charlotte noted that the Charlotte on the other side of the door was talking about the child in the third person, and it did seem to her, as she looked through the keyhole, that there was another face emerging: a weary, workaday face, which did not have the child's stubborn look, but was only tired out and terribly miserable. She looked like she needed a good holiday. Which, of course, was just what she couldn't have. Being miserable and soldiering on was what she was for. Charlotte had a brainwave.

'Listen, Charlotte, how about this: I'll take the baby. She can stay with me. The two of us can be down here, while you stay alive up there, and keep things going for all of us.'

'That's quite a responsibility,' Charlotte said in a voice that no longer had the piping quality of a child. 'And hard work, too.'

'I know. But you've got to face it,' (and from the new look of her, it seemed she might have) 'you're the one who does all that. You're the one who isn't mad. You can't be. I'm sorry, but there it is. You're sane, and you're responsible. I know you're depressed and fed-up with everything, but that's what you are. You're the miserable but managing adult, you can't change. *I'll* take the child, *you* keep us alive and out of the clutches of the wrong kind of medicines. *You* can't kill us. Don't you see, you're the survivor out of all of us.'

'That's funny, I thought *you* were the survivor. That's why I couldn't keep going without you. How can I be it when I've just committed suicide?'

'You forgot yourself, that's all. And you had too much to cope with taking care of the baby. Don't worry about which of us is the survivor; you just concentrate on not dying, for the time being. All right? All right?'

It wasn't clear whether the deal was done or not, because suddenly everything became very grey indeed. The already sombre light dropped to an almost complete darkness, both through the keyhole and, when Charlotte turned to look, in the corridor, too. As dim faded to black, so did the sound. There was just a brief final second when Charlotte heard very faintly the voice of Jenny Orang.

'Uh-oh, hang on to your hats, everyone. Here we go . . .'

And then all of them and everything was enfolded in a deep black silence.

Chapter 17

A SLOW SORT OF COUNTRY

*Alice looked round her in great surprise. 'Why, I
do believe we've been under this tree the whole
time! Everything is just as it was!'
'Of course it is,' said the Queen: 'what would
you have it?'
'Well, in our country,' said Alice, still panting a
little, 'you'd generally get to somewhere else – if
you ran very fast for a long time, as we've been
doing.'
'A slow sort of country!' said the Queen.
'Now, here, you see, it takes all the running you
can do, to keep in the same place. If you want to
get somewhere else, you must run at least twice
as fast as that!'*

Charlotte FitzRoy looked as if she had not a care in the world. She
had tried to arrange for it to be so, and it seemed to those whose
business it was, that she might very well continue in her carefree state
indefinitely.

Not that *carefree* was the word they used to define her condition;
comatose was how they described it. But every now and then, one of
the older, more experienced and busier nurses allowed herself a dark
moment of envy towards Charlotte, who not only did not have to race
about sorting out every emergency that came up, but did not even
have to bother to do her own breathing.

Charlotte was the very essence of the lady of leisure as she lay
hooked up to the machines which fed her, ventilated her, carried her
wastes away, told stories about the activity in her brain, the strength
of her heart, and the condition of the blood which had been pumped
into her to replace her own poisoned plasma.

So far as anyone could tell, Charlotte could neither receive signals from the physical world, nor respond to them. It was supposed, when anyone did any supposing, that she was frozen, as it were; suspended in a no-man's-land of oblivion where darkness and silence replaced the light and sound of the world of the living. And there were people – tired people, troubled people, anxious people – who might well have wished themselves in her place.

Their wishes, of course, were aimed towards only what was apparent and visible. Charlotte did look peacefully asleep. Her face still carried the marks of her fifty years, but the lines and wrinkles had no depth as they would have had if her face had been alert and mobile. Her hair, brushed every morning by a nursing assistant, spread out, curling on the pillow. She lay in repose in the small ward where the only disturbance was the ticking and clicking and bleeping of machines which gave the clinical surroundings the peaceful, comforting rhythm of an old clock in a silent house. There was the sound of traffic outside, but from behind the double-glazing, high above the street, it could be mistaken for the pleasant rustling of the wind. Charlotte was all stillness and, at times, most people could pass by and feel the tranquillity of her condition. It was what Charlotte herself had been trying to achieve, and it certainly looked as if she had been successful. She might have thought so herself if she had been on the other side of her experience.

But the tranquillity *was* only apparent, and the stillness merely all the naked eye could see. It was certainly true that she had very little inkling of what was going on around her. The physical world had, indeed, been put aside. Charlotte felt and saw nothing of it. Which was what she had intended when she decided to kill herself. To that extent, she had succeeded. But she was not dead, and her suspended animation only mimicked the visible aspect of death.

Of course, there was no guarantee that death itself would have provided the eternal nothingness she was after. In that sense, all suicides are the result of disturbed and faulty thinking, for no one in their right mind would take a one-way ticket to a distant land from which no visitor had returned, without first demanding to see the brochures. It is a reckless act which supposes that nothing could be worse than present conditions – a curiously optimistic view for a desperate person to take.

What Charlotte had been trying to get away from was – everything. The present, the past, the perpetual beating of her heart, the emptiness of the future, and, most of all, she had been trying to get away from herself.

In fact she found herself trapped in a place which had her at its mercy. All she had managed to kill was time, which, as it turned out, had the valuable attribute of ordering past and present in a way that prevented them from jostling for the attention of the troubled soul who wished only for peace and quiet. And the future, although it seemed to have disappeared, continually disturbed Charlotte with a distant, insistent sound of ticking, clicking and bleeping which she could not place, but was, in fact, the future getting itself fit and ready to come out of retirement.

A world without time is a world without sense, and senseless Charlotte found herself in a senseless place where past and present howled at her, and paraded before her, the voices and shapes of then and now twisted together, vying for prominence. All her experience and all her fears tumbled in on her, having lost their order, and each demanded she look and listen. Blood battled with ghosts: FitzRoy and her father; Julian and Matthew; the gardening lady and Karl Marx; the old tramp and Charles Darwin; Dr Davies and Sigmund Freud; Jackie and Jamie; doctors and nurses; Elaine and a ridiculous-looking monkey in a frock which, like all the rest of them, kept shouting at her as if across some vast derelict wasteland. And beneath all the cacophony, a baby cried incessantly as if its heart was breaking. The confusion was horrible and there was nothing she could do to escape. Try as she did to slip away into silence, to where she really wanted to be, bellows pumped air into her, creatures called and grabbed at her, blood and plasma, not hers but fresh, life-giving stuff swirled through her, forcing her to continue to exist among the noise and the fury. All of them cried out: *Listen to me. Listen to me. I must be heard. You have to come back*. And none of them whispered: *It'll be all right. We'll take care of you*.

It had been touch and go, but the casualty doctor and Jackie were right about the power of the will to live, even though that power did not reside in the comatose form of Charlotte, but somewhere or in something else. Charlotte began to make a gradual but definite recovery, though she herself was hardly to be found among the tubes and associated hardware that kept her body going. They did the living for her and she was left stranded in her clamorous nowhere. All that could be done was to allow the body – with the aid of medical science – to mend the damage it had done itself.

She came back very slowly, in incremental parts, and as she did so, the noises and chaos of the other place faded into silence. A hazy form of consciousness began to emerge, a sudden half-awareness that she existed, though without any sense of what or who she was, let alone what or who existed outside her. There was merely a waking to a sense of her own physical presence, and then only in disparate pieces. She would become aware of the mattress beneath her shoulders, or her buttocks. Not that shoulders or buttocks existed, or even mattress. But there was a pressure (a combination of the mattress and the gradually enlivening nerves in certain parts of her body) which she felt occasionally, instead of feeling nothing at all. Then she would be aware of discomfort in certain parts, where bits and pieces that were attached to her and then to machines of one kind or another made themselves felt. Irritability about these inconveniences signalled the beginnings of a more solid kind of consciousness that began not only to separate the thing which was herself from those things which were not and therefore caused disturbance, but to connect the physical disturbance to the bad temper which was her reawakening mind. Before long she was an entity, distinct from all the other things in the universe, and not long after that, the specific entity called Charlotte FitzRoy (though she was not yet conscious enough to be concerned about the spelling of it).

Still, for a while, she remained no more than that. Questions about why she was here, what her condition was, and what it would be, were not for her. She did not recognise herself except as a physical body which was not behaving as it was supposed to. She tried to speak, but her voice wouldn't work. She tried to move parts of herself, her hands, her feet, her head, but it was as if she was paralysed. Indeed, she took herself to be paralysed, but was too ill and too perplexed to be alarmed about it. Only her body wanted to move; the rest of her was perfectly content to remain where and as she was – for ever.

But then Charlotte's mind leaked back and she remembered who and what she was, and how and why she had got here. Her history returned to her, along with the feeling in her limbs, and shortly she became the person she had been before she had taken the overdose.

Almost.

She felt that something was missing, though, at first, she couldn't put her finger on what it was. She remembered how her sense of the loss of some part of her had caused her to take the overdose in the first place, but now there was a further loss, another depletion, and it was unclear whether its disappearance was a good or bad thing.

It was when she finally remembered the circumstances before taking the pills, that she recalled the helpless, frightened child whom she had seen in the mirror. It had gone. There was no child any more. She knew it would not bother her again. All that was left was a weight which, paradoxically, signified absence rather than substance.

The grimness and despair she had felt, the necessity for getting rid of her life, for which she could think of no use, came back to her. She still felt exactly the same way, but lacked the energy now even to mind about having failed to die. So in addition to not caring if she died, she no longer cared if she lived. But there wasn't the feeling of *desperation*, the terrible need for *help* from no one she could imagine, that she'd had immediately before the suicide attempt. She was not overwrought; not anything at all. She was without emotion, except for a dull ache around the place where her unstoppable heart pumped heartlessly away.

She felt herself to be stranded, an astronaut beached on a dead asteroid far out in space. Like an astronaut in a hostile environment, machines still supported her life, so that it seemed the very air she was surrounded by was inimical to her system. Somewhere, on earth, people lived and laughed and used their existence to some purpose, but for her there was only the simple, neutral fact of being alive, rather than dead. And what she knew now was that there was no prospect of rescue.

As her body recovered, Charlotte considered where the drama of attempted suicide had got her. What was odd was that it was as if nothing very much had happened, and there had been no more than the tiniest blip on the measuring device which had been recording her life. Her suicide attempt had barely jolted the pattern. It had had no effect and therefore, it gradually came to her, everything would carry on as usual. Charlotte was not bitter about this. It was true. She had tried to kill herself, and she was not dead. Somehow, a failed suicide was as irreversible as birth. There was nothing else to do but carry on.

Charlotte had some fleeting thoughts about pointlessness, but decided they were pointless. She grew a practical casing around her mind in those first few days of returning from the grave. The idea that there might be some purpose, some ordained conclusion to life was, she was certain, an illusion manufactured by the way that time and memory were organised in the brain. Both appeared to move in a single direction, from the past to the present, and that gave the impression there was a story, and so one had the feeling there ought to be some denouement. In reality, Charlotte told herself, she had already done what any creature born on the planet was *supposed* to do: reproduced herself. Now, all that was left was to wait the time out; to meander on until the body gave way and let her go. It was the same for all organisms. She would be doing only what she had to do: living in her body, feeding it, breathing it. Just those things which all living creatures had to do by order of their instincts. And yet she felt that she did not fill to capacity the vessel she had been forced to reinhabit. It was a bad fit, her inside herself; there were missing parts. She had shrunk and the carcass seemed to slip around on her, like a pair of adult shoes on a small child; too big and too heavy.

But she put that depleted feeling out of her mind, determined not to let herself be beguiled again into wanting to find a purpose – a fit – for all the events of her life. There was to be no finale, no point to the events that her meaning-seeking brain had made into a story. She had made a mistake in allowing herself to recollect her life during her sessions with Matthew. It merely deceived her into giving significance and shape where there was none. The post-suicidal survivor who was Charlotte, was doing just that: surviving. Why should there be more to do?

During this time, when, in any case, Charlotte could barely speak, the doctors left her alone, and catered purely for her physical needs. Julian came and sat beside her bed, sometimes, but not for very long, and he didn't say much.

'How are you feeling?' he'd ask in a curiously muted, almost shy voice.

She would attempt a weak smile and something like a nod.

'Good, I'll come by tomorrow. Anything you need?'

Charlotte would shake her head and Julian would leave, both of them relieved to have been released from the obligation of conversation for this time, at least. And yet there was a new note in Julian, barely there, but as if he had been touched in some way by something. Only very slightly, of course, but it was there – the faintest shadow of compassion.

Jackie sent a card signed by everyone at the lab, and some flowers.

There was no word from Matthew, even though this was his own hospital.

Eventually, it was decided that Charlotte was strong enough to consider her future, and Davies arrived at her bedside to have, as he said, a bit of a chat.

'Being at home doesn't seem to have worked, does it?' he said, more in sorrow than in anger. Though it was the sorrow of the adult faced with an irresponsible child.

'I suppose I ought to apologise,' she said, trying to think of the right thing to say.

Davies gave a small shrug.

'Well, of course, you've worried a great many people. Do you understand how close to the line you got?'

She did understand, but she did not tell him how very difficult it had seemed to be actually to step over it.

'And how much you've cost the NHS?'

About that, she felt genuinely guilty.

'Yes, I'm sorry,' she said, feeling that at last she could say what he wanted to hear.

'But are you? Are you going to try again?'

'No, I won't do it again,' she said with conviction.

'Because I think we ought to start again and readmit you to the psychiatric unit.'

Charlotte knew that this had to be avoided, that she would have to face Matthew, and that they would give her treatment which would be detrimental to . . . To what, she couldn't decide, although it was, she was sure, still essential to protect it. Though even in her weakened state she could see that was a funny thought for someone who had just tried to kill themselves.

Charlotte negotiated. She apologised again, and spoke of her regret at what she'd done, and how relieved she was that it hadn't succeeded. It was a kind of required recantation, a confession designed to get absolution from a demanding Lord. Charlotte, in fact, had no such feelings of regret or relief. She had no feeling to speak of at all, other than alarm at the idea of being put on medication. But her words did their work.

It seemed, according to Davies, that her suicide attempt *might* be seen as a phase in the process of recovery. Davies explained that the state of extreme depression was often too debilitating for people to organise their own suicide, and, paradoxically, it was when they were getting better, once the antidepressants had begun to do their work, that there came a point when suicide was a real danger. It was then when there was enough energy to plan out the practicalities of how to do it, without there yet having been enough rehabilitation not to want to. Davies suggested that having survived this episode, it might be that Charlotte was now past the point of killing herself on the mental recovery curve. He said he would think about it. Charlotte thanked him.

He had not mentioned Matthew.

Once Charlotte was out of danger and off the machines, Julian seemed to revert to his former, angry self. He had a lecture ready on the selfishness of people who cause immense difficulty for others, who make themselves troublesome and demand time, when time was money and what it could buy.

'*And*,' he told her at her bedside, quite aggravated, 'you've messed up my relationship.'

Charlotte was surprised to hear this.

'I have? How?'

'Elaine's dropped me. It's very annoying. I'm not used to being chucked by women,' he said with real inner pain.

'Why did she do that?'

'I had to cancel dinner with her when they phoned about you. Not that there was anything I could have done, the state you were in, but they said I had to come and sign something or other. She went very funny when I told her what you'd done. Then I couldn't get hold of her on the phone at her office for a couple of days. God, it annoys me to chase after a girl. Then I got a letter.'

'Saying what?'

Charlotte was intrigued. Elaine's unannounced visit to her was the last memory she had before taking the tablets and coming round in the hospital. It had been the final grey hair that broke the camel's back.

'The most extraordinary nonsense about how she thought we had been meant for each other because of you. How you were trying to tell her something or other. Some rubbish like that. She went on about you that first time we met, when we got together. But now, she saw she'd been wrong about you. About *you*, mark you. What that had to do with me, I don't know. She said she could see now that you were a fake, that you were trying to be something you weren't and that she'd been caught out, and her life had nearly been ruined by listening to you.'

Charlotte's spirits rose.

'So she dumped you?'

'Yes, thank you, Mother, she dumped me,' Julian agreed with a small, surprising grin flitting across his face. 'It wasn't the greatest relationship of my life. She did go on something awful about goodness, and I suspect she had marriage on her mind, but, even so, I don't like getting the shove.'

'No, I can see that. So she's not going to give up her job and become a saint, after all? I suppose the new vogue for grey hair won't see the light of day, either,' Charlotte mused, entertained for the first time since she had come round.

'What are you talking about?' Julian said. 'Anyway, it doesn't matter, there are plenty of good-looking women around. I've been seeing a long-legged systems analyst for the last few days who, unlike Elaine, hasn't got the slightest interest in being good.'

'No, dear, you wouldn't want that kind of nonsense.'

'No, I wouldn't. I had enough of that crap growing up with you, thank you. And look where it got you. Megan likes good living, good food and good sex. And she doesn't ask questions about the future, or talk about *us*, like Elaine. I'm better off without her.'

'So I did you a favour, really, trying to kill myself. The only thing that spoiled it was that it didn't work.'

Julian gave her a sweet/sour look that suggested he didn't fervently disagree, though there was still a new irony in the look which intrigued Charlotte. Had these faint notes of humanity and humour always been there, or were they new? Oddly, she found little consolation in the thought that her son might have had a modicum of quality all along. There was some comfort to be found, however, in the thought that Elaine would not be turning up for hot chocolate and chats about Life.

'I've had to sell the Porsche,' Julian said, as if admitting to something shameful.

'Oh, I'm sorry,' Charlotte said, and wanting to mean it, tried very hard to understand how painful a loss it was. 'I really am sorry, Julian.'

He gave her a quick glance, as if checking to see whether she was mocking him, and was surprised to see something quite real in her eyes. For a moment, they looked at one another with an approximation of warmth. Then Julian shrugged.

'It's OK,' he said boldly. 'There'll be more and better Porsches. You'll see.'

And from Matthew, there was silence. But that was just as well, Charlotte thought, her feelings for him before her overdose were not anything she wanted to think about. It was best, she told herself, not to think about anything, but simply to prepare herself for going home and getting on with the business of getting on with it.

Chapter 18

WOW! WOW! WOW!

Speak roughly to your little boy,
And beat him when he sneezes:
He only does it to annoy . . .

CHORUS
Wow! Wow! Wow!

Out of the blackness into which Charlotte-the-Irresponsible, Jenny Orang, the three elderly gentlemen and the entire landscape of Charlotte's imagination seemed to have disappeared, a sound began to emerge which made the dark very slightly less impenetrable. A wet, rhythmic clucking broke through the absence of light, and Charlotte noted it. And in noting it, she noted also that she *was* noting it, and therefore was not non-existent, after all (or was it 'any more'?).

'My goodness,' a voice said, over the other noise. 'That was a close thing. Well wheedled. There's none so canny as those who are mad.'

With some delight, Charlotte recognised Jenny's voice, and as she did so, began also to see through the blackness, which was melting away like smoke. Now, she could see where the apparently life-saving noise was coming from. It turned out to be the sound of the Little One, the new addition, sucking away on her thumb as if her life depended on it.

They were back. The corridor was back, the door, the marble floor. And there was Jenny, elegant again in her floral tea-frock and hat, tapping her high-heeled, not so elegant foot impatiently, to indicate to whomever it might concern that the gloom was not disappearing fast enough for her.

'Here we are again, then, but only just, I reckon. What's *that*?'

228

Jenny curled her top lip up over her protruding upper jaw, showing her teeth and gums to the child on the floor.

'The Baby,' Charlotte explained. 'I had to make a deal. That's why we've come back. The Baby stays with us.'

'With you, you mean,' Jenny said tartly. 'I don't do baby-sitting. I'm one of those liberated orangs. No apron springs or off-strings for me. What are you going to do with it?'

'She'll be all right. She just needs to be comforted from time to time. Charlotte wasn't up to it. Keeping going is as much as she can manage.'

'And she hasn't managed that very well,' Jenny said, huffily. She was finding it hard to be generous about her near-non-existence experience.

The Baby was looking from one higher ape to the other, sucking on her thumb with such ferocity that Charlotte feared she might implode. It was a funny turn of events, she thought, when a mad person was made responsible for a baby. That didn't seem to be right at all. But mad or not, Charlotte remained something of a realist. No one, she still knew, got away from it all completely.

She walked over to the child and picked her up. The sucking rate seemed to treble as she took the child in her arms.

'It's all right,' Charlotte said to her, and propped her comfortably on her hip.

Suddenly the sucking stopped, the thumb dropped out of her mouth and great tears welled in the child's eyes as her chin and lower lip began to tremble.

'Oh, no!' Jenny said, alarmed and dismayed. 'Now what?'

The baby glared at the bad-tempered orang, opened her mouth to an enormous extent and began to howl, hugely and inconsolably.

'Whatever's the matter with it?' Jenny asked, astonished at the power of such a small thing to make such a large noise. She had thought only baboons were capable of such an out-of-scale racket.

'Abandonment,' Charlotte explained, swaying her hips from side to side, and bouncing gently up and down at the same time in what she hoped was a comforting sort of rhythm.

'Wild abandonment, I should say. Does it do this often?'

'Most of the time, I'm afraid. It's what she's for. She's the Cry

Baby. The one who does all the crying; the only one, really, who *feels* all the pain. She hasn't got any words to dull the pain with, and howling is all she can do, but Charlotte can't cope with it so she has to keep quiet and pretend not to be there.'

'Quite right,' Jenny snapped. 'Cry Babies should be not seen and not heard. Especially,' she added, raising her voice over the ever-increasing wails, *'not heard.'*

'It's not her fault, she's only doing what she's supposed to do. If she didn't, we'd have to, and that would make a pretty mess of life, wouldn't it? Best to let her have a good cry and cuddle her. She'll quieten down when she's had enough.'

'Cheer up, do you mean? It's not going to start going "goo, goo, goo" and being cute all over the place, is it? Because if that's what it's going to be like round here, I'll have to find myself some other madwoman to keep company with.'

'I don't think there's any danger of actual cheerfulness,' Charlotte explained. 'She can be quietened, but she can't be cheered up, because she hasn't got anything to cheer up about. It's a case of what's lost is lost with the Cry Baby. She's stuck with all the fear, and all the helplessness and none of the rationalisation.'

'And now we're stuck with her, thanks to you. No wonder the other one up there took an overdose. I hope you know what you're doing. And I hope, most of all, she doesn't spoil my tea-times. I suppose I'd better order extra milk. There aren't any more of you up there, coming down here, are there? It's getting quite crowded – to say nothing of noisy,' Jenny said grumpily.

Actually, the crying had taken on the rhythmic quality of Charlotte's swaying hips, and was much quieter. It had lost its jarring edge and had become almost a hum. Quite soon, there was silence. The Cry Baby, having had her cry and allotted comfort, dropped off into a fitful sleep.

Charlotte suspected it might not be easy to put the Baby down, and she was right. When she tried, it opened its eyes wide and dangerously and made an enormous, preparatory black hole of its mouth.

'See?' Jenny said. 'She only does it to annoy. Little pig!'

But the baby fitted quite well around Charlotte's hip and was snug enough against her shoulder, so she hoped it might be possible to continue with her idyll, after all.

'So what are we going to do now?' Jenny asked Charlotte, finding something delightful to pick in her ear. 'It must be getting close to tea-time. I'm not mad about this corridor of yours.'

Charlotte thought about returning to the beach, but she remembered the way the dark fog had dimmed it, and the foul, foaming stuff which had covered the surface of the sea. She supposed it would be all right now, but the image was spoiled for the time being.

'I don't know,' she said, rather plaintively.

'That's the thing about you humans. Haven't got a clue what you want. The whole underworld at your disposal, mad as a march hare, and you can't think what you want.'

'Nothing very exotic,' Charlotte said. She felt a bit of a failure as a mad person. 'I'd rather like to be in one of those English hotels. There must be one close to that beach we were on. You know, with over-stuffed armchairs and badly dressed people wandering aimlessly about talking in whispers?'

'No, I don't know,' Jenny said, rather grumpily. 'It doesn't sound like much to me. Why not a nice rain forest?'

But since it was Charlotte's psyche they were inhabiting, an English seaside hotel was what it had to be. Charlotte was quite surprised herself at the sedentary nature of her madness. She did wonder why she wasn't bolder. She knew now that she could be anywhere her fancy took her; any kind of adventure was at her disposal, and yet her fancy only took her to places of rest and repose. She realised it was a little dull, but she had not the slightest desire for an exciting environment. The truth was that, mad as she might be, she was still Charlotte and she could only be mad in a Charlotte kind of way.

'Well, if it's an English hotel, at least there'll be tea,' Jenny said, trying to cheer herself up.

'Plenty,' Charlotte said, encouragingly. 'Buckets of it.'

Jenny was seated in an overstuffed, chintz-covered armchair, one of several with big pink and red roses afloat on greyish green leaves on an off-white background. Jenny looked quite colourful, and just the thing in her sprigged blue tea-dress and fruited hat against the floral background. She was sitting straight against the cushioned back of the armchair, which was of such huge proportions that only her court-shod feet dangled beyond the edge of the seat. Charlotte didn't think she looked all that comfortable, but hoped that tea would make up for it.

Charlotte sat opposite her orang friend in a matching armchair, in which she was a better fit. The Cry Baby had remained gratifyingly asleep, clamped against her older, madder self. Charlotte spoke in slightly hushed tones, however, not wanting her to wake until she had to. The large room was empty apart from the three of them and it quite hummed with a heavy, upholstered silence. There was a grand piano behind Jenny's chintzy chair and cushions of a different floral pattern on the polished wooden window-seats. A dense pale-green Chinese rug covered most of the floor, again with a pattern of roses. And the walls, too, though painted cream, carried the floral motif on a frieze two-thirds of the way up, all around the room.

It was just as Charlotte had imagined, although she had never been to a place such as this in all her life. It was dead and hushed and fat with pile and self-satisfaction. Oppressive, some would say. She would have said so, too, normally, but, very oddly, it was *exactly* what she wanted, and where she wanted to be.

She supposed it was in somewhere just like this that her father and mother had met and conceived her. It was hard to imagine passion taking place here, and yet it might be a great, perverse pleasure to fill one of its silent, heavy rooms with cries of desire and know the sound couldn't escape through the thick walls. Charlotte could see that. What she couldn't see was the cries of desire coming from her mother. But then, she told herself, who can see such a thing?

'Well, now,' said Jenny, in her usual strident voice, and then, noticing the echo it made, dropped it to the back-of-the-throat whisper which was more appropriate to the atmosphere, and less likely to wake the Cry Baby which she emphatically didn't want to do. 'There's not a lot happening here. I do hope tea will be soon.'

She waggled one of her feet a little and hummed a bit of a tune very softly, so as not to disturb the room.

Luckily, it *was* tea-time almost as she spoke, and it was signalled by people beginning to appear through the big oak door and settling themselves in twos and threes in the little groups of chairs and sofas dotted around the room. Nobody spoke above an undertone, and although one or two individuals acknowledged Charlotte and Jenny in their corner with a vague nod, no one seemed perturbed about taking tea with an orang-utan.

They were all in their late middle-age or elderly and mostly in couples, apart from one or two small groups consisting only of women. What connected them all was respectability and a self-conscious display of propriety. It became harder than ever for Charlotte to imagine her own engendering among the lowered voices and slightly shifty sidelong glances to check that everyone else was behaving properly.

Charlotte looked at a couple preparing to sit on the sofa nearest to her and Jenny. The man was big – both overweight and naturally large – with stiff old-aged joints which caused him to walk awkwardly and need the help of a stick. His lumbering slowness across the room made his obviously short temper reach its limit by the time he sat down. Petulantly, he elbowed away his wife's attempts to help him down into the sofa.

'I'm perfectly all right,' he hissed at her, jerking his arm out of her reach before falling back heavily on to the cushions.

She didn't react at all to his sullenness, but clung on to his withdrawn arm with dogged determination until he was settled into the sofa, although whether she was actually of any assistance to him, Charlotte doubted. The wife sat beside him and slipped her black handbag off her wrist, putting it on the floor just touching her feet so she would know where it was at all times.

'Well, I hope we aren't kept waiting long,' she said to her husband in a noisy attempt at a whisper. 'Yesterday, the wait was quite unacceptable. I really thought I was going to have to find the manageress to complain.'

'No consideration,' her husband growled, although it was not clear whether it was the late tea or his complaining wife whom he was berating. The woman's lips pursed prissily several times in answer to this. A silence followed while Charlotte admired the total anonymity and shapelessness of the wife's clothes. It really looked as if they had been carefully designed to be that way; that someone had sat down and drawn with great skill the cardigan, jumper and below-the-knee-length pleated skirt, so that for colour, style and fabric, nothing could ever match them for invisibility. In the shop of such a designer, one could roam around with eyes shut, taking this, that and the other off the hangers, and no matter in what combination they were put on, one could be assured that they would all look exactly alike, which is to say, like nothing at all. Great and terrible crimes could be committed in such clothes without any fear of witnesses being able to describe or ever identify what the criminal had on. A very special talent was required both to make and to find such clothing.

'Well, you can talk,' Jenny snapped in a whisper, although Charlotte had not spoken out loud. 'And what do you think *you* look like, may I ask? Not everyone can be as stylish as, for example, I am, but at least they look tidy. Look at you!'

Charlotte, of course, was still in her skirt and shirt which had not been improved any by their afternoon on the beach.

Another woman, across the room, said in a hushed undertone of anxiety to the man beside her, 'Not cold are you, dear?'

To which he grunted that he wasn't.

After several moments of silence, she spoke again.

'If you are, I could get your cardigan.'

'No, I'm not,' he snapped, and they sank back into silence.

A young nurse came into the room with a tray of tea.

'What?' Jenny demanded. 'A what?'

Charlotte blinked.

'Oh, I'm sorry. A waitress, a young waitress . . . .'

She was a pretty girl in a neat black uniform and white apron. The couple near to Charlotte watched in heavy disapproval as she passed them by and went to the furthest corner of the room to put the tray on a table in front of a pair of elderly ladies. The wife in the anonymous clothes turned to look at her husband and raised her eyebrows knowingly at him.

'You see what I mean,' she hissed loudly enough for the far end of the room to hear. 'We were *certainly* sitting down first. There's no question at all.'

The wife of the other couple turned to her cardigan-less husband.

'You're quite sure you're not feeling a chill?'

'Tell her I want cucumber sandwiches *and* cake today,' he replied.

Charlotte felt a great calm settle over her.

Soon the waitress brought a tray of tea and cucumber sandwiches to their own table, which mollified Jenny somewhat. She had been glaring at Charlotte with her lidless eyes, making it clear that this was not at all her idea of a good time. But Charlotte revelled in it, sitting back and listening to the tinkling of teaspoons against flowery china, and the snatches of conversation that floated across the room towards her.

' . . . of course, they've never even heard of contraception in those places. There'd be *plenty* of food for everyone, if only they didn't have so many children. Perfectly absurd . . . '

' . . . don't go much, these days. It's not the theatre I used to know. Not the theatre of Larry Olivier . . . Saw a play once, one of those modern playwrights. Peggy Ashcroft up to her neck in a pile of rubbish. Such a waste of a lovely actress, and she could *move* so well.'

'Can't expect them to be able to own their own houses and manage. No notion of providence, do you see? It's all "What can I have *now*?". No real background. As for those unmarried mothers who get themselves pregnant just to get somewhere to live from the council . . . '

'Of course, they *like* living on the streets. Don't want to work. There are plenty of jobs about if you really want one. Look at Justin, got a job, just like that after university. Give them a neat uniform and get them clearing the place up, that's the answer.'

'Yes, dear.'

'No, dear.'

'Quite.'

'Humph.'

Conversation was not the right word for what was happening in the room. Befogged opinions, untouched either by experience or information, floated through the air like fluffy clouds between the floral decoration. Each statement was responded to not in order to answer or discuss what had been said, but merely to confirm that speech had occurred.

Charlotte, who once might have sunk into despair at being surrounded by people such as these, looked from face to face and saw their complete bewilderment with the life they had passed through and which was now passing through them, as if they were no more than ghosts. Every clipped and confident pronouncement was contradicted by the glazed, befuddled look in their eyes as they struggled with incomprehension and the enormous difficulty of

235

understanding anything at all. They were all utterly confounded by the life they found themselves living in. Charlotte was surprised to find herself moved by the plight of these dimly lit creatures for whom the world was far too complex and fast-moving and who had retreated, like Charlotte herself, into a cosy, insulating world of teacup-tinkling madness.

Jenny was enjoying her tea.

'They do know how to make a good cup of tea,' she said with her mouth full of cucumber and thinly cut white buttered bread. 'Do you want that last sandwich?'

Eventually, she sat back in the voluminous chair, sated.

'Now that unpleasant business with her up there has been sorted out,' she said. 'What's next?'

'Since it's tea-time again, let's have more about your forebears,' Charlotte said. 'What about Jenny the First, after she had tea with the Queen?'

'Not much to tell,' Jenny said. 'She went back to the Zoological Gardens, and the visitors came and went.'

'Did she mind being in England?'

'Did she miss the rain forest, you mean? Well, we all miss the rain forest and England was not a very warm place to be, although the dampness was familiar enough. I believe she rather enjoyed her new environment. There was none of the tedious business of hunting for food. You humans are rather romantic about living in the wild considering how much effort you've made to get yourselves out of it. There is nothing quite like getting three meals a day – plus tea – put in front of you. Ask any orang if they'd mind having their food brought to them. We aren't stupid, you know. It's true there wasn't the space she was used to, but, you see, we only need all that space because we have to find enough food. Jenny didn't object to sitting about all day studying the human race as it came up to her cage and gawped at her. Between them and Hunt, her understanding of the world was considerably broadened. And knowledge is always a good thing, isn't it?'

Charlotte wasn't completely sure if that was true.

'But what about her natural dignity? She couldn't have liked being displayed like that.'

'Oh yes, natural dignity. You humans talk about natural and

dignity a lot. Why on earth should Jenny feel undignified because people came and stared at her and made funny faces and peculiar noises? She didn't do any of that sort of thing. She just watched and studied. Being a zoo creature is a contemplative life, with freedom from hunger and fear, which leaves a great deal of time for meditation. The loss of dignity was all on the human side. She felt sorry for you, and, I can assure you, her compassion has been handed down through all the generations of Jennys. We hope for better things for you. I genuinely mean that. Jenny was certain she saw some latent quality in some of you that gave her reason to hope that in the future you would develop into something a little more . . . Well, something a little more. But she realised it would take time. These things do.'

Charlotte felt she couldn't argue with this, although it took her a little by surprise.

'But what about companionship? The company of more of her own kind?'

Jenny shook her head, making her goitre-like lump swing from side to side, and the cherries on her hat jiggle.

'I've told you before. We're solitary. We're natural contemplatives. We only get together for sex and, frankly, that's not all it's cracked up to be. The worst time for us zoo animals is when they take the barrier down between the females and males. But Jenny back then didn't have a male to put up with, and being in a cell simply provided her with the right kind of meditative environment.'

'But she had a good relationship with Hunt, her keeper, didn't she?'

'She studied Hunt, like all the rest. Of course, Hunt *adored* her. There's no question of that. When she died he was quite devastated. They say that he was unable to speak her name afterwards. Inconsolable, they say. Human beings are not like us, they haven't achieved detachment in the way that we have. It rather holds them up. It makes them prone to confusion.'

Charlotte looked around the hushed drawing-room filled with the quietly deranged and thought that Jenny and her kind might have a point.

'Do you think we could carry on like this for ever?' Charlotte wondered.

'Having tea, you mean?'

'More or less. Being beside the seaside. Lazing around.'

'It depends on her up there.'

'You mean, she might try and kill herself again?'

'It's possible. But most people don't, you know. Look at all this lot. They've settled quite nicely into the excruciating boredom and pointlessness of their lives. They're not exactly unhappy. Well, no more unhappy than they expect to be. People adjust to disappointment. Most likely she'll become like them.'

'What about all Charlotte's (the other Charlotte's) hopes and fears?'

'The political idealism and the curse of the FitzRoys, you mean? The real curse is overcapacity in the brain box. Nature did a little experiment: give this species more than it needed and see if it could fill the gap between capacity and thought. As a rule, you know, a species has slightly less than it needs. Didn't work. That's clear enough. All the extra space just filled up with garbage: mostly self-delusion and grandiose plans. Hot air filling a vacuum. Nature abhors them, they say. What's the use to the individual of a sense of individuality when that's not at all how the world works? What you get are hopes and fears, expanding, as hot air will, until it reaches its limit and *then* what you get is an awful headache. Which is more or less Charlotte's condition right now. She's given herself a terrible headache about nothing. Look around you. Every one of these people is waiting out their lives, more confused with every passing day at what they were supposed to do with them. But every one of them was filled with hopes and fears once. It's the disease of your kind. One of those which causes terrible itching in unscratchable places – like thrush or pruritus. Most people get over it, take the pills, once they've given up on natural yoghurt, and learn to sit still and enjoy the regularity of tea-time. Some don't, and make a great fuss about it all, scratching all the time, and embarrassing other people. Fact is, it doesn't matter a hoot what runs through Charlotte's veins. You know why? Because it doesn't matter, that's why! It's not the point. And you know why *that* is? Because there isn't any point!'

Charlotte began to feel very glum as she looked about her and realised that there were not so many years' difference between herself and most of the partakers of tea in the drawing-room.

'But, then what am I doing here?'

Jenny cocked her head to one side, but remembered to hold on to her hat.

'Interesting, eh?'

Charlotte let the question go. One of the best features of madness was not having to confront awkward questions like: interesting, eh?

'You're very cynical.'

'Very pure. No overcapacious brain. Just the ability to enjoy life's little pleasures and not have daft thoughts about destiny.'

'But you have a sense of your own history. Your stories of the Jennys . . . '

'Nothing wrong with a what-happened-next sort of history, but it's no more than that. Just give me a nice cream tea and a decent frock and I'll be happy. That's what's wrong with your Charlotte; she doesn't know how to have fun.'

'So she'll end up down here with them, you think?'

'With us. Probably. And nothing wrong with that. But that baby's a bit of a problem. What about when it grows up? There aren't any education facilities here, you know.'

'Oh, it won't. The Cry Baby doesn't grow up, any more than I stop being mad or *she* loses her misery. Everything just goes on being what it is, I think. But, you know, I can't help feeling sorry for them – for us.'

'Stuff and nonsense. Best thing. Everybody getting on with what they know best. No disturbances. Except –' Jenny turned her head at a commotion which had begun just outside the drawing-room door. 'What do we need *them* for?'

The three elderly gentlemen marched into the room, looking quite distraught.

'We demand to know what's going on!' Karl boomed.

'What's *really* going on,' Sigmund insinuated.

'Yes, if it's no bother,' Charles said feebly.

The tea-takers froze, cups in mid-air, grunts in mid-voice, and stared in horror at the furious, bearded threesome.

'Good God!' the man with the stick said, finally. 'Hooligans! Here!'

Even Charlotte felt there had been some breach of decorum by the three enraged old men. They had no business arriving and speaking above a whisper in this place of psychic rest.

'Shhh,' she said.

'I will *not* shush!' Karl said stamping his foot. 'I demand an explanation. *We* demand an explanation.'

'Yes, we do,' Charles agreed.

'We were sleeping peacefully, doing nobody any harm and then, without a word of warning – nothing! And as if that wasn't enough, after the nothing, things became very unpleasant. Indescribably mucky. Not a thing to eat, or drink, no sun, and something horrible coming in towards the shore. Muckiness! And here you are in a comfortable hotel taking tea. What about us? We won't be treated like this.'

'And,' Charles added, 'I've got a terrible stomach-ache.'

Unfortunately, the noise of the angry old gentlemen woke the Baby, who stared round at them, immediately stiffened and began to cry with all her tiny might. It was enough to silence the threesome, who hadn't noticed her clamped against Charlotte's shoulder.

'Now look what you've done,' Jenny shouted above the noise.

'Call the police!' the man without the cardigan cried.

'Is this the revolution, dear?' a sweet little old lady asked of her companion, a rather more assertive elderly party.

'Damned if I know. They look dressed for it. I say,' she called out, pointing to Karl whom she had picked out as the ringleader, 'what are your grievances? I suggest we thrash it out like sensible people.'

'Bloody English,' Karl muttered.

'The thing is,' Charles said, having rather taken to the old dear, who looked to him like someone who could get things done, 'we don't have anything to eat or drink. Nor anywhere to go, really. We seem to be at the mercy of circumstances quite beyond our control.'

'Although,' Sigmund said, 'it is probably the case that we have internalised our initial infantile helplessness on to a mysterious mythic power. In reality – '

'In reality,' Karl interrupted, 'we've wandered from pillar to post all day long and we haven't got anything to eat. Whereas these useless appendages – these dogs of capitalism – these ravening hyenas preying on the rotting corpse of the working class have full bellies and somewhere nice and warm to sit.'

'Oh, I say,' said a gentleman at the back of the room. 'That's no way to talk in mixed company.'

'I don't suppose anyone has any powders for the colic?' Charles asked.

'As a matter of fact . . .' The sweet little old lady, delighted to be of use, got her bag from the floor and rummaged around in it until she found a folded packet. 'Yes, here you are. It's just the thing for a bad tummy. Works a treat.'

She held it out for Charles with a sweet-little-old-lady smile.

Throughout all this the Baby bawled its head off, and Jenny had stuck her fingers in her ears.

'Will you please *do* something,' she screamed at Charlotte, quite forgetting her ladylike pretensions.

Charlotte looked thoughtful for a moment, before she spoke.

'Yes,' she said. 'I do believe I will.'

She stood up and putting her hands around the Baby's middle, removed it from her shoulder and pushed it against Karl's chest. Then she took each of his arms and positioned them so that the child was held securely.

'Now,' she said, in a voice so filled with calm authority that in spite of her quiet tone, everyone stopped speaking and listened. Even the Baby stopped crying. 'Karl, Charles and Sigmund, you will take care of this child. When she screams you will rock her and comfort her and sing her lullabies. You will do this downstairs in the kitchen, where, so long as the Baby is taken good care of, I will ensure there is all the food and drink you could possibly want. There will also be a very nice couch where you, Sigmund, can give regular treatment to the other two to ensure the Baby receives the best quality care and doesn't suffer from their neuroses. You, Charles, will have an entire medicine cabinet for yourself, filled with every kind of remedy for belly-aches, and a regular supply of barnacles to study for the rest of eternity. And, Karl, you can have every May Day off, and organise the other two to demonstrate against injustice, so that once a year, those of us above stairs can be woken out of our self-satisfied torpor and reminded of all the wrongs and imperfections we can't bear to face. I think that's everything. I won't take any questions. You can go. Now, I wouldn't mind if it was tea-time again.'

With that Charlotte sat down to a stunned silence. The three elderly gentlemen stared at her aghast. Karl opened his mouth and raised a hand, his finger pointing towards her, but after a few

241

moments when no words emerged he shut his mouth again and his hand returned to encircle the Baby, who had begun to wriggle. Sigmund also looked as if he was about to speak, then looked as if he had changed his mind, but did finally find some words.

'Um . . . I was wondering if I might have a supply of tobacco for my pipe.'

'You may,' Charlotte said.

'Thank you,' Sigmund murmured gratefully.

'Off you go, then,' Charlotte ordered.

The three men and the Baby turned and made their way out of the room, treading quietly so as not to disturb anyone.

'Sigmund,' Charles whispered as they reached the door, 'I wonder if I could tell you about a dream I had. I was sitting on this giant tortoise, you see, and all of a sudden a huge white pigeon that I'd been breeding flew down and, before I could do anything . . .'

The silent drawing-room exploded with the sound of clapping as the door closed on the rest of his dream. The cheers were deafening.

'Bravo!' one of the old men said. 'That's telling 'em.'

'Leadership, you see,' the man with the stick explained to his wife. 'Must have leadership. No one'll disturb our tea-time with that kind of captain at our helm.'

Charlotte acknowledged the cheers of her grateful fellows.

'Thank you,' she said, giving a special smile to Jenny, who responded with a very satisfied nod of approval. 'Now that's been sorted out, and we've found something useful for them to do, let the tea commence!'

Charlotte, mistress of the underworld, conductor of tea-time, felt very contented with her lot. She had truly found her place in the world. Being beside the seaside suited her nicely. She knew she was going to stay. Charlotte up top, she decided, would have to manage as best she could. When something was right, it was right. Down here was where she belonged and where she planned to remain. Sensible Charlotte of the real world would just have to manage without her.

Chapter 19

DREAMING AFTER A FASHION

———

. . . Alice got up and ran off, thinking while she
ran, as well she might, what a wonderful dream
it had been.
But her sister sat still as she left her, leaning her
head on her hand, watching the setting sun, and
thinking of little Alice and all her wonderful
Adventures, till she too began dreaming after a
fashion . . .

Charlotte spent the first few days back at home considering her options. They did not seem to be many, nor to be very different from what they had been before that morning when she had visited the Zoo and returned to dishevel her garden. She was still almost fifty, and sturdy enough to live for anything up to fifty more years. She still had a skilled though routine job if she chose to return to it. Her son was alive, her daughter was dead. She may have been a descendant of Robert FitzRoy, but then again, she may not, and there was no way she would ever know for certain. And the silence from Matthew had continued.

The list, aside from the last item, was exactly as it would have been had she made it when there were still shrubs and grass outside her front door. Since nothing had changed even after what had seemed to her an extremely unusual period of her life, there was no reason to suppose it ever would. She had tested the definition of her life and found it to be very definite indeed. A life, she supposed, was what it was, for all that it seemed to her, in the living, to be quite mercurial in its ungraspable drift.

Matthew's silence confirmed her in this certainty. Weeks had passed since she wrote the letter, and with them went all the rationalisations which rose pitifully to protect her. She could no longer imagine him ill, on holiday, called away on a family emergency. She believed in none of these thoughts, but as each surfaced a small hope had lit up; though not for long, and now it had been entirely extinguished. The silence still pained her, not in itself, but because it was a continuous reminder of a last absurdity which had hung on even after all the other absurdities had left only the reality of doggedly getting on with it in their place. She still blushed at the memory of the impetuous, revealing letter she had sent him. She knew it was foolish for a woman of her age to fall in love, more foolish to declare it, and perfectly idiotic to feel dizzy with shame at his rejection of her. There were moments of anger towards Matthew – he might, given his profession, have found a better way of dealing with it; indeed, it might never have happened if he had not been so relaxed, so forthcoming about himself during her sessions. But when she put herself in his position, she understood how not responding to her might seem the most effective method of non-encouragement.

The funny thing was that the passion had abated. Her sudden sexual arousal seemed to have died of embarrassment. His image no longer floated into her mind; the longing had left, as if it were a drug which had been injected into her and whose effect had now worn off. She experimented with deliberately thinking about Matthew in the way she had in the hospital. All that remained was a surge of discomfort at her own silliness. Perhaps, after all, writing the letter had had its real intended effect and set her free from her middle-aged moment of folly. If so, it was certainly not conscious. But it had also deprived her of Matthew as a friend. She had liked his company, he amused her and she missed the warmth the two of them sitting in his room had created. Still, the truth was that he had disappeared. His silence diminished him. He could have managed it better – except he didn't, and therefore couldn't, and that made the loss of her brief reawakening of love more bearable. It was her momentary craziness, the last burst of spontaneous life, not his absence she had to come to terms with. If it was a final attempt to light her existence up with excitement, it had failed. But, finally, the death of expectation was a relief. There would be no further opportunity for disappointment.

All that remained of Charlotte – the one who with gritted teeth got on with things for no reason she could or would try to understand –

settled down to a future which needed no further thought. If she knew herself to be abandoned in some fundamental way, she did not mind. She did not mind about anything. This was how it was to be. It was, after all, how life was for most people. Usually, in a quiet sort of way, they survived.

Charlotte, dressed and ready for her uneventful day ahead, ate her toast and honey and sipped her tea as she looked at the front page of the morning newspaper. She glanced at the headlines. Her eyes slid over continuing reports of the breakup of the Russian empire and ominous trouble in most of its former territories in Europe. Every day Europe cracked a little more as the crazy paving of its boundaries heaved like ancient tectonic plates, crushing together and pulling apart. Even now, the reports juggled words like *freedom* and phrases like *the rebirth of hope* with a description of the rise of murderous small-scale nationalism and religious fundamentalism. To Charlotte, the map of Europe was coming more and more to look like the ones she had seen in history lessons at school depicting Europe and the Balkans prior to the First World War. It was also clear that the new leaders had, as it were, been awoken from their beds and been asked to take charge at a moment's notice. All of them looked dazed and bleary-eyed at the burgeoning chaos they had suddenly to preside over. Who was to be in charge of a mass of murderous weapons? Where were the jobs to pay the millions who wanted to participate in the grand new market economics which had appeared from one day to the next? Who was attending to the vicious rage that had been simmering between ethnically different neighbours forced to lived side by side by post-war treaties? Did anyone notice anything happening in Iraq? And how were things in Africa? People were hungry – for food, for power, for their share. Yes, yes, we must think about it all . . . Still, Mandela was free and Yugoslavia and Romania had cast aside their repressive masters. Yes, freedom was on the march, no doubt about it.

The headlines were fearful confirmation of Charlotte's worst fears. She no longer chose to read the texts. But she stopped chewing her toast and honey when her eyes reached the bottom of the front page. In the space often reserved for odder light-hearted items of news, there was a report which riveted her attention. It was headed: *Non! Non! Non! Says Eurocentred Ape*, and concerned an elderly couple

245

who had been found in a cage at the London Zoo early the previous morning, standing ankle-deep among the debris of broken lumps of safety glass, passionately pleading with a female orang-utan to go off with them. Mr and Mrs Tyringham had broken into the Zoo in the early hours and, using Mr Tyringham's knowledge – gained from his years in the Army – of explosives, had blown out the window of the orang-utan's cage in an attempt to kidnap it. They were well known to the keepers, and, indeed, had named the very orang-utan (and her baby) whom they were trying to entice out of her cage to go and live with them on the Sussex coast. They could not accept, so the keepers explained, the fact that Suka and her baby, Jago, were about to be sent to a French zoo which had more funds and better facilities. But the plan had gone wrong when, the window having been blown out, the orang-utan had tucked her baby under her arm and sat herself down in a far corner of her cage with her back to her would-be liberators, flatly refusing to budge. Mr and Mrs Tyringham had pleaded, reasoned and cajoled, but all to no effect; the orang-utan had adamantly refused to follow them to freedom.

A police psychologist suggested that the pair were suffering from a sort of *folie à deux* not uncommon among elderly, childless couples, but which usually took the form of an excessive adoration of a family dog or cat. The psychologist declined to comment, however, on the orang-utan's stubborn determination to remain in her cage. The Zoo authorities said they would not be pressing charges, since Mr Tyringham had promised to pay for the damage and both had agreed to attend regular counselling sessions. 'Nothing would be gained,' a spokesman for the Zoo was reported as saying, 'by locking these people up. They need help and understanding from society.'

Charlotte remembered Mr Tyringham's loden coat and his pained reserve, and how Mrs Tyringham had tried so stoically to put the Zoo's point of view for sending Suka and her relations away to France. She struggled to recollect where they had said they lived, and couldn't, but she thought she'd recognise it if she saw it on a map.

Charlotte sat watching London slide away behind her. She thought how surprisingly active this uneventful day had turned out to be. It had been a long time since a day had been more than a morning slipping towards an afternoon which dimmed into night, while she merely watched its passing, uninvolved, from her living-room, or a hospital chair. Today had been full of achievement. She had put on her coat and walked to the bookshop on the high street where she bought a map of the south coast. She took it home and studying it, remembered that it was Hove where the Tyringhams lived. She had called directory enquiries but been told that they did not give out addresses, though if she looked up the name (providing it wasn't Smith or Jones or something impossible like that, or the subscriber was not ex-directory) in the Hove phone-book it would give her the address.

'Where could I get hold of a Hove phone-book?' Charlotte asked.

'In Hove,' the impatient voice told her.

One further call got her through to a slightly friendlier voice at British Rail who informed her that Victoria was the terminus she wanted for Hove and that trains left at twenty-one minutes past the hour.

'Which hour?' Charlotte asked, hoping she hadn't missed it.

'Every hour,' said the man at British Rail.

What a busy place Hove must be to have trains going to it so often, she had thought, going into her bedroom to take the twist of tissue paper from the drawer and putting it in her handbag. Then she'd shrugged on her coat, locked the front door behind her and, stepping over her new paving stones, headed off to the bus-stop.

And now, at twenty-five minutes past the hour, she was on a train gathering speed away from London and heading for the south coast. It had been a quite remarkably busy day.

She opened the map she had brought with her and unfolded it. She didn't know why she'd brought it, nor why she was looking at it. Hove was the train's destination, and when she got off she'd be where she intended to be. She didn't need to find her way there; the train would do it for her: on at Victoria, travel along the rails, and off at Hove. She had no use for a map. But she stared down at the one resting on her knees.

'It's interesting, isn't it?' a voice with a German-American accent said.

Charlotte looked up. She was certain she'd been alone in the cariage when the train had pulled out of Victoria. She was surprised that her attention was so caught by the map that the man sitting opposite had come in without her noticing. He was leaning towards her; a rather shapeless, overweight elderly man with a dramatically unkempt hairstyle.

'Not very,' Charlotte said, slightly alarmed. 'Just as you spoke, I was thinking it was quite uninteresting. It's an almost smooth curve from Beachy Head to Selsey Bill. And, frankly, it's not much more eventful to either side.'

The plump, white-haired man beamed.

'Yes, that's exactly what is so interesting about it.' He pushed out an arm towards her. 'Mandelbrot,' he said.

Charlotte took his hand and received a firm single shake.

'I'm Charlotte FitzRoy.'

'The man who invented the weather forecast was called FitzRoy. Did you know that? Didn't have a hope in hell. But he didn't know he didn't have a hope in hell. There are too many unknown factors having unknown effects on each other ever to hope to make a guaranteed accurate forecast. We know that, now. There's progress for you.'

Charlotte was more than a little surprised to find this stranger talking to her of her ancestor, but wished to keep her relation to herself, so she simply smiled and said, 'Really?'

'It's a matter of scale, you see.'

'Weather forecasting?'

'Everything, but I was talking about map-making. What you're looking at is just an approximation of the coast. But then, of course, that's all it could ever be.'

'Unless the map was detailed enough,' Charlotte suggested.

'Madam,' Mandelbrot said with a very satisfied smile on his face, 'that is just what it could never be.'

'Actually,' Charlotte said, 'I don't really need to know it in any detail. I don't really need to know at all.'

'It never *could* be detailed enough,' Mandelbrot continued, ignoring her indifference. 'Because the true shape and length of a coastline alters at every scale up to, down to, and including infinity. Fractals, you see. It's my own invention.'

'Fractions?' Charlotte said, trying to grasp his drift.

'Fract*als*. It's a name of my own devising. Now look . . . '

He took out a notebook and a propelling pencil from his jacket

248

pocket, and began to draw a continuous line that altered in its degree of smoothness as he spoke.

'Irregularity, you see? From a distance, the coastline looks smooth. Get closer, and you see inlets and coves. Closer still, rocks, and then stones. Now we're down to tiny pebbles, and now sand. And everything, madam, has its own irregular outline.'

For some reason that she didn't understand, Charlotte's heart began to beat harder.

'Yes, I see,' she said. 'The measurements actually change, don't they, until you get to the smallest grain of sand.'

'No! Even that is not the end. Examine the grains under a microscope and what do you find? Bumps!' he crowed triumphantly. 'Bumps! Bumps! Bumps! Increase the magnification and: more bumps! Now, what about your smooth and boring coastline?'

'Yes,' Charlotte said thoughtfully, 'it does rather change things, doesn't it?'

'It certainly does. And not just coastlines. Everything is infinitely regressively bumpy. All bumps have bumps on them. So nothing *really* fits together, you see. That is what we call the Humpty Dumpty Effect.'

'All the King's horses and all the King's men . . . '

'Didn't have the slightest possibility of putting Humpty together again,' Mandelbrot said with a very satisfied grin. 'No truly continuous surface exists. Therefore there can be no mending of anything once it's broken. Things must stay separate.'

'But then,' Charlotte brooded, 'that wouldn't matter very much, because nothing would really ever get broken, would it? Because it wouldn't have been truly together in the first place – not with all that infinite bumpiness.'

'Madam, you are a woman after my own heart.'

'None the less, we'll still get to Hove.'

'Not me. I get off at Brighton. I have to attend a conference on Chaos and Predictability, otherwise I'd accompany you to Hove and we could verify the paradox of its reality together. But you're right in essence. Things go on going on in spite of underlying reality. There's glory for you!'

'I do believe there may be, Mr Mandelbrot, I do believe there may be. I'm very pleased to have met you.'

There was only one entry for Tyringham in the Hove phone-book. It was for the Tyringham Guesthouse: prop. A. Tyringham, and the woman in the ticket office at the station gave Charlotte clear instructions how to get to the address.

'You can't miss it,' she said. 'It's directly off the front.'

Charlotte walked along the front until she came to Welgarth Avenue, but she didn't turn into it. Instead, she turned in the other direction, towards the sea, and walked down the steps that led on to the beach.

It was empty, of course. It was too late in the day for people to be exercising their dogs and far too cold, this being early March, for anyone to be swimming. Charlotte had the beach to herself as she walked down the stony slope to the edge of the sea.

Charlotte crouched down, just out of reach of the waves which broke, foaming, a foot or so in front of her. The edge of the sea was choppy but not violent. It was a still, grey day, and when Charlotte looked out to the horizon it was hard to distinguish sea from sky. But the greyness was soft and not threatening. It was not a day for rain and storms, and the sea went about its business unruffled by dramatic weather. Far off, it looked as if the sea was quite motionless, almost glacial, though Charlotte knew this was a trick of distance and perspective, and that, in reality, every part of it heaved and surged with movement created by the force of its own depth.

Charlotte squatted, staring out to sea, and felt herself being drawn into the middle distance, as if the breaking waves on the shore pulled her along with them as they withdrew. Once she stopped resisting the pull of the waves, she found herself far out there, submerged beneath the weight and mass of the accumulated water; her eyes, ears, nostrils and mouth filling with salt water as the pressure of the weight above her and the drag of the sea bed below tussled for control, making her body spin around its axis, spiralling but never travelling in any direction. She might remain like this for an age, while the friction of the water against her skin wore her layers away, thinner and thinner; flesh to muscle, muscle to bone, bone to soft viscera, viscera to cell, cell to nuclei, nuclei to chromosome; the chromosomes themselves distintegrating into chemical essence until everything of her was sloughed off and washed away into the sea and there was no longer any distinction between Charlotte's molecules and the drops of water which massed together to force all things to become themselves.

The sounds of the pebbles at her feet, knocking against each other, dragged by the tide backwards and forwards, brought her back to the shore. She ran a flat hand over the shingle, listening to the pebbles clink together, stone sliding harshly against stone. Spaces in between, she remembered with a slight smile, bumpiness leaving gaps, irregular shapes rolling and shifting for position, leaving a network of tiny voids which could never be filled. Not even by the water washing through them, only seeming to fill the cavities but – look closer, and closer still – in reality, in *reality*, never making smooth, complete contact between the surfaces of all the varied, dancing atoms. And even the space between was not space, but discontinuous particles also leaving gaps between themselves.

A great dichotomy of all things striving to become one thing, and all things infinitely separate, filled her with the most extraordinary surge of hope, which had no name or purpose, but which spread through her, being itself, and needing, therefore, to be nothing else. It was now perfectly clear to her how everything fitted together and never would, and how movement and stillness, light and dark, truth and deception, feeling and numbness were created out of that single contradiction which kept winds blowing and hearts beating and minds racing to and from conclusions which never could, would or should be conclusive.

Chapter 20

WHO IT WAS THAT DREAMED IT ALL

---

*'Now, Kitty, let's consider who it was that
dreamed it all. This is a serious question, my
dear . . .'*

Welgarth Avenue was one of a dozen streets which ran perpendicular
to the seafront like the teeth on a comb. Charlotte passed by the
houses, up away from the sea, counting off the numbers. All the
houses were similar; modest bay-fronted structures set back a little
from the pavement by a small area bordered with low walls topped
with small privet hedges. Every window was screened by net
curtains, not suggesting, as they might, secret lives hidden from the
casual public gaze, but a desire not to stand out, not to jar the passer-
by with suggestions of individuality. The houses were all of a piece,
small, ordinary, undistinguished, but secure and solid: Welgarth
Avenue being their collective noun, just as Hove was the collective
noun for the sum of all such streets.

But number 23 was different. A sign above the door proclaimed it
the *Tyringham Guesthouse* and its low street wall ran straight across
the boundary, without a dividing wall, to number 25 which, being
part of the guesthouse, had no front door any longer but an enlarged,
flat-fronted ground-floor window instead. Charlotte stopped at the
wrought-iron gate. The front garden was well tended, with a large
central bed of shrubs and a border on either side of the paved path to
the front door, filled with rose bushes and flowering plants. Charlotte
guessed that Mr Tyringham was the gardener, and that he spent a
good deal of time weeding and pruning. It was the kind of front
garden Julian would despise; it was not arty, there was no attempt to
make sculptural statements or to coax along plants no one had ever
seen growing on this side of the equator. Charlotte liked it, however.

A bell over the lintel jingled a welcome and a warning as she opened the front door and let herself in. A few moments later the woman Charlotte recognised as the one at the Zoo came from a back room to the reception desk. She smiled welcomingly.

'Can I help you?'

She was probably in her mid-sixties, but looked older and more weary than she had at the Zoo. Had their adventure taken it out of her? She didn't seem one of nature's terrorists.

'Do you do tea?' Charlotte asked, though she hadn't planned to. But it was mid-afternoon, and she needed to say something. All her plans that day had been remarkably efficient; she had only omitted to consider what she would do when she tracked down the Tyringhams. Tea seemed as good a start as any.

'Yes, you're just in time,' Mrs Tyringham smiled, and came round the reception desk to lead Charlotte into the lounge.

It was the ground-floor room of number 25, which had been extended and had the picture window Charlotte had seen from the street. Plump armchairs, a couple of sofas, a writing desk and several small, highly polished mahogany side-tables filled the room, and three or four elderly people already eating sandwiches and sipping tea, turned their heads at Charlotte's entrance. Mrs Tyringham settled her new guest and asked if she wanted the full tea.

'Yes, please. And – do you have a room free?'

'Oh, yes. It's a very quiet time of year. Half our rooms are let to permanent residents, but we've got several rooms vacant.'

'People live here, then? It's not just for holiday-makers?'

'No. Quite honestly, there's not very much of a holiday trade any more. People going abroad, you see, although we do have a few regulars who've been coming here for decades. Most of our guests are retired people who don't need their own big houses any more and like to live quietly in the sea air. Not very much happens, you see. There's nothing to keep youngsters entertained.'

'We met once, you know,' Charlotte said to the smiling, pale woman standing beside her.

'Oh?' She looked nervous suddenly.

'At the Zoo, by the orang-utan's cage. You told me how you named them . . .'

253

Mrs Tyringham looked flustered and started to back away. Then she stopped and sat down in the chair opposite Charlotte.

'You're not from the press, are you? It's been a bit much . . . We're very sorry for what we've done and all we want is to get on with our lives. We don't like being in the papers.'

'No, no,' Charlotte assured her. 'It's really as I said. We talked about . . . Suka. When I read about you – well, I don't know really – I wanted to find the two of you. I don't have any bad intentions, I promise you.'

'Yes, I think I do remember you,' Mrs Tyringham said, examining Charlotte's face closely. 'And you say you want a room?'

It had been no plan of Charlotte's, especially since she hadn't known the Tyringhams ran a guesthouse, but she did want a room.

'Yes, please, and tea.'

Mrs Tyringham went into the kitchen with Charlotte's order and after a few moments Mr Tyringham's head peeked around the door, then disappeared. Not long afterwards Mrs Tyringham arrived with a trolley and set the stainless-steel teapot, hot-water pot and milk jug on the table in front of Charlotte, then a Royal Doulton floral cup, saucer and plate, and finally a plate of thinly cut cucumber and fishpaste sandwiches and another of small iced cakes on top of a lace-paper doily.

'There you are, then,' she smiled. 'Tea. And it'll be all right about the room.'

Charlotte took the room she was shown, explaining to Mrs Tyringham that she had no baggage because a short break by the sea had been a sudden whim, but that she would go out in the morning and buy what she needed. Mrs Tyringham said they could find her a new toothbrush and toothpaste for the time being. She liked the room; it was a reasonable size and bright with light and cleanliness; Charlotte wouldn't have chosen a blue candlewick bedspread or chintz scalloped curtains with a matching cover on the winged armchair for herself, but it was, she realised as she stood in the doorway, exactly what she had hoped for as she followed Mrs Tyringham up the stairs to inspect the room.

She phoned Julian at work and told him she was taking a short holiday by the sea. An impulse, she said, truthfully.

'Oh,' Julian said, disturbed by the word. 'You didn't book or anything?'

'No, but I knew it would be all right. It's only early March.'

'Yes, I suppose so,' Julian said doubtfully, though he couldn't quite put his finger on what was troubling about it. 'Well, the air will do you good, I suppose. You have got your pills with you, haven't you?'

Charlotte assured him she had.

'And you're not up to anything . . . funny?'

'Silly, you mean? No, really, there's nothing to worry about. I'm just having a break.'

'Well, OK. But why Hove? I mean, you've got enough money . . . you could have gone to the Seychelles or somewhere.'

It took almost a week before Charlotte realised that she wasn't going home; that she had never intended to go home, not even as she boarded the train at Victoria.

The Tyringhams – Arthur and Rose – had lost their fear of Charlotte. They had chatted with her at breakfast and during tea, and finally, after a good deal of persuasion, they agreed to let Charlotte take them out to dinner. She suggested The Grand in Brighton.

'Oh, we haven't been there since . . . Oh, so long ago.'

Rose's eyes lit up at the prospect of dinner at The Grand, and Arthur smiled at her pleasure.

Over dinner Charlotte brought up the business at the Zoo.

'It was terrible, terrible,' Arthur said. 'I really don't know what came over us. We're just an ordinary couple. I think we must have gone mad. I mean, how could we have thought we could keep Suka at the guesthouse? And to break in like . . . criminals . . . hoodlums . . . '

He was completely perplexed at their behaviour.

'Of course, now we have to see a social worker once a week. It's a bit silly, to tell you the truth. She talks to us as if we were naughty children, and tries to make us see – how does she put it? – the *underlying motivation* for what we did. I just say to her, "Look, Miss Hampton, we went potty, I'm afraid, but we're all right now and we promise not to do it again." Quite honestly, it's embarrassing having to think about it. Best to get on with running the guesthouse and hope everyone will forget.'

'We *won't* forget,' Rose said, plaintively.

'Yes, we *will*, Rose,' her husband told her sternly.

'It was because you loved the orangs,' Charlotte said. 'It's not mad to love something.'

'Mmm, that's what I said to Miss Hampton, but she said it was *inappropriate* love. A substitute.'

'For the children we didn't have,' Rose explained. 'I expect she's right, but I don't fancy a dog. That's what she said; that we should get a dog.'

'Or a cat,' Arthur added. 'But we don't want a dog or a cat. It was the orangs. They were who we loved.'

'And now? The orangs, I mean?'

'They've gone,' Rose said, and had to put her knife and fork down to concentrate on letting the pain pass. 'They're in France. We thought we might go and see them, but it's difficult with the guesthouse, leaving it. Perhaps after the summer, we might visit them. It's not the same. But as Miss Hampton says, we have to come to terms with it.'

'What Miss Hampton doesn't know is all the things a person has already come to terms with by the time they're our age. How could she? She's not out of her twenties,' Arthur said, his eyes lowered.

Charlotte looked from one to the other before she spoke.

'I've got a suggestion,' she said.

Before she put it into the envelope and sealed it, Charlotte untwisted the tissue paper and took out the seed-pearl. She knew now why she had taken it with her on her journey to Hove, although it had surprised her when she found herself retrieving it from the drawer. Now, she held the tiny seed-pearl in her palm, letting the gold chain dangle to either side of her hand, far too short, now, to fit around her neck. She looked closely at it as she had that first time, long ago, when her father brought it for her. She understood again what it was for and why her father had given it to her, even if her father himself had had no such deliberate motive. As if no time had passed between her nine-year-old self and the present, she saw its iridescent singularity, and remembered how it had told her that she was what she was, irrevocably: a creature made by other creatures, and of them, yet, until the first splitting of that first cell, an entirety which would never be completely obliterated by complexity and event. It was what she was before life happened to her, before the first thing happened to her, and would always be, in spite of anything and everything. And it was that elementary single entity alone, out of all the matter and circumstance in the world of large and small, which was not subject to the Humpty Dumpty Effect. It was the only thing which, beneath its bumpy surface, did not have infinitely receding surfaces within it. It was the single unity, and would remain so. She knew that at nine, and she knew it again, now.

She put it back in its twist of paper and slipped the seed-pearl into the envelope on which she had already written Julian's name and address. Then she wrote on the back of a picture postcard of the Hove seafront.

Dear Julian, I was wrong about having a short holiday. I've decided to stay. I'm going to sell the house in London and invest the money in a half-share of this guesthouse with the present owners. They want to spend part of the year in France, and I'll take care of the place while they're away. I think I'll be very contented here. It's very quiet and right by the sea. I'll explain it all to you over the phone.

In the meantime, this is for you. My father – your grandfather – gave it to me when I was small. He said it was like me. I should have passed it on to you a long time ago. But I forgot about it. It's the nearest thing we have to a family heirloom. Certainly, it's the most precious thing I have to give to you. I'd like it if you came and spent a few days here, by the sea, with me. The air will do you good, and it would be nice to walk along the front and talk together. It's time we did, and perhaps we can, after all.

Charlotte signed the card with her love and put it in the envelope. She had a moment of anxiety as she sealed it: what if he throws the seed-pearl away, or simply loses it, not realising its value? But it didn't matter, she thought, pushing a fallen lock of hair out of her eyes and securing it with a hairslide she had bought at the chemist. She had done with the seed-pearl what she could, and she had passed it on. It was all there was to do, and perhaps, after all, it might be enough.